D0455251

OUT NOW

QUEER WE GO AGAIN!

**Books edited by Saundra Mitchell
available from Inkyard Press/Harlequin TEEN/HarperCollins**

Out Now: Queer We Go Again!
All Out: The No-Longer-Secret Stories of Queer Teens throughout the Ages
Defy the Dark

OUT NOW

EDITED BY
SAUNDRA MITCHELL

CANDICE MONTGOMERY

CALEB ROEHRIG

ELIOT SCHREFER

CB LEE

WILL KOSTAKIS

MARK OSHIRO

JULIAN WINTERS

KATE HART

KATHERINE LOCKE

JESSICA VERDI

TANYA BOTEJU

HILLARY MONAHAN

KOSOKO JACKSON

TARA SIM

SAUNDRA MITCHELL

MEREDITH RUSSO

FOX BENWELL

inkyard
press

Recycling programs
for this product may
not exist in your area.

ISBN-13: 978-1-335-01826-7

This edition published by arrangement with Harlequin Books S.A.

For questions and comments about the quality of this book, please contact us at CustomerService@Harlequin.com.

Inkyard Press
22 Adelaide St. West, 40th Floor
Toronto, Ontario M5H 4E3, Canada
www.InkyardPress.com

Printed in U.S.A.

CONTENTS

For every queer kid out there—in, out, questioning;
rocking it, hiding it, getting used to it; holding the line
for your generation and the next:

You are beautiful.

You are valid.

You are loved.

KICK. PUSH. COAST.

by
Candice Montgomery

EVERY DAY, SAME TIME, SAME PLACE, SHE
appears and doesn't say a word.

Well, she doesn't just appear. She takes a bus. You know she takes a bus because you see her get off the bus right in front of 56th Street, just in front of the park where you skate.

You know she takes a bus and gets off right in front of the park at 56th Street because you are always at the park, waiting to catch a glance of her.

She—her appearance—is a constant. Unlike your sexuality, all bendy like the way your bones got after yesterday's failed backside carve.

Bisexualpansexualdemisexualpanromanticenby all bleeding bleeding-bleeding…into one another.

That drum of an organ inside your chest tells you to *just be patient.* But now, here you are and there she is and *you can't help yourself.*

She's beautiful.

And so far out of your league.

You're not even sure what she does here every day, but you probably shouldn't continue to watch her while trying to nail a Caballerial for the first time. Losing focus there is the kind of thing that lends itself to unforgiving injuries, like that time you broke your leg in six places on the half-pipe or the time you bit clean through your bottom lip trying to take down a 360 Pop Shove It.

You're still tasting blood to this very day. So's your skateboard. That one got split clean in half.

She looks up at you from underneath light brown lashes that seem too long to be real. She reminds you of a Heelflip. You don't know her well but you imagine that, at first, she's a pretty complicated girl, before you get good enough to really know her. You assume this just given the way her hair hangs down her back in a thick, beachy plait, the way yours never could.

Not since you chopped it all off.

That's not a look for a lady, your mom says repeatedly. But you've never been very femme and a few extra inches of hair plus that pink dress Mom bought you won't change that.

You hate that dress. That dress makes you look like fondant.

Someone nails a Laserflip right near where you're standing and almost wipes out.

Stop staring. You could *just go introduce yourself to her.*

But what would you say?

Hi, I'm Dustyn and I really want to kiss you but I'm so confused about who I am and how am I supposed to introduce myself to you if I can't even get my label right, oh, and also, you make me forget my own name.

And in a perfect world, she would make eyes at you. She'd

make *those* eyes at you and melt your entire fucking world in the way only girls ever can.

Hi, Dustyn, I'm in love with you. Eyelashes. All batting eyelashes.

No. No, the conversation probably wouldn't go that way. Be nice if it did though. Be nice if anything at all could go your way when it comes to romance.

You push into a 360 ollie while riding fakie and biff it so bad, you wish you possessed whatever brain cells are the ones that tell you when to quit.

If that conversation did go your way, on a realistic scale, she'd watch you right back. You would nail that Caballerial.

Take a break. Breathe. Breathe breathe breathe. Try something else for a sec.

Varial Heelflip. Wipe out.

Inward Heelflip. Gnarly spill.

Backside 180 Heelflip. Game, set, match—you're finished.

That third fail happens right in front of her and you play it off cool. Get up. Don't even give a second thought to your battle wounds. You're at the skate park on 56th Street because there's more to get into. Which means, you're not the only idiot limping with a little drug called determination giving you momentum.

Falling is the point. Failing is the point. Getting better and changing your game as a skater is the point. *Change.*

But what if things were on your side? What if you'd stuck with that first label? What if *Bisexual* felt like a good fit and never changed?

Well, then you'd probably be landing all these 180s.

If bisexual just fit, you'd probably have been able to hold

on to your spot in that Walk-In Closet. But it doesn't fit. It doesn't fit which kind of sucks because at Thanksgiving dinner two years ago, your cousin Damita just *had to* open her big mouth and tell the family you "mess with girls." Just had to tell the family, a forkful of homemade mac and cheese headed into said mouth, that you are "half a gay."

That went over well. Grams wouldn't let you sit on her plastic-lined couches for the rest of the night. Your great-uncle Damian told her *gay* is contagious. She took it to heart.

No offense, baby. Can't have all that on my good couches.

You glance up and across the park, memories knocking things through your head like a good stiff wind, and you find her taking a seat.

Oh.

Oh, she never does this. She never gets comfortable. She's changing things up. You're not the only one.

Maybe she plans to stay a while.

You love that she's changing things up. You think it feels like a sign. It's like she's riding Goofy-Foot today. Riding with her right foot as dominant.

The first time you changed things up that way, you ended up behind the bleachers, teeth checking with a trans boy named Aaron. It felt so right that you needed to give it a name.

Google called it pansexual. That one stuck. You didn't bother to explain that one to the family, though. They were just starting to learn bisexual didn't mean you were gay for only half the year.

You pop your board and give the Caballerial another go.

It does not want you. You don't stick this one either.

If pansexual had stuck, you'd introduce yourself to the beautiful girl with a smaller apology on your tongue. *Hi, I'm*

Dustyn, I've only changed my label the one time, just slightly, but I'm still me and I'd really love to take you out.

And the beautiful girl would glance at your scraped elbows and the bruised-up skin showing through the knee holes in your ripped black skinny jeans. She'd see you and say, *Hi, small, slight changes are my favorite.* And then she'd lace her bubble-gum-nail-polished hand with yours.

But you changed your label after that, too. It was fine for a while. Your best friend, Hollis, talked you through the symptoms of demisexuality.

No wonder holding the beautiful girl's hand seems so much more heart-palpitating than anything else. A handhold. So simple. Just like an ollie.

You take a fast running start, throwing your board down, and end up on a vert skate, all empty bowl-shaped pools that are so smooth, your wheels only make a small whisper against them.

A whisper is what you got that first time you realized sex was not for you. Not with just anyone. This was…mmm, probably your biggest revelation.

It was like you'd been feeding your body Big Macs three times a day and suddenly—*a vegetable!*

Tic-tacking is when you use your entire body to turn the board from one side to the other. It's a game of lower body strength, but also a game of knowing your weight and knowing your board. You are not a tic-tac kind of girl.

You are not a girl at all. You are just…you.

That. ´

That one's sticking forever. You know it all the way through to your gut.

You make one more attempt, which probably isn't super

wise because you are so close to the spot where she's sitting that not only will she *see* you bite the dust, but she'll *hear* that nasty grunt you make when you meet the ground.

You coast by.

The friction vibrates up through your bearings and you know you're going too fast because you start to feel a little bit of a speed-wobble, that lovely, untimely, oscillatory behavior that means *bro, you are about to lose control.*

And you hate that word. Control. You hate that word because it is so very rare that you have any. Over your life, your sexuality, your gender, your pronouns, your heartbeat when you're around your beautiful girl.

But then you do.

You gain control. And you nail that Caballerial.

And the three guys who've been watching you make an ass of yourself all afternoon pop their boards up, hold them over their heads and let out wolf shouts.

And you're smiling so hard. You get like that when you nail a particularly difficult one. You're smiling so hard you don't notice the someone standing behind you.

Beautiful girl. You don't even *want to* control your smile here.

"You did it," she says.

★ ★ ★ ★ ★

WHAT HAPPENS
IN THE CLOSET

by
Caleb Roehrig

VAMPIRES MIGHT BE UNPOPULAR THESE DAYS, but apparently nobody told *them* that. They keep showing up at our parties anyway.

Orchard Bay isn't even that big of a place, but the blood-thirsty jerks can't seem to leave us alone. Monsters: They're real, and they're annoying.

You'd think that at some point, after the third or fourth serious attack by the undead, the city council would get its act together and pass some sort of public safety ordinance. But our local political scene is a "complete nightmare," (according to my dad) and the mayor "has her head up her ass," (according to my mom, after two glasses of red wine).

When the recession hit, the municipal government had the bright idea to create jobs by hiring and training a volunteer squad of vampire hunters. Spoiler alert: It was a lousy idea. And if you know anything about the Salem Witch Trials, you can maybe guess what happened when they gave paranoid,

desperate townsfolk a bunch of weapons and a blanket direc-
tive to destroy human-faced monsters.

The truth is, vampires aren't a constant, terrifying scourge.
The smart ones rarely Turn anyone. It's in their best inter-
ests to lie low, so they're mostly a nuisance. They mesmerize people, drink a little blood, and move on. But once in a
while, some vamp comes to town looking to raise an army
and take over—like four years ago, when a group of newly
Turned undead swarmed the senior prom at Orchard East
and ate a dozen people.

But four years is four years, and about the only thing shorter
than the span of an Orchard Bay resident's life is the span of
their memory. So this year, instead of holding our homecoming dance at the school—which is actually equipped
for lockdown procedures—they're having it at a country
club.

"What could possibly happen?" My best friend Taisha scoffs
as we show our tickets at the door. She's a lesbian, but she's
my date tonight because neither of us has a lot of options.
Besides me, there are only two other out gay guys at Orchard
East, and they're together. And they've *been* together since
eighth grade. "There are vampire emergency kits all over the
place, and you've got your crucifix, right?"

I shoot her a dirty look as I hold out my hand to get it
stamped. "Did you seriously just ask, 'What could possibly
happen?' Why not read aloud from the *Necronomicon* if you
want to jinx everybody!"

She rolls her eyes. "Don't be so dramatic, Austin."

"He has a point, Taisha," sniffs Julie Whitmer—senior class
president, chair of the homecoming committee, and royal

pain in the ass—who happens to be holding the stamp. "This is a vampire town. You should take jinxes more seriously."

This time, Taisha and I *both* roll our eyes, because *Julie.* She's one of those people that makes you want to argue against stuff you believe in, just so you won't be on the same side.

Once we're inside, we wander the dance floor, looking for our friends.

The Harbor Haven Club is gorgeous. Big and modern, it's got a whole wall of windows that look out over the water. We're not members here—"on *principle,*" (my mom again, three glasses of wine). I've come with Julie's family once or twice, because the Whitmers live next door to us and Julie doesn't exactly know that we're enemies. Anyway, it feels very sophisticated, even if the DJ for the dance tonight is talking to us all like we're fifth-graders.

We find Katie and Joshua right away, and then Miyu arrives with a hip flask she managed to sneak past Julie. Taisha really wants to find Gabi, because they kissed after rehearsal last weekend, and my best friend is hoping for an encore. Only, when we track Gabi down, the night takes an immediate nosedive, because she's dancing with none other than Lucas Coronado—my sworn rival.

Here's the thing about Lucas: He's one of those guys who's funny and nice (to everyone except me), a super talented actor (I say I don't see it, even though of course I do), and he's, like, unfairly hot. Nobody as obnoxious as Lucas has any right to be that attractive on the outside. Oh, *and* he and Gabi take dance together, so they're doing this complicated salsa thing when we find them, and the way he moves is unreal. Even though I hate him, it turns me on.

When they're done, Taisha is fanning herself theatrically. "Ohmygaw, you guys, that was sexy as hell!"

"Hey, Taisha!" Lucas greets her with this huge, megawatt smile. Then he glances at me and his tone gets, like, fifty degrees colder. "Klein."

"Coronado," I reply, so frigidly my tongue almost gets frostbite.

Here's the *other* thing about Lucas: He says he's not gay. I can't believe it, because the signs are all *right there*. His skin is flawless, his eyebrows are perfectly shaped, and when he starts talking to Taisha and Gabi, his hands wave everywhere like he's conducting a symphony, but if you so much as hint he's gay, he gets all furious and offended. When we first met freshman year, I thought he was cute and tried to flirt with him. He gave me a look like I was covered in diarrhea and snapped, "I'm not *like* you."

So we're not friends. Plus, there's a chronic shortage of guys in the Orchard East Drama Club, and we're always competing against each other for the same parts. There was an incoming senior who was arguably a better actor than both of us, but he got eaten by a vampire in July.

The three of them strike up a conversation that almost deliberately doesn't include me, so I turn away and take a look around. A disco ball throws light against the walls, the bass thumps, and people stand in awkward clumps because nobody but Lucas and Gabi actually know how to dance. Joshua and Katie are making out, and Miyu has joined up with some other kids from the Asian Student Union, so I head for the refreshments table by myself like a sad loser reject.

Unfortunately, the refreshments are almost as sad as I am.

Some kind of off-brand potato chips, store-bought brownie squares with the consistency of Lava soap, and a pile of withered grapes on a plastic tray. If the night was in a nosedive already, then one of its engines just exploded.

"Dude. Is this not the most pathetic thing you've ever seen?" The voice is right at my shoulder, and I jump, spinning around. Standing behind me is a guy I don't recognize, and he's definitely not dressed for the dance. In a polo shirt and flip-flops, he looks like he came in on one of the boats moored outside. "Someone on the dance committee needs an intervention."

He acts and sounds very, very straight, and I shift a little, uncomfortable. Straight guys don't usually talk to me, but I force a smile. "I'd rather eat the table."

The guy laughs, harder than my joke warrants, and gives me a sly little grin. His eyes are locked on mine, and, oh man, I can feel that look in the pit of my stomach. Something inside me wakes up as he reaches out to shake my hand. "I'm Kenton."

"Austin," I stammer, suddenly terrible at flirting. Because that's what happening, right? His hand lingers in mine, and little sparks dance up my arm. "I'm... I, uh, do I... I don't know you, do I?"

It is literally the most awkward I've ever sounded—my brain and my mouth are going through an acrimonious divorce—but Kenton's smile only gets wider. He still hasn't let go of my hand. "Nah, I'm new. We just moved here, and I started at Orchard East a couple weeks ago."

"F-from where?" His eyes are the most amazing color, storm-cloud gray fading into pale blue—or maybe the other way around. Or maybe both. They're magic.

"Different places," he murmurs. He steps closer, and his free

23

hand touches my chin, tipping my face up. I didn't have anything from Miyu's flask, but I feel drunk as Kenton's thumb traces my jawline. "Has anyone ever told you how beautiful you are, Austin?"

"N-n-n..." My tongue doesn't have the energy to finish the word, and I swallow it, just as Kenton presses his soft, perfect lips to mine. I can't believe I'm kissing this boy I barely know—and he's a total bro, too, not at all my type—and yet I can't imagine doing anything else. It's like magnets are locking us together, and it feels utterly *right*.

His hand squeezes my waist, his tongue presses against my own, and then he sucks my bottom lip into his mouth. And then his teeth bite down, *hard*, and the sudden burst of sharp pain breaks the spell. I stumble back, cold everywhere, sweat breaking out on the back of my neck. Kenton is grinning at me, shaking with silent laughter, his eyes lit up from the inside and his teeth smeared with my blood. My shoulders sag. *Ah, shit.*

"VAMPIRE!" I shout, but I'm already too late. Whatever the signal was, he's already given it, and chaos erupts inside the Harbor Haven Country Club. The windows facing the bay shatter as creatures of the night leap through the glass. People scream and run for the exits, only to find their way blocked by more cackling bloodsuckers sporting Greek-lettered sweatshirts and Roman numeral tattoos.

Bros. It's always bros. Whenever this sort of thing happens, people immediately blame the goth kids, but they're never right. Every time, it's the bros: Dudes with hemp bracelets and cargo shorts, and horse girls with super blond hair. Bros are gonna fucking kill us all.

Kenton dives at me, his true face showing at last, fangs gleaming and eyes burning like hotplates. We crash into the refreshments table and topple to the floor. Desiccated brownies and mushy grapes rain down on us, and I'm only barely able to wrestle my crucifix free from my pocket in time. I slap it against the vampire's forehead, and he roars as his unholy flesh burns on contact with the sacred object.

Retreating into a crouch, he snarls at the cross in my shaky grasp. All around us, people are screaming and fighting for their lives, vamps feeding with frenzied abandon. I really hate school dances.

"I thought we were gonna make out, bruh," Kenton taunts me, twisting his neck until the vertebrae give a sickening, unnatural crack. Vampires can be killed by decapitation—and fire, sunlight, and stakes through the heart—but their bodies can take a lot of punishment. They love showing off their messed-up physiology, because it grosses mortals out. "You tasted so sweet!"

"Go back to hell," I snap, but my confident tone is a sham. We're in a corner, and he's blocking the way out—and as for my protection…well. A crucifix is like bug repellent: No matter how well it works, you eventually get bitten anyway. If I make the mistake of looking directly into his eyes again, he could even mesmerize me into dropping it—which is why I'm looking him in the chin instead. "Ugh. I can't believe I couldn't tell you were a vampire. You're wearing a *puka shell necklace!*"

"Hey, man, these are the real deal—I bought them on a beach in Kauai!" Kenton scowls. And then, without warning, he pounces again—teeth bared, fingers elongating into claws—and I shrink back as my life flashes before my eyes.

But I'm saved by a tremendous crash, a chair slamming sideways into the vampire's head and sending him off-target at the last second. Lucas stands over me, his eyes so wide they're almost jittering. Before Kenton rises again, Taisha appears out of nowhere with a metal canister, and she sprays its contents into my attacker's face. It's holy water, from one of the country club's regulation emergency kits. It sizzles like acid when it hits the bro's ungodly flesh.

"Come on!" Lucas shouts, hauling me to my feet.

The three of us take off through the chaos of the dance floor—past Miyu and the Asian Student Union kids as they wrestle a vamp to the floor, past the helpless DJ as a monster in deck shoes and a backwards hat rips his throat out—but before we make it very far, a group of cheerleaders fighting a second group of *undead* cheerleaders crashes into us and sends us sprawling.

I'm back on my feet in an instant, charging for the first exit I see that isn't blocked. A wide, half-lit hallway, it leads past a dining room and bar, and then makes a sharp turn into a dead end. There are some closed doors, though, and the first one I try opens into some sort of walk-in closet that smells of artificial lemon. I dive inside, and only realize Lucas has been at my heels all along when he dives in after me. He slams the door shut and then curses loudly, panting. "Shit. *Shit.* This door doesn't have a lock!"

"W-where's Taisha?" I gasp out, my heart hammering my rib cage so hard the bones might crack. The space is dark, but enough light leaks in that I can make out my sworn rival's terrified expression.

"I don't know," Lucas snaps, bracing himself against the door. "I think she stayed with the ASU kids when we got separated. Why the hell did you trap us in a room without a lock?"

"I didn't trap *us* anywhere." He's making me wish I'd stayed with the vampires. "*You* followed *me*, remember? And how was I supposed to know this door doesn't lock?"

Lucas lets out a grunting breath and rubs his face. "The other rooms down here are offices…it might not be too late to sneak out and—" He's interrupted by a scream from up the hallway, frighteningly close, and then the blood-curdling sounds of some pretty hideous violence. His eyes bulge, and his voice becomes a terrified squeak. "And now we're stuck here! I could die in a *supply closet*, thanks to you!"

"You're welcome to leave anytime," I rasp through my teeth.

I'm worried about Taisha. She's tough, but none of us have ever faced a full-scale attack before. I hope she did stay with the ASU kids; Miyu's dad was part of the recession-era vamp hunting squad, and I know he taught her some tricks.

"How did they even get in here?" Lucas demands. "Vampires need an invitation to enter any non-public building, and Harbor Haven is privately owned!"

"You saw them—it's a whole pack of bros. Most of them probably belong to this fucking place." Only, even as I say it, I know it doesn't totally make sense. In order to Turn into one of the undead, a person has to actually die first and stay that way for at least twenty-four hours; after that, their fatal vulnerability to sunlight pretty much keeps them out of regular circulation. There's a lot of vamps here tonight, and Orchard Bay is small enough that we'd have noticed that many missing people. So, either they've been lying dormant for years, gathering numbers, or…and when it hits me, I actually smack my forehead. *"The banner."*

Strung across the entrance to the club, a giant banner greets everyone who arrives tonight with an enormous message: Welcome, One and All, to the Orchard East Homecoming Dance! Harbor Haven might be members only, and the school might require tickets for admission, but *Welcome, One and All*, is a loophole big enough to fit a dozen thirsty vampires through—and the homecoming committee put it right there outside the front doors. Even though we can't stand each other, Lucas and I share a look and roll our eyes, because *Julie.*

A moment passes before Lucas speaks again, his tone full of disdain. "I can't believe you were making out with a bro."

"Hey! He *mesmerized* me, okay?" I'm indignant, my cheeks heating up. Along with their immortality and other superpowers, vamps also have this special pheromone thing that they use to subdue their prey. It triggers a chemical response that makes people docile and swoony and compliant, so that even if you live in a vampire town and you're naturally suspicious of bros, a pretty face with dreamy gray-blue eyes can still render you helpless. "I was in a trance!"

"*I* can't believe you've lived in Orchard Bay your whole life and you still don't know how to avoid being mesmerized."

I bite my tongue on what I really want to say, but what

comes out as a result is what I really, really *don't* want to say. "I was lonely, all right?"

Immediately, I hate myself for admitting it out loud. It's exactly the kind of thing enemies love to hear, but Lucas just huffs out this weird breath. "How is that possible? You've got, like, a billion friends."

"You're the one with a billion friends." My tone is unattractively sullen. Everybody loves Lucas—teachers, directors, the other drama kids—and there are days I think I'm losing my mind because I'm the only one who sees how fake he is.

"Oh, please! You're always the center of attention at rehearsals, you're always making people laugh…even Mr. Lutjen likes you better than me." He's talking about the director of the fall show, and making no sense. "'Austin, your line delivery is perfect!' 'Austin, your instincts are spot-on!' 'Austin, if you didn't exist, we would have to invent you!'"

Although his attempt at Mr. Lutjen's Dutch accent is satisfyingly awful, the quotes are all real. And yet. "He still picked you for the lead over me."

"Yeah, well, I'm a better actor," Lucas snits, without even trying to make it sound like a joke.

I'm so outraged I swear I feel a blood vessel burst open in my eyeball. Thanks to my brain/mouth divorce, I'm once again saying exactly what I shouldn't. "Are you kidding? You can't even figure out how to act straight!"

I regret it immediately, of course. There's not a single person in the drama club who doesn't think Lucas is gay—well, except for Jenna Holcomb, who thinks they're going to get married someday, and we all cringe when she brings it up— but nobody says it out loud.

Everybody likes Lucas too much to talk about him behind his back, and everybody feels bad for him on account of his older brother getting eaten by a vampire at prom four years ago, so no matter how blatantly he checks out Katie's older brother when he picks her up from rehearsal, everyone agrees not to notice it.

"Screw you." Lucas turns his face away from me, but his breathing thickens, and I can just see the silvery glimmer of a tear when it rolls down his cheek. I am the worst possible person.

"I'm sorry." I hate saying it, though, because I still can't forget our first encounter. "I didn't… I shouldn't have said that."

"Screw you, Austin Klein," he reiterates, getting angrier. "Everything's so easy for you, isn't it? Making friends, getting laughs, flirting with whoever the hell you want. You don't even stop to think about it, do you? You just do *whatever* and it all falls into place!"

"Yup, exactly. My life is perfect." I hurl it back at him, louder than I should, and I check myself. All the screaming from down the hall is loud enough to drown out a marching band, let alone our bickering, but it's better safe than sorry. "I'm trapped in the closet with a homophobe because everything just 'falls into place' for Austin Klein."

His shock is almost palpable. "Ho—*homophobe*? Did you just call me a *homophobe*? How *dare*—"

"'*I'm not* like *you*,'" I interrupt, mimicking the same mordant tone he'd used the day we met. "I told you I thought your outfit was cute, and you glared at me like I was a sex criminal. Then you said, 'I'm not *like* you.'"

For a moment, Lucas struggles to find his voice, and when

he does his tone is haughty. "You weren't really talking about my outfit."

A mirthless laugh erupts from me because, of course, he's right. We were fourteen, and I was barely out of the closet, and I said his outfit was cute because it was easier than saying *he* was cute. Because I didn't know how to safely admit it wasn't his clothes, but the way he filled them out, that I liked so much. "Nope. I wasn't. But you were definitely talking about me being gay when you acted all disgusted by me."

"It wasn't like that." He sniffs again, crossing his arms over his chest. "It's just… I'm sick of people always assuming that I'm gay because I like acting instead of sports. I'm sick of people gossiping about me, or thinking they can tell me my own business."

"The only thing I was trying to tell you is that I thought you were cute," I state curtly, not sure how to explain that it isn't his love of theater that had me convinced he was gay. It was seeing my own mannerisms mirrored in Lucas—his sibilant *S*, his way of talking with his hands—that made me sure we were on the same page. Frankly, it had been a relief that first week of school, to hear another voice that sounded just like mine. And then he ruined everything with the first words he spoke to me.

Rather suddenly, I realize that the screaming and violence in the hallway has ended—and I'm pretty sure it wasn't the good guys who won this particular fight. But Orchard Bay kids are really good at compartmentalizing bad news, so Lucas just lets out another sullen breath and lowers his volume a little. "Sorry. I should've been nicer. But I'm not a homophobe, and I'm *not gay*."

Maybe it's because all our friends could be literally dying on the dance floor right now, but my resentments suddenly seem pointless. I've been angry because he made me feel more alone; angry because his denials suggested that what I am is shameful; angry because he frustrates me, mentally and sexually. But maybe I should let it go.

Whatever Lucas Coronado's deal is, he saved my life from Kenton the Vampire Bro, and at the very least that evens the score.

"Fine. I don't care," I say. And then, because I'm a shameless liar, "I didn't really think you were all that cute, anyway."

He might be about to respond, but footsteps in the hallway shut the both of us up quick. The corridor doesn't extend too far beyond the supply closet, and it ends in a blank wall. The only reasons to come down here during a massacre would be to run from vamps—or hunt for victims.

And whoever is out there isn't running.

The footsteps draw closer on what seems like a beeline for the supply closet, and Lucas and I stare at each other with dinner-plate eyes. Then, just as a shadow breaks the light passing through the gap under the door, he dives at me and tackles me to the ground.

I'm laid flat in an instant, his fingers tangled in my hair before I can react, and as he yanks my head back and bares my throat to his teeth, I think, *Of fucking course Lucas Coronado would turn out to be a vampire.*

He plunges his face into the crook of my neck, his mouth latching on to the flesh over my jugular—and I brace my hands against his shoulders for a futile final struggle, just as the closet door is flung open wide.

Lucas is snarling, pulling my hair and sucking at my neck as hard as he can…but he's not actually biting me. A figure looms above us, outlined by the light from the hallway, a black silhouette with burning golden eyes—a vamp.

My head spins, my heart surging with terror, my body giving me a familiar fight-or-flight ultimatum, but Lucas is delivering the performance of a lifetime. His teeth graze my skin, his tongue slides warmly over my pulse, and he grunts with animalistic passion as he pantomimes feeding.

He's pretending to be a vampire, pretending to have cornered me in the closet and subdued me. It's a gambit that shouldn't work—vamps can smell the difference between mortals and the undead—but I'm so suffused with terror right now that it's actually possible my scent overwhelms Lucas's.

I force my head to loll back, my lids to slide shut, and my body to go limp. Well, most of my body. Honestly, I know it's messed up, but Lucas is making out with my neck, and I can smell his cologne, and one of his hands is just slightly touching my butt… We could die at any second, but have I mentioned how hot he is?

The light from the hallway glows red through my eyelids, Lucas tugs at my hair…and then the door creaks shut and the closet goes dark again. For a long, agonizing moment, we don't move. Finally, the footsteps outside recede, and we separate, both of us panting as if we've just completed a hundred-yard dash.

Lucas hovers over me, his lips swollen and his eyes hidden by shadows, but I can feel him studying my face. I'm flustered and shaking and *still totally erect*, and the only words I can manage are, "I can't believe that worked. We should both be dead right now. Maybe you *are* a better actor—"

But I can't finish, because Lucas tackles me a second time, covering my mouth with his. Suddenly, we're making out— and I mean, *making out*. It's the mixed martial arts of kissing. He's pulling my hair again, our legs twined together, and his tongue is so deep in my face it nearly touches my uvula.

We roll one way and bump into some shelves, then roll the other and collide with an empty bucket, and the whole time our teeth are clicking together and our breaths huff out in steamy blasts.

Whatever vampire magic Kenton worked on me earlier, this kiss is a hundred times more exciting, because this one is *real*. I rake my fingers through Lucas's silky hair, he grunts deep in his throat, and I press my hips against his so hard that if you put a piece of coal between us, I'd give you back a diamond in two minutes. I'm dizzy and breathless, and only have about fifteen percent of my virginity left by the time we split apart again.

"That was…you're really good at that," I manage, my lips raw.

Lucas breathes hard for a long moment, and then quietly begs, "Please don't tell anyone."

I push up onto my side and find him in the darkness, my fingers tingling with latent excitement. What I feel isn't frustrated, but confused. "Why not? Lucas, your friends would totally accept you—and, you know, look: you and I could have been doing *this* for the past two years, instead of whatever it is we *have* been doing."

"You don't even like me."

"You don't like me either, what's your point?" I retort, and it dredges a soft laugh out of him. "And maybe I would like you, if you gave me the chance."

"You don't get it." His voice is tired and miserable. "My brother was this...superhero. He was athletic, smart, he dated nice girls, went to church, helped with cleaning and chores and stuff...when he was around, my parents didn't even notice me. And then he died at the Prom Night Massacre, and now my parents don't have anyone to notice *except* me." In the dark, he heaves out a bone-deep sigh. "It was hard growing up in his shadow, but it's even harder in his spotlight. All the expectations they had for him, they've transferred to me—and I'm not Gabriel. I can't do what he did. I can't be who he was."

"That's not fair."

"Nothing is fair." He sniffles. "I miss him. But now my parents expect *me* to go to law school, and church, and...and to date nice girls. My mom already gave me her grandma's ring, because she wants me to use it when I propose to my future wife."

"They can't put all that on you! You have to be able to—"

"But they have put it on me." Lucas states it flatly. "And I don't know how to escape from it. I don't know how to tell them...the truth. I don't think they can take it."

I feel bad for Lucas Coronado, something I never thought would happen, but lots of things are changing tonight—even us. With difficulty, I admit, "I was pretty sure my parents would be cool with it, but telling them I was gay was terrifying anyway. So I get it. Or, I get being scared." My face heats up. I'm so bad at this, at knowing what to say. "But you can't live a lie forever to please someone else, or it'll destroy you. And you're a good kisser, Lucas." Now my face is *really* hot.

"I mean, after tonight, do you honestly think you can go the rest of your life without kissing any more boys?"

"I think I'll have to." He gives a defeated shrug that breaks my heart. But before I can argue, the closet door explodes open again—wrenched with so much force it's torn clean off its hinges, flying sideways down the dead-end hallway. Kenton the Vampire Bro steps into the small, stifling room.

"Hope I'm not interrupting, dudes. Nah, don't get up." Moving faster than I can take in, he lifts Lucas up, sending him crashing into a set of shelves. In the next heartbeat, Kenton has me pinned to the wall, my toes barely touching the floor. His chin and neck are sticky with blood, his shirt ripped and untucked, and his eyes shine like a forest fire. He's been busy since the last time we saw each other. "Are you cheating on me, bruh? That hurts my feelings."

"The rest of you is gonna hurt worse," I choke out, fumbling my crucifix free from my pocket and shoving it under his shirt. Pressing the metal to his bare stomach, I hear the bright hiss, and the closet fills with the gamy odor of burnt skin. This time, Kenton is expecting the move, or he's consumed so much adrenaline-filled blood that he doesn't feel the pain, because he barely flinches.

"Mmm, whatever that smell is, it's making me hungry!" Kenton laughs wildly, baring his fangs, his eyes getting brighter as he prepares to feed. My heart rising into my throat, I squeeze my lids shut and wait to be eaten.

There's a whistling sound, then, and a loud crack as something wooden breaks apart against Kenton's head. He turns, irritated, and I open my eyes to see Lucas standing nearby, clutching one end of a snapped broom handle in his shaky grip. "Get away from him, Dracu-loser!"

"I spent, like, twenty minutes doing my hair for this dance!" Kenton snaps, holding me up with one hand while he uses the other to smooth his coiffure. "You're gonna pay for that, you dick!"

And that's what gives me a brilliant idea. Yanking open Kenton's shorts, I drop my crucifix into his boxer briefs, and let the elastic waistband snap back into place. With an abrupt shriek, he jolts away, releasing me so he can grab for his crotch—which is now giving off smoke and the telltale crackle of cooking flesh.

Kenton yelps and dances, jamming both hands into his shorts, his back arching as his most delicate parts are seared like ahi tuna—and Lucas doesn't need a written invitation.

Lurching forward, he plunges the sharp end of the fractured broomstick into the vampire's chest with everything he's got. It's a perfect blow, piercing beneath the sternum and angling upward to find the undead creature's heart.

When it sinks home, Kenton looks up in horror, his face going slack. "Oh, fu—"

He never finishes. His tongue and lips shrivel, his jaw dislocating. His eyes bulge as his lids peel away; his nose collapses and craters. Kenton the human has been dead since the day he was Turned, the normal processes of decay held in check by supernatural forces, and now they're catching back up with a hyper-accelerated vengeance. He rots at warp speed, muscles and tendons disintegrating until he collapses at our feet—nothing but a pile of dry bones and clothes from Old Navy.

Lucas and I stare—at the remains, and at each other—our

bodies keyed up and trembling with leftover nerves. For the second, or third, or maybe even fourth time tonight, I can't believe we're still alive.

And then we're kissing again, and it's like I'm trying to inhale him, our mouths mashed together until I don't know where his ends and mine begins. His hands grab my butt, and I jump up to wrap both legs around his waist, and we almost knock over a stack of cleaning supplies.

"Austin? *Austin*?" A familiar voice sounds in the corridor, and we break apart a half second before Taisha, Miyu, and Gabi appear in the doorway.

"Oh, thank God, Austin!" Taisha hurls her arms around me, weeping. Between halting breaths, she tells me it's over—the vamps have all been killed or chased off. "When I lost track of you, I thought... I was so worried!"

"I'm all right," I assure her. "Oh man, I'm glad you're all right, too."

"It was ugly out there." Taisha shakes her head, wiping a tear from her eye. "Miyu saved my ass twice."

As if on cue, Miyu interjects, "We should go. The city's sending an emergency response team to sweep the building, and they want all the humans outside."

"We're right behind you." I give Taisha a look that she reads loud and clear. With a nod, she leads the other girls back up the hallway. I turn to Lucas.

"Thanks for saving my ass—"

"You were right," he blurts at the exact same moment. Flushing to the tips of his ears, he adds, "If there's anything I've learned from my brother, it's that I could die before my life even starts, and I like… I like kissing you. I don't want to stop. I'm tired of being lonely."

Smiling, my face as warm as his looks, I nod. "Me too."

"I'm not sure I'm ready to tell everyone, though." He swallows nervously. "And I'm definitely not ready to tell my parents. Is…is that okay? Are you…is it okay if we keep it just between us, at least…for a little while?"

"It's okay." I could have died kissing a bro tonight, and I've got a whole new perspective on life. Fishing my crucifix out of Kenton's bone pile, I blow the dust off and slip it back into my pocket. "What happens in the closet stays in the closet."

The joke is terrible and he flips me off, but he's grinning when he does it.

★ ★ ★ ★ ★

PLAYER ONE FIGHT!

by
Eliot Schrefer

Player One, Choose Your Fighter!

> Name: Blake Bailor
> Height: 5' 6"
> Weight: 145 lbs.
> Fighting Style: Default
> Strengths: Towering Self-Confidence
> Weaknesses: Towering Insecurity
> Difficulty: Hard

My summer of video games led right into the day I met my first boyfriend.

It's not as dramatic as that might sound. Here's the break-down: I played *Uppercut* all summer, got well past the finger callus stage, and pretty high up the world ladder. That all ended because I had to go to my first day of high school, and that's when I met Carson Hahn. No cause and effect at all.

All the same, here's the crux of the whole thing. I should probably save it for the end of the story and pass it off as my big revelation, so that you can put this down, rest your glasses on top, put some tea on, and say "that crazy kid, at least he learned something from all this."

And you can still say that, I'm not stopping you. Here goes: What draws me to video games is what is lacking in my actual relationships. Video games are only joyous, and relationships are only hard.

When middle school started, I was an unapologetic gamer, but by the end it felt like I had to closet that nonsense. At the right lunch table, sure you could let loose with your *Assassin's Creed* theories, but otherwise you had to pretend you didn't spend half your nights in the Animus.

If I was around someone I wanted to impress, I'd talk bashfully about my years of gaming, how I "used to be a big dork." This implied that I was no longer that dork. Did it work? Probably not. I still wore *Minecraft* tees. But as I started high school, I realized it's not a bad way to gain some nice new friends, making sure I got teased in just the right way. It worked on Carson Hahn.

My favorite thing about one-on-one brawlers is selecting your character. Like on *Uppercut*, they all have numerical values for how much they're worth, from strength and constitution down to charisma. Your dexterity isn't "pretty good," it's fifteen. That's it. You could put it on your résumé.

If Carson were an *Uppercut* character, I could look up his Blake Receptivity Score before making any potentially embarrassing aggro moves.

My dad thought the *Uppercut* stats were interesting, and for a time that made me just beam. He would whip through the character sheets I printed off the internet, squinting at them, his hand scratching through his dress shirt to the small of his meaty back. Then he'd laugh and say "Well, Blake boy, I could use these when I interview people."

I photoshopped some blanks and printed a stack for him. He made them disappear somehow.

The best games are the ones that have a stock of ready-made characters. I don't care if it's some hokey low-budget tennis game, where the only difference between players is the color of their shorts. *Somewhere* in the game's development, a programmer had thought about each one of these people. These characters had *purpose*. We should all be so lucky.

My favorite fighter across canons is Chun Li. She's one of the regulars on the *Street Fighter* series, the first girl to hit the two-dimensional fighting scene, so to speak. My friends would ask, "So you're the chick again?," and back when I was in the closet I'd answer "she's got great legs" (thereby affirming my masculinity and also referencing her strong kicks), but inside I'd be thinking "this girl had to struggle to make it, the world's stacked against her, and *someone* killed her father," and so on.

She's a complex character, Chun Li. Although most virtual women wear halter tops and fuchsia thongs, she dresses in a ceremonial Chinese coat that probably has some official name I don't know. It disguises her curves like a stiff carpet, and she wears what appear to be pit-bull collars on her wrists.

When she defeats her enemy, the game randomly shows one of two animations: she either jumps up and down and giggles or gives you this haunted look and bows her head. These are pretty much the two moods I live in.

45

Player Two, Choose Your Fighter!

Name: Carson Hahn
Height: 6' 2"
Weight: 180 lbs.
Fighting Style: Open palms, close range
Strengths: Soccer, Popularity
Weaknesses: Unknown
Difficulty: Hard

I met Carson during soccer tryouts. I had never really played soccer (not unless you count digital versions, obvs), but I figured I should get in shape so guys would want to have sex with me, and soccer is one of the few sports short people can play.

As I stood on the field, trying to touch my toes for twenty minutes while we waited for the coach to start things, I stealthily checked out the other guys. If I was going to finally be openly out to everyone in high school, and not just my faithful core friends, there were sure going to be some hard choices to make about who to date first.

Though, who am I kidding? I'd have definitely hooked up with most any of these guys. I'd have hooked up with most any homo *homo sapiens*. These new soccer teammates were giving off straight vibes, though.

Carson, though. Man, that was not a hard selection to make. Top stats, all the way. He's tall, and plays goalie with rare talent. I can be very accurate about that because I spent the week on the bench, watching him.

I was equipment manager, which really meant benchwarmer (soccer doesn't have much equipment, you might have noticed). I made myself Carson's cheerleader. I couldn't help it.

Whenever he glanced to the sidelines, I would give him a big wave, and from time to time he would wave back, confused at first and eventually energetically, his already big hands made four inches longer by his gloves. (I can be accurate about their size, as well, because I had his extra pair in my lap and ran my hands up and down the fingers.)

After practice, Carson and I would sometimes hang out with Lisa from the girl's team. I guess she was his girlfriend? They never used that word, though. Lisa was technically an A+ amazing human being, totally funny and charming, but she's also one of those people who are "friends with people for what they can *do*, rather than who they *are*," or so I enlightened Carson.

She and I would playfully pull him between us as we walked, and he would let out these peals of baritone laughter. Soon everyone on both soccer teams knew that Carson, Lisa, and I would be together forever.

I haven't talked to Lisa for ages.

One time after practice, we raided the old yearbooks that Coach kept on his shelf. Carson showed us a picture from two years ago, when he was in ninth grade, so we could see how out of shape he used to be. He gave us these sad eyebrows, like it was some tragedy, but I knew the true message was "I'm so hot now, huh?" Couldn't disagree with that.

Carson and I seemed a perfect match. Take it back to *Street Fighter*: he was the Ryu to my Ken; two men from distant worlds, but alike in force and power. Ken and Ryu were tied by an intense bond, alone in their deep characterizations amidst a shallow avalanche of sumo wrestlers and capoeira artists and well-endowed marines.

There was an awesome backstory there—they studied

under the same master when they were young, only Ken left Japan to train in freewheelin', cigarette smokin', sexually saucy America. Ryu, on the other hand, calmly kept about his business being the most amazing fighter in the world.

The two meet for the first time in years, only now they're battling to the death. Powerful stuff. People say that video games have recently become more cinematic, and I say "bullshit!" Games have had screenplays for years.

One night, Carson and I kissed in front of the gym while Lisa was inside getting her homework out of her locker.

Round One. Fight!

Carson and I tangled for the weekend following that kiss.

His parents were out of town, and we basically spent two days in their bed. Sunday night, I asked if he wanted to meet up before first period the next day and he hemmed and hawed and then said, "I'm not sure if I'm gay," as if that was an answer to my question about first period. Who are you kidding, buddy?

I answered in what I thought was a very caring manner, full of soft words and understanding. But inside I was imagining Carson and me in our Manhattan apartment years from now, sipping cocktails off of cork coasters on blond wood tables, laughing about that time Carson said that he "wasn't sure if he was gay."

What a silly thing to say! Some things in life are obvious, and Carson's being into me is one of them. At least it's obvious to me.

When I walked into the cafeteria before first period the next day, Carson was sitting with Lisa, head down, avoiding my eyes.

He may think she's funny, but she's not.

Round Two. Fight!

The problem with Carson and me was that I couldn't ever tell who won. There had obviously been a battle, and I sure as hell felt beaten, but I didn't see how that meant he had *won*.

Maybe winning doesn't apply to relationships, like as a concept? I mean, I had performed really well, I thought, really done all the moves right. Carson just needed some time to come to terms with who he was, and all that groovy stuff.

And it's not as though Lisa and I were fighting over Carson. She sure as hell didn't win Carson through any charms of her own. She just happened to be what he was attracted to. My loss was coded in from the start.

I spent the next half of the school year doing this trick where I appeared never to notice Carson Hahn and simultaneously obsessed about him at all moments. When I was supposed to be writing in-class essays, half the time I'd actually be imagining the scene when Carson returned.

My head bowed against a strong headwind, eyes clenched in disavowal, I would cross my arms and face away from him. He would appeal to me, ask to team up again, and promise to begin to see, to really see, all the good in me that no one in the world had yet seen. He would be sorry for what he had missed the first time around. He would be sorry he left.

I would remain still for a dramatic and pregnant pause, at which point I would say the perfect thing, depending on my mood:

BLAKE *[Without opening his eyes]*: I could have fallen in love with you.

(This would not be psycho like "I loved you," but would still be profound).

Or...

BLAKE *[Without opening his eyes]*: You've always gotten what you wanted, your whole life...until now.

Or...

BLAKE *[His eyes open, releasing a single tear]*: What we have is a song, and although we haven't reached the chorus, I can't stop singing.

Definitely some high drama there, I hear you. What actually happened, though, was this. I'm going to tell it quickly, because it's honestly kind of sordid.

During winter break I finally came out to my dad (Him: "I'd love you even if you were polka-dotted!" Me: "Thanks?") and began dating this kid, Matt.

He went to a different school, but was the son of one of my dad's coworkers—I met him at the work holiday party Dad made me come to. He was kind of vapid (his big phrase was "that was quite an experience," which he used to validate lame story after lame story), but he had these angular green eyes and an elfin expression that I couldn't resist. He would have made an awesome mage.

He liked me but I wasn't into him (I hate to say that; it makes me sound like a prick, but it's true!), and by the time break was over I knew that relationship was a goner. So, when

I returned to school in January, it was with the cheerful step of the jilter. I had a win under my belt.

This attitude seemed to turn Carson on, because he started texting me nonstop (well, at least once a week), and he returned my messages really quickly. Although he didn't make any moves or anything, and stopped texting back eventually, it was clear that he still had a thing for me.

Late one February afternoon, I'm waiting outside school for my dad to pick me up to go to the orthodontist. Lisa walks by, gives a wave that makes her skull rings tinkle, returns to her phone. Then Carson follows a minute later, face totally blank, even after he notices me. He's trying so hard to be chill that a stranger watching could almost think that the sight of me standing there, available, didn't bother him.

Technical Knockout

My dad won't buy me a graphics card, so my computer has never run *Street Fighter V* all that well: after I begin a special move, I can put the controller down and watch the frames of animation pass like slides until the move finishes seconds later.

It takes Chun Li so long to do her lightning kick that the blur of feet in the console version is revealed to be only one foot, bathed in blue pixels, striking first the top of a person's body, and then the bottom, then the top. Ear and chin, ear and chin, knee and shin, knee and shin.

On consoles she makes this jubilant "huzzah!" sound, but on my slower computer the sound breaks down into a "heh heh." Ear, heh, and chin, heh. When her move is slowed down and the elements of it became distinct, the truth appears— Chun Li is feverishly laughing as she slaughters.

I call Carson's disappearance from my life a *technical* knock-out, for a number of reasons.

One is that I like Lisa, I really do. No one believes me when I say that. Maybe some of my warm feeling for Chun Li just passed over onto her.

Second, I technically couldn't have hooked up with Carson again, anyway. Matt and I hadn't officially broken up, and as far as Carson knew I might have been in love with the guy. So, Carson probably didn't even realize that I was available. Typical Carson.

But really, there's never supposed to be any clean conclusion between two perfectly matched fighters. Look at Ken and Ryu—they went head to head for years from the original *Street Fighter* all the way through *Street Fighter V,* one never beating the other. Ken's *shoryuken* may have had flame while Ryu's had none, but they were both just as good. Two fighters facing off, identical in body, chests heaving and eyes narrowed. That was chemistry, that was power.

I was glad to see that in the latest *Street Fighter,* Ken finally has his own look and fighting style. He's no longer a Ryu copy. After battling so long, coming head to head but never coming to terms, Ken and Ryu have finally found some other way to be, that doesn't involve holding on to each other as enemies.

It gives me hope for Carson, that we might get past this stalemate before he graduates and goes away forever.

In the meantime, I'll take a pause from this whole hooking up thing. *Fortnite*'s plenty to fill my time these days.

★ ★ ★ ★ ★

LUMBER ME MINE

by
CB Lee

JASMINE CLUTCHES HER BACKPACK STRAPS A little tighter as she exits the bus. *This is it. Senior year,* she thinks, the words somehow falling flat even in her head. The drab gray buildings look the same as ever; the warning bell ringing sounds exactly the same, and the rush of students joking and laughing and lingering on the front lawn could be indistinguishable from any other day at Garden Bells High School.

She didn't know why she expected it to be different.

You're not different, a lingering voice inside her says. *You're the same mousy doormat you've always been, and a summer abroad wouldn't change that.*

"I'm going to have a good year," Jasmine mutters softly to herself. "I am confident, I am strong, I don't need anyone to—ah!"

Jasmine startles as a blur of red and black zooms past her. She barely manages to catch her balance in time. Ahead, the blur turns into a girl in a plaid shirt and jeans, swerving on her skateboard and narrowly avoiding crowds of students. She turns back and waves at Jasmine with a sheepish smile. "I'm sorry! Didn't see you! Are you okay?"

"Yeah, I'm—I'm fine," Jasmine says.

The girl nods and zooms off.

"It's okay," Jasmine says, more to herself than anything, not that the girl can hear her. She looks familiar; she probably was on the same bus just now. "No one really sees me anyway."

Jasmine shuffles forward, keeping her shoulders tucked in as the kids from the bus rush past her.

"Did you see that new alien movie?"

"Football game on Friday, yeah!"

"We're gonna crush Garden Heights!"

"Look at my new boots!"

She lets the conversations wash over her as she walks into her first class, ignoring the cacophony of friends greeting each other, hugs and fist bumps, trading gossip and asking about summer.

"Did you hear Janet dumped her?"

"I don't blame her, she could do so much better."

"What is she wearing, anyway? She looks twelve."

The giggles stop when Jasmine looks up; the three girls don't meet her eyes, but they change the subject to basketball.

Jasmine thought her outfit was cute this morning—a blouse with a Peter Pan collar and a denim skirt she found at Goodwill—but now she isn't so sure. Her pink backpack covered in her enamel pin collection suddenly seems childish, and looking around, everyone else's backpacks are cool—black or gray or sleek muted colors.

It shouldn't bother her, the comments, but they do. Those girls—Jasmine can't remember their names—they're on the basketball team, she thinks. Janet would know who they are; in a school of thousands, she'd remember not only their names but something nice about them, something special. It's what made Janet—Janet.

A sudden pang of longing courses through her as a couple holding hands walks into class, completely lost in one another. They take their seats, hands lingering, as if they're loath to leave each other even for a moment.

Did Janet ever look at her like that?

Maybe Jasmine didn't think this through properly, what it would be like, going back to school after the breakup.

That bitter voice echoes at the back of her mind again. *Did you really think you could handle this on your own? What are you without her, really? You're nothing.*

"No," Jasmine whispers to herself. "I am strong and confident," she repeats. The words sound weak even as she says them, just like how she feels.

Jasmine tries to shake off the doubt coursing through her and rushes into her class, ignoring the heat of eyes on her and the whispers in the hallway.

"Settle down, we're going to get started. Jackson, that's inappropriate. Come on now, don't make me report you both on the first day." A sandy-haired man in his fifties sighs, standing up reluctantly from his desk, and looks at the time. "Alright, I'm Mr. Thompson, this is economics, and the seat you've chosen is going to be your assigned seat for the year."

Jasmine taps her pencil on her desk, and the boy next to her turns and gives her a friendly smile.

"Hey," he whispers. "Cool backpack."

"Thanks," Jasmine whispers back.

"You're Jasmine, right?"

"Yeah, I—"

"Roger," he supplies helpfully.

Jasmine studies him a bit more; he's got a wide forehead and messy hair, and he seems nice. Maybe he could be a friend. Maybe this year won't be terrible after all.

"You know um, Janet's friend, Stacey? Do you think she'd be into me?"

Roger gives her a winning grin, and Jasmine's stomach sinks.

Nope. It's going to suck.

For as long as Jasmine could remember, they'd always been a pair—Janet-and-Jasmine, J2, J-squared, double-Jay-trouble. It seemed inevitable they'd be best friends, going from long afternoons playing pretend in Janet's backyard or creating elaborate stories with Jasmine's stuffed animals to trading stories about what they'd be when they grow up. For Janet, sometimes it'd be President, or an astronaut, always something fantastic. Jasmine had no doubt she'd do it. Janet was that kind of girl: the kind teachers and parents liked, smart and confident and good at sports and making friends.

Jasmine's mom loved Janet.

"Why can't you be more like Janet?" she'd say, right in front of Janet when they'd have her over for dinner.

Jasmine would scoot back in her chair, twiddling her chopsticks idly in her hand, and Janet sitting next to her would laugh and insist that Jasmine was talented too and she was lucky that they were friends.

Being friends with Janet was like being friends with the sun. Wherever they were, people would always be drawn to her, her warmth, her smile, her ideas.

And Janet *always* had ideas: let's go hiking, let's go see that detective noir marathon, let's go eat too much food at all-you-can-eat Korean barbeque, let's go to the zoo, let's go, let's go, let's go. She would plan these elaborate adventures, coordinate with people for carpools and pickups and everyone would have a good time. Jasmine didn't quite understand how she did it, how she got along with everyone, how she knew what different people needed to enjoy themselves, how everyone—*everyone* wanted some of that sunshine.

Being her girlfriend was no different—Janet could sweep excitement into any ordinary day with her wild ideas, and Jasmine would always go along, always say yes. That's how it was between them. Looking back, Jasmine can't even remember properly if it was ever a question to begin with.

They were both sixteen, studying at Janet's house on afternoon when Janet sighed, put down her book, and looked up at her with a serious expression.

"You okay?" Jasmine asked. They had only been studying for twenty minutes; it was out of character for Janet to tire of homework that fast. Then again, she'd been distracted all day by something, staring at Jasmine occasionally with an intense focus, like she was trying to figure out something.

Janet blurted out like it was nothing, "Do you like me?"

Jasmine's mind raced with a whirlwind of thoughts—all the times she thought about Janet, holding her hand, imagining what her lips would taste like, imagining the two of them getting married and what that would be like, if Jasmine could still be a wildlife photographer if she was First Lady. Years of thoughts and daydreams and hopes and dreams flitted through her mind in the split few seconds before Janet spoke again.

"Because I like you. I um, I like girls. And you, specifically." Janet looked down shyly at her chemistry book, and twirled her hair in her fingers.

Jasmine always remembers this: how nervous Janet was, how she'd never played with her hair before, how she'd always been confident and knew exactly what she wanted and there'd never be any doubt that she'd get it.

It's strange, thinking about that afternoon now; it was barely two years ago, but now it's like a dream that happened to a different person, someone who just got swept up and carried away by a bright promise.

Jasmine's first two classes fly by in a blur of teachers and conversations that she feels are somehow about her. It's probably gone around the school twice by now, whatever Janet's been saying.

She walks into yearbook with a relief. There's a few "Hey, Jasmine's", Harry Wu gives her a nod, and Bonnie Owens waves at her. Jasmine smiles back at Bonnie and drops her backpack next to her, taking her seat.

Jasmine listens intently as Ms. Park gives a one-minute spiel about yearbook before handing it over to Bonnie, the editor-in-chief.

"This year, we're going to meet our deadlines!" Bonnie starts. It's pretty much a carbon copy of the speech Joey, their editor-in-chief last year, gave, and then a few months later they promptly derailed into missing deadlines and frantically trying to catch up, but it's always nice to pretend in the beginning anyway.

Jasmine grins despite herself as Bonnie starts brainstorming on the board about how best to get the most features squared away so they can keep on schedule. Jasmine marks up her schedule, chatting with the other photographers about who can do what this week.

It's a familiar rhythm, and Jasmine loves it. Yearbook is the one place people recognize her for her own talent, as a photographer, as an editor. Nobody here ever forgets her name or calls her Janet's girlfriend.

"Hey, how was China?" Bonnie asks, plopping into the chair next to her, speech done.

"Oh," Jasmine says, surprised and a little pleased Bonnie remembered this conversation. They'd never been super close—Jasmine was always spending time with Janet—but Bonnie's always been nice. "It was really pretty."

"Your family has like, a farm, right?"

"My great-aunt's side, yeah," Jasmine says. "I ate so many lychees, it was amazing."

Jasmine had gone to China only once before, when she was ten. While it was great to see the sights, a good chunk of the time was spent visiting relatives she didn't quite know how to talk to, sitting and holding her tea in silence while her parents laughed and talked and caught up. So when her great-aunt invited them again for the summer, Jasmine hadn't planned on it.

But she needed a change, and this time *was* different. Instead of trying to cram visiting endless relatives and sightseeing in one week with her parents, Jasmine spent the entire summer trying to learn Chinese, spending time with her cousins and going for long walks in the countryside. It'd been perfect; she needed time away from this town, from Janet and her attempts to include Jasmine in all her summer plans out of pity.

Ugh.

It had been so humiliating, as if *Janet* was the one to want to break up—and somehow at the end of that conversation, it was like everything Jasmine had said had gone over her head, and Jasmine breaking up with Janet—became about Janet somehow. Like everything always ended up being. Even Jasmine's one, final attempt to stand up for herself and do what she wanted for once, still ended up feeling like it's what Janet wanted all along. It was as if she dumped herself for Janet, who just hadn't gotten around to it.

"How was yours?" Jasmine asks Bonnie, racking her brain to try and remember that conversation before school ended. "Robots?" she ventures. It was some sort of science camp.

"Yes! It was brilliant. I took first place and I made a bunch of friends! Did you know how many different batteries are used in robotic combat?" Bonnie grins, waving her hands, taking the conversation forward.

It's nice, charting out schedules with Bonnie and the yearbook crew. No one asks her about Janet.

Bonnie falls into step behind her as Jasmine heads toward the vocational buildings at the back of the school. "Do you have Nutrition and Household Planning too?"

"Woodshop," Jasmine says, gripping the straps of her backpack even tighter. She signed up for it on a whim; it'd been right after the breakup, right before school ended, and she knew for sure that Janet was taking NHP. She doesn't think she could handle it, a year of Janet being perfect and holding court with her friends as they baked cookies or whatever.

Jasmine just isn't strong enough; she can't handle Janet seeing her, she can't handle another year feeling like she's not good enough.

Bonnie whistles. "I heard Harrelson can be super strict, and you don't get to build anything until like, after the break."

Jasmine shrugs.

"Are you sure you don't want to switch? You still can, right? It'd be fun, I heard we're making empanadas today."

Part of Jasmine does think it would be much more fun to be in a class where they would get to cook every day and then eat their creations. And there's like useful stuff too, like learning to do taxes.

"Mrs. Caldwell won't let me switch," she lies easily. Her counselor probably would if she asked and made a strong case for it, but Jasmine really doesn't want to.

Bonnie nods. "She's still holding a grudge after all the drama you gave her about yearbook counting for your PE credits?"

"Hey! Taking photos is very aerobic," Jasmine says, snorting. That petition saved her high school experience, seriously. She couldn't stand another year of being picked last for pointless scrimmage games in sports that confused her.

Bonnie snickers. "Just tell that to Jason and Harry, they

were so mad they couldn't get credits either. It'd start a precedent, apparently."

"Going to class, ladies," a voice booms at them. It sounds like it's supposed to be a question, but it isn't.

Jasmine looks up. This must be Mr. Harrelson; he's wearing a sawdust-covered apron and crossing his arms at them.

"Yep!" Bonnie says. "I was just walking her to class and now she's here. Bye!"

Harrelson looks at Jasmine, and she shrinks back, hoping he isn't judging her. He probably is. "Well, sit down. We've got a lot of safety to cover."

Jasmine follows him inside, feeling very self-conscious.

The classroom smells like wood and the faint sharp tang of metal, and it's completely different from any class she's been in before. The building is older, for one, the window frames rusted over and glass clouded with age. Multiple workbenches line the main classroom area; at the front is Mr. Harrelson's desk, a chalkboard, and behind it, a locked cage filled with power tools.

It's funny how many kids here Jasmine knows by name and some random detail about them because of yearbook—she's never talked to any of them.

Well, here's your chance, a voice inside her says.

Jasmine tells it to shut up and looks for a seat. There's an empty one next to a long-haired girl in one of the middle rows. She's leaning backwards on her chair, chatting away with the two boys behind her. Her baseball cap is nonchalantly flipped backwards on her head, and she laughs, throwing her head back. She looks completely at home in the woodshop class already, unlike a few of the other students, who sit quietly at their desks and look apprehensively at the tools locked away behind Mr. Harrelson.

"Hey," Jasmine says, her heart leaping into her throat. "Can I sit here?"

The girl touches her hat, adjusting it with a wide grin, balancing effortlessly on one leg of the chair as she sprawls out like the class is her kingdom. "Sure," she says easily. She squints. "Oh hey, you take the Persimmon Grove bus, right?"

"Yes," Jasmine says, sitting down. She looks familiar, but Jasmine's only just started taking the bus. Janet always drove her to school before.

The girl looks at her, biting her lip like she wants to say something, and for a brief moment of panic Jasmine wonders if it's going to be something like *are you a new student* or *how come I've never seen you before* and she'd have to explain.

"Sorry about earlier. Sometimes I go way too fast because if I don't make it to the quad before the warning bell, it's filled with people and I can't practice any of my jumps." She grins, broad and sunny. "I'm Ash, by the way."

"Jasmine." She waits for it, for some semblance of recognition, or the inevitable question about Janet, but it doesn't come.

"Cool. Excited about woodshop?"

Mr. Harrelson coughs and glares at the classroom. "Before anyone asks, no, we're not building anything today. This class is serious business, and our first week we'll be covering safety. If you don't pass the safety test on Friday, you will not be allowed to handle the tools, is that clear?"

The class groans, but there's a good-natured air of energy in the air. Everyone does seem to be looking forward to this.

"I am, actually," Jasmine says to Ash, surprised at herself.

She turns to look at Ash, who's looking at her with some sort of calculated amusement, her lips quirking up in a smile. It's a nice smile, and she has a nice face and she's *cool* and oh no. No. This is not happening.

Jasmine spent the whole summer being independent and confident and she's going to have a good senior year, none of which involves having a hopeless crush. Jasmine already decided: the life of a wildlife photographer is a lonely one, and she just will be single forever. She doesn't need *anyone*.

Ash's smile lights up her whole heart-shaped face, and she adjusts her baseball cap at a jaunty angle. Heat rushes to Jasmine's cheeks, and she turns determinedly back to Mr. Harrelson in the front.

It's not going to be a crush. Nope.

Lunch in the yearbook room is pretty nice, actually; Jasmine's never done it before. She'd always poked awkwardly at her food while Janet and her friends chatted about student government policies or volunteer activities or whatever it was that Janet was organizing. No one talked to Jasmine at all; she was just there.

Bonnie's looking at her with a strange expression and Jasmine realize she's been staring off into space.

"You can ask me, it's okay," Jasmine offers.

Bonnie shrugs. "I figured you knew that I knew. The whole school knows. Janet was telling Priscilla this morning it was a—" and she does finger quotes— "'mutually amicable thing at the end of junior year, and we both agreed to go our separate ways, of course we're still friends', which everyone is taking to mean that she dumped your sorry ass by the side of the road. No offense." She pats Jasmine on the shoulder. "Are you okay?"

Something inside Jasmine splinters, a hard, angry thing rising inside her. Of course. Of course, Janet would spin it the way she wanted to in front of her friends.

Oh.

Something actually broke.

"If you need a new pencil for class, I can give you one," Bonnie says, taking the broken pieces of the pencil out of Jasmine's hand gently. "I take it that it wasn't exactly mutual?"

"Last year—wasn't good," Jasmine says. It feels strange to admit it out loud, that their picture-perfect relationship was anything but. "And I was telling myself for months to get out and I finally did and I still can't—she's everywhere," she admits miserably.

Bonnie takes a thoughtful bite of her pizza. "Well, I'm glad you did. You're doing your best, don't be too hard on yourself," she says with a small smile.

"Thanks," Jasmine says, grateful.

A few other students sit down with their lunches, and Bonnie changes the subject. "Anyway, so Harry says he's afraid of water, can you cover the swim meet next Tuesday?"

"I am *not* afraid of water!" Harry insists. "I just am creeped out by those plastic floaty things—"

"You mean the lanes?" Jasmine teases.

The yearbook room erupts into laughter. Harry rolls his eyes as Preston elbows him good-naturedly.

The rest of lunch should be forgettable—Bonnie and Harry discuss the finer points of pool equipment; Preston asks her—

Jasmine, of all people!—for advice on how to ask out Jimmy Veracruz; Ms. Park surprises them with Halloween candy. But it's so nice, laughing and joking with her friends, that Jasmine wonders why she wasted so much time being someone else's shadow.

Woodshop becomes, surprisingly, the one place she can relax and have fun. Jasmine's other classes start piling on the homework and yearbook is starting to ramp up in intensity; she's often out every afternoon taking photos for features and interviews.

Mr. Harrelson is finishing a long-winded story that Jasmine lost track of ten minutes ago. "And that's how I lost my finger. Not fighting the bear, but because I didn't read the safety manual properly and wasn't watching the saw."

"Do you really think Mr. Harrelson did all those things?" Jasmine whispers to Ash. "He keeps talking about the war, but which one? How old is he?"

Ash chuckles. "He could be immortal."

"Getting lost in a snowstorm in Russia? Losing a bet in Spain? He's like, traveled the world. He just might be." Jasmine laughs. "Or maybe he is part of a secret underground crime ring. I wonder if he has anything to do with that fake wig shop."

Ash tilts her head at her. "That one on Persimmon and Walnut? I always thought that place was creepy!"

Jasmine's never been inside, but the dusty storefront has always seemed strange to her. She turns and grins at Ash. "Wanna go check it out with me? There's also a boba shop a block away, we could go get some boba and then do some reconnaissance." The words fly out of her before she realizes it sounds suspiciously like a date.

No, no, she and Ash are friends now—they make jokes about Mr. Harrelson's mustache and study the safety manual together, draw blueprints for ideas and designs of stuff they could build for their project when they actually get drawing. Ash rips out pages from her notebook and shares them with Jasmine before she can even ask, and always saves the seat next to her for class.

It's always on the tip of her tongue to ask if Ash wants to eat lunch together, since their class is right before, but Ash always waves at her goodbye and speeds off on her skateboard.

Jasmine has seen her a few mornings, walking to the bus as well, but she hasn't struck up the courage to say hi or even sit next to her.

She doesn't want to admit it, but she's been enjoying it, getting to know someone on her own, as herself.

"That sounds like fun!" Ash says, grinning at her. "You take the Persimmon bus home, right? I see you sometimes in the morning but I never see you on the three o'clock bus going back."

"Oh, I usually stay after for yearbook. I'm covering all the fall sports so I have to get good shots of the home games this year," Jasmine says. "But uh, this Thursday I don't have anything."

"Thursday it is," Ash says.

Thursday comes too soon and not soon enough. Jasmine tries three different outfits before settling on a floral-print sundress and high-top sneakers. She stares at herself in the mirror, wondering if it's too much. No, plenty of girls wear dresses to school. It's cute. She's cute. She's hanging out with Ash, who she likes.

Like like? a small annoying voice in her head pops up.

"Shut up," Jasmine says aloud.

She walks to school, lingering on the corner of Persimmon until she sees Ash skateboarding toward her.

"Hey!" Ash says brightly. She slows to a graceful stop, kicking her board up and holding it nonchalantly. "Guess what, I was watching the History Channel last night and I swear in the documentary on cryptids there was a guy who looked just like Mr. Harrelson."

"Why is a documentary on cryptids on the History Channel?" Jasmine asks. She also can't stop smiling at Ash, she can't help it.

Ash usually wears her baseball cap over her hair down, but today her brown hair is pulled up into a high ponytail. A few wisps frame her face, falling around her dark skin in soft curls. It's cute, she's always cute, why is Jasmine even thinking about this—

"Wanna sit with me?"

"Yeah, sure," Jasmine says, following behind her onto the crowded bus. They get a seat near the back, and for all that Jasmine thought it'd be awkward, it isn't. It's just like wood-shop, conversation flowing easily.

Ash points to the enamel pins on Jasmine's backpack. "These are cool! I like this one the best." She chuckles, flicking a cat riding a Roomba.

"That's one of my favorites," Jasmine says, catching her

breath. Ash is leaning close, close enough for her to smell her hair. Jasmine freezes, going unnaturally still.

"These are all awesome," Ash says, flicking a rainbow pin with the slogan *SOUNDS GAY, I'M IN.*

Jasmine blushes. "Thanks. Do you have any?"

"Yeah, I've got a few on one of my jackets, but I like how you have all of yours here."

Ash's knee knocks against Jasmine's own, their thighs brushing together the entire ride to school.

"Today, we will practice hammering nails into these boards. Remember to be aware at all times. Got it?" Mr. Harrelson glares at the class before passing out hammers to everyone.

"The mythical Cage of Tools is finally open," Ash says, in a deep dramatic voice.

Jasmine chuckles, marking her board with a row of neat dots, matching the diagram on the board precisely.

"No loose clothing, Miss Rodriguez," Mr. Harrelson says, his face twitching at Ash's plaid overshirt.

"We're not using any power tools, I don't think it'd be a problem." Ash rolls her eyes.

"Safety first!"

"Fine, fine," Ash mutters, taking off the flannel. She's wearing a tight black t-shirt underneath, stretched tight over her toned arms and—

Oh no.

Jasmine blinks and misses with her marker, messing up her row. She grits her teeth and tries again, holding a nail still. She grips the hammer in her hand, concentrating as she aims for the head of the nail, tapping it lightly.

She looks up to find Harrelson watching her. "You'll have to use a bit more force, Ms. Chau," he says. "Try again."

Jasmine raises the hammer back up and bites back a laugh; Ash is holding her hammer up to her face in the semblance of a mustache, and is wobbling around, doing an impression of Mr. Harrelson.

Harrelson narrows his eyes at her. "Something funny?"

"No, just uh—I'll try to use more force, thanks." Jasmine bursts into giggles as soon as Harrelson leaves their workbench and continues his walk around the class.

"Yeah, Jasmine, use the Force to draw a straight line," Ash teases.

"I can't do anything straight," Jasmine says.

Ash stares at her for a long moment before she bursts into laughter, throwing her head back with bright, joyful chortles.

"That was a good one," she gasps, reaching up to wipe her eyes. "Am I crying? I'm crying. You're too funny."

Jasmine's never been called funny before, and she feels hot all of a sudden, all her blood rushing to her face with pleased surprise. "Not as funny as you. That Harrelson impression was spot-on. I'm going to forever remember your hammer mustache."

Ash grins, turning to her board with intense focus as she starts to hammer all her nails in a neat row.

Mr. Harrelson's voice booms from the front of the room. "Now, once we finish with this, we'll move on to handsaws, but we can't until everyone has demonstrated their ability to complete the first task."

Oh, right. Jasmine's been too busy laughing with Ash to do any sort of hammering. She swings it again, getting the first one to go in, albeit a bit crookedly. Four more to go. Jasmine tries to settle into a rhythm of it, and then looks up to see how Ash is doing.

Ash's arms are built up, her biceps high and rounded, tight with muscle, and she looks so capable and beautiful, her hair gathered up at the top of her head, her ponytail bobbing with every swing. A few strands of hair have escaped her ponytail, falling down to the nape of her neck in soft, delicate curls that Jasmine wants to touch—

A white-hot scaring pain suddenly blossoms from her thumb and forefinger and Jasmine lets out a high-pitched scream. Tears spring to her eyes, and the pain is so sharp and intense that it's all she can do to just hold her hand there, lip wobbling. She's vaguely aware of Mr. Harrelson shouting and classmates gathering around her, and Ash stepping forward with a worried expression.

"Jasmine! Are you okay?"

"Hold your arm up to the ceiling, Ms. Chau—"

Jasmine doesn't want to cry in front of everyone in class, and she knows tears are already falling down her face, it hurts *so much*—

Mr. Harrelson is saying something, and there's pressure on her hand, but it feels like it's pulsing, like she's got a whole new heartbeat just in her hand and it's radiating red-hot pain.

Jasmine squints at her hand. Mr. Harrelson's pressed a wad of paper towels to it, and he instructs for her to hold it steady. "Now keep your arm raised and pressure on this." He shakes his head. "You better head down to the nurse's office." He scribbles a note and hands it to Jasmine.

"I'll go with you," Ash offers. She grabs Jasmine's backpack and her own, and the plaid shirt. "Come on." She grabs the other wad of paper towels Harrelson offers them and gently leads Jasmine out the door.

The hallways seem strangely empty and quiet, in this in-between, and Ash babbles to fill the silence. "One time, I was trying a flip and landed on the edge of the ramp. I did the thing where I tried to break the fall with my face, ended up with this. It bled like a river and hurt so badly." Ash points to her right eyebrow, where a long, thin scar streaks down from her forehead.

"I don't think I'll get a cool scar, though," Jasmine mutters.

Ash laughs. "That's okay, you're plenty cool enough."

Jasmine blushes.

Ms. Sugihara, the school nurse, tuts appropriately as she undoes the makeshift paper towel bandage and tosses it in the trash. "Did Mr. Harrelson do this? I swear, just because that man took a few first aid courses doesn't mean he knows everything." She squints as she cleans the small cut on Jasmine's hand with an alcohol swab. "Well, I've certainly seen worse."

It's not as bad as Jasmine thought it would be, now that her hand has stopped bleeding. There's a small tear in her skin where the hammer struck her hand, and it still hurts, but it's more of an angry throbbing now.

Ms. Sugihara bandages her cut neatly with gauze and medical tape, and gives Jasmine an ice pack, instructing her to press it in place. The cold relief is immediate.

"I don't think anything's broken, but you're welcome to call your parents and have them take you to the doctor if you like." Ms. Sugihara smiles at them both.

"I think I'll be okay," Jasmine says.

"Do you have any candy, Ms. S?" Ash asks, swinging her legs as she sits next to Jasmine on the exam bed.

"Of course, Ashley," Ms. Sugihara says with a smile, pulling a bowl out from under her desk. "You're both welcome to stay here through lunch. Jasmine, if you need a note for fifth and sixth period, let me know."

"I think I'll be fine," Jasmine says. "Thank you!"

"Okay. I'm going to check on another student, okay? If you need me, I'll be over there." Ms. Sugihara nods at them before heading over to the bed at the other end of the room, taking a groaning boy's temperature.

Ash is looking at her feet, almost shy. "I uh, I did an independent study last year and helped out in the main office."

"That sounds nice," Jasmine says. "I've never had a free period."

Ash shrugs. "It's not so bad. I did my homework, helped file some stuff. Got to know some of the teachers. Ate a lot of Ms. S's candy."

"What else are you taking?"

Ash rattles off her classes; they're similar to Jasmine's, aside that Ash is in AP English. "And theatre," she adds. "Been in the program since freshman year."

"That's cool!" Jasmine says wistfully. "I've always wanted to go see the shows." She'd always ended up with the sports beat for yearbook, so never really had the time.

"I'm gonna be Lucy in the Charlie Brown musical," Ash says quietly and looks up at Jasmine with a soft smile. "It opens right before the winter break."

"Okay, I'm definitely gonna go now," Jasmine says. "Do you sing?"

"You bet."

Ash beams at her, and Jasmine could swear her hand is healed already.

There's a long moment that's only broken by the sound of someone coughing in the other room, and Jasmine ducks her head, trying not to blush.

Ash sits down next to her, the paper on the bed crinkling as she sits down. "Can I see?"

Jasmine offers her hand.

Ash's fingers are gentle, holding her bandaged hand carefully. She rearranges the ice pack, folding it around Jasmine's hand, and then slowly winds her plaid shirt around the ice pack, tying a knot. "There. Now you don't have to hold it," she says brightly.

Jasmine wants to say something, like ask Ash if she would hold her hand instead, but Ash is already standing up.

"I'll go get you lunch and bring it back for you before I go to class," she says, giving Jasmine a luminous smile.

Jasmine shakes; no wonder she missed, she never stood a chance.

For having smashed her hand with a hammer—well, not completely smashed, but it still hurt—Jasmine's having a great day. She and Ash share a bus ride back to their neighborhood and then instead of walking home, they idle down Persimmon Grove, chatting and laughing.

"For real, I can't believe we've never had any classes together!"

Ash gives her a wry grin and shrugs. "Sometimes that's just the way the cookie crumbles." She flips her skateboard over, holding it so the wheels are facing outwards, spinning one idly with her hand. She catches Jasmine watching her and holds out the board with a smile. "Wanna try?"

"Oh, I don't know, I've got terrible balance," Jasmine says, giving the board a wary eye.

"I'll be right here!" Ash winks at her.

"All right."

Jasmine lets Ash walk her through how to stand, trying not to tremble when she puts her hand on the small of her back, and then she's standing on the board, balancing and everything. "Look! I'm doing it!"

"You are certainly standing on it," Ash teases. "Okay, now push off with your—which is your dominant foot?"

"Uh, right, I think—like this?"

Jasmine takes a tentative step, pressing off the sidewalk with her foot, and then the skateboard rolls forward a few feet. Ash runs behind her, steadying her by the shoulders and laughing. Jasmine laughs too; she can't remember the last time she's felt this happy just fooling around. She feels light and free, with the sun shining down on her and Ash by her side.

"That's probably enough for today," Ash says.

Jasmine follows her gaze to where Persimmon is starting to climb upwards. "Oh yeah, good idea. Let's save hills for another day. Boba?"

"Yeah!"

BOBA READY FOR IT is crowded already, as Jasmine expects at this hour. She's about to push open the door when she spots a familiar asymmetrical bob through the window.

Jasmine freezes, her heart beginning to pound out a panicked rhythm.

Janet looks perfect as always, not a hair out of place, casually sipping from her drink and giggling with—Jasmine doesn't know who she is, but she's pretty, with long, flowing curls.

Jasmine really, really doesn't want to be here. She hasn't talked to Janet since the breakup, not that Janet hasn't tried, sending her cutesy little text messages and invitations to her parties and whatever. Jasmine doesn't know what she means by it, why she's trying to be overly friendly. She's spotted Janet out of the corner of her eye a few times at school, and Janet's always smiled and waved, but it felt hollow, strange, and Jasmine would just turn and find another route to go to class.

"Hey, can we go get ice cream instead?" Jasmine asks, stepping away from the window like she's been burned.

"Oh—okay, sure." Ash gives her a worried look, but follows Jasmine right past the shop, but not before looking curiously in the window.

Jasmine walks as fast as she can, anxiety giving her speed as she hurries to the end of the block.

Ash keeps pace, falling in step next to her. "Are you okay?"

"I—" Jasmine catches her breath, staring at the sidewalk, at the splotches of old gum on the pavement, on the hamburger wrapper trying to fly into the gutter. She doesn't really want to talk about it, especially not with the girl that—oh god, here she is admitting it to herself—that she *does* have a crush on.

Maybe she doesn't deserve this, maybe she should be just alone forever. After all, Janet was perfect, and if she couldn't be happy with Janet, then she couldn't be happy with anyone.

"I get it. I have so many exes that like, I can't go to half the eating establishments in Garden Heights," Ash says brightly, with the tone Jasmine's come to recognize as her unique brand of entertaining bullshit. "I may have to move out of this town as soon as possible. It's not big enough, you know?" Her tone is playful but the hand she places on Jasmine's shoulder is kind, like a question. Asking her if she needs help.

"I'm just kidding," Ash says, leaning against the shop with her. This end of the block is quieter, away from the popular restaurants and stores. "I've only dated like, two people, and we're all still friends. We'd never run each other out of town." She glances at Jasmine, pausing for a second. "I'm totally ace, by the way."

Jasmine turns to Ash and finds her looking back with a sincere, open expression. "Cool," Jasmine says with a smile.

"Bet you're surprised! Because I'm so extroverted and charming and witty and funny!" Ash says, pointing two finger guns at Jasmine.

She laughs in spite of herself. "I don't think any of those things are mutually exclusive with being asexual."

Ash's grin only widens. "Oh, do you know many asexual people then? Am I not the most charming of them all?"

Jasmine laughs, relaxing into the easy camaraderie with Ash. "I mean, I guess I know a lot of people, but it's not something I would know, right? I mean, our school is huge. It's likely I know a bunch of ace people."

"And I'm the coolest."

"You are the coolest person I know, period."

Ash's eyes are warm and brown and she's standing close enough for Jasmine to see little flecks of gold, and she's so happy, right here in this moment, just the two of them smiling at each other, a moment stretching out into infinity.

"You know," Ash says conspiratorially, leaning closer. "I would totally date someone, if I really liked them. And I'm into kissing, too."

"Oh?" Jasmine says, hope fluttering in her heart.

"Hey! You kids can't lean against the store window like that. You'll leave smudges on the glass," a cross voice says, the door to their left opening.

Jasmine and Ash step away from the door and the angry shopkeeper, laughing as the mystery of the fake wig shop beckons onward.

"You have a crush on her, don't you?" Bonnie asks, turning to her in and giving her a sly look.

"Shh!" Jasmine shushes her frantically. She glances about the yearbook room, but no one else is listening, laughing and gossiping over their lunch or busy on a computer. Well, only Harry is—wait, no, Harry's checking sports scores.

"I think it's cute," Bonnie says. "So woodshop's going well, huh?"

"Yeah," Jasmine says, thinking about Ash helping her hold a piece of her birdhouse steady as she screwed it in place.

"You gonna ask her out?"

Jasmine sighs. "I don't know. We've hung out a few times, but…"

"Not officially?" Bonnie tilts her head.

"I mean, we went to the movies. And another time she recorded this documentary about cryptids and we watched it at her house. But, uh, I don't know if I can actually just be like, do you want to date me? Be my girlfriend?" Jasmine frowns. Even just saying it sounds impossible. And the more time they spend together, Jasmine likes her more and more.

"Ah, the old is-this-a-date-or-not-a-date question," Bonnie says.

"Right? How do you know?"

Bonnie squares her jaw and gives Jasmine a definite look. "I feel like, unless both parties know it's a date, then it's not a date. It's a matter of like, having a clear declaration of intent."

"I don't know if I can do that," Jasmine says. She's never done anything like that before. "Plus, we haven't really had a lot of time lately either."

It seemed like the year just got started and then it got way too busy; it's already Homecoming week, and yearbook is frantically trying to keep up with deadlines. Jasmine's been busy every day after school either photographing or editing, and she knows Ash's schedule is just as packed, practicing for the upcoming musical. "I want to," Jasmine admits, "but...time."

"Time," Bonnie agrees. "I think my boyfriend is a myth at this point. But you can ask her to Homecoming, right?"

Jasmine gives Bonnie a wry grin. "You're not putting me on feature duty?"

"Nah. Harry's got it, considering how often you had to cover for him. Go ask your girl."

Jasmine is so lost in thoughts about Homecoming, giddy with nerves, which is why she doesn't see it coming. In hindsight, she should have recognized that power-walk anywhere. She's heading to woodshop thinking of a way to smoothly ask Ash to go to Homecoming when Janet intercepts her, right in the narrow hallway.

"Hey, Jazz," Janet says smoothly, like they're still best friends, like they're still together, like nothing ever happened. "Heading to the P building?"

"Yes," Jasmine says warily. She looks around; she's in one of the narrow hallways, and to head back down that way means she'd have to go around the whole building to get to English. "Hi. Good to see you."

In some way, it is good to see her; Jasmine can't turn off that part of her that still cares for Janet, that grew up with her and wants the best for her.

"It's always great to see you," Janet says, with that smile that Jasmine knows so well. She knows all of Janet's looks, from the I'm-going-to-destroy-you glare she uses on opposing teams at basketball and anyone foolish enough to run against her in student government, the how-sweet-of-you-I'm-secretly-planning-a-way-around-this smile she often employed around their parents, and Jasmine's least favorite, the I-want-something-from-you lip curl.

"How are you?" Janet asks sweetly. It almost feels sincere. Maybe it is, who knows?

"Busy. Yearbook and all. How's presidenting?"

There's an easy conversation switch, with Janet's favorite subject: herself. "Oh, good! We're right on schedule with fund-raising, this is going to be the best Homecoming yet! I think the theme I came up with works out so well—Priscilla thought we'd never get the student council to agree, but you know me!" Janet giggles a little.

Jasmine hasn't heard the humblebrag in so long that she's almost charmed by it. She chuckles. "*Beyond the Stars*, right? I've seen the posters. Looks great."

"Thanks," Janet preens. "By the way, toffee is still your favorite, right? I saved you one."

She hands Jasmine a chocolate bar, one of the kinds from the student council fund-raiser.

Jasmine takes it, because she does love chocolate with toffee bits.

"Look, I know that you usually do the interviews for the student council and such after the winter break, but we're all going to be dressed up for Homecoming and I think it would be wonderful to get a few shots of us and this marvelous event we organized for the yearbook spread." Janet smiles at her and leans in close. "Did you know I'm on the Homecoming court this year?"

Jasmine's seen the posters. *JANET WU FOR HOMECOMING QUEEN* on every hallway, every building, decorated in glitter.

"Congratulations," she offers.

"Thank you!" Janet squeals. In another life, her excitement might have been infectious, and Jasmine would have bounced along with her, jumped up and down, but she's remembering it all now, the way Janet ignored her, the way Janet never made time for her the way she made time for any of her other activities, the way Janet would brush aside her ideas, her opinions, her thoughts, like it was nothing. Like she was nothing.

Jasmine is bristling now, marinating in all the memories, and waiting. Because Janet isn't going to ask, she's going to lay it all out, whatever she wants, and at the end of the conversation Jasmine would find herself volunteering to do whatever it is she wanted.

But no. Not today. Janet can say all she wants about how

she "thinks it would be wonderful" or whatever but if she wants Jasmine's help, she's gotta ask for it.

"I've missed you, Jazz," Janet says, her eyes going soft and stepping closer, and oh if Jasmine doesn't know this Janet too. "Do you remember last Spring Fling? We slow-danced in the aquarium, and the light was so pretty, shining through the water and making everything sparkle. We looked so lovely together."

It had been one of those rare mostly-nice nights. "Yeah. I still can't believe you got them to rent to our rinky-dink school."

"It was *Under the Sea*, I had to," Janet says, with a smirk.

Jasmine scoffs, and Janet rolls her eyes, and for a second it is like the old times.

"I think it would be wonderful to dance with you again. Like at Homecoming, maybe? Of course, with the theme *Beyond the Stars* you wouldn't go wrong with a blue dress." Janet taps her chin thoughtfully. "Then again that dress of yours was more cerulean, which would be acceptable, but I'm sure you could find something in a navy, with some sparkles, that would be lovely, although not black, since my dress is black and we wouldn't want to be matching exactly, but complementary—"

"Did you just—are you even hearing yourself right now?" Jasmine blurts out.

"Why yes, I was saying you'd look wonderful in a navy dress," Janet says breezily.

"And there's the part where you just assumed I'd go to Homecoming with you!" Jasmine says, her voice cracking, but she holds steady. "You can't just—Janet, this is why I said it wouldn't work, you never listened to me at all! I never said yes, you can't—I don't want to go with you. We're not together anymore!"

"Every couple goes through their rough patches," Janet says, eyes glinting. "And I'm sorry that you felt that way—"

"That's *not* an apology, and you know it," Jasmine says, gripping her backpack tighter.

"I promise I'll listen more," Janet says. "I know I wasn't the most attentive—"

She keeps going, spinning promises and promises, reaching out and taking Jasmine's hand, stroking it just like she used to, and for a second Jasmine thinks about it, thinks about Janet promising to change and it'd be like the good times, when they'd laugh and joke and watch movies and skip rocks at the lake.

Jasmine isn't even listening to Janet anymore, just watching her smile and promise, like she's done before, and she knows Janet's not going to change.

Jasmine's changed.

She doesn't have to take this anymore, she doesn't have to just be Janet's girlfriend, the wallflower, the one uncomfortable at parties and large gatherings where Janet thrived, the one convenient ear to listen to, a shoulder to lean on, but never there when Jasmine needed her.

Maybe Jasmine hung on to that relationship so long because she was afraid—afraid of being single, afraid of being left out, at having to define who she was without Janet. But Jasmine knows her worth now; she doesn't have to put herself last.

"No," Jasmine says.

"What?"

"No." Jasmine pulls herself up to her tallest height, standing strong. She lets go of her backpack and makes a no-way motion with her hands. "Look, I appreciate being asked, but I'm not interested in going to Homecoming with you, or getting back together, or any combination of those." She hands the chocolate bar back as well. "You can keep this too, or put it back in the fund-raising box you took it out of. Sell it for funds to make Homecoming look great, whatever."

Janet tilts her head, a confused look on her face; she's really not used to people saying no at all. She coughs. "All right, then. I—would you be able to photograph the student council at the dance, then?"

"Ask Harry. I hear he'll be there." Jasmine turns around and starts down the hallway for class.

"But his pictures aren't as good as yours!" Janet calls after her.

"I need to get to class," Jasmine says, a feeling of triumph coursing through her veins.

The handsaws are ridiculously loud, and the class takes turns heading up to the power tool area to do any cutting under Mr. Harrelson's watchful eye.

"How's it going?" Jasmine asks loudly.

"What?" Ash shakes her head, laughing and pointing at the saw.

"I said how's it going?"

"It's going!" Ash says.

Ryan is behind them in line, and he's saying something to Jasmine that she can't quite make out.

"What about a limo?" Jasmine asks.

Ryan repeats again, "I said, do you and Janet want in on the limo for Homecoming?"

The handsaw turns off, right while Ryan's talking in an unnaturally loud voice, and it makes several people stop to stare.

"We've only got six so far and Priscilla says we need at least four more to make it so it's not really expensive," Ryan says imploringly, looking at Jasmine.

"Oh, you're going to Homecoming with Janet," Ash says, a little too casually.

"No, I'm not— Ryan, what?"

Ryan blinks. "Priscilla told me that Janet was taking you, I don't know." He backs up, looking between Ash's cold stare and Jasmine's confused one. "So um, let me know by Wednesday about the limo, okay?"

He slinks back to his seat.

Ash and Jasmine are left alone in line for the recently vacated handsaw. "You go," Jasmine says, jerking her head forward.

"No, you take it. I'll wait for the next one," Ash says dully.

"I'm not going to Homecoming with Janet," Jasmine says softly.

"He just said—"

"Janet probably told all her friends that, but she just asked me and I said no." Jasmine sighs, running her hands through her hair.

Ash turns to look at her, raising her eyebrows. "Really?"

Jasmine takes a deep breath. She's been holding on to her feelings for so long, afraid of what might happen, what might change, but if she doesn't do it now she'll never know. "I like you."

"Oh," Ash says, a pleased flush starting on her cheeks.

"I like your face and your hair and the way you laugh, and joking around with you during class and having lunch with you and hearing about your conspiracy theories, and I've never been brave enough to try skateboarding before, but you were really nice about it and I just—I like you, okay?" Jasmine is flustered, this is nowhere near the cool and fun and flirty vibe she wanted to throw off but she's trying her best.

"I like you too. A lot," Ash says, with a small smile.

"And I'd like to use the handsaw, and get an A in this class," mutters Jimmy behind them.

Ash catches Jasmine's eye, and they laugh, shuffling out of the way and back to their workbench. They try their best to do the assignment, but they just keep talking and laughing and every time Jasmine looks at Ash she can't help but smile, and then Ash is smiling back at her, and they don't make it back to the handsaw at all the whole period.

"And what do you call this?" Mr. Harrelson asks, scrutinizing the pieces of wood glued together to make—well, Jasmine's not sure what it is.

"A curio display case," Ash says smoothly.

"You didn't cut any of the pieces at all," he observes.

"It's more of an art statement. The display case itself is meant to evoke feelings of doubt and existentialism," Jasmine adds.

"All right," Mr. Harrelson says. "I suppose it's better that you're taking this handsaw business slow, Ms. Chau."

Jasmine chuckles. "Yes, I wouldn't want to have to go to the nurse again."

Ash elbows her playfully. "You know I'd go with you if you did."

"Thanks," Jasmine says with a smile.

Harrelson nods at them before moving on to the next bench for his critiques, shaking his head and muttering "Existentialism," to himself.

Ash reaches for Jasmine's hand, gently stroking the light scar at the base of her thumb. "What did I tell you? Cool scar."

Jasmine laughs. "That's probably gonna fade in like, a week."

Ash hums to herself. "Who knows?"

Jasmine's hand seems to tingle under Ash's touch, every time her fingers graze across her skin sending sparks down her spine. "You know, I'm really glad I decided to take this class."

"Me too." Ash smiles at her. "It's such a big school, I don't know if we would have had the chance to get to know each other."

Jasmine thinks of all the classes and all the buses and all the maybes in the world, and how this almost didn't happen, how she almost didn't ask because she was ready to accept the world as it is.

Jasmine leans in close, takes in the incandescent way Ash is smiling, her whole face radiating with joy, and interlaces their fingers together.

It turns out that she does have the strength for this after all.

★ ★ ★ ★ ★

FOLLOWER

by
Will Kostakis

IT'S THE SECOND LAST DAY OF THE SUMMER holidays and everyone's had the same idea. The beach is packed. You can't take two steps without tripping over a sunbather or a phone somebody's stuffed inside a plastic cup to amplify their streaming playlist.

Not everyone had the *exact* same idea though. I brought two extra towels and laid them on either side of me. It looks as if I have two friends in the ocean, but really, I just wanted the option to sprawl.

I don't get enough credit for using my genius only for personal gain and not all-out evil.

I have no intention of giving up my territory, at least, not until I think I recognize the guy tripping over sunbathers and phones in plastic cups. From afar, he looks like moderately famous internet celebrity and bisexual legend @London-FromBrooklyn. I haven't decided whether it is him or just wishful thinking, when the guy stops close to me, *really* close to me. Like, the side of his foot is grazing one of my territory-preserving towels. He scans the area. He's wearing a pair of pineapple-print boardshorts. He has a tripod over one shoulder.

I reach for my phone, wipe the sunscreen grease off the screen, and pull up @LondonFromBrooklyn's profile. I compare the guy in the latest pic with the guy in the pineapple-print board shorts in front of me. Same curly hair. Same unnecessarily ripped physique.

It's him.

"Are you…?" The words are barely audible. I clear my throat and try again with fifty per cent more masc. "Are you looking for a spot?"

He turns away from the ocean and beams down at me. "Yeah." London's accent is every bit as amazing as his video posts have led me to believe.

I peel back the towel between us with an urgency the situation dictates. "You can hang here," I say, committing to the ridiculous-sounding deep voice.

"Your friends won't mind?"

I'd forgotten about my fake friends in the ocean. "Oh, they'll be a while. They're not very good swimmers. They've probably been pulled out by a rip or something."

That makes him laugh. He tells me he won't be long. He just needs somewhere to take a photo.

He plonks down the tripod and fixes a camera to it. He aims the lens towards the ocean—the tumbling, frothing waves breaking against the shore.

"You're London, right?" I ask.

"I am." He doesn't turn away from his camera. "Have you heard of me?"

"A little." The understatement of the year.

When I first signed up for WeGlo, I kept it a secret. The app took over my school, but Mum skimmed the user agreement and was adamant I wouldn't download it before I turned thirteen. I wasn't going to miss out though, so I downloaded it...several hundred times.

Every time I wanted to see my friends' posts. I deleted it the moment I was done. That way, Mum never knew I had it. After I turned thirteen, it took me a solid few weeks to stop accidentally deleting the app out of habit.

At first, I was only on it to know what my friends were up to. Then I started following famous people. That was cool. Then I visited profiles I wasn't following. I was very careful never to accidentally follow them. I would stay up late scrolling through their feeds.

They were guys on the beach, guys playing video games. I was beginning to wrap my head around this maybe-being-gay thing and I had this app that tethered me to all these guys... Gymnast guys, nerdy guys, other-side-of-the-world guys.

I told myself I wanted to look like them—a lie. I wanted to kiss them. Especially the shirtless ones. I started to risk liking the occasional post, hoping they would see my pics and like me back. Some did. Ego boost. The first time I followed a random shirtless guy from Spain, my heart was beating out of my chest. I was worried what someone might think if they noticed.

Now I don't care. I'm gay. It's in my profile bio.

Jason. 18. Sydney AU. Gay.

Stalk my following list, you'll see lots of random shirtless guys. London's one of them, but that's not how he pitches himself:

London/19/BKLYN/Influencer/Travel Lover/
Travelling Lover

He's an *influencer*. Groan. A *travelling lover*. Double groan. He's one of those people with brands and aesthetics. His is about love. Falling in it. Embracing it. He's WeGlo-famous for travelling the world, sharing snaps kissing people he meets along the way. He calls them his scattered soul mates. Every week, a different kiss, a different soul mate. He pitches it as romance. Sponsored by Grinners Breath Mints. It's good for a laugh.

I'll forgive a lot when a guy's shirtless, and London's shirtless *a lot*.

I'm sure some people think he's sincere though. He has more followers than seconds I've been alive. Well, not really. But he has a ton of followers.

He's squatted by the camera, adjusting its settings. They'd kill for an opportunity to be this close to him, to see him in action.

He springs up. "Do you mind watching this for me?" he asks.

"Sure."

He needs to fetch his scattered soul mate, someone he met yesterday and "fell in love" with. They're probably waiting in a shady spot on the edge of beach.

When he springs up, he doesn't walk anywhere with purpose. It's more of a wander. He's stepping over sunbathers and phones in plastic cups, his head snapping from side to side. He's searching. I sit up a little. I always thought his profile was a *little* cynical, but this is next-level. He's looking for a random person to kiss him on camera, so he can call it love.

He's talking to some dude whose skin glistens in the sun. I can't make out what they're saying, but I mutter the sales pitch under my breath.

"Hey, I don't know you, but wanna play tonsil tennis for WeGlo? I'll get $0.01 per 100 likes from a breath mint company and you'll get to feel famous for a fleeting moment."

The dude with the glistening skin shakes his head.

"Aw? That doesn't appeal? What a shock."

London steps over more sunbathers, more phones in plastic cups. He ends up chatting to this girl. She looks about my age. He must've tweaked the sales pitch, because she seems far more into the idea. He leads her over.

"Eve, this is…" London's brow creases. He's realised he never asked my name.

"Jason," I say.

"Hi."

London directs Eve to kneel in front of the camera. He checks the framing of the shot and sets the timer and then crawls over to join her.

This is really happening right in front of me.

There's some umming and ahhing about their pose. He trials a hand on her waist and reconsiders. She wraps an arm around his shoulder. He tenses so his muscles bulge.

As the timer nears its end, they lean into each other and kiss. I mean, they really go at it. I hear the smacking of tongues and everything. The camera takes a series of shots in rapid succession and then they immediately pull apart. There's an awkward laugh to diffuse the tension. He crawls over to the tripod and squints down at the camera's display to check the quality of the image.

I'm in awe. It's one thing to believe his profile is fake and cynical, but it's another seeing how fake and cynical it actually is. I'm impressed. My trick with the towels seems pedestrian compared to the evil-genius levels on display.

I must be staring because Eve gives me a little wave. "Are you two friends?" she asks.

"He's a follower," London answers for me.

Eve's beaming. "Like me. There are heaps of us," she says. "We're the population of a small nation." I can tell by the way she says it...*that* was the appeal of kissing someone she's known a whole five seconds. The audience. The likes. "Isn't his stuff so romantic?" she asks.

"Yeah, that's why I follow him. The romance."

I can see London biting back a smirk. After Eve says her goodbyes and retreats to her towel, I ask him if that's what all his shoots are like.

"Yeah, pretty much," he says.

I recall the captions, the long stories of how he meets his latest soul mate. "But what about the captions?"

"Oh, they're made up. The sponsored content deal is for a pic and fifty words."

"You don't feel weird about it?"

He laughs. "No one thinks it's real."

"Eve thought it was romantic."

"And then she kissed me and wandered off. Deep down, no one genuinely believes I fall in love with a different person every week. It's content. It's clicks. Everyone knows it's fake."

I laugh.

"They do, right?" he says.

"I'm not sure."

He shrugs. "Well, I'm done for the day. Thanks for letting me use your friend's spot."

"Oh, they don't exist. I plonk two towels down for extra room."

He opens his mouth to speak and says nothing. "While everyone's tripping over everyone looking for a space to lie down?"

I nod.

He seems impressed. "That's cold."

"And I do it for free. No breath mints are sponsoring me."

He laughs. All right, that's a few times I've made him laugh. It's enough to make me think he might enjoy hanging out, like I should be bold and suggest he stick around longer.

"So, you're not even cold for cash?"

"If you feel bad about it, you can take the spot," I say. "I have a towel you can use. And you said it yourself, you're done for the day."

"I have to edit the pic and upload it."

"That'll take five seconds. How often is it that you get to hang with a follower?"

I know the answer is, "Pretty often." But he humours me, says it's a once-in-a-lifetime opportunity. I lay the towel back over the spot he used to take the photo and he hops down.

We get to talking, both on our fronts, staring out at the sea. I steal occasional glances. I like to think he steals occasional glances back.

London Alvírez is—in news that is surprising to no one— from Brooklyn. He took a year off between high school and college to see the world. It's been eighteen months.

"That's more than a year," I say with a laugh.

"Mom's annoyed, but I figure, my posts are still getting likes and I'm still getting paid, why not see more of the world while I can?"

I can't fault the logic. Part of me wants to ask how somebody goes about getting a sponsorship deal for photos and how much money he makes, but before I can, he has a question for me.

"Can you explain something to me?"

"Sure."

"The guy I went over to, before Eve, I explained my profile and asked if he wanted to be on it and he asked me if I was taking the piss."

"Sounds about right."

"I get that he didn't want to kiss me for WeGlo, but I don't understand *what* he was asking."

His face is all confused lines, and it hits me he probably thought the dude was accusing him of stealing his urine.

I say, "It means to make a joke out of someone, test someone or something's limits, or to do something without really considering the consequences."

"Right."

"*Piss* is our go-to word for everything."

"In America, you can be *pissed* as in *angry*, and you can *piss* something away, but I've never heard of someone taking it before."

"We can also be *on the piss*."

The confused lines are back. "I can't even guess."

"It means to be drunk."

"Right. That's confusing. I thought Australians just said *mate* a lot."

"That's a misconception. Very few people can pull it off without it sounding aggressive."

He pushes up off the towel a little. "Mate," he tries.

It's not a bad first effort. "Okay, now I can ask you a question."

"Sure."

"I know your profile is super cynical, but do you believe in romance? Proper love?"

"Oh, you're going straight for the heavy stuff. My question was about vernacular."

"It's not my fault you wasted your question."

"Well, @LondonFromBrooklyn was voted one of the year's top romantic profiles," he says.

"You fake intimacy with strangers every week and you promo breath mints or slap a discount code for the sneakers you're wearing in the caption," I say. "That isn't romance."

"It's not fake, it's…brief."

"Romance is losing track of where you are, when you are, and being so sucked in by the other person that for a moment, nothing else matters. It has to happen organically. You can't set up a tripod, pose for a shot. And you can't just force it every week wherever you go."

"And you want every kiss in your life to be that?" he asks.

"Yeah. And that's a second question I've answered, and you haven't answered mine."

"Haven't I?"

"No. That's three. Do you believe in romance? Like, being so caught up in someone you're smiling involuntarily."

He sighs. "I've…only ever been in love once, I think. I'm not sure though."

I stay silent enough that he knows he needs to elaborate.

"There was this guy, Justin," he says. "We went to the same middle school and then high school. We kissed at a house party in junior year, but that's about it. Nothing major.

"Dad saw him working at the mall, and I'd told him about Justin. And he was like, 'Why didn't you ever date Justin properly?' and I didn't have an answer. The next day, I saw him walking down the corridor at school, holding hands with a guy and it hit me: I waited too long."

I exhale. "That's your love story?"

"I think so."

"That's bleak."

"Sometimes they're bleak."

"I don't think I've ever been in love, but I did once bully Hugh Mason off the debating team, and then realise months later that I had an intense crush on him."

He stifles a laugh. "I don't know about you, but that sounds like love to me."

I cackle. "Right?"

He shares another story, one about a guy he met on summer camp. I reply with one about the first guy I kissed at school. Time escapes us. It isn't until someone trips over me while looking for a place to lay her towel that I remember there are others on the beach besides us. She apologises. I tug on my spare towel and roll it into a ball.

"You can chill here," I say.

"Really?" She doesn't wait for me to change my mind.

I turn back to London and realise, in the commotion of being tripped over, we've edged closer to each other. He rests his hands on the towel.

His left pinkie finger grazes the side of my hand. It's an accident, but he doesn't pull away. We keep talking and I find myself squeezing his forearm for emphasis.

The world around us evaporates—the sounds of shrieks and waves and amplified playlists go quiet.

"Would you kiss a random on the beach?" London asks. His face is inches from mine. He blinks.

"If I was properly wooed, maybe."

I take a breath. I erase the space between us. My lips meet his. We kiss.

When we come apart, he's smiling.

REFRESH

by
Mark Oshiro

This is a very bad idea.

MY TEXT TO ROSIE HANGS IN THE BALANCE,
and for a moment, I wish I could pull it back. I know what
she's going to say to me. And sure enough, the dots appear
below mine and to the left, and the message comes through:

Don't be a baby, Rodrigo. Eres un bebe, ahora? Should I get
you a bottle?

Ah, Rosie. She's so…detailed.

I'm serio. I hear there are people into that. Quieres un pañal?
I can facilitate that for you.

And now I'm wishing she wasn't so detailed.
I put my phone back down on the table and push it away

from me. More texts are coming through, but I can't look at them now. That's a bad idea, too. It'll just make me more nervous, and this is nerve-wracking enough as it is. What if he doesn't show? What if he *does* show up, but he doesn't like what he sees?

Maybe I should update the photo.

I grab my phone again and open up the front-facing camera. This makes me wince immediately, and I'm plunging. Plunging into those terrible, dark thoughts, the shadowy recesses I often cling to. *This is not going to go how you want it to.* The thought was uninvited, but familiar. *You haven't dated anyone yet, so what makes you think this is the start?*

No.

No.

I take a deep breath, then adjust a few of the curls on my head. *I love my hair,* I tell myself. And I do! My curls are one of my best features, and I always make sure they show in all the photos I put online. Rosie knows not to post anything without consulting me first.

It had taken me over an hour to pick a photo I was pleased with before I stuck it on the app. A warm smile. My curls. The light hitting my brown eyes just right. A colorful flannel, but not too bright. It matches my brown skin so well, and makes me look dignified. Approachable. Nice.

And I love how soft I look, how my curves give my body a shape that is *mine*. I struggle with my body like anyone else, but having Rosie in my life has made me appreciate being a big guy. It's who I am! And I love feeling confident about myself and my body.

That's what other boys want?

Right?

My phone vibrates again.

I open the app.

Refresh.

Is he here yet? I've still got five minutes, but maybe Erwin is like me and likes getting places early. I click on his profile— saved in my favorites, of course—and look at his photo.

Tall. Close-cropped hair in a slick fade. Skin slightly darker than mine. He's got on a tight-fitting tank top, and it's clear why. And those lips…

Okay, Rodrigo, calm down. You're in public, and you can't be staring at him when he gets here. I didn't want to be in public to do this, but Rosie wouldn't let me link up with this guy unless I was somewhere with lots of people. So when Erwin told me he wanted to meet, I picked a coffee shop downtown.

6' 1". Love the movies. Looking for someone new…someone refreshing. Surprise me.

I could surprise him. I could be new and exciting!

I…think.

I look around the cafe, but I don't see him or anyone who could believably be him. There's a noisy family in the back of the store, and the mom is trying to calm down her whining child. Most everyone else has their headphones on, their heads bowed, their eyes locked on their laptops.

So he isn't here. And I am trying not to panic, and maybe this double shot was one of many bad ideas currently occupying my life. I swipe down on my screen.

Refresh.

He isn't online.

Oh, this is *definitely* a bad idea.

I open my messages again.

He's still not here, I text Rosie. You think he'll show up?

Those three dots.

Rodrigo.

Oh, damn. Just my name, nothing else. I can hear Rosie's voice in my head. *Why you bein' a fool, Rodrigo? Why you asking me a question you know the answer to?*

I switch over to the app.

Swipe down.

Refresh.

Still not online.

I hadn't given Erwin my phone number. I wasn't going to trust a stranger with that. You never know who anyone is online. But as Rosie fires off text after text to me, I wonder if this was another mistake. What if he wasn't going to trust me because I had not trusted him with my phone number? In a burst of anxiety, I open his DMs, and this must be the thousandth time I've read them since this morning.

Erwin: We been talking a while.

Me: I know! Like a whole month.

E: You think it's time?

Me: ...for what?

Me: Are you talking about meeting?

E: Of course!

E: But only if you want.

E: I was thinking of it.

E: A first step.

Me: Like on the moon?

Me: A first step for gaykind?

E: Lmao your too much.

E: But I was thinkin...

And then, of course, Mom had me come help with dinner, and I didn't want her to see my phone blowing up with notifications, so I had left it back in my bedroom. For an *hour*. When I came back to my phone, much later that evening, there were only two unread messages.

E: Well, damn. I see how it is.

E: Its okay, maybe its too early to meet.

A familiar panic slipped into me. I shot off a few messages, all in rapid succession:

Me: Ah! Lo siento, Erwin, I had to go make dinner. I promise!

Me: I didn't understand what you were referring to.

Me: I think it's a good idea. You really want to meet me?

But there was nothing, not until this morning. I kept refreshing his profile, hoping to see that green dot come back again, but it stayed gray. He stayed inactive. And my hope evaporated. I slept terribly that night, and I woke up this morning certain that I'd just blown my shot with this beautiful guy. When would someone as attractive as him find me appealing ever again?

I rolled over. Picked up my phone.

Six unread messages.

All from Erwin.

I dreaded opening them. I switched on the lamp by my bedside and squinted as light flooded my vision. I braced myself. Took a deep breath.

Opened my phone.

Opened the app.

Swipe down.

Refresh.

And the little message count went up, and I went straight to them, and, just as I was doing now, I read them. Over. And over. And over.

E: I do. Sorry if I seemed salty earlier. Sometimes folx don't wanna meet. They just wanna talk.

E: And I like our conversations. I feel an energy. You feel it too?

E: Maybe its just me. But maybe not.

E: Maybe we can take a chance.

E: Today. This afternoon. Let's just be ourselves.

E: But in each others presence. You down?

This happened.
Saying it in my head helped. If he really didn't want to see me, if there wasn't some attraction there, then would he have sent me those messages?

No.

No one would do something like *that*.

I sip my coffee, which isn't as hot anymore, and I put my phone facedown, and I tell myself that I just have to wait. I just have to believe that Erwin will show. It's possible. It's real. This is not a mistake.

I follow this inspirational plan of mine for the whole of a minute, and when the door to the coffee shop opens, my heart nearly thumps right out of my chest. Is it him???

A slender but older man, his beard tightly lined up around his face, slinks into the shop, letting the door shut behind him. He seems me staring, gives me one of those nods of acknowledgment, then makes his way to the counter.

This is a disaster.

When I open my phone, it goes right to his messages again, so I back out of it and—

Oh.

Oh, *shit*.

The icon is bright green.

He's online.

Underneath that, it reads:

486 feet away.

It's like every emotion I've ever felt is now rushing through my body, all of it a torrent that spills out. I nearly drop my phone, and I *absolutely* drop my coffee, which pours onto the tabletop. I stand up and scoot back my chair, which scrapes against the floor loudly, and now, everyone's staring at me.

Great. Just what I needed.

I rush to get some napkins, and I'm cleaning up when I realize my phone is still open, still on his profile page, and I don't even care if anyone sees it.

I glance at it.

212 feet away.

It's a rapid procession now, one thought colliding with another as they all scramble for attention in mind.

What if he hates me?

What if he isn't showing up at all?

What if I make a fool of myself?

I text Rosie, my comfort and my certainty:

He's almost here omg. I'm dying

The dots appear.

Bitch!!! You're gonna be fine. Seduce him, honey. You got this.

The door opens.

My heart stops, I'm sure of it.

I sit up straight, put my phone to the side, give the entrance my full attention.

Three of them walk in like they're in a group, but it's clear in a moment that they don't know one another. The first person is...one of the employees. They lift an apron over their head and slide it down so that it hangs from their neck. They look nothing like Erwin.

Then there's a taller guy behind him. Young, possibly my age. And he's *thick*. Not like the way some people misuse the term online, who think that having abs, pecs and a size 31 waist makes them thick. If I didn't know better, I'd think he was a linebacker on my school's football team.

His skin is a light brown, with a line of facial hair tracing his baby face, and he's got a close-cropped fade. He's *really* cute. He glances at me, then keeps walking toward the line by the counter.

Figures, I think. *I don't really get guys hitting on me in public.*

So I look to the third one, who *must* be Erwin, and he...

...is a FedEx delivery man.

My heart drops all the way to my stomach, and I let out a rush of air. Why do I keep doing this to myself? I see more texts from Rosie, but I ignore them to open the app one last time.

0 feet away.

What?

What?

I turn back around. Did I miss him somehow? The mother and surly child are gone. But the other tables are still occupied by those deep at work on their computers. The *same* people. Was it the employee? I look back down at the app—

0 feet away.

—and it's clearly not him at all. Erwin said he was Puerto Rican, and the employee is definitely white.

0 feet away.

Perhaps he is next door. Or just parked. Oh, God, does he even *drive*? This is Fresno. He probably *has* to.

And in that moment, I realize just how little I know about this guy.

His name is Erwin. He said he was Puerto Rican when we talked about being Latinx and how people thought everyone in California was from Mexico. (We're really not.) He lives across town, closer to Clovis. And…

And…

And…what else?

What else, Rodrigo???

How did I not know more? We had talked every day, for hours and hours, and I had vague impressions of him, and he *seemed* cool, and—

"Rodrigo?"

I look up.

The guy is standing there.

The thick one.

The one with the thin facial hair.

The light brown skin.

The hoodie stretched over his torso.

The one who is most definitely *not* Erwin.

He's lighter; still brown, but definitely the tone from the photo. His shoulders are wider, his face is round instead of long, and his head is full of bushy curls.

There is no *way* that this is the same guy from the profile photo.

"Uh…hi?" I say, arching my eyebrow up at him.

"It's me," he says, and I look down to see his hand shaking at his side.

What?

What???

No.

No, this can't be happening.

"Who are you?" I ask, hoping I've misunderstood this.

"Erwin," he says. "We've been talking on—"

I raise up a hand to him. "You're joking, right?"

He sits down across from me, and when he smiles, I can see fear ripple over his face. But his smile is cute...sort of. But *whose* smile is this? Is this even Erwin?

"No, no jokes," he says. "I'm just glad that we could make this happen."

My mouth is on the table. At least, it *feels* like that's the case. "But..." The words fail me. I open my phone with my pass code, and there's his photo, and I know right then that I am not imagining this.

I look at the photo. Study it.

I look up at this...person.

Different facial structure. Cheekbones. Different hair, different body shape. In fact, this guy looks younger than me.

They're 100% different people. I have no doubt about that.

"I'm so lost," I say. "This has to be a mistake."

"It's not."

When he says it, he stares at me, refusing to break contact. "It's me, Rodrigo." He smiles again. "Making our first small step for gaykind."

Oh my god.

It *is* him. "But you're not..."

His brows crease together. They're thick, too, and I want to admire them. But now I'm *angry*, my rage pulsing under my skin.

"No," I say, "this is whack, man. Did you...did you *catfish* me? Did I just get catfished?"

I know I'm being loud; I know that other people are probably staring at me; I know their eyes are on the two of us. But it's like my spirit is leaving my body, floating above the two of us, and I am observing this unfold from afar.

I'm brought back down, though, when he replies. "It's not that bad," he says weakly.

"You're not the one being *catfished*!" I hiss.

"But it's all still *me*," he insists, and his hand is on his chest over his heart, a gesture I would probably find attractive in any other context, but right now, I hate him all over again.

"How can you say that?" I shoot back, holding up the phone, pointing it toward his face. "This is *definitely* not you."

"But everything else...that's me. I just use the photo so people will talk to me."

My mouth drops open for the second time since he's arrived. "What? *Really?*"

"No one wants a big dude," Erwin says. "At least, not like me. So, the guys feel better talking to me if they think I look like that."

I'm speechless. I sip at the paltry remains of my lukewarm coffee because I don't have anything meaningful to say. Does this *work*? Does he meet up with guys all the time with this technique?

No.

I *have* to say something.

"You saw my picture, Erwin. *I'm* a big dude!"

I wave my hands at him, and it feels so pathetic. "I would have felt fine talking to you…like…*this*. I would have definitely still replied to your first message if you had just put up a photo of yourself."

"No one has before! Why you think I did this?"

I don't know why I feel compelled to do this, but I hold my phone up and open up the camera. "I'm taking your photo."

"What? Why?" He stands up then. "Please don't, I'm sorry—"

The words are rushing out of him. He's mortified. I dismiss him with a wave. "No, I'm not doing anything with it."

"I'll leave," he says, and his hands are up, palms facing me.

"That's not what I meant," I say, and I sigh. "I just think you're perfectly fine the way you are, and this…this *thing* you're doing is pointless. I just wanted to show you what you look like. I mean…does it ever *work*?"

"Work? What do you mean?"

"Do guys ever stick around after you show up?"

"Well…" He sits back down. "Technically, no."

I sigh. "*Technically?* What does that mean?"

"I haven't ever *met* a guy off the app before today."

My palm hits my forehead. Why is all of this happening at once? My phone buzzes; it's one of what must be a million unread texts from Rosie. I'm shaking my head as I unlock my phone and shoot off a quick text.

Erwin here. Not who he said he was. Will update in a sec.

"So…" he says, and I ignore the succession of vibrating notifications. "Should I leave?"

I frown. "Erwin…"

"No, I get it, I shouldn't have even tried. I'm sorry, Rodrigo."

I don't know what to tell him. This wasn't what I was preparing myself for. Just minutes ago, I was terrified that no one would show up. But...who is this person? If he hates his body this much, is he gonna hate mine? Was anything that he told me *true*? What about all the things we spoke about? Was any of that true?

I stared at Erwin, at the worry lines forming at the corner of his eyes, at his thick lips as he licks them. He's cute. *Really* cute. And if I am being honest, he's cuter than the photo. Softer around the edges.

Real.

He's not a profile. He's a person. And maybe there's a part of him that I understand. A part of this that makes a terrible sort of sense.

Would I use a different photo if I could?

Maybe.

No.

Probably not.

But I just spent half an hour actively trying to convince myself that no one would actually find me interesting or attractive enough to want to meet me.

And here Erwin is, proving me wrong.

(If this is Erwin.)

(It is, right?)

"You should leave," I say.

He stands again, too sudden, and this time, his chair is squeaking on the tiles. "I'm sorry," he says again. "Really. I promise."

"But come back."

He stops. Shakes his head. "What?"

I shrug. "Let's do it again. A new start."

He scratches at his head. "You mean that?"

Is this another mistake?

Or is this an opportunity?

"Yeah," I say. "I do mean it."

A grin spreads over his face, and it lights up the room. Maybe this isn't such a bad idea.

And then Erwin walks out the door and he lets it shut completely. A few seconds pass, and my heart is racing again. *What am I doing?* I think. *Why don't I just kick this guy to the curb and leave?*

But the door swings back open again, squeaks as it does. He walks in, his t-shirt clinging to his body, and I love how he has a shape like mine. He makes eye contact immediately, but this time, he doesn't look away or rush past me. He grins, just a little thing that makes his face look warm.

When he walks up to me, there's no shaking nerves, no uncertainty. Just those full lips and his round cheeks and a light in his dark eyes.

He sits down, a smirk growing, and he sticks his hand out.

There are texts from Rosie. So many of them. I'm sure I've ruined her day, but I have to live in this moment, this chance to refresh, to try again.

I take his hand in my own, and it's surprisingly soft.

"Hi," he says. "I'm Erwin."

"Rodrigo," I say.

"You come here often?"

I roll my eyes at him. "So you're cheesy?"

"Maybe," he says. "You wanna find out?"

"Maybe," I say back to him.

And maybe I do.

★ ★ ★ ★ ★

VICTORY LAP

by
Julian Winters

I AM CAPITAL, BOLD, UNDERLINED, AND ITAL-
icized THE WORST at finding a date to anything.

I'm a wiz at pre-calculus. I can do a perfect handstand. I can run the 5km in under fifteen minutes. Last year, I was the first-ever sophomore on South Perry High School's cross-country team to win the state championship.

But when it comes to something simple like asking a guy to the winter formal, I'm hopeless. Negative-twelve in the game department.

Luke Stone, eternally single.

"What about Dean Watkins?"

Thankfully, I have best friends like Aiko and Skyler to save me.

"Dean Watkins?" Aiko repeats.

"No," Skyler says from my other side. "He's a superior douchebag. And he's always *staring* at me."

Aiko smirks. "Because you're so fierce."

"Duh." Skyler rolls their seafoam-blue eyes. "All non-binary people are. That doesn't make him an acceptable date."

Aiko stares at me expectantly.

I half shrug, frowning a little.

Okay, maybe the reason it's so hard to *find* a date to the winter formal is because I'm not actively trying? I spend more time watching YouTube on my phone or trolling Instagram for cool anime art than stalking the guys who are out at our school.

Aiko and Skyler, on the other hand, are on a mission.

We're exiting La Mesa del Abuelo, this awesome Mexican restaurant in Main Street Plaza, which is a blink-and-you'll-miss-it shopping center on, you guessed it, Main Street. The main attractions of this plaza are a farmers' market on the other end and the barbershop my dad owns.

Aiko and Skyler are trading names back and forth while I carry a takeout bag for Dad. Chicken burritos with extra jalapeños, his favorite. If I don't grab him food, he'll forget to eat. He's always so focused on work. Entertaining his customers.

"Okay. DJ Yang." Aiko's holding up her phone with DJ's Instagram opened. "Very date-worthy."

"Very straight," I tell her. "He's always throwing heart-eyes at Jaliyah."

She rolls her eyes. "He could be bi. Pan. Questioning."

"What about Dylan Johnson?" Skyler interjects, shaking their phone in my face.

I frown.

Dylan could be my twin. We're the same height and build. Identical curly hair. Except he's got this wide grin, pale brown skin and hazel eyes. Also, Dylan's a year younger and has the perfect nose and eyebrows for his face.

Me? I have dark curls, but my hair is shaved super-close on the sides. And my eyebrows are outrageous. I have a small scar over the left side of my mouth people mistake for a dimple. At least my smooth brown skin is over the acne stage, and the rest of my body is catching up with my long legs.

"He's not my type," I lie.

My type is simple: *guy*. That's it.

We stroll lazily down the sidewalk outside the shops. December exhales a cold breath against our cheeks. The sun's dipping, flicking a thick gold rope across our faces. Another phone is thrust into my face, but I ignore it to watch the colors melt across the sky.

Aiko offers, "Rico? He's hot."

He *is*, but I still say, "Nope."

"Jay?"

Definitely not queer.

"Scott from the basketball team?" Skyler says.

Definitely not from planet Earth.

"Terrence Newton?"

I stop and gape at Aiko. The *Terrence* she's referring to is my cross-country teammate. *Was my teammate.* It's weird to think like that. I quit the team in early September.

For a good reason. I did the right thing.

My brain likes to repeat this mantra, like it's an achievement.

Anyways, Terrence is like family. I can't ask him to the formal.

Even though Aiko's giving me her infamous You Will Not Deny Me stare, I say, "I'm not going with Terrence," with only a hint of squeakiness in my voice. I'm blaming that on allergies.

I'm allergic to my own bullshit.

127

The truth is, I want to stroll hand-in-hand with a guy into the formal. Dress up and smile stiffly for photos and dance awkwardly together. To kiss him good-night. To not worry what anyone will think about that.

And I want it to be someone I know.

I'm kind of out at school, depends on whether you check my Instagram likes or who I follow on Twitter. But none of the students in my class see me as date-potential. I'm just Luke Stone, the guy with the curls and eyebrows who ran cross-country.

I check the time on my phone: 5:06 p.m.

"Damn. I'm late," I say hurriedly.

Aiko blinks at me. "How're things with your dad?"

I shrug. I always get this question, even though it's been four years since Mom died. I get it—Aiko cares. Skyler, too. I know they're concerned that I haven't been honest with my dad about *why* I quit the team. Why I'm doing what I'm doing.

I just don't like talking about it.

"FaceTime me later?" I offer, avoiding further interrogation.

"We'll think about it," Aiko says, yawning.

Skyler elbows her. "Don't work too hard, Luke."

I nod, jogging backwards. And I'm so invested in waving while balancing my phone and the takeout bag that I spin around almost a second too late. I nearly collide with someone blindly shuffling in the opposite direction.

"Whoa. My bad."

"I'm so sorry."

It's Milo Leone. We sit together in the back of world history every day, not that we speak. We're not friends. Not enemies, either. Since freshman year, I've been in the cross-country crowd. Or the Aiko-Skyler crowd.

I'm carefully holding him upright by his shoulders as he tries to untangle from his red apron. It has a giant GROUND FRESH logo in the middle of it. Ground Fresh is the farmers' market hugging the corner of the plaza. There's something about his voice, deep but squeaky, if that's a thing, as he repeatedly tries to apologize.

I grin.

Milo's chestnut hair is wind-wrecked. He's wearing a black turtleneck, which makes his watercolor-paint green eyes stand out. He gently bites a chapped bottom lip.

"Are you okay?" I ask him, head tilted.

His hands shake while tying his apron. A dust of pink frames his cheeks. His nose is red, too. He sniffs and presses out this too-shy-to-exist smile. "Uh, yeah. Thanks."

I release his shoulders. He stumbles back. I almost reach for him again, but he straightens. And I laugh under my breath as he wiggles around me.

Over his shoulder, Milo gives me a quick look.

I nod, and he trips on his feet but, thankfully, he doesn't faceplant into the sidewalk.

Still… Milo Leone is kind of cute.

My phone buzzes in my pocket and I'm reminded, no matter what Milo is, I'm late.

I shouldn't know who Tevin Campbell is. Or New Edition. Frankly, I shouldn't know every lyric to "Waterfalls" by TLC, but I do.

Thanks, Dad.

Dad's shop, Razors & Blues, is sandwiched between a nail salon and a shoe store. It's a cornerstone of Main Street Plaza. Generations of families have built shops around it for almost two decades. Some have come and gone, but Dad's business is notorious.

Everyone knows Darwin Stone. "Uncle Dee" to the kids who hop in his chair every Saturday, crying at the slightest swipe of alcohol against their freshly-cut skin fades until Dad gives them a lollipop.

Dad's chair is booked from 8:00 a.m. to 7:00 p.m. Monday through Saturday. Never Sundays.

"It's the Lord's day," Dad insists, even if he spends his Sundays in sweats watching sports and listening to old-school R&B. "Jesus died so I could have one day of relaxation."

No, Dad, the Lord didn't create Sundays as your free-pass to laziness.

But Dad doesn't need a pass. He's earned more than just Sundays off. All his life, he's been a hard worker. His dad was too. His dad's mom. It's the legacy of every Stone.

It's why I'm at the shop now, sweeping hair as Dad finishes Mr. Whitaker's perfectly-shaped high-top fade. The Stones work; everyone else plays.

Overhead, Shanice sings about loving some guy's smile. I kind of dance—the Stones are also credited for creating the two-step shoulder-shimmy—while sweeping. It's the only way I survive in the shop. The music and the "war stories" Dad recites to all his clients, about trudging five miles in the snow to cut hair during the brutal Georgia winters.

For the record—it doesn't snow enough in central Georgia to build a proper snowman. And every year, when winter drops a fistful of flurries on the South, it turns into a national emergency.

"Smooth, Dee." Mr. Whitaker checks himself out in the mirror behind Dad's chair, leaning on his cane. He's easily sixty years old. "There's no one like you, brother."

Dad grins. "No one *cares* like me."

It's true. Dad's devoted to his craft, unlike the other barbers who duck out the shop promptly at 4:00 p.m. Dad won't leave until the very last walk-in is complete.

Once Mr. Whitaker has limped out the shop, Dad turns to me and says, "That man looks ridiculous. Who does he think he is? Bobby Brown?"

"Bobby Who?"

"Luke Zion Stone," Dad says in that annoyed-but-amused voice I love. He's hard-core serious, but after you've caught your dad dancing to Whitney Houston in the middle of the night, it's hard to fear him.

"Was he a rapper?"

"He was *everything*. An icon. Don't you forget it," Dad says, half laughing.

I fake a chuckle, too. But one word echoes in my head: *Zion*. Mom gave me that middle name. Suddenly, I'm somewhere else. Floating between the shop and an emptiness.

"Hey." Dad's voice is soft. "What's up?"

I force myself out of a daydream of Mom's voice. Her fingers in my curls. The warmth of her laughter. "You're right," I say, ignoring the roughness in my voice, "he looks flippin' ridiculous."

It's not the word I want to use, but Dad's old-school about

swearing. If you're not paying bills or don't own a car, you can't swear around adults.

"Can't tell Mr. Whitaker nothing," Dad mumbles.

I exhale a laugh but nothing inside of me is amused.

"You're distracted."

"I'm not."

Dad raises an eyebrow at me. "You've been sweeping that same pile of hair since you got here," he shakes his head, "*late*, with cold chicken burritos."

Oh, wait. What's that weight piled on my shoulders? Hello, guilt!

"I don't pay you to be late *and* distracted."

I wrinkle my nose at him. "You barely *pay me*."

"It's entry-level wages."

"Dad, I've been sweeping hair in this place since I was old enough to crawl—"

"When I was your age," Dad interrupts, thick arms crossed over his chest, "I had to…"

Right on cue!

But I tune out Dad's childhood horror stories to stare out the shop's giant window front. The plaza is dead, like always. Endless gray from empty parking spots. Moms carrying take-out to their minivans. Old men ambling into a gas station to play the lotto. A girl dances down the sidewalk to her own beat while snapping selfies on her phone.

None of them worried about finding a date to a stupid winter formal.

"Luke?"

"I'm cool, Dad." And I am. Mostly. "I'm cool," I whisper again to Dad. To myself.

But Dad obviously isn't listening. "Come on." He smacks the worn leather of his chair repeatedly.

"Dad," I whine, suddenly possessed by four-year-old Luke. "Let's go."

"I just got a line-up last week."

"And you look a hot mess. Fire your barber."

"You're my barber!" I say, half laughing, half mortified.

"Then tip better." Deep wrinkles crowd Dad's pale brown eyes. His grin overtakes most of his face, the way mine does on a good day. Gray hairs are scattered through his neatly-trimmed beard. A constellation of freckles on both cheeks stands out against his light brown skin.

Firmly, he says, "Luke Zion" and I sprint over before he can finish. Dad's "means business" tone still scares me a little bit.

Every moment of this is like home. The neck strip tied loosely below my Adam's apple. Dad's flimsy black cape draped over me. The jerky lift of the chair as Dad's foot pumps the pedal, lifting me higher. The click of the clippers as they come alive. The first ghostly brush of them against the back of my head loosens a shiver up my spine.

We never talk at first. Dad needs to find his groove. I need to find courage. This has been Dad's method of breaking down my walls since I was a kid. When I admitted to him I was terrified of the dark. My preteen confession about acne ruining my school life. Fifteen-year-old Luke shyly asking about condoms, even though I had no intention of using them. I just needed Dad to know that, when the time was right, I'd be safe.

That warm September morning when I told him I quit the team.

"So," Dad says, the clippers humming near my ear, "what's up?"

Cool metal teeth graze my skin. I need to keep it cool. One false move and I'm finished. There's no way I'm walking into school with a jacked-up haircut.

I try to swallow the words in my throat, but they bubble back up. "The winter formal is coming up."

"And?"

"And it's a pretty big deal." To my best friends and the whole effing junior class, I guess.

"Do you need money for a ticket? A suit?"

"No." Being Dad's assistant doesn't pay much, but it covered the cost of tickets. Yes, plural. *Two*, for me and my future social media stalker if I let Aiko or Skyler have their way.

"Have you found a date?" Dad asks.

"Not exactly."

"You don't have to have one, you know."

"Yeah." But everyone seems to think it's cooler if I do.

"You can go with friends."

"Yep."

Except I want a date. I want to tell Dad all about this amazing guy I haven't met yet.

But Dad doesn't even know I'm gay.

This is my big moment, right? The one in every teen coming-of-age where the main character comes out and there's tears and singing and glitter. You know, where the main character experiences approximately thirty seconds of anxiety and fear before they're swinging out of the closet on a chandelier.

Look at me! Out, proud, and loved!

Yeah, okay. Thanks, TV.

I've thought about coming out to Dad. A lot. But it hasn't happened.

Dad's not conservative or anything. But he also doesn't pay attention to the news segments about LGBTQ rights and marriage equality. He doesn't mention any queer friends or family members.

It's just…not a big deal to him. It's not a *deal* to him at all.

"I want…" My right leg bounces frantically. An ache burns behind my eyes. My palms are coated in sweat.

"Do you *want* a date?"

"Yeah?"

"So?"

"Well, I…"

The clippers quiet. I can feel Dad's patient stare. My pulse breaks records in my ears. Whitney sings about wanting to dance with somebody. This is it. Where's my glitter and parade and Big Moment?

This is a lifetime of anxiety suffocating me until Dad says, "There isn't a boy you can ask at school? Or do they all have dates?"

And everything stops.

"What?" I choke.

The clippers buzz back to life. "Are you having a tough time finding a boy to ask?"

Wait, what the actual…

In true pre-puberty form, my voice hits an alarmingly high note when I ask, "You know? About me?"

I turn my head slightly to get a glimpse of him. Thankfully, he doesn't slice off my ear.

Dad shrugs, like it's no big deal.

It's a big-effing-deal, Dad!

"I didn't always know, but I knew," Dad says nonchalantly. He's killing the unbothered father game.

I cough harshly, eyes bitten by tears.

"I had to do some research first," Dad continues. "Google is my friend."

A laugh creeps up my throat, tickles the roof of my mouth. Darwin Stone, professional comedian.

"I wasn't sure how you identified—gay, bisexual, ace, aromantic, greysexual…" Dad rubs his face, sighing. "I had to learn a lot of terms and what they meant. I had to make sure I knew *who* you were."

I blink hard. Luckily, nothing warm and wet slides down my cheeks. But the pressure-before-the-break is there.

"Why didn't you ask?" I say, my voice thick. "You've never talked about any of this."

Dad frowns. "I wanted to make sure I knew how to make you comfortable and safe first."

I nod. "Are you," I stutter, heavy words weighing down my tongue, "Are you comfortable with it?"

"This isn't about me."

"Dad," I say in that tone he's used with me at least four times today.

"I'm trying," he confesses. We're quiet. Too quiet. Then he says, "I am. I wasn't raised to understand different sexualities. Everything was very black and white, and often unfair to the black."

It's a joke, sort of. But the truth behind it, how everyone is made to believe white is good, pure, a ray of light while black is bad, tainted, the ugliest darkness, is ridiculous.

Dad carefully turns my head to finish buzzing my sides. "I'm changing. For myself. For you too."

We edge back into silence. The music of the clippers and that one Montell Jordan song played at every sports event fills the gaps.

"I can find you a date," Dad finally offers. "I've joined a few online communities for parents of LGBTQ youth."

A rush of blood burns my cheeks. "Dad, no."

"What? There are so many amazingly supportive groups!"

A shudder tickles my spine, draws a smile to my lips. Dad talking to other parents about me, online? I can't even imagine. I won't be attending any local PFLAG meetings with him, but it's kind of epic that he cares that much. That he's trying.

He touches up my hairline with a razor, then swipes my skin with far too much alcohol. I hiss, tears hanging on my eyelashes. Dad smiles at me in the mirror, dusting off loose pieces of hair. He rips the cape away like a matador deflecting a bull and I hop down.

I whisper, "Thanks, Dad."

I wonder if he knows what I'm thanking him for. What he means to me.

I quit the team for Dad. He'd never admit he needs an extra hand around the shop. To clean and schedule appointments and maintain the atmosphere his customers love. The other barbers don't care enough to help.

This shop's all Dad has besides me now.

I couldn't watch him die slowly again like he did after

Mom, so I lied. Said I was bored of running. I wanted to learn how to build a future.

Everyone says it's a parent's job to protect their child, but why can't I protect him? Why are there roles when it comes to protecting the ones we love?

"I'm gonna finish up," I say, grabbing the broom.

It's nearly closing time. Exhaustion is weighing Dad's shoulders down.

The silly jingle bell above the door rattles and in walks...

"Milo?"

Milo jumps, then shyly ducks his head. He's still wearing his red apron. Black turtleneck. He plays with the zipper of his ocean-blue hoodie, ivy-green eyes moving from me to Dad in a slow, hypnotic motion.

He clears his throat. "Is it too late for a haircut?"

Dad sizes him up, then cocks his head at me. Something sparkles in his eyes. I don't like it.

"You need a cut... Milo, is it?"

"Yes, sir." Milo nods jerkily, sneaking another glance at me. Pink edges up his cheeks.

Dad laughs under his breath, leaning on his chair. "And you trust me with your hair?"

Milo raises an eyebrow. "Sir?"

Dad waves a hand around at all the framed photos on the wall—Dr. Martin Luther King Jr. Oprah. Langston Hughes. Dad's forever crush, besides Mom: Michelle Obama.

"Oh!"

I chuckle into the crook of my arm at Milo's wide eyes, embarrassingly squeaky response. Cute isn't the right word for what this is.

Milo starts, "I mean…"

Dad briskly waves him off. "I'm kidding." One heavy, calloused hand thumps his chair. "Sit. I'm a pro. I used to cut that Justin Timberlake's hair, you know."

Mortification has a death grip on my larynx as I squeal, "Dad!"

"What? Wrong Justin?" Dad has a little too much amusement in his voice. "Is Bieber still the cool one?"

I want to die. But Milo cracks this smile that reminds me of the first clear inhale after completing a race. The adrenaline of first place. The pride of finishing *anything.* He shrugs off his hoodie, detangles from his apron. His thin fingers pull through his deep brown hair, messing it up some.

Dad makes small talk with Milo as he begins his usual prehaircut routine. I kind of tune him out.

Milo Leone. Why haven't I noticed him before?

Well, I've noticed him. Duh. But I haven't *noticed-noticed* him. In an attractive way. A dateable way.

Our only shared class is world history. It's the best class for a nap. Mr. Johnson constantly rambles about stories of the world from, you know, *one perspective.* Not one I can relate to. I always grab the most low-key desk—the one in the corner— next to Milo. He's painfully shy in class, which is why he sits in the back. He freezes whenever Mr. Johnson calls on him.

He clearly doesn't like the attention. I don't know why. He has all my attention right now.

"What do you like to do outside of school?" Dad inquires.

It's weird—Dad's learned more about Milo in the last five minutes than I have an entire semester sitting next to him.

I feel bad about that.

Milo's good at talking to his feet rather than making eye contact in the mirror. He rambles about tech stuff and online games. "And anything *Star Wars*."

Damn it.

Thing is, Dad's hard-core about *Star Wars*. The attends-national-conventions kind. Wins local trivia contests. As in I'm named after his favorite character—Luke Skywalker. But that's confidential info. Since middle school, I've told everyone I'm named after Luke Cage, the comic book character.

"Milo!" Dad shouts. "Shut the front door."

Milo startles, but he's smiling, wide-eyed. A-*freaking*-dorable.

They geek out over Jedi stuff while Dad carefully trims Milo's sides. Fanboy over General Leia. Analyze the latest films with laughter and enthusiasm. It's the nerdiest thing ever. It's also the first time Milo's eyes meet Dad's.

I sweep around the shop, my mind drifting. It'd be cool to bring a guy home to meet Dad. Someone who makes Dad laugh. That would listen to Dad's endless stories with a smile and equal interest. Someone I could find the quietest moments with in the noise of the world.

A guy to attend winter formal with.

Someone like… Milo?

"Vader or Kylo Ren?" Dad asks.

"Vader, obviously." Milo's tiny, cocky smirk lights a flame in the darkest corners of my wishful thoughts. "But Ren is still cool."

"More like whiny," Dad corrects with a grin. He brushes stray hairs from Milo's cheeks and temples, spinning him around. Then he gives two sharp nods at his work—the Darwin Stone stamp of approval.

I nod, too. Milo didn't look *bad* before. He was this geek-tastic cloud of awkward-cuteness. But this haircut enhances his softness. His sides are clipped, and Dad's swooped a section of hair over his brow. It sharpens his cheekbones. Emphasizes his wide shoulders.

Milo steps out of the chair, smiling at his feet. "Thanks."

Dad pats his shoulder. "Looking sharp."

If a new shade of red existed, it'd be called Milo Leone. It's everywhere, from his nose to his big ears.

"Yeah," I whisper. Clearly it wasn't as quiet as I thought because Milo's head jerks in my direction, our eyes meeting, a prickly wave of embarrassment scorching my skin.

"Uh…" My tongue malfunctions. Lips numb. Vocabulary decimated.

"Nice, right, Luke?" Dad says too suggestively.

Am I that transparent? That even Dad knows I'm into Milo?

"Sure," I mumble, nose scrunched.

Milo's eyes drop, but his smile doesn't.

His smile is a hurricane, dangerous and relentless and inescapable.

Milo's fumbling with his wallet, fishing out money, when Dad says, "No charge, son."

"What? No, I couldn't—"

Dad holds up a hand. "It's on the house."

"But—"

"*No charge*, Milo," Dad says, firmly. "I couldn't possibly charge a loyal member of the Rebellion."

I snort. "Better take him up on that offer. Dad doesn't do freebies." A complimentary haircut from Darwin Stone is like finding a unicorn at a coffee shop. He doesn't even do birthday haircuts. After all, he has a shop to pay for and all my cross-country gear wasn't cheap—not that it's earning him any money back hanging in my closet or stuffed under my bed.

Milo's hand drops, but there's a small lift to his mouth. A quiet *thank you* in his sagging shoulders.

Dad leans on the headrest of his chair, grinning a little too hard. "If you really want to repay me, maybe you could hang out with Luke sometime?"

Oh no.

"Go for coffee."

He's not…

"Dinner and a movie?"

This is happening.

"Dad," I hiss, jaw tight.

Dad shrugs. "Just a suggestion." Then he *winks* at Milo.

"I, uh…" Milo's flustered again. Tangled words and twitching hands and skin burnt crimson.

A faint kind of ache hums in my chest. It's for the way Milo looks at his hands, then at me, through thick eyelashes. We share equally embarrassed smiles. Our shoulders are wire-tight. Our feet shuffle like we're learning a new, clumsy dance.

I can't believe this.

Darwin Stone, certified wingman.

Except, Milo says, "I should go," waving in a disjointed, clumsy way. At the door, he glances back at me. Blinks one too many times.

I smile a little, but not enough to make him stay.

How am I supposed to ask a boy to winter formal when I can't properly flirt with one that's ten feet from me?

Is that even what Milo wants? I don't know his sexuality.

I sit next to him all the time and only know he smells like gym sweat under a layer of mango-scented deodorant. That he has nice handwriting. That, sometimes, he looks at me with this tiny, unreadable light in his eyes.

Milo finally whispers, "See you around," to Dad, promising to follow his Millennium Falcon blog. Then he disappears.

And I go back to sweeping. To wanting something I don't have the guts to ask for.

"Luke Zion Stone," Dad says, loud and annoyed, "is that how I raised you?"

"Huh?"

"You're seriously going to just stand there?"

I tilt my head, eyebrows creased. "I'm doing my job, Dad."

"No, you're doing a terrible job of being a teenager." He drags a hand down his face. He looks tired. No, agitated. "You're not going to quit on this one. Run after him. Three years of cross-country should pay off for something."

"Dad?"

"Milo. Go." He points stiffly at the door. "Give this a chance."

I shake my head, confused. "I can't—"

"Yes, you *can*." All the wrinkles around Dad's eyes can't hide his pleading. "He obviously likes you."

"Okay, joining a few online communities for parents of queer kids doesn't make you an authority on whether a guy is into me or not."

"It sure as hell doesn't." Dad laughs. "That's decades of watching romcoms with your mom."

I shut my eyes, but a laugh squeezes past my lips.

"It's okay to take a risk," says Dad, soft but earnest. "If it doesn't work out, that's fine. Life goes on."

I lean on the broom, refusing to acknowledge the dizzying spin of my stomach. The thunderstorm of my heart behind my ribs.

"Luke," Dad says, and I finally open my eyes. Stare at him. A knowing grin crinkles his mouth. "Don't quit before you start. You've done enough for everyone else. For me. Do something for *you*."

It's as clear as lightning in the dark. As loud as marching bands after a touchdown. *Dad knows.* Why I quit the team and why I'm always at the shop now. But a heaviness in his eyes, masqueraded by a warm smile tells me we'll talk about that later. That Dad wants me to focus elsewhere instead.

"Go," Dad demands, amusedly. "Or I'm firing your lazy ass."

I run as if I'm breaking a new record.

As if I'm winning this race for Dad. For both of us.

"Wait!"

An aching heat roars in my lungs. My heart's sinking in the acid of my stomach. Every muscle in my legs stings. I barely have the speed and focus to catch Milo under an orangey street lamp outside his car. It's an old, greenish two-door compact with a Stormtrooper bobblehead on the dashboard.

Milo jumps when my fingers catch his elbow, squeezing a little too tightly.

"Wait," I wheeze.

I'm distressingly out of breath. A few months off the team and I'm a winded rookie incapable of completing the 100m dash.

Milo stares at me with these wide eyes, partially concerned but slightly pleased. It centers me. Endorphins explode in

my system. My heart's suddenly a dormant volcano return-
ing to life.

"I want to," I pause, sucking in more air. Milo raises an
eyebrow and courage leaps into my throat. "I want to go to
the winter formal."

"Yeah?" He's almost laughing, nose wrinkled.

"With a boy."

He nods slowly, nibbling that chapped lower lip.

"I want to take a boy to the formal."

"I think I got that."

Right. Here we are, standing under a tangerine street lamp.
A pattern of fuzzy glowing stars swims in an endless gray-
black sky. The moon is a broken halo. I haven't thought any
of this through. What to say. How to ask. Or the fact that
it's way past chilly outside and I'm standing in a pair of black
running tights under loose basketball shorts with nothing but
a red thermal to keep my chest and arms warm.

Not exactly Ask a Boy to Winter Formal apparel.

"I'd like…"

Just effing say it, Luke Stone.

"Luke?"

I shake my head at the concern in Milo's voice. My teeth
chatter. Goose bumps layer my skin.

"I don't know if I'm reading this right. If you're interested."
I inhale deeply. "But would you like to go with me to the
winter formal?"

"With you?" Milo repeats. Not angry. Not ready to report
me for harassment.

To be certain.

The jolt in my stomach is nauseating. I nod a little too happily. "With me." I step closer, wait to see if he backs away. He doesn't. My cold fingers cautiously slide to his wrists. He turns his hands over, palms out—giving me permission. I take them in mine. I whisper, "As my date."

Something hopeful shines in Milo's eyes.

"Your date?"

I'm still shivering. But I focus on the curl of Milo's mouth.

"Would you like to go to the winter formal as my date?"

"Um."

"It's okay if, like, you don't want to. Or that's not your thing? Maybe I'm not your 'thing,' which is super cool. No sweat." My rambling has hit an all-time high.

"No."

"No," I repeat, sadly.

Dad's so wrong. Rejection isn't okay. Rejection effing sucks.

"Wait, not like that," says Milo with a nervous laugh. "You are. My thing, I mean. Wow, that came out wrong."

A grin sneaks over my lips. "It didn't."

"I've had a thing for you since forever." His laugh is perfect—not too loud; the nose-scrunching kind.

"Really?"

His eyes clench shut, quiet breaths sneaking past his lips. He's that Milo-shade-of-red again. "I didn't think you…"

"Yeah. Definitely. I'm kind of bad at all of this."

I free one of my hands to brush hair away from his forehead. He doesn't flinch away.

A sudden snap of wind attacks us, and I howl, "Damn, it's cold out here!"

But Milo takes my other hand in both of his. He squeezes

tight, all his warmth tingling up my arms. Headlights shine over us, passing cars ignoring our existence.

Nothing to see here. Just a boy asking another boy to a dance.

"I've always wanted to..." Milo's words die on a breath. On a nervous smile.

I return it, bigger, with slow-lifting eyebrows.

"Wanted to...?"

He licks his lips. Another wave of crimson darkens his skin.

And now it's just a boy—Milo—standing on his toes to lean up and quietly ask if he can kiss another boy—me.

I let him.

It's not one of those cinematic kisses. Not even a Netflix one. Our noses bump, I'm still shivering but then...we fall into it. The barest press of cold lips. I cautiously tuck a hand behind his head, a thumb behind his ear. Milo smiles against my mouth to let me know it's okay. His hands squeeze mine and my fingers undo Dad's perfectly-styled haircut.

Even in the cold, this feels like melting candy in my palm. Like the crest of summer.

Kissing Milo—my first real kiss—is finishing a race I didn't know I was running until now.

"Well?"

Dad doesn't allow me two seconds to warm up once I'm back in the shop. My toes are numb. I'm sniffling. But my mouth buzzes with heat. My head's ready to explode.

I kissed Milo.

Bonus: I'm going to winter formal with Milo.

"Luke Zion Stone," Dad says impatiently.

Finally, I look at him. And grin. I nod sharply, twice. The Luke Stone stamp of approval.

Dad crows, already tapping away on his phone.

"What're you doing?" I ask.

Dad flops into his chair. "I have to tell the other parents about how I got my son his first real date."

"No."

"Wait 'til I post photos of us shopping for suits on the community board."

"Dad, you will *not*—"

"Should we get Milo flowers? Do you think he likes flowers?"

I groan loudly but Dad ignores me. His thumbs are moving slowly, tongue between his teeth as he types. No doubt, he's already trolled Milo's social media accounts for photos to post on his support group's community page. He's probably already found a suit and tie to match Milo's eyes. I hope he doesn't brag about how he gave me The Talk and a pack of glow-in-the-dark condoms that look like light sabers.

Yeah, my seventeenth birthday was an epic tragedy, but this is going to kill me.

Not before I walk into winter formal holding Milo's hand.

Not before I kiss him again.

I sweep as Dad laughs while typing. Old-school music fills the shop like it does every day.

Eventually, Dad says, "Your mom would've loved to have seen this" quietly with a sad smile.

"Think so?"

He nods, twice. "She'd be so proud of you." Then, softer, he says, "I'm so proud of you."

I look away. A familiar sting assaults my eyes. But I'm hardcore smiling.

When I'm done cleaning, I text Milo all the Pinterest ideas Dad's already found for suits. I also text Aiko and Skyler about having a date, but I don't tell them who. They're going to be insufferable when they find out they failed as matchmakers.

Milo texts back a link to a photo of a *Star Wars* tie that I immediately reject.

He also sends a selfie of his newly-wrecked hair. I'm not ashamed I did that. I text him back a heart-eyes emoji.

"Okay. Let's go." Dad's standing in the middle of the shop. Prince is playing overhead.

I cock my head at him. "What?"

"If you're going to impress Milo, we've got to perfect the Stone Shuffle." Dad's already bopping side-to-side. "I can't have you shaming our name."

I laugh so hard, the tears finally come. I don't try to hide them, and Dad smiles like it's okay.

I can't believe this. Out of all people, Dad found me a date to the winter formal. A boy that I like. That Dad has met and likes, too. Dad loves me enough to ensure I have a great night with Milo.

I shake my head, still laughing. "Thanks, Dad."

★ ★ ★ ★ ★

A ROAD OF ONE'S OWN

by
Kate Hart

CASS IS ALREADY WAITING FOR THEM AT THE Tote-a-Poke in Poteau. The gas station chain exists, with the exception of one store, solely within the boundaries of Le-Flore County, Oklahoma, on the edge of the Ouachita Mountains. If Eliza weren't dreading their destination so much, she might find the landscape comforting: it's similar to the Ozarks she's grown up in, the hills just a little lower, with more sky in between.

But she's been dreading this entire trip, really, and agreed to tag along only out of spite. Her boyfriend, Nathan—*ex-boyfriend*, she reminds herself for the millionth time—is on a "guys only" road trip to Arizona before all their friends leave for school. Eliza doesn't want to go to the Grand Canyon with the boys any more than she wants to go with Nathan back to college in Texas, but it's the principle of the thing.

So when Keri and Rosa and Mindy decided to launch a counterprotest, Eliza played along, because a guys only road trip is bullshit and they know it. Keri is calling it the GROSS Club, after the old Calvin and Hobbes cartoon, with Get Rid of Slimy girlS altered to Sexist boyS instead. Mindy suggested "Sisterhood of the Traveling Van," which was vetoed immediately, and Rosa has admonished them that the gender binary is a patriarchal construct in the first place.

Eliza is just calling it a bad idea at this point. If she'd known Mindy's cousin, Cass, was coming along, she never would have agreed, but there's no way to argue against including her. They're driving to the Rockies, and Cass needs a ride back for her sophomore year at the Colorado School of Mines, maybe the most badass and intimidating college name Eliza's ever heard. So, while the Tote-a-Poke in Poteau, Oklahoma makes an excellent tongue twister, it's the last place she wants to be, and its approach is twisting her stomach into knots.

"What does that even mean?" Keri's in the driver's seat of the minivan they've borrowed from her parents. "How do you tote a poke? Or is it like 'totem pole'?"

"A poke is a bag," Mindy says. She pronounces it *baig*, her accent a little flatter and stronger than the others'. "Like a grocery sack."

"In what language?" Rosa demands.

"In *English*. Okie English, anyway." Mindy is from Oklahoma, but moved to Arkansas when her parents divorced. She points as they pass the Choctaw Travel Plaza. "Maybe it's a Choctaw thing, I dunno."

The word alone re-reminds Eliza that the last time she saw Cass, she made a huge fool of herself. She tries to wash the feeling down with a swig from her water bottle, but it's difficult to swallow.

"How do you say 'gas station'?" Keri asks.

"In Choctaw?" Mindy snorts. "I can only say three things: 'hello,' 'thanks,' and 'I am Choctaw.'"

"Wait, are you really?"

"Yeah, believe it or not." She gestures at her dirty-blond hair. "Chahta sia hoke. I have a membership card and everything."

Eliza's mouth falls open. If she'd known, she could have asked all sorts of questions to avoid looking like an idiot in front of Cass again.

"I wish I had a card," Keri says. "Then when I say 'y'all' and people stare, I can hand it over and introduce them to the concept that both Korea and immigration exist."

"Ha," Rosa says, "me too. Mine'll say 'Yes, I am Latina. No, I cannot do your Spanish homework.'"

"Okay, but you totally *can* do my homework," Mindy says.

"Yeah, until Señora Brazos is like, 'Where did you learn Costa Rican slang in an Iberian textbook?'"

"That only happened once."

"*Your destination is on the right,*" the navigation app announces, and Keri turns at the black-and-yellow sign. "*Tote-a-Poke, Poteau, Oklahoma.*"

"Thank god," says Rosa. "I have to pee like crazy."

The girls pile out and Mindy hugs her cousin, who's waiting out front with a backpack and half a corn dog. "I'm glad y'all are here," Cass says, careful not to get mustard in Mindy's hair. "That a-hole over there has been watching me like a hawk."

A large man stares from beneath the hood of a car he's not fixing. Eliza bristles, remembering Nathan's warnings—that a car full of young girls is creep bait, that she needs to be careful, that she'd better pack the mace her dad gave her when they left for Texas last year. She doesn't want to have to use it, not just for the obvious reasons, but because she doesn't want Nathan to be right. About anything.

"And this is Eliza," Keri says, making introductions.

Eliza jerks back to the conversation with an awkward wave. "Hi."

"Hey." Cass's eyes hold hers a little longer than necessary, but no dislike, or even recognition, registers on her face. Then she tosses her corn dog in the trash. "So where are we heading today?"

"Hopefully Palo Duro," Mindy says. "It's about seven hours—if we make good time, we can get there by dark."

Cass snaps in her direction, somehow making finger guns look cool. Eliza has never felt cool in her life, and here's Cass on a ninety-five-degree day, looking effortlessly amazing in tight jeans and honest-to-god cowboy boots, a sleeveless Zeppelin shirt with a strappy black bralette underneath, dark hair twisted upon her head, on her way back to a cool school in a cool state while Eliza...

Okay but she didn't make you wear khaki shorts, Eliza interrupts herself. The other girls aren't *cool*-cool but they all match, in their plastic shorts left over from cheerleading camps of days past. She looks down at her MDA Muscle Walk shirt. *At least it's not band camp.*

Keri claps her hands together. "Let's get your bags in."

"I just have the one." Cass hoists it onto one shoulder. "It can ride wherever."

"Oh good," Keri says. "We're pretty crowded." The van is crammed with camping gear, another fact making Eliza's anxiety flare. She's been camping lots of times—just never without Nathan. He loves the outdoors, revels in roughing it, and it's always been easier to let him set up camp and cook the food and do the dishes and...

And all I've really done is lay out sleeping bags and gather kindling. Part of her wants to reject the hobby entirely, to cut it out of her future the way she wishes she could cleanly excise him. *But the boys already took bets that we won't last a day. So screw that.*

"Oh man, I thought I was gonna pop," Rosa says, emerging from the store with a bright red ICEE.

"You are not drinking that in my parents' car," Keri says.

Rosa shrugs. "I'll chug it here."

Eliza heads inside for her turn in the bathroom and sends a quick text home, updating on their progress. When she returns, Cass is already wearing headphones in the back, while Rosa clutches her head in the middle seat, cussing the world's worst ice cream headache. "You want to drive? Or risk getting covered in red barf?" Keri asks.

Eliza shakes her head. "Let Mindy drive. I'll take my chances."

Back on the interstate, the land levels out quickly, forests dwindling into small clumps of gnarled trees, then down to rolling plains. Signs along the roadside announce their crossing of each tribal border: Muscogee (Creek), Seminole, Kickapoo, Citizen Potawatomi. Eliza has never understood the designations. The highway patrol still gives tickets all over the state, a fact Nathan learned from speeding on the Cherokee Turnpike to Tulsa. She's not sure who's really in charge of each area, but there are specific headquarters and health centers and other tribal businesses that make clear they're moving through distinct territories.

"Prague?" Rosa reads aloud.

"It's pronounced 'prayg,'" Mindy says.

Rosa laughs. She's been making fun of all the unusual town names: Tenkiller. Weleetka. Okemah. Wewoka. "Bowlegs?"

Mindy doesn't answer, but Keri leans forward. "Listen, Tica."

She doesn't finish, but they all know what she's implying: Rosa hates when the Mexican kids at school make fun of her Costa Rican accent, so she should knock it off. Trying to lighten the mood, Eliza says, "You wouldn't believe how much the people at UT made fun of us for being from Arkansas."

"As if Texans have much room to talk," Cass says, crossing her arms on the back of the middle seat. "You're already in school?"

Eliza twists around to answer. "Yeah, but back at the U of A. I transferred at semester."

"Your boyfriend too?"

She forgot that Cass met Nathan last summer too. "No, he's still at UT. And he's not my boyfriend anymore."

"Oh," Cass says, eyes widening. "I thought y'all were basically married."

"So did he," Keri pipes up. "That was the problem."

The other girls have known Nathan as long as they've known Eliza, but Keri, who met him later, has fully taken Eliza's side, and Eliza is grateful. Even her own parents are mourning the loss, and her sister sobbed when she broke the news. "I didn't want to do the long-distance thing, either," she adds.

Cass nods and starts to ask another question, but Keri interrupts. "This trip still needs a name. Cass, what should we call our all-girl road trip?"

Cass thinks for a moment. "Get Your Dicks Off Route 66?"

The whole van erupts in laughter, except for Mindy, who says, "I can't use that as a hashtag," which makes everyone laugh harder.

"What about 'A Road of One's Own?'" Eliza asks, when they calm down.

Mindy frowns. "I don't get it."

"Virginia Woolf?" Cass asks. "As in, who's afraid of?"

Rosa pats Mindy on the head. "She didn't take AP Lit. A Road of One's Own it is."

Somewhere west of Oklahoma City, they stop at a rest stop and Cass takes over driving. Mindy insists Eliza take shotgun, since she hasn't ridden up front yet. "What do you want to hear?" Cass asks, handing over her phone.

"I'm easy." Eliza tries to give it back.

Cass waves her off. "You do it. I never read and drive."

"Me neither." Scrolling through, Eliza's surprised to recognize many of the artists, and finally spies the blue and white cover of an album she loves.

"Ooh, good choice," Cass says, to her huge relief. "Who's navigating?"

"Eliza is," Keri says from the back. "Front seat responsibility."

Eliza considers claiming that it'll make her carsick, but decides to just suck it up. *How hard can it be to type in a destination?*

Surprisingly hard, it turns out. Several hours, albums and hundreds of passing windmills later, the app tells them to turn south, and soon it's insisting they've reached their destination—only there's no state park in sight. "There's a sign for Antelope Flats," Cass says, pulling off the road. "But that's not what we want, right?"

"I have no idea." Eliza's face burns.

Keri is asleep, but Rosa leans forward, pulling out her own phone to check their route. "Um, this says we're way off course," she says, showing them her screen. "The park is over here."

"At least it's not too far," Cass says.

"I mean, it looks close, but..." Rosa adjusts the display. "There's no roads going straight through. It's another hour and a half."

"It's what?" Mindy squawks, waking Keri up.

"Oh my god, I'm so sorry—" Eliza glances out the window at the fading light. "I don't know what—"

"You put the wrong place in," Rosa says. "You just said 'Palo Duro Canyon,' not 'State Park.'"

Eliza blinks, determined not to cry.

"It's an easy mistake," Cass interrupts, and pulls back onto the road. "The canyon is really big and it sent us to the wrong end. We just have to drive around it."

Rosa groans and sits back roughly, while Mindy takes a picture of the Antelope Flat sign, the electronic click like a tiny admonishment. Keri yawns. "It's fine," she says. "An hour's not that much longer."

"And a half. We'll have to set up camp in the dark," Rosa grumbles.

Cass glances in the rearview and hands her phone back to Eliza. "Find us some more music."

Embarrassed, but stung, Eliza spies an album she knows they'll hate. But if it's in Cass's music library, so she must like it, and the first plucky guitar notes make her grin.

"Ugh, what the hell is this?" Mindy demands as a strident voice kicks in.

"Listen, cousin," Cass says over her shoulder. "We sat through your jock jams playlist, you can put up with this."

Mindy sticks her tongue out and puts her headphones in.

"I can't believe you listen to Camp Cope," Cass says.

Eliza shrugs. "It's not my usual thing, but the lyrics are…"

"Yeah," Cass agrees. She bobs her head for a moment, then joins in singing the second verse. Eliza mouths the words, letting her volume rise a little as Cass wails along with the bridge.

"What is wrong with y'all?" Rosa demands, covering her ears.

Cass sings louder, and for the first time today, Eliza laughs.

It's twilight by the time they reach the park gate, and Rosa suggests they stop at the Visitor's Center so they won't have to double back for a hiking trail map in the morning. The adobe building clings to the canyon wall and when the sun is out, the view must be amazing, but right now it's just dark shapes against a dark sky. Mindy takes a picture anyway.

Inside, Rosa chats with a park ranger while Keri and Mindy check out the gift shop. Eliza and Cass linger behind, looking at the historical displays. A black-and-white video plays on one wall, telling the story of the Comanches who controlled this territory until the late 1800s, when the US Army tracked down the last band who hadn't been forced onto the reservation. "Where did they…" Eliza starts, afraid to misphrase the simple question. "Were they moved to Oklahoma?"

Cass nods. "Down around Lawton and the Wichitas."

"Ouachitas?"

"*Wich*-itas. Different mountains, in the southwest." She points to a map, then reads a nearby sign titled *The Final Blow.* "The army captured about 1,400 horses from the hostiles in Palo Duro Canyon. *Hostiles,*" she repeats, snorting.

Eliza reads on.

To prevent the Indians from recovering the herd, General Mackenzie had his men shoot over 1000 of the animals. Without their large horse herd, the Southern Plains tribes lost their mobility and had no choice but to surrender.

"Wow," she says. "It makes the Indians sound like the animals." She stops. "Is it even okay to say Indian?"

"Depends on who you ask." Cass moves to the next sign, and points to another use of the word *hostiles*. "I'll take it over this crap though."

"I've never heard of any of this," Eliza admits.

"That's the public education system for you. Hey, we missed a room."

Cass leads her into an exhibit about how the Civilian Conservation Corps built the park in the 1930s. Eliza musters her courage and when she's read every display, she forces herself to ask, "Cass...do you remember meeting me last summer?"

Cass turns around slowly and studies her. "Yeah," she admits, "but I'm surprised you brought it up."

Eliza's face flushes. "I know. I'm so sorry. I just didn't know any better and when I said—"

"Wait," Cass interrupts. "What did you say?"

She can't meet her eyes. "You...um...you said something about taking Choctaw language classes, and I said..." She glances up, hoping Cass won't make her repeat it, and sighs. "And I said, 'Oh, you don't look Indian.'"

Cass throws her head back and laughs. "Oh my god."

Eliza covers her face. "I know! I'm sorry—"

"Eliza," Cass says, pulling her hands away. "Do you know how many people have said that to me?"

"I knowwwww," she says miserably. "Afterwards I researched and—"

"I only snapped at you about it because I was flustered by your boyfriend cockblocking me."

Eliza's defense trails into sputtering. "What?" she manages.

"He totally caught me checking you out so when I started trying to make conversation and he came over I just...spun out."

Eliza can't stop shaking her head.

"For real. I'd only been out for a few months so I didn't know how to play it cool at all."

This explanation makes absolutely no sense. "The whole way to Poteau I felt like I was going to barf because I thought you hated me."

Cass laughs, but not unkindly. "Girl. Half the people I meet say I don't look Indian, and the other half tell me they have a Cherokee grandma. It's an occupational hazard of being Native."

Eliza doesn't know how to answer that, so she says, "Nathan never mentioned anything about it."

"He probably knew you hadn't realized I was hitting on you and didn't want to freak you out."

"Why would that…" The true meaning starts to sink in. Cass was hitting on her? On *her*? "I mean… I'm flattered."

"Well," Cass says, looking down at her boots. "You never can tell how people are going to react."

"I don't know how to react," Eliza admits, and rushes on, not wanting to offend. "I mean, nobody ever hits on me. Girls or boys."

"Yeah but how long has Nathan been around to cockblock?" Cass grins, and when Eliza doesn't answer, says, "I rest my case." She turns to join the other girls, then stop and adds, "But he's not here now, is he?"

Eliza watches her walk away. No. He most certainly is not.

The campground is crowded, but only with RVs—nobody wants to tent camp at the height of summer in the Texas panhandle. "We should have brought more lanterns," Mindy complains, holding up one end of the tent she's sharing with Rosa.

"Look on the bright side," Keri says. "It's cooling off. And at least it's not raining like the forecast said."

Rosa huffs. "We're car camping, you wusses. And it's nice enough we don't even really need a tent."

Mindy drops her end to slap a mosquito and holds out a bloodied palm in response.

Eliza isn't confident her own tent is going to last the night.

It's a one-person model she reluctantly borrowed from Nathan, since her own family doesn't do much camping, and she's never put it up before. Laying out her sleeping bag, she realizes it still smells like him, and quickly unzips all the windows to let it escape.

"You're gonna need your rain fly," Rosa calls, her headlamp illuminating Eliza's progress.

"I'll put it on before bed," she says. "The tent's kind of musty."

Despite the dark, Rosa somehow manages to make calzones on a single burner stove, and the meal greatly improves morale. "How'd you learn to do that?" Cass asks. "All I can cook in the woods is canned soup and beans."

"I spent last summer at a survival skills camp," Rosa says.

"Well that explains it." Cass stands up. "What should I do with these dishes?"

"I'll take them," Eliza says, happy to have a way to contribute. But it only takes a minute to realize she can't even wash dishes without help. "Should I just take these to the water pump?"

Rosa shakes her head. "I brought tubs—you're going to want to boil some water first, to get the dishes clean."

This presents another problem: There's a burn ban, so she can't build a fire, and relighting the stove involves potential explosives. Her options are to ask for help, or risk blowing herself up. The latter seems less embarrassing.

Ten matches later, Cass comes over. "You need help?"

Eliza shrugs, knowing the answer is obvious, and feels even stupider as Cass simply turns the knob a little more.

"It's easier if you can hear the gas," she explains, turning the flame back down once it ignites. "Just don't turn it *all* the way up. Assuming you want to keep your eyebrows."

She forces a smile, noting that even Cass's eyebrows are cooler than hers. She's never understood how to shape them the way everyone else seems to. "Thanks."

"No problem. Here, I'll fill this." She pours water from a jug while Eliza steadies the pan. "We can scrub while we wait."

Eliza takes the dirty plates and dumps leftovers into a trash bag, careful to be tidy—she doesn't think Palo Duro has bears, but nobody wants javelinas and raccoons either. She tries not to think about how many bears there will be when they get to Colorado.

She's trying not to think about lots of things at the moment. Cass had to be kidding, or at least just trying to make her feel better. Eliza knows she's not horrid looking, but thanks to a jerk on the baseball team, she also knows her pale, bony face can be described as "rat-like," complete with fake cheese eating and whisker stroking. Besides, no one as cool as Cass would bother being friends with a dork like Eliza, much less…

Much less is too much to ponder. Dishes are easier.

But Cass insists on helping. When the water is hot, they work in tag team, Cass rinsing and Eliza drying. "I'm sorry if I made things weird," Cass says, handing over a plate.

"No, no," Eliza says, flipping a hand and showering Cass with dishwater. "It's…it's fine."

It's not fine. All evening, her mind has gone around in circles, evaluating every friendship and celebrity obsession and harmless crush she's ever had. Sure, she's always been a little *too* into a couple of her favorite female musicians, and sure, she can admit that those women are drop-dead gorgeous, but does that mean she might want to...?

Even putting words to it feels like standing at the edge of a cliff. A canyon, even.

"Look, I knew the chances were good that you were straight," Cass says. "And I want you to know that unlike a lot of dudes, I am totally able to be friends with someone I find attractive."

Friends, Eliza thinks, surprised, then: *Find attractive?* It seems such a stiff and clinical way to express it, but what else can she say? *I think you're hot? I find you ridiculously appealing? I want to kiss you?*

Why does she want Cass to say that?

She blinks and lets herself admit it. *I might want Cass to want that.*

"So just like—don't feel like you have to—" Cass is saying.

"How did you know?" Eliza interrupts.

Cass stops. "How did I know what?"

"About girls. That you like them."

"Oh." She thinks for a moment. "I just...always did. Guys never did it for me."

"Oh." Eliza picks up another plate, one she knows she's already dried, and wipes it with the towel. "Never?"

"Not really. I mean, I don't rule out the possibility that one might someday, but if he exists, I haven't met him yet."

"So you..." Eliza pauses, then just admits the obvious. "I don't even know how to ask this, but what do you call yourself?"

"I'm a pansexual Choctaw feminist," Cass says, adopting a professorial tone. "Though I usually just say I'm a lesbian.

Folks in Poteau don't know what pansexual means unless they're on the internet."

Eliza nods. "I guess that's a benefit of living where I do."

"Big Springs is pretty liberal, huh, especially for Arkansas."

"College town," she says. What she wants to ask is, *What am I? What did you think I was?* But instead she says, "Our friend Randy is gay."

Cass cracks up.

"What?"

"Nothing."

Eliza's ears burn. "No really, what?" When Cass doesn't answer, she reaches for her arm, realizing a moment too late that her hand is wet.

Cass sobers herself, letting Eliza's hand rest where it fell. "It's just funny, how people always want you to know. 'I have a gay friend.' 'I know an Indian.'"

Eliza pulls away and stares into the water, wishing it could drown her anger and shame. "I'm sorry."

"I know you didn't mean it like that," Cass says.

"Yeah I did," Eliza admits. "I didn't know what else to say."

"Well," Cass says, taking the twice-dried plate out of her hands. "Now you do."

The predicted rain arrives not long after the girls go to bed. Eliza remembered her rain fly, but she's still nervous the tent will flood. *Keri left the van unlocked just in case that happens, so chill out.* She puts her phone in her pocket, just in case.

Without those worries, though, Eliza is stuck in a different storm of questions. What does it mean if she wants a girl to like her? What does it mean if she wants to kiss a girl? What does it mean if she likes and wants to kiss Cass, specifically? What would the other girls think? Does it even matter, if they're all moving to different towns anyway?

What would her parents think? Or her sister?

Or Nathan?

Eliza sits up. *Who cares what Nathan thinks?* But she knows she still does. Their breakup has been amicable, making it all the more heartbreaking. Nathan thinks this is just a phase and they'll get back together, because he still loves Eliza. And of course she loves him too. She always has. Just not in the way she should.

Is that because she's…bi? Pan?

What the hell would she even call herself?

A gust of wind whistles through camp, pushing one side of the tent against her shoulder. For all Mindy's griping about the heat, the phone says the temperature has dropped thirty degrees. Eliza digs through her backpack and pulls on the puffy jacket she packed for Colorado. As the rain becomes a downpour, she digs for socks, too, wondering if she should put on shoes just in case.

A loud crack of thunder makes the decision for her. Giving up on socks, she grabs her backpack and braces for the rain— Eliza hates being wet, hates swimming and doesn't even like putting her face into the shower. Lightning flashes, temporarily blinding her as she crawls out of the tent into the red mud. Beside her, Cass's tent has collapsed, and it's flailing like the cocoon of a very pissed butterfly.

"Cass?" she yells over the storm. "Hey! Are you okay?"

She can't tell what Cass says in reply but suspects it's mainly profanity. Eliza ducks to the corner of the tent and runs her hand along the bottom until she finds the zipper, then peels the soaked nylon apart. Cass jumps up and throws her arms around her. "I was freaking out!" she yells.

Together, they run for the van and struggle inside, slamming the door behind them. Eliza rummages through her bag for a towel, but Cass hugs herself tightly. "Here," Eliza says, wrapping her towel around Cass's shoulders. "Hey. You okay?"

Thunder crashes down the canyon like they're the pins in a bowling lane, and lightning illuminates a falling tree branch that narrowly misses the picnic table. "That's why Rosa told us not to pitch our tents beneath them," she says, but Cass doesn't answer. She's shaking.

Eliza scoots closer and wraps an arm around, rubbing her shoulder bracingly. "Cass," she says, forcing her to look her in the face. "It's okay. It's just a storm."

"But...what if..."

"My phone has signal," Eliza says, holding it up. "I'll get a weather alert if things get too dangerous."

Somehow, this reaches through Cass's haze. She stares for a moment, then feels for her own phone. "I have an alert set too," she says wonderingly, like she's just realized they speak the same language.

"The joys of growing up in tornado country."

Eliza watches as Cass deliberately slows her breathing until she can meet Eliza's eyes. "Thanks, for that," she says. "Sometimes I just—" She trails off and shakes her head.

"It was scary." Eliza looks out the window just in time to see her own tent collapse. "Annnd there goes mine."

Cass giggles. It's so at odds with everything that Eliza laughs too, and then they're both cracking up. Dripping all over Keri's parents' seats, their clothes soaked, one semi-dry towel between them. Someone's tarp flies by the van and they laugh even harder. Their eyes meet and the laughter stalls, then Eliza takes a breath and leans and then.

They're kissing.

They're kissing. And it's different, not because it's a girl, or not just because it's a girl, but because it's not Nathan, and Eliza had dreaded this moment from the minute she considered breaking up, because how could she ever kiss anyone else? But now— now it's the greatest decision she's ever made, because this is…this is not what she's used to, this is being wanted, being *desired*, this is…connecting and—

Cass breaks away. "Wait. Is this…are you okay—"

"It's fine. Great," Eliza breathes. "Yes."

Cass grins and leans in again.

The next morning, Eliza wakes up with a crick in her neck and a sneaking suspicion that she's been drooling on Cass's shoulder. The sun breaks over the canyon rim, revealing rock walls striped like the layers of a cake, deep red at the bottom and fading to yellow at the top. Cottonwoods' silvery leaves shine along the creek bed, and small mesquite and juniper trees dot the canyon floor. Rock formations—hoodoos, Eliza knows from the visitor center—stick up at random like twisted lighthouses in a sea of yucca and prickly pear.

She tries to move, but Cass wakes up immediately, and they smile shyly at each other. Outside the van, they survey the damage: both of their tents are down and soaked, and Keri's has collapsed on one side. "She must have gone into Mindy and Rosa's," Cass whispers.

Eliza nods. She's not sure what to say in the light of day. But Cass isn't acting weird, so she follows her lead, helping drape their waterlogged things over the roof of the van to dry and getting coffee started. The other girls emerge, yawning, and they compare notes on the night. "Keri got mud all over my sleeping bag when she came in," Mindy complains.

Rosa hands her a mug of coffee. "You'll survive."

Eliza wonders if they can see it on her face: I KISSED A GIRL. ALL NIGHT. It was just kissing and cuddling, but it feels more intimate than any of the making out she ever did with Nathan. She doesn't think it's because he's a guy. They were together a long time, but Eliza did kiss other boys before him, and last night makes her remember that some of those early awkward fumbles also felt similar—frantic and wonderful and scary. Maybe it even felt that way with Nathan, originally. It's impossible to remember now.

"Can we get a hotel tonight?" Mindy asks.

Rosa rolls her eyes but Keri beams at the rest of the group. Cass just shrugs and looks to Eliza.

"Um..." It sounds great, but she doesn't want to admit to the boys that they wussed out after two nights. Then Cass smiles, and Eliza reconsiders. Everyone would notice if they shared a tent, but sharing a hotel room wouldn't be weird... "I'm fine with it," she decides. "There's no way my sleeping bag is going to dry out in time anyway."

They take a long hike, giving their gear time to dry enough in the sun to hold off any mold. The heat returns with a vengeance, and everyone is grateful that Rosa forced them to carry extra water, especially when the trail climbs to a large hoodoo with a view of half the park.

Eliza takes a seat in the shade, watching Mindy snap photos from every possible angle. Service is spotty, but while her phone has signal, she sends her parents an update text: Survived storm at Palo Duro—hiking then headed to Pueblo today.

Her mom's reply buzzes back: I saw on Mindy's Instagram, so scary! Glad you're okay. Drive safely and let us know when you arrive.

Eliza snorts. She forgot her mom was a social media addict.

Cass plops down beside her. "I hope Mindy is planning to work at *National Geographic*."

"She actually has a pretty big following online," Eliza admits.

Rosa takes a spot on her other side. "You wearing sunscreen, gringa?"

"Trust. I wear it to bed." She holds out her arm, ridiculously pale. Almost translucent next to Rosa's.

"You look more Indian than I do," Cass says.

Rosa shrugs. "Latinxs are indigenous too."

"I always wondered how that was pronounced," Eliza says, and Cass laughs.

"You have a lot to learn, Grasshopper."

Eliza can't decide if she's insulted or not, but Cass offers a hand and she takes it, following her down the slope. "What will you be doing," she asks Rosa, "while Mindy's off being a photojournalist?"

Rosa shrugs. "I dunno. Maybe I'll be her keeper."

There's a bitter undercurrent there that Eliza doesn't know

how to address, so she turns to Cass. "And you'll be a miner, of course."

Cass laughs again. "With a degree in engineering."

"What will you do with it?" Rosa asks.

"Depends." Cass holds a branch back so it won't snap Eliza in the face. Eliza does the same for Rosa. "It's a five-year master's, so I can go on to academia, or just get a job."

"Our education program is a five-year master's too," Keri says from behind, catching up.

Eliza wonders why she feels uncomfortable in so many conversations lately. *That's because in the past, you'd just start a private convo with Nathan.* Breaking up with him had felt like letting go of a safety rail, but it's really more like peeling back a security blanket bit by bit, exposing unexpected parts to the air.

Cass bumps her shoulder. "Hey."

"What?"

"I was asking what your major is."

Eliza's stomach sinks. Another of her least favorite topics. "I'm undeclared." Noticing her shoe is untied, she steps to the side and crouches down. "Go on around me," she says, letting them pass.

Cass lingers, adjusting her ponytail so her baseball cap sits comfortably. "Undeclared, huh?"

She even looks cute in hats, damn it. "To be honest, I have no idea what I want to do with my life."

"Me neither."

Eliza snorts. "Sounds like you have it pretty well figured out though."

"It sounds good on paper," Cass says. "The problem is that

I want to go back to Poteau and help the community, but you need money to help and there's not much there, so..."

The trail narrows, forcing them closer together, and their arms bump. Eliza thinks about how natural it seems to just take Cass's hand, but she can't make herself do it out here in the open. "I guess my situation is sort of similar, in a way. When I'm home, I want to leave, and when I leave, I want to go home."

"Is that why you left UT?"

"Half of it. The other half was Nathan, but I let him think it was just my family." She looks at Cass. "Do you know about my sister?"

Cass shakes her head.

"Well, she has muscular dystrophy. She uses a wheelchair and—"

"Oh, I'm sorry."

"Don't be," Eliza snaps, then catches herself. "It's just—that's who she is, you know? She's really clear on that. She's a disabled person whose lifespan will probably be shorter than average, but she's not—"

"I'm sorry," she says again, and Eliza knows it's a different apology. Then Cass laughs. "I'd say 'I have a friend who uses a wheelchair,' but to be honest I don't."

Eliza relaxes, almost relieved to find that Cass has blind spots too. *Wait, is okay to call them blind spots?* She shakes her head. "Well, anyway, I kind of let Nathan think that she and my family need my help more than they really do." She shuffles her foot in the sand. "Actually, I kind of let myself think that, too."

"I'm sure they appreciate it," Cass says.

"Oh, they do, but..." It's hard to say out loud what she's

only said to herself. "They can get by without me just fine. And I think I was hoping that… I don't know, it's stupid."

"What?"

Eliza stops and takes a drink. "I was hoping…he would miss me more, I guess."

"He didn't miss you?"

She shrugs. "I mean, he did. But not in a way that like… changed my mind about the future. I mean, the thing is, he has his all worked out." She only meant to leak a secret thought, but now they're pouring out in a torrent. "He wants to go to law school and then settle down and support a family and it's not like I'm *against* any of that, but it's just not—I didn't want…" She looks up. "I didn't want it with him, is what I finally realized."

"And he can't understand that."

Eliza shakes her head. "No. And now…" She gestures between the two of them. "He's going to think I really left because I was secretly gay and like, maybe I am, but that's not why, but then again why does it even matter if he—"

Cass takes her upper arms and squeezes.

"My entire life is one big open question right now, and everyone acts like that should be exciting but it just makes me feel tired. But I also have it so much easier than so many people…"

Cass turns her hat backward and rests her forehead against Eliza's. "You do, but that doesn't mean it's not hard. It's just perspective. Both those things can be true."

Eliza nods awkwardly. "I'm sweating on you."

"Who's sweating on who?" Cass pulls away. "Oh my god, Mindy is such a piece of work."

Eliza looks up, to where Mindy is waving them forward. "Did she take our picture?"

"Of course she did. She probably already posted it with eighty-seven hashtags."

Eliza's stomach gives a lurch.

The girls pack up their gear and head north, Mindy waxing rapturously about the shower she's going to take at the hotel. Keri hopes they can find one with a pool, Eliza just wants a night of decent rest, and even Rosa has to admit it's a good plan. "Our reservations for tomorrow night are at Longs Peak, and that's at 9000 feet. It'll be good to acclimate in Pueblo for a night—it's only at 4K."

"Good call," Cass agrees. "My school's at 5600 and even that makes me sick if I do the drive all in one day."

"Thanks for planning so much of this trip, Rosa," Keri says. "I didn't realize how much you had done."

"Me neither," Eliza admits, feeling guilty. "You're amazing."

Rosa actually blushes. "Well," she says brusquely, "you can repay me by not getting altitude sickness."

That, Eliza's not sure she can promise. A quick search says their hometown is only at 1400 feet, but another search says preventative measures include eating carbs and drinking water, so at their next stop, they load up on snacks.

The drive passes fairly quickly, but Eliza can't stop checking Instagram to see what Mindy has posted. So far, there's just a group shot, but Eliza is hyperaware of how Cass's hand curls around her hip, and how her own face is turned toward Cass, not the camera.

She glances over. Cass is beside her, taking in the scenery, which for now is still desert and weird rock formations. Their hands are inches apart on the seat. She wonders more what the sleeping arrangements will be, and how she feels about sharing a bed...or a room.

But the latter is a non-issue. The girls get a semi-decent meal at a greasy spoon in northern New Mexico, where Eliza is surprised to find that green chile is delicious, and by the time they get to Pueblo, Keri's found them a deal on a hotel room with two beds and a pull-out couch. They take turns in the shower, have a microwave popcorn fight, and spend another half hour cleaning it up because Keri insists it's unfair to leave for the cleaning lady.

No one thinks it's strange that Cass and Eliza volunteer to share a bed, or notices that they're holding hands under the covers, but it still takes Eliza hours to fall asleep.

"It seems a little weird that we drove here to do more driving," Mindy says.

Rosa looks up from the map. "Did you want to hike?"

"Fair point," Mindy says. They're still tired from yesterday, and with the altitude, Rosa has planned for them to drive the Trail Ridge Road.

"'Rocky Mountain National Park's heavily traveled highway to the sky!'" Keri reads from a brochure. "Damn, it goes up four thousand feet in a couple of minutes."

"Why are so many of the trees dead?" Mindy asks.

"Beetle kill," Cass says.

"That sounds like a band," Keri says.

Cass snorts. "It took out almost all the lodgepole pines.

Like, over a space the size of Rhode Island." Mindy gives her a quizzical look. "We learned about it in school?"

"Oh right." She looks out the window. "God, these little lakes are so freaking blue. Pull over, Keri, I want to take pictures. Whoa, a moose!"

Keri groans but obliges. It's not every day you see a moose, at least where they're from.

The road winds up and around, making long curves around the tallest peaks. Walls of snow have been bulldozed to the shoulder, and the shady sides of the mountains remain white, but the sunny sides are either sheer gray rock or green slopes. Tall poles mark the road's edge every few feet, and Eliza marvels that snow regularly gets so high, much less that people still drive on it.

Cass is sitting in the backseat without her, and it's weird that the separation already feels wrong. They've barely spoken at all, but of course they've been with the other girls the entire time, so Eliza tries not to let it bother her.

They reach the Alpine Visitor Center, where tourists are speaking every language imaginable. Ravens swoop overhead, grabbing dropped snacks from the parking lot. "You want to do the trail?" Cass asks, pointing. A paved sidewalk leads up the closest peak. "I think it's the highest point on the route."

Rosa starts to reply, but Keri interrupts. "Let's see if they have gum," she says, and grabs her arm. "Mindy?" Mindy follows cluelessly, taking pictures of the birds as they walk.

"Wow, that wasn't obvious at all," Cass says.

"What?"

"You didn't see Keri? She might as well have yelled 'Let's

give them some alone time.'" Cass laughs. "We should have called this trip 'Life Is a Biway.'"

"She knows?" Eliza asks. Her first instinct is panic, and Cass's smile disappears. "I just... I don't know. I haven't thought this part through."

"Let's walk and talk." Cass pulls out a stocking cap. "It's windy up here."

Eliza puts on her gloves and they start toward the summit. It's hard to breathe, but a few feet up she blurts, "What happens now?"

"Right now?" Cass asks. "Or when you go home?"

"Both. Either. I don't know."

"I dunno. What do you want to happen?"

"I have no idea."

Cass doesn't reply. At the top, a sign reads *12,005 feet*, and another says *Protect the Tundra*. Eliza had no idea there were tundras in the United States, at least outside of Alaska. Purple and yellow flowers grow everywhere, and she points at the small rocks lying scattered around. "What's with those?"

"Glaciers."

She doesn't elaborate. Eliza can't tell if Cass is mad or winded or just thinking. But she's clearly waiting for Eliza to speak up, and after a minute, Eliza decides to just say exactly what she's thinking.

"If you went anywhere else, I'd offer to transfer," she starts, "but I don't think mining is for me."

Cass doesn't laugh, but she gives her a half smile. "That would probably be a little fast, anyway."

"And I've already gone that route once before," Eliza admits. "I like Big Springs. I might not always live there, but..."

"I understand." Cass gestures for them to step away from the sign so a family can take a photo. When they're out of earshot, she says, "I wouldn't want to be your mistake."

"You wouldn't be a—but yeah. I get it."

Cass looks down. "I mean, I like you a lot. I hope you know that."

"But…" Eliza says, bracing herself.

"But I'm not the only girl who's going to like you. Not the only person," she amends, looking up. "I'll definitely call you, next time I'm home—Big Springs isn't that far from there. But I know you're not into the long distance, so if you're with someone else, or if I am…"

Eliza swallows hard but nods. "Yeah." She desperately wants to throw herself on top of Cass, insist that she loves her and never wants to leave her, but she knows only the second part is true. The first could become reality, under the right circumstances, but for now they're a fling and that's all there's time for. "There's so much more I want to know about you."

"Well, there's always texts and FaceTime and stuff." Cass gazes out over the mountains. "Isn't it wild that the hills back home are technically mountains too?"

Eliza nods. Even these don't look like the triangles in children's drawings, but like the ones at home, they're all connected—the peaks are higher, but they're still in lined up like long arms hugging the valley below. "They make me homesick even though I don't want to leave," she says, unable to express what she really means.

"It'll be hard," Cass says, and Eliza's glad she understands. "But listen. If we do, you know…going forward… I'm out. And I don't want to pretend that I'm not." She takes Eliza's hands, and Eliza forces herself not to check and see who might be watching. "I'm not asking you to like, put on a rainbow flag and come dance on a float at Pride, but…but that part's up to you." When Eliza doesn't answer, she tries to step back. "I won't rush you, but I won't be your secret, either."

Eliza knows she should let go, but she can't. They just stand there and stare at each other, while Eliza's mind races, wondering what all the reactions might be. Her parents: surprised, but probably supportive. Her sister: the same. Her girlfriends: giggly but delighted, she hopes; weirded out and weird, at worst.

Nathan: shocked and hurt.

But that's not what makes her decision. What makes her decision is the realization is that the only reaction she hasn't considered is her own. *How will you feel, if you go home like this? If you left Cass at right this second?*

She already knows. She feels it right now. It aches and it will just get worse.

It's not something she can live with. Or without.

"Hey," Cass says, pursing her lips toward the steps. "Mindy strikes again."

Mindy's taking their picture, turning her phone, aiming for just the right angle. "Smile!" she yells, as a tourist hurries to get out of the way.

Eliza smiles and pulls Cass forward, then kisses her at the top of the world.

★ ★ ★ ★ ★

SEDITIOUS TEAPOTS

by
Katherine Locke

I DON'T KNOW WHERE IT STARTED.

(That's a lie. I know exactly where it started. The Museum of the American Revolution in Philadelphia. Pretty cool museum, to be honest. I thought it was going to be like the same old crap we've been learning about the Revolutionary War since we were like six years old or whatever, but it wasn't. I learned a lot there.

Honestly, why do they even bother teaching us the Rev War in school? Just shred the textbooks and send every kid to the museum. Museums tell stories so much better than textbooks do. And that's what history is, isn't it? It's just a really big story. That's what makes it important. And museums get that. Textbooks don't.

I have feelings about museums. And history. Apparently.

Anyway. That's where it started.)

I saw this teapot.

No Stamp Act.

I laughed, aloud, right there in the museum, at this little teapot with those words.

Like, I get it. You throw out the tea, but also you still want tea, but you want to be subversive and edgy, so you put what was the equivalent of an anarchist bumper sticker on your teapot. It was like the eighteenth-century version of keyboard activism. Cheeky, but not really productive. Still buying the tea with all that tax from England, right?

I don't know why—maybe it's the part where I got it— the throwing out the tea, but needing the tea, but wanting to subvert the whole shebang—but I needed the teapot. They didn't have it in their gift shop so I bought it online.

My mom stared at me, and then at my teapot when it arrived.

"I didn't even know you *liked* tea," she said at last.

"You don't know a lot of things about me," I said. I meant it to sound mysterious but mostly it sounded super defensive.

There's something about my mom that always makes me sound super defensive.

She opened her mouth to say something, and then shut it. She tried again. "I'll buy you some good loose leaf tomorrow."

I had no idea what she was talking about but said, "Thanks," because it seemed like the right thing. She was trying and I was trying and we were both failing, but it was the thought that counted, right? That's what I was told for years. I'd be pissed if it turned out it wasn't true. A for effort and all of that.

Anyway.

That was just the first teapot.

Then I bought one online that had an anarchist A slashed over it, but on a teapot made in China.

I'm not even sure the maker had any idea how ironic that was.

The third teapot got a little macabre. My mom made a face when I unpacked it. It had one of those old-timey paintings of a dutiful housewife, and she's smiling as she slides a plate onto the table. Only on the plate is a man's head. He's smiling too, like everything's great. The text says *Serving the Patriarchy with a Smile.*

"Rory," Mom started.

I stared at her.

She stared back at me.

She sighed. "It's a little *violent*, don't you think? For a teapot?"

I did not say, *That's the point*, even though *that was in fact the entire point.* What I said was, "It's just a teapot."

(It's not just a teapot. You know that. I know that. My mom knows that.)

Anyway.

It turns out that "loose leaf" was tea not in those little bags. It never really occurred to me that you could buy tea that wasn't already pre-portioned out for you. It made sense once I thought about it—I mean, obviously the people dumping the tea in the Boston Harbor weren't dumping little satchels of tea—but it just wasn't one of those things I thought about, you know?

The one Mom got me was good, so I asked her where she got it and she said, "That little tea shop in town."

I did not know we had a little tea shop, but of course we did. Sometime between freshman and senior year, I realized that the little run-down "too far off the main highway for city folk" town I'd grown up in had become chic. Trendy.

Instagrammable. So I should have guessed we had a TEA SHOP now. Like a proper tea shop with little teacups, and little tasting cups, and flavors with names like *Vanilla Sunrise*.

Vanilla Sunrise. These things don't go together!

But when I taste it, it's not so bad.

I'm getting ahead of myself.

I went because I wanted more tea, even though I didn't know if I liked tea, or wanted to like tea, or just liked the act of making tea. When I stepped up the small marble step into the shop, the doorbell tinkled behind me and it was weird, because it was such a *cheerful* noise and I wasn't feeling *cheerful*. I was feeling—apprehensive?

I don't know what I expected but I guess something that felt like it was from a *Pride & Prejudice* set, or something? I don't know! I've never been in a tea shop before! How do you form expectations about something with which you are completely unfamiliar?

A girl with glossy red hair—natural, I think—cut into a bob with a black bedazzled headband and a soft little black feather looks up from the register where she's stickering teapot boxes and chirps at me, "Welcome to Indy Tea Shop! Revolutions in a cup!"

I consider walking back out. No one should be this cheerful. Or pretty.

I can't make eye contact with her.

"Can I help you with anything?" she asks, like she doesn't notice how awkward I am.

"No," I mumble. "I'm good."

"Okay!" She is practically bouncing with every word. "Let me know if you have any questions!"

Each tea is in a little tin, silver with a dusty rose-pink ribbon around it, and pretty matte silver labels. In front of each tin, tea leaves sit in a little glass dish. I'm not sure what the purpose of that is, but I sniff a few and they smell good. Maybe I should do that in my room. It does smell funky. And laundry's a drag. I don't know if tea can help with it, but maybe.

There's a collection of teacups in the corner and I examine them, but they're mostly really pretty flower patterns and gold edges. There are a few that say, "Tea is the most important thing," but none of them are really connecting with me. I keep wandering until I reach a back room where there are more gift ideas. Another employee's back there, rearranging oven mitts and tea towels and—teapots. And teapots. Shelves and shelves of teapots.

"Oh," I breathe out before I can stop myself.

The employee jumps, turning around to look at me. A bright blue name tag says *LANE*. I look at Lane. Lane looks back at me. We stand there, frozen in this weird time warp, staring at each other. Lane's tall with medium brown skin, short dark hair, a chiseled jaw, a full mouth, and big brown eyes. Taller than me by at least two inches. Maybe six.

I am bad at guessing height and we're across the room from each other, but I'm pretty sure that Lane could drape an arm over my shoulders comfortably. I don't know why I'm thinking about that but it's the first thought that pops into my head. That Lane looks *comfortable*. Standing there, looking at me. Just *existing* there, like it's *easy*.

I blink again, and Lane scowls. "Can I help you?"

I look away, like a coward. "Just looking at teapots."

"*Lane*," hisses the perky girl at the counter, and the way she says it, I know it's a rebuke for Lane's tone.

They, I assign Lane in my head. It feels...strange. Uncomfortable. Like it makes my tongue thick in my mouth. I can't swallow. How can they just stand there, like this, without wanting to crawl out of their skin? Without wondering what the chipper girl thinks of them?

"They were staring," Lane mutters as they pass me back into the main room of the tea shop.

My head jerks up and I stare, wide-eyed, at a teapot depicting Amelia Earhart riding a dinosaur. *THEY*. They used they for *me*.

"What?" I say, before I can stop myself.

I turn, and so does Lane. They frown, tilt their head, and then soften, their whole body slumping down. "Oh. You—ah. I see." They consider me for another brief moment, then nod. "I get it. I'm sorry. I didn't mean to snap at you."

What do they see? I try to make the words form in my mouth, but my head's buzzing too much for me to find the sounds. I make myself swallow and clear my throat. "Okay."

It's a little pitying, the look Lane's giving me, and in the back of my mind, I think I know why, but I also don't know why. All I know is that I need to get out of there, right now, immediately, as fast as I can. So I grab the Amelia Earhart teapot and shove it in front of me, a barrier between me and the look on Lane's face.

"I'll get this one."

Lane looks amused now. "Okay. Emily will ring you up. Em, I'm taking my break."

Emily looks helplessly after them as they head for the front door. "We've only been open an hour..."

But Lane's already out the front door, the bell twinkling behind them.

Emily fixes a cheerful smile on her face and rings me up. I pay an absurd amount for the teapot, and I don't even mind. With a hand-stamped paper bag filled with golden tissue paper and the teapot, I step back out onto the street and the bright sunlight.

Lane's leaning against a brick wall, scrolling through their phone. They glance up at me and slip their phone into their pocket. "Hey."

"I have to go," I say automatically.

They nod, like they knew I'd say this. "You go to Pleasant View?"

"Yeah," I say warily. "Why?"

"I graduated last year. You looked a little familiar." Lane's lying. I can see it on their face. They just want to talk to me. About—nothing. Teapots, probably. Tea, maybe. Nothing. They hesitate and step a little closer to me. They smell like the store. I take a step back and Lane's face scrunches up a bit. Their voice drops low. "I hang out at Grounds for Change. Around the corner? With some friends. On Friday nights. You should join us."

I don't know why they're offering this. "Okay. I'll think about it. Thanks. Bye."

I can hear their sigh as I turn away, and I can feel their gaze on my back as I hurry as fast as I can down the street and around the corner.

The teapot goes on the shelf, next to my other teapots, and I realize only when I'm home that I never bought more loose leaf. I tell myself it's fine. It's not like I really wanted the tea anyway.

I look up Lane online. It's easy to find them since it turns out we do, in fact, have mutual friends. I guess that makes sense because we went to the same high school, but I didn't recognize them at all. I don't know if they were telling the truth about me, but I think it's unlikely. I keep to myself at school. I have a handful of friends in band with me, but I'm the quiet nerdy one doodling on the edges of the music while the band director's prattling on. I know Lane's not a band person. I'd remember them if they were.

I feel a little more like myself now, like the distance from the teashop and elapsed time have let me breathe again. My tongue feels like a normal size and I inhale, then exhale, rinse, repeat.

I hesitate and send Lane a friend request.

They accept *way* too fast.

I shut my laptop.

Inhale, exhale. Stare at the teapots. Consider making a cup of tea.

I open my laptop again.

They sent me a message.

Rory, eh? How's the teapot?

My fingers hover over the keys, and then I reply, joins the other teapots. I have a bit of a collection.

Really? Teapots?

It's weird, I know, I type. Aloud, I say, "WHY AM I TALK-ING TO THEM?"

Mom pops her head in my room. "Why are you talking to *who*?"

"No one," I say, which is a stupid answer because *obviously* I was talking to someone and now she's just staring at me in that way she does, like she thinks we should have a conversation but we don't, so I stare back until she shrugs and moves away from my room.

I turn back to my computer.

Lane's replied. I mean, everyone has their thing. Why teapots? Do you use all of them?

I don't use any of them. I mean. I guess, occasionally, that I use one or two? But it's not like I'm that into tea. I think I want to be into tea, but I'm not even sure where to start. But it feels like if I have teapots, I ought to be into tea.

There's a long, long pause.

I can see Lane typing but they haven't hit enter.

I add quickly, never mind. Pretend I didn't say that.

The dots pause.

Resume.

I should unfriend them right now. I should delete all of my social media right now.

But it's too late.

Lane says, that's a thing with you isn't it.

Like the idiot I am, I reply, what's a thing.

Thinking you need to be into something when you really don't have to be.

Lol, it's just teapots.

You totally know what I'm talking about.

My hands are sweaty.
WHO HAS SWEATY HANDS? I do.

I really don't.

I can almost *hear* Lane's sigh through the computer. It's cool. I'm just saying. I looked at you, and I understood. I've been there. And I know school isn't always the best place for people like us so if you ever want to talk or hang out, I'm here.

You don't even know me, I type back.

There's another long pause, and then Lane says, okay, it's two things. One, I don't, you're right. But people were really really kind to me. People helped me figure my shit out. And it's so much easier with people to talk to. I promise you. And second, I never want anyone to get into the same dark place I was in a few years ago.

It's hard to swallow again.

I tap my fingers lightly over my keyboard. I don't know how to reply. I know how I want to reply.

I'm not nearly as brave as I want to be. Cool. Thanks.

No problem. Lane lets me off the hook.

We both know it.

Tuesday crawls into Wednesday, Wednesday into Thursday, Thursday into Friday. I lay on my back and stare at the ceiling. Stare at the teapots. Stare at the laptop I haven't opened today.

Here's the thing about wanting things.

You have to know what you're wanting.

That weird ache between your ribs? Indistinct and constant, unattached to any organ in particular but a part of your chest muscle, stretching painfully tight so you can feel it every time you breathe? That's a want without words.

I am full of wants without words. It's painful, all the time, I've just gotten so good at ignoring it. At buying teapots instead. At directing all of that aching at something I can *hold* in my own two hands.

I want to exist in all those spaces without names but the thought makes me explode with panic.

I open my laptop. The browser's still open, and there's a message from Lane.

Lunch? 12? Grounds for Change?

It's 11:45. I reply back before I can stop to think, see you there. Might be a few minutes late.

I stare at my closet. I don't know what to wear. This is the other thing. I'm making a choice here, aren't I, in front of this closet. This is how Lane and their friends will see me forever now. I'm labeling myself in front of them, and everyone else who sees me, every single day with whatever I put on. And I hate that. I hate that feeling. I just want to wear my clothes.

So wear your clothes, I tell myself.

But I can't. I overthink, check the time, quash the panic that rises like bile in my throat, and grab a Captain America shirt and my favorite pair of jeans. I don't look in the mirror before I leave. I just grab my wallet and car keys and get out of the house. Otherwise, I might never leave again. That's a little dramatic but I'm a little dramatic and I wouldn't put such drastic actions past me.

Lane's in the corner with three others. They see me and wave me over and I approach, hesitantly. I shove my hands into my back pockets so no one will try to shake my sweaty, shaky hand.

"Hey," Lane says easily, their dark eyes disappearing into their smile. "Margot, shove over."

The girl on the bench scoots over, moving her coat next to her. "Hey. Lane told us you'd be joining. Want anything? My girlfriend's working. She'll make your drink for free."

I blink. "Um. I—I don't know."

"Tea?" Lane asks.

I shake my head. "No. I think I'm good for now."

If I get a drink, I might have to stay. This way I can leave if I need to.

Lane gestures to the guy across from me. "Ian. And this is Ari."

I'm afraid I will ask Ian something stupid like *DID ALL OF YOUR PIERCINGS HURT AND WHY DID YOU GET THAT PIERCED* but Ari's soft smile is safer. They ask me, "And you're Rory right?"

"Yeah."

"And you collect *teapots*?" Margot asks. "Why *teapots*? No offense, Lane. But this whole revival of tea seems like a hipster conspiracy to me."

Lane laughs, and Ian says, "Hipsters are *not* organized enough for conspiracies, Margot."

Ari adds, "Also, that's rich, coming from you."

"What does that mean?" Margot cries.

"You're a hipster, Margot," says Ari, in a tone that's an almost pitch-perfect imitation of Hagrid's *yer a wizard, Harry* moment.

I laugh, despite myself. Margot elbows me, like we've

known each other our whole lives. "You can't agree with Ari. That's the first rule of hanging out in the queer corner on Fridays. Ari's head is big enough, thanks."

I freeze when she says *queer corner*, and Lane's eyes leap from Margot to mine, but we're the only two who stop moving. The other three continue on in their whirlwind of banter and fun. Lane's watching me for my reaction. I don't know what my reaction should be. My stomach feels tight, and the ache between my ribs spreads to my left arm. Maybe I'm having a heart attack.

Breathe, Lane mouths at me.

I exhale. I inhale. The pain eases.

"Teapots!" yells Margot. "We were talking about teapots!"

"Margot, do NOT piss people off," hisses a girl behind the counter.

Margot blows her a kiss, and the girl blushes but turns away. Margot turns back to me. "Teapots."

"Seditious teapots," I say, without thinking.

"Why seditious teapots?" asks Lane.

I frown up at the ceiling. "I don't know. It's like…a teapot seems so prim. Proper. Like you expect it to be one way. But then it says *FUCK* on it, or has Amelia Earhart on a dinosaur, and then it's not prim and proper anymore. It's unexpected."

Lane smiles at me. "Yeah. That's cool."

"Obvious metaphor is obvious," says Ari, grinning at me like we have a shared inside joke. And what if we *do*?

Then they look back at Lane, saying something that I miss. I blink, grappling for something to say so they'll look at me again. I want them to look at me again. I want them to talk to me like that, like they know me. But they don't. Because they all know each other and I don't even know me.

"Jesus, Ari," Lane mutters, but they're smiling at something Ari's said. Something I missed. I feel like I've missed so much.

"Not my guy," Ari says cheerfully.

I close my eyes. It's too much, all at once. All of them. Their banter. Their ease of being. That twinge beneath my ribs has teeth and it is eating me alive.

I open my eyes, and then took a deep breath. "I think I should go."

Ari bites their lower lip, looking down into their paper cup. Margot's face falls. And Ian's finger stops turning the ring in his eyebrow. Lane swears under their breath. I hesitate and slide out from the bench, standing up. I wipe my hands on my jeans. "Thanks. It was nice to meet all of you. I'll, um, see you around."

"Rory," says Lane.

"Lane, let them go." Margot.

I walk toward the door, picking up the pace as I reach it. I have to get home. I have to get home. Everything's the way it's supposed to be at home. It hurts less at home. I pull open the door and step into the hot, humid summer air. I breathe it in, and my chest eases a bit.

"Hey." Ari's behind me. Not Lane. Ari. "Hey, Rory. Look, I'm sorry. We can be a lot."

"It's fine."

"Rory, please, hold up. Was it me? When I mentioned the metaphor?"

I stop and they come around me so I'm staring at their shoes. They're glittery sneakers. I kind of love them. They're unexpected against the black jeans and black Henley shirt.

"I can't," I say to their sneakers.

Ari makes a frustrated noise. "You can. I promise. We won't even talk about it."

So they do know. They know what I can't even say yet, not even to myself.

"We can't *not* talk about it. It's…" I press my hand against my breastbone, against my beating heart, against the muscle ache pulling my ribs farther and farther apart. "I can't."

"Okay," says Ari finally. And that's that.

I spend the weekend in bed, scrolling aimlessly through the internet, reading and seeing nothing in particular, looking for something I can't find because the internet doesn't give you what you need, it gives you only what you search for. You have to know what you want, what you're looking for, what words to pin to it, and I can't. There's no teapot for this. No pithy saying for this ache inside my chest.

My mom checks on me, worried, but she has to go to work, and I stay home, face creased from my pillow.

I ignore the messages from Lane.

Hey. I'm sorry. That wasn't cool. I mean, what I did. I shouldn't have pushed you. I know they're a lot and it would have been too in your face.

Do you want to talk?

Rory, I'm worried.

At that one, I type back. Don't worry. Nbd.
They reply, okay. You're good? You're safe?
I reply, yeah.
And then I mute the conversation.

★ ★ ★

Mom comes in on Sunday night, wipes a hand over my brow. "You feel warm."

"I'm fine."

"Rory," she says warningly.

"I'm fine," I insist.

She doesn't know what to say. "Okay. Will you come down for dinner?"

I have to. I skipped Friday night and last night. She will totally freak if I skip tonight too. I nod, and she leaves me alone for a blessed five minutes.

I stare at the teapots.

I close my eyes.

I open them. And before I can talk myself out of it, I open up the muted thread with Lane on my phone. They've sent me like a million messages since Saturday AM when I muted it, but I don't read those.

I just say I'm not stupid. I've read all the posts, I've watched the vlogs. It's that—If I reject ONE label because it doesn't feel big enough for me, doesn't that mean I have to pick a new label? And like, how many labels can one person have? And just because the label people assign to me when they meet me isn't big enough doesn't mean that it's wrong. Maybe I'm the one who doesn't fit into it, maybe I'm the one that's wrong, not society, you know? Like maybe *my* perceptions of what that label means are the wrong perceptions? Maybe I'm taking up space I shouldn't take up. What if this is all because I'm depressed and if I actually saw a shrink then it'd all be fixed? It was easier when it was just me and the teapots and the tea and my mother's weird looks.

I close the window.

I go downstairs and I eat dinner with my mom. I feel muted though, like everything around me is in sepia, and I'm forcing cheerfulness, like I'm pretending everything is normal and in color, into every word with my mom. I cannot will the world around me into color again though, which is really annoying because I've gone *seventeen years* being able to will myself into denial and into color and *now* that superpower fails me? Fine. Okay. I get it.

I do.

Upstairs, I open my laptop.

Was it? Was it easier? Lane had asked. But I hadn't replied, so just a few minutes ago, they asked, would this be easier in person?

I type back, no. I think I'd vomit if I had to talk about it in person.

Okay, says Lane. It's not your fault that the label you were given doesn't feel like you. Or big enough to include you. It's not because you're depressed—though it might be contributing to your depression—and it's not because your own worldview is narrow. It's not your fault that the label you think you need to replace it with—like nonbinary, or enby, or agender, or gender nonconforming, or whatever you've read on the internet—also doesn't feel right. It is not your fault that language hasn't made a word that fits you yet.

I can't breathe.

I can only watch the three little dots on my screen run like a little wave over and over again.

And I'm sorry I pushed you into that. It was clear that you weren't ready, and I thought I could help, and I made it worse. I'm sorry.

You didn't make it worse, I say. I think I was heading for this breakdown all summer.

Lane sends me back an unsure slash unhappy face.

I reply, I hate that I have to pick labels. I hate that humans like labels.

Who said you had to pick labels?

I did. I mean, if I say I'm not this, but I'm not anything, it feels like...god, like I'm untethered. Like I'm not real.

The dots again. Then, You're real. Even if you don't pick a label. Even if you pick a label that feels close enough for now. Even if you understand yourself more next year, or ten years from now, and that label changes.

I drum my fingers on top of the keys, trying to think about how to ask my next question. It feels uncomfortable, like I'm admitting something I'm not supposed to admit. What if it's like...a phase?

Then it's a phase. It's still YOU, Rory. Whatever you experience is still you.

I hesitate and ask, Can I ask what labels you use?

Lane responds immediately. Sure. I'm agender, use they/them pronouns. I'm also pansexual.

Oh god. MORE labels. I swear it's like my anxiety's reaching through the screen and having a panic attack in Lane's living room.

Lol. I know. But the beauty of the internet and language is we're learning how old some of these things are—like really, screw anyone who tells you that they/them as a singular pronoun is weird and new and they can't handle it. It's been around for literally centuries—and also, like...we can find words and make words that fit us. Language is growing more inclusive. It'll catch up to all of us, eventually.

I press my hand against my chest again. The pain is a dull throb.

You think?

Yeah. I do.

The first teapot I bought says NO STAMP ACT on it. It's a reproduction of an Am Rev war teapot.

The same people who threw tea in the harbor made a teapot?

Probably not the same people but yes, exactly.

I get it.

I smile. It's hard. Wanting the tea, but also not wanting the tea, but feeling like you should want the tea, but knowing you should protest the tea, so you put the protest on the teapot and throw all the tea in the harbor, and I guess the teapot... stays empty?

extreme Ari voice It's a metaphor.

It's a metaphor, I reply.

Throw out the tea, and protest all you want, you rebel.

Patriot, Lane. I'm a patriot.

Yeah you are.

Smiling, I lean back against my headboard. I don't know how to figure it all out.

You don't have to figure it out in one go. You play with it. Test it.

You used they/them for me in the teashop. Right away.

Yeah...you're...androgynous/ambiguous enough that it felt safer. I didn't mean for you to hear it though. I'm sorry about that. I should have asked. Actually, I've never asked, have I. What pronouns do you want me to use?

A choice. I know what they said, that I can change pronouns and labels, and what fits me now doesn't need to fit me forever, but it still feels important. They/them doesn't fit, but none of the options I know about fit.

Then I remember Lane telling me that it isn't my fault language doesn't have words for me yet.

I type slowly. That...works for now. It doesn't feel totally right, but it's better than the alternatives I know about right now.

Lane sends a smiley face and then after a pause adds, is there anything I can do to help slash make up for my earlier missteps?

I hesitate and then say, can I come back next Friday?

Of course.

Thank you.

The pain in my chest does not go away, but I breathe easier. I don't notice it every breath that week. Maybe every other breath. That might be dramatic. It definitely decreases for a few days, but Thursday night I can't breathe and Friday, I want to tear open my skin and find the source of the pain and yank it out with my bare hands. (That IS dramatic, I know.)

I stare into my closet.

I hate that I don't know what to wear.

I hate that it feels worse this week, now that I've given Lane pronouns.

I wear a Loki shirt and my favorite jeans again.

When I find the group at their usual table, Ari says coyly, "Rory's gender is Marvel."

I grin, surprising myself and from their expressions, everyone else. "Wait, is that an option? I will absolutely take that."

"How many of these things do you own?" asks Ian, scooting over on the bench.

"As many as you have piercings," I say.

Lane crosses their arms over their chest, leaning back in their chair. They have a very self-satisfied smirk on their face. "Look at this confidence. Where did that come from? Oh wait, I know."

"*Lane,*" warns Margot. Then, she gives me a bright smile. "Hey. Glad you're back."

"Thanks for not holding last week against me," I reply with a smile.

Ari pitches forward, whispering conspiratorially. "Heard you're trying different labels."

Lane winces. "I was *trying* to say that we shouldn't push you to ID yourself." Lane meets my gaze. Every inch of their expression pleads, *I'm sorry, don't hold this against me.* And I don't. I get it. The group seems used to asking for pronouns, labels, like everyone sails into their orbit knowing them. And I don't.

"I am," I tell Ari, and the rest of them. I hesitate and add, "I did a lot of research into nonbinary and asexuality this week."

"Oooh another enby," says Ian.

I frown. "But not that word. That's…that does not fit."

"It's a shorthand," Ian begins.

"They said it doesn't fit, Ian," Ari cuts him off crisply.

"Can I tell you what I think?" Ari says, dropping their voice even lower.

Lane, Margot and Ian groan. "Ari…"

Ari ignores them. When they stare at me, it's like it's just the two of us at this table. I can feel their sparkly sneaker against my boot underneath the table. *So maybe more on the gray-ace side of the spectrum,* I think as heat rushes over my face. I need to do more research.

"Just saying that you're not cis helps, doesn't it," Ari says. "Like letting a little pressure out. Turning the valve a bit. Gives you room to breathe and think."

I blink. They're right. "Yeah."

They don't lean back. Not yet. "Want to hear a not–cis secret?"

I can't help it. I whisper back, "Yes."

Their smile's slow, hypnotic. "No matter what anyone tells you about what you look like, or what you wear, or how your name sounds, or what they think you are, you'll always have that. That's enough."

I wait, expecting a *for now* but there isn't one. That's enough. Enough to make me feel like enough. Enough for me to settle into. Enough of a label for me to call home, without feeling boxed in.

I take a breath, and it doesn't hurt. Ari sits back, a satisfied smile on their face. I exhale slowly, glancing around at everyone. They're all staring at me. Lane's worrying their lower lip. Ari looks proud. Ian and Margot look like they expect me to head for the door.

Instead I say, "Want to hear about the rest of the teapots?"

★ ★ ★ ★ ★

STAR-CROSSED IN DC

by
Jessica Verdi

CLICK-CLICK-CLICK-CLICK-CLICK.

Cameras shutter and bulbs flash, a random series of tiny explosions.

I make sure not to squint or blink too much—there's no use doing a publicity event if the papers are only going to end up with unflattering, eyes-half-closed pictures to run alongside their articles.

"Yes, Genevieve," I say, pointing to a reporter in the front row, all the way to my left.

Genevieve stands up on spiky heels and smooths her gray pencil skirt. "Congratulations, Squeaky. How does it feel to officially be a registered voter?"

I flinch internally at the nickname, but don't let it show. Another skill I mastered ages ago.

I don't think anyone's called me Savannah in years.

"It feels fantastic," I say truthfully, my high-pitched, "squeaky" voice reverberating back to me through the speakers. "It's never felt quite right, spending my whole life around government and politics but not being able to cast my own vote. I've tried to contribute in other ways, of course, but I have to admit I'm pretty excited to go to the polls in November."

Genevieve smiles. "I bet!"

More hands shoot up.

I call on them one by one, answering all the questions I knew they'd ask.

Of course I'll be voting for my father! He's done incredible work during his first three and a half years as president of our country and I know he'll continue to do so if granted a second term.

It doesn't matter whether you're a Republican, Democrat or Independent—the important thing is for all eligible citizens to get out there and do their civic duty.

My birthday yesterday was great, thanks for asking!

The press routine is necessary, but it's exhausting. With each question and answer, I feel my smile shift from easy to the slightest bit pinched. They won't notice.

Another reporter stands. "Hi, Squeaky. Word on the Hill today is that the House vote on the controversial First Amendment Reinforcement Act is set for tomorrow, now that the bill's details have been released to the public. Have you read the bill? What is your opinion of it?"

Everything stops. The room is too quiet. I blink back at the reporter, trying to scramble together a response. They *never* ask me questions like this.

The First Amendment Reinforcement Act is a bill my dad and his Congress have been working on for a few months now. I haven't read the specifics yet, but its purpose, from what I understand, is to even more staunchly protect the right to free speech and free thought in America.

Dad told me that if he could ink just one stamp on the country during his time as president, he'd want it to be this. That made me proud, to see him fighting so hard for *all* his constituents—even if they use said free speech to disagree with him and his policies.

But no one's ever asked me my opinion on political issues before. My job as First Daughter is to represent the Chamberlain family, *not* the Chamberlain presidency.

For the first time in a long time, I'm not sure what to say.

I glance at Meryl, the communications director. Her nod is almost imperceptible, but I know what she's telling me:

Go neutral. Diplomatic. Feign confidence.

"I have the utmost respect and appreciation for my father's vision for our country and its citizens," I say into the mics, and make a personal vow to keep more informed on what's happening in Washington now that I'm a voter.

The reporter scribbles in his notepad. The others do too.

"That's all we have time for today." Meryl steps in seamlessly. "Thank you for coming, and congratulations again, Squeaky."

The bright lights are killed, the reporters record their tags back to the anchor desks, and the crews begin to pack up. With a quick, over-the-shoulder wave goodbye and a deep breath of relief, I slip out of the room.

My head hurts from the tight milkmaid braid pinned across the crown of my head, and my first impulse is to pull the pins out and let my hair free, now that I'm not on TV anymore. But there are usually public tours coming through at this time of day. You can bet your last penny that every single one of those people is going to have a camera at the ready. Which means I must be ready, too.

I make my way through the East Wing, nodding at the occasional Secret Service agent stationed outside of closed doors and at certain junctures in the labyrinth of halls, all the way back to the Executive Residence.

What I really want to do right now is change out of this dress, wash the makeup off my face, and take a long nap before dinner. But as soon as I close my bedroom door, my phone dings with a new text message. I glance at the display, and my heart beats out the three most perfect syllables in the world:

Emily.

She's the one person I always want to hear from.

But her message is just a series of about ten question marks, attached to a news article. I'm surprised, because politics is the one subject we usually don't touch.

First Daughter Squeaky Chamberlain Voices Support for Controversial Free Speech Bill, the headline reads. *Controversial.* That's the same word the reporter used. The piece has accumulated over a hundred comments in the last five minutes.

Huh.

A new text pops up on the screen, from my best friend, Hudson: Are you OK?

Why would he ask me that? What is going on?

I scan the article Emily sent, but it's brief and relies on the reader already being familiar with the ins and outs of the proposed bill, which were only released yesterday. Opening my laptop, I type "First Amendment Reinforcement Act" into an internet search.

A lengthy description of the bill tops the news feed, but I can't help myself—I bypass it in favor of search result number two. It's a video interview, posted earlier today, with Senator Phyllis Bautista, Dad's rival in the upcoming presidential election. I don't usually follow the Bautista campaign, but this interview is with the entire Bautista family.

And.

Emily is Phyllis's daughter.

And.

I'm in love with her.

Talk about star-crossed.

Emily and I first met a year ago, at the annual fund-raiser for the Millennials in Politics Initiative. We hit it off immediately, and have had a pretty consistent text thread going ever since. We've seen each other a few times too, but it's always been at official events.

With the Secret Service breathing down my neck and reporting back to my parents, it's not like the daughter of the enemy and I can just meet up any old time for coffee or a movie.

I came out to her as bisexual a few months ago; she was only the second person I've told, after Hudson. She was every bit as amazing and supportive as I'd known she'd be. But I haven't dared confess my feelings for her.

Emily's been famously out and proud for what seems like forever, even though she's only nineteen now. I, on the other hand, am very new in this incredible, shiny world where girls flirt with each other and kiss each other and fall in love with each other.

In the video, her hair is up in a messy topknot, and her lipstick is so pink and bright that if I saw it in a store I'd wonder what on Earth the makeup company had been thinking. But when I see it on Emily, I know—they had someone like her in mind. Someone gorgeous and fearless.

I stare at those perfect lips, and my face warms.

"I wanted to give you an opportunity to comment on the pending First Amendment Reinforcement Act vote," the interviewer says to Phyllis.

Phyllis's expression goes somber. "I appreciate that, Nia. As you may know, President Chamberlain has vowed to sign the bill if it passes the House and Senate. We *cannot* let this happen. If enacted into law, this bill would be extremely detrimental for our country."

Slowly, the rational, not love-struck part of my brain shifts from *Emily!* gear into *Pay attention!* gear. What does Phyllis mean, *detrimental*?

"Can you explain that a bit more?" Nia asks. "I know many Americans are confused as to how and why you might be against further protection of the First Amendment."

Yes. I am one of those Americans. Thanks, Nia.

"Well, that's because the wording of the bill is confusing. Intentionally so, I might add. This so-called 'First Amendment Reinforcement Act' is only about protecting the First Amendment in the most *technical* of senses." She sounds tired, as if this is something she's had to explain many, many times, to negligible effect. "In reality, the bill will allow businesses to discriminate against LGBTQ people, citing religious beliefs.

"Doctors and hospitals will be able to turn away gay and transgender patients, even in cases of emergency. Employers will be able to fire queer employees without cause. Banks will be able to hike up mortgage rates for LGBTQ families. And so on."

My face has gone from warm to full-on hot. What she's saying can't possibly be right.

I press the space bar to pause the video. Out the window, across the North Lawn, past the fountain and the fence, tourists crowd the sidewalk, pointing their cameras this way. I lean back a bit, out of view.

Yes, Dad believes in the "traditional" definition of marriage being between a man and a woman, but it's not like he's *mean* to LGBTQ people or anything. Once a lesbian pastor from a church here in D.C. came to visit the White House and Mom and Dad were perfectly pleasant to her. Surely Phyllis is just doing the politician thing—molding the narrative to suit her purposes, demonizing the opposition.

If your parents are so accepting, Savannah, why haven't you told them about you?

I stuff the traitorous question back down inside, where it belongs, and press space bar again.

"Here at the network we've heard from many citizens who feel that if this bill becomes law, they'll no longer be welcome in their own country," Nia says. "How do you respond to them?"

Phyllis puts an arm around Emily and tugs her close. "We understand what you're feeling. This is a very real concern in our family as well." Emily nods in agreement. "But I promise you, even if Congress votes in favor tomorrow, the fight is far from over. We are working hard in the Senate to ensure the bill moves *no further.*"

"And if you don't succeed?" Nia presses.

"Well, then the American public will show the incumbents how they feel about their choices come Election Day, won't they?"

Another text from Emily comes through.

I can't BELIEVE you went on TV and said you support this bill. After everything you confided in me?? I don't understand.

It's followed by a sad face emoji. The really heartbroken one.

I pull up the Google Alerts I'd set for myself. The proclamation of my support for the apparently anti–LGBTQ bill has spread fast.

A piece titled "Squeaky 'Respects' and 'Appreciates' Father's Bigoted Agenda" is trending on Twitter. Side-by-side photos of me and Emily, making it look like we're standing off, with "Vs." scrawled in the center are plastered all over the web.

My Instagram handle is tagged in dozens—no, hundreds now—of images of people's middle fingers, with the hashtag #RespectAndAppreciateTHIS. Known hate groups are releasing statements commending me on my bravery and thanking me for my support.

Everyone knows the internet is filled with hate and jealousy. With baseless opinion and "fake news" and manipulative wishful thinking. I don't have to believe any of this.

But.

There's so much here, from reputable sources. Non-American ones. And in that video, Phyllis spoke off the cuff, impassioned, without a pre-written speech, embracing— literally and figuratively—her gay daughter in front of the entire world. She said the word *queer* like it was as common and regular as *cheeseburger* or *school bus*.

It doesn't *seem* like political posturing.

Reluctantly, I open a new window and bring up the bill. It's long-winded and, like Phyllis said, a little confusing. But I keep reading, going over the same sentences three and four times in spots. By the time I'm done, the sun has begun to set. I flip my desk lamp on, close the window shades, and sit back in my chair.

There's no denying it; it's all there, in black and white. This bill my dad loves so much is aimed at hurting people. People like Emily. People like *me*.

And now the whole world thinks I'm all for it.

I slam my laptop shut.

The room is silent, but my ears are pounding. My head hurts. My stomach hurts.

How did this happen? All I said was I trust and respect my father. I was doing what I was supposed to do. What's expected of me.

I stare at my phone for a long while, deciding what to say to Emily. Finally, I just write, I'm so sorry.

It's the truth; I'm sorry I hurt her. I'm sorry I said anything to that reporter at all.

She doesn't write back.

"Dad," I say as soon as he joins me and Mom at the dinner table. He got back from France this morning, so this is the first family dinner we've had in over a week. And I need to get this out before I lose my nerve. "Um, I was wondering if you could tell me a little more about the First Amendment Reinforcement Act?"

He selects a bottle of wine from the list one of the kitchen staffers has presented him with, then glances at me. "Why?"

I force myself not to break eye contact. "I don't know if you've seen the news today, but I'm kind of being raked over the coals right now for saying I support the bill. Not that I *actually* said that, in so many words, but…" I shake my head. "Anyway, I'm just trying to understand what it's all about." More to the point, I'm trying to understand what his intentions are with it.

In my opinion, there's a difference between a law that's meant for good but some jerks finding a loophole and using it for bad, and a law that's *designed* to cause people harm. After my hours of reading, I'm pretty sure I know which this is, but there's still a huge part of me that wants to give my dad the benefit of the doubt.

"It's about protecting our base human right to freedom of speech." He tilts his head. "I thought you knew that."

"Yes, but isn't the First Amendment already pretty solid? There's tons of precedent in the justice system, and apart from cases of treason—"

"No, Squeaky. It's *not* solid. You just said it yourself—you shared your opinion on a political matter, which is every American's prerogative, and yet the press is… How did you put it?"

"Raking me over the coals?" I mutter.

"Exactly." Dad tastes the wine, and nods to the server. She pours Mom a glass, then Dad. "We're living in an era of such inane political correctness, that a person can't share his or her opinion without a witch hunt."

Of course it took Dad only about five seconds to completely turn my argument back on myself. The man is a born politician. But he's not only my president. He's my father. I know him better than most.

I take a deep breath. *Say it.* "I read that the bill will make it easier for people and businesses to discriminate against the LGBTQ community. Was that purposeful?"

Mom coughs. "Squeaky! This is not appropriate supper conversation."

But Dad studies me curiously. Whether it's because I'm pressing him on an issue for the first time in my life, or because I said the phrase "LGBTQ" in my parents' presence, or—oh, God—because my mention of LGBTQ has made him suspicious about why this subject might be important to me, I'm not sure.

I start to itch under his surveillance, my temporary bravery making a hasty retreat. "It's just that I'm old enough to vote now," I add quickly. "And, um, reporters are starting to ask me my opinion on this stuff. I need the facts."

I hate myself. For backtracking, for cowering under my powerful father's gaze, for avoiding an opportunity for an honest conversation.

Hudson once asked me when I'm going to tell my parents I'm bisexual.

My answer was simple: Never. They don't need to know.

It'll be easy to pretend I like only boys—because I *do* still like boys. Sometimes. I just happen to also like girls. One girl in particular. One stunning, radiant girl.

I take a sip of ice water, wishing I was twenty-one and could have a glass of wine, too.

Finally, Dad replies. "Your mother's right. This is not an appropriate topic for supper, Squeaky." Dad turns to face

Mom, and the two of them begin a quiet conversation about his visit to Normandy.

It's not an answer. But it speaks volumes.

I sit there, my heart beating hard. The food on my plate looks about as appetizing as a bucket of concrete.

My phone buzzes from where I'd tucked it between my thigh and the chair cushion. For one sweet moment, I hope it's Emily texting back, telling me it's okay and she understands. But it's Meryl.

The annual Millennials in Politics Initiative banquet is tomorrow evening at six. I'd originally RSVP'd no because of the busyness with the campaign right now, but after today I think it wouldn't hurt to foster some goodwill with the media. Any objection or conflict in your schedule I don't know about?

The Millennials in Politics fund-raiser! The spark of hope comes back.

Will the Bautista kids be there? I type. She'll think I'm asking because if they're there, it will look good, optics-wise, for me to be there too. But I couldn't care less about my father's campaign at the moment.

Yes, they're on the guest list, she replies.

OK. I'll go.

Your car will be leaving at five thirty. Dress is cocktail attire.

I do everything I'm supposed to do. I pose and smile on the step-and-repeat, I wave to the small crowd outside the venue, I let the Secret Service forge a path in front of me and trail closely behind me, I speak to the reporters.

The House passed their version of the First Amendment Reinforcement Act this morning, and it's now headed to the Senate. I get a lot of questions about that. This time, I keep my answers so neutral they're flat-out *beige*. I suppose I could, at any moment, give the reporters my real feelings about the subject, now that I *have* feelings on the subject, but this isn't the venue. Besides, there's only one reason I'm here right now, and I won't be able to concentrate until I find her and set things right.

It takes ages to make my way through the hundreds of mingling attendees; I have to stop every few feet to shake a hand or give a hug or sign an autograph or exchange pleasantries. But finally, *finally*, I spot her, standing with her sister Tess and some other people I don't recognize. She's laughing at some unheard joke, and my heart beats those three lovely syllables again.

I'm still a couple yards away when she looks up, and our gazes lock like magnets. Even with everything that still needs to be said, even with the way her smile falters into a little frown when she sees me, all I can think is, *There you are.*

I stop walking. Give a little wave. Try to keep my breathing level.

The corners of Emily's pink-lipped mouth turn down, but she excuses herself from her group and comes over to me. Her slinky gold dress leaves very little to the imagination. I swallow.

"Hey, Squeaky," she says, softly enough that no one except the two of us would hear. She knows exactly what it's like to have the world's eyes on you.

"Hey!" I wish we could hug hello, but her body language is still standoffish.

"I didn't know you were going to be here."

"It was a last-minute decision."

"Oh."

"How are you?" I ask.

"Honestly?" She searches my face. "I'm...confused."

Fair enough. I take a small step forward. "Emily, I am so, so sorry."

"You said that." I watch as she catches her sister's eye. Tess raises her eyebrows in a *You all right?* way.

Emily nods, and turns back to me. "You know, when we first started texting, and you said you didn't want to talk about politics, I figured it was because you're around it all the time and needed a break. Or because you didn't want our friendship to be defined by who our parents are. Not because you're one of those self-hating queers who secretly believes in all the stuff that makes life a hell of a lot harder for anyone who isn't cis, straight, white and rich." Her tone is biting.

What? I wave my hands frantically, trying to keep up. "Emily, *no.* You've got it all wrong."

The hurt in her eyes pierces my soul. "Squeaky, did you or did you not say you respect and appreciate what your father is trying to do with this bill?"

"No!" I shake my head. "I mean, yes, I did, but I didn't *mean* it."

"Right. Of course." She doesn't believe me.

I want to grab her shoulders and rattle her. Shout the truth so loudly that she'll have no choice but to accept it. But we can't do that here. I quickly assess our surroundings and make a decision. "Follow me," I whisper. "Please." And without waiting to see if she does, I take off, ducking and bobbing through the crowd, and slipping through a door marked Employees Only.

I find myself in a long, stark hallway, empty apart from a few suited servers en route to and from the kitchen. Jennifer and Sandeep, two of my Secret Service agents, are right behind me. At the end of the hall is an exit sign. I march in that direction, looking back only once, when I hear the door to the banquet hall open again. It's Emily.

I push the exit door open, and the oppressive summer heat hits me in the face. The small alley is lit by street lamps and passing headlights. There's no one out here. It smells a little like garbage, but it's quiet and private, and that's all I need right now.

"Where are we going, Squeaky?" Emily asks, clearly unsure if following me was the right choice. "What is this?"

"Can you give us some privacy, please?" I ask Jennifer and Sandeep.

They exchange one of their "looks," in which they hold an entire discussion with no words at all, then turn back to me in unison.

"This is not a secure location, Squeaky," Jennifer says. "We can't leave you alone here."

"This is *way* more of a secure location than inside that hall with all those people!" I counter. "Or in the car, which we'd have to go back through the crowds to get to, broadcasting to everyone exactly where I am." I never argue with my agents, but the past two days have been a lot, and I've had it with being the good girl.

Sandeep is shaking his head, but before they can say anything else, I say, "You guys know I could just give you the slip, right? The Bush twins did it to their agents all the time. It's not that hard, especially in a room full of hundreds of people. Let's see you explain that to my father." I cross my arms and let the threat sit there. Emily's wide eyes dart back and forth between the three of us.

Jennifer and Sandeep exchange another look.

"Fine," Sandeep ultimately says. "We'll be stationed at either end of the alley. Don't do anything stupid," he warns. And they stalk off in disparate directions.

When they reach their posts, I can still see them, but they're far enough away that I know they can't hear us.

I turn to face Emily. "Thank you for coming with me. I know all of this is weird, and it doesn't smell great out here, but I thought we should talk in private."

"Go ahead." She nods.

"I promise you, Em. I don't believe *any* of that stuff." My voice suddenly sounds way too loud, in the relative quiet of the alley, but I keep going. "I don't support the bill."

She grimaces. "Then why would you say you did?"

"Because that reporter had me on the spot and I had to say something. But the details of the bill were released on my birthday when I was hanging out with Hudson, so I hadn't read it yet. And everything I knew about it—which, okay, in retrospect wasn't very much—was from my dad and his team, and of course they'd made it sound like it was a good thing.

"As long as I can remember, my job has been to support my father. When I gave my response to the reporter, I thought I was doing that. But I also thought I was being neutral. Which is obviously my fault. I just… I wish it had all gone differently. I wish I'd been more informed, or that I didn't answer the question at all, or…"

I drift off as Emily blinks, assessing me. My body is so tense my knees are locked; I'm starting to get light-headed. I lean against the brick wall for support, watching emotions flicker over Emily's face.

Believe me. Please.

What the rest of the world thinks of me doesn't matter. There are always going to be people who think my family and I are the worst. But I can't just go home, knowing Emily Bautista, the epitome of everything good and beautiful and strong, hates me.

"I *swear*," I say.

When she opens her mouth to speak, I brace myself.

"Um, yeah…" she says slowly. "You were *not* being neutral."

I give a wry smile. "So I've learned."

We stand there for another suspended beat or so, and then Emily starts to laugh. A real laugh, filled with the entirety of this ridiculous situation. I start laughing too. The lingering tension breaks, and just like that we're back to being *us*. Emily and Savannah. Two girls who come from very different places but who have a remarkable amount in common.

It's so nice to hear Emily's voice and not just be looking at her texted words. To see her smile without it being filtered through a TV or computer screen.

When our laughter subsides, Emily says, "I should have heard you out. I've seen how the press has twisted my mom's words at times too. I'm sorry I jumped to conclusions."

I shake my head. "No more apologies, okay?"

She smiles—big. My tummy gets warm and molten, in the best way. "Okay."

Emily holds her arms out for a hug. I fall into them a little too willingly and hold on a little too long. She's taller than I am, so I'm at the perfect angle to breathe in the perfume she'd dabbed on her neck before the party. She smells even better than I'd imagined. If I had to go through all of *that* to get to *this*, it was worth it.

"I guess we should go back in," she says when we part, shrugging toward the door.

I nod. "After you."

I lie on top of my bed, unable to muster the energy to get under the covers, staring at a ceiling that Chelsea Clinton and Sasha Obama once slept under. In a building built by enslaved people, as a supposed symbol of freedom and liberty.

Why does everything have to be so complicated?

I've been glued to the news since I got home from the banquet. There's a lot of talk about the bill moving on to the Senate, and how it's expected to pass there as well. The rash of attention sent my way yesterday has died down a bit, but only a bit. There's one tweet thread in particular, from a well-known, left-leaning pundit, that I can't get out of my mind.

@The_Real_Max_Mitchell:

Imagine if Squeaky Chamberlain had a backbone.

Think about it: Have we ever seen a teen or adult First Child who used their platform to support the direct opposite of their president parent's position—while the parent was in office?

No. We haven't. There've been children of presidents who didn't agree with their parents' politics, sure, but they've at best stayed in the shadows, and at worst stood up next to the president with a smile on their face anyway.

Squeaky is eighteen now. She has every right to let her opinions be known, ESPECIALLY if they're more progressive than her father's.

I, for one, would love to see her go out and fight for what's right. To campaign for the other side, even. To be a role model for her generation. What an impact that would make.

Of course, that would require that she CARES about what's right and good. And we've seen no evidence of that.

But a boy can dream, can't he?

He's right. This random person I've never met, whose show I've never watched, has me pegged. I *do* care about what's right and good, but it's true that he's never seen evidence of it.

I roll onto my side and call Emily. It's after ten p.m., but I don't want to go back to texting. It feels, oddly, like going backward.

She picks up on the third ring. "Hey! Everything okay?"

Good question. "Yes? No? I don't know."

There's someone talking in the background. I think I hear "Is that her?" But it's muffled, and Emily shushes whoever it is. "Tess says hi."

"Hi, Tess."

"So, what's up?" Emily asks.

"I wanted to run something by you." My idea is still only

partially formed, but I'm hoping Emily will tell me if it's completely bonkers. "I'm thinking about…maybe…calling a press conference."

"About what?"

"About the First Amendment Reinforcement Act. Specifically, about how I don't actually support it. And how I'm very pro-LGBTQ rights. And how I think it's important to stand up for what *you* believe in, regardless of who your parents are."

There's pure silence on the other end of the line. No response from Emily, no Tess in the background. I check the screen to make sure the call wasn't dropped.

"Em?"

"Sorry, I'm here. I'm just…surprised."

"Well, I'm still thinking about it. I haven't made any decisions yet."

"Will you come out as bi? If you do the press conference, I mean."

That thought is terrifying. "No… I mean, someday, maybe. But…baby steps?"

"That makes sense."

"So, what do you think?" I ask. "About the press conference idea." *Tell me what to do.*

She lets out a wistful little sigh. "I think it would be so brave. Important. And would mean so much to so many people. But…"

"But?" I press.

"I can't tell you to just go ahead and do it, no big deal. I would *love* it if you did, but it also needs to be completely your decision. I don't want you to hate me if things go badly."

"I could never hate you, Em." My voice is soft.

"I could never hate you either, Savannah." Her voice is even softer.

"You called me Savannah," I whisper. If I wasn't far enough gone before, that just clinched it.

"Yeah. Sorry, was that weird?"

"No! I love it."

"Okay. Savannah." I can hear the smile in her voice.

"Okay. Emily." My own grin is unstoppable.

There's a pause, and then, in a rush, she asks, "Are you dating anyone?"

As if. I haven't even kissed anyone since Jacob Schwartz at summer camp when I was thirteen. Hudson had a crush on me in the early days of our friendship in ninth grade, but as much as I would have liked a boyfriend at the time, I didn't feel that way about him. Which turned out for the best, because he and I are much better as friends.

"You still there?" Emily says, and I realize I haven't actually responded.

"No. I mean, yes, I'm still here. No, I'm not dating anyone."

Emily clears her throat, and when she speaks again, her tone is almost businesslike. "Okay, I have no idea how to say this, so I'm just going to say it. I like you. I've liked you for a long time. I can't stop thinking about you."

Oh my god.

My heart starts pounding. *Hard.* It's the only part of my body I can feel.

Oh my god oh my god.

Somehow my legs find their way to standing, on the bed,

and I pace in a little circle, the mattress giving beneath my socks.

"Savannah? Squeaky? Say something. Please." Emily sounds worried. Maybe even embarrassed.

I *want* to say something, tell her everything. But I've forgotten how to form words.

"It's okay if you don't feel the same way," she says quickly. "I get it. Just forget—"

"Is this real?" I whisper.

"What?"

"Did Emily Bautista just tell me she feels the same way about me as I do about her?"

She inhales audibly. "You do?"

"Of *course* I do!" I've gone from mute to whisper to shout in no time.

"I wanted to dance with you tonight," she confesses, relief and happiness flooding her voice.

"I would have loved that," I confess back.

I want to ask her to go on a date with me, just her and me and no security detail or paparazzi or prying eyes. I want to ask her to come over for dinner with my family. I want so many things that are probably impossible.

But Emily Bautista *likes* me. And that's enough for now.

"So…this press conference," she says after a minute. "Are you going to do it?"

"Yes." I've made up my mind. And not only because it will make Emily happy, though that's a small part of it. I'm doing it because I *do* have a backbone. And conviction. And apparently people do care what I have to say. Who knew.

"Really?" she says. "When?"

"Tomorrow." I put her on speakerphone and open a new text window. "I'm texting Meryl right now to ask her to set it up." I leave the details out, simply letting Meryl know I'd like to speak to the press again. I hit send on the text. "Done."

"Wow."

"Yeah." My stomach goes a little queasy. I probably won't sleep tonight. But I'm not going to change my mind. "Will you watch?" I ask.

Emily laughs. "Of course I'll be watching! I'll make sure my whole family does too. My mom is going to be so proud of you."

At least *someone's* parents will be.

"Okay, then." I nod, determined. My whole life, I've been in front of cameras and crowds, representing something big, something I didn't choose. This moment is new. Scary. But I've never felt more myself. "Let's do this."

★ ★ ★ ★ ★

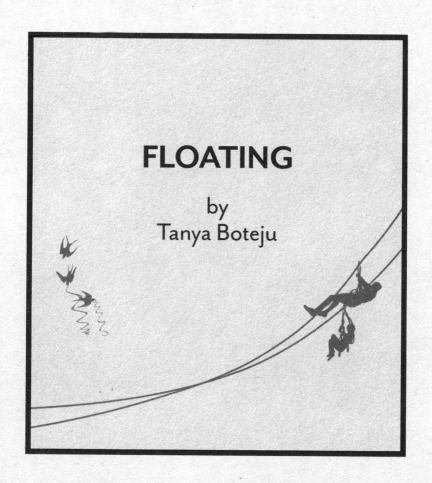

FLOATING

by
Tanya Boteju

SHE FLOATED. THAT'S WHAT SHE DID. SHE
floated from one place to the next, from one group to the
next, from one idea to the next. She didn't know why she did
it. Some days she wished she could just land. Two feet. Solid.
But instead, she drifted—a dandelion gone to seed, looking
for its next spot of soil but never finding it.

At lunchtime, she would float toward whichever area in the
school was empty. Sometimes this was the computer lab—
cool and whirring. Sometimes the stairwell behind the cafeteria gave her a few moments to herself. Once in a while,
the lounging chair in the library would open up to her like a
small oasis, but this was rare. Mostly, she floated from floor
to floor, moving on as others slipped into her space.

When she was forced to land—when she was in class, for
instance—she let her mind float instead. Through the windows, into the clouds. Beneath the teacher's desk amongst
the dust bunnies. Sometimes along the books lining the back

shelf—dropping into the Signets and Penguins. Never resting. Just tiptoeing in and out of the pages.

She'd get caught, often.

"Shanti. Where are you?"

"Shanti, please join us."

"Shanti, eyes up, please!"

Her floating self would seep back into her body, but not for long.

This morning, she arrived to school early, as usual. One of her parents would drop her off before heading to work each day, so early only the cafeteria staff and a security guard occupied the building with her. She loved this time though. So many places to roam, undisturbed.

Today, as she made her second round of the first floor—circling the ninth-grade lockers, dipping into the bathroom to ignore herself in the mirror, tightrope walking along the benches lining the entryway—she came to one of her favorite spots.

At the end of a long hallway, a window had been decorated with swirls of paper, each ribbon of color tightly wound and tucked in against the next. A mass of the spirals bunched at the bottom and gradually sloped upwards along one side of the windowpane, as though climbing each other to escape through the top corner but never quite making it.

The swirls reminded Shanti of whirlpools and she allowed herself to pause here, to dip into the curls and out again. She wished she had been the one to create the maze of looping paper, but that would have required staying in one place for far too long. She couldn't imagine winding each long strip, one by one, then building the creeping pattern in front of her. But someone had been able to. She envied them.

"Like them?" a girl asked. She sat with her legs folded beneath her, on a bench Shanti had been balancing on only minutes before. Where had she come from?

Shanti recognized her, of course. The school wasn't that big. The girl was in the tenth grade. Shanti was in the ninth. The girl played sports, made pottery, had friends. These few things Shanti knew. What she didn't know, was why she was here, so early, so close, in the middle of her floating path.

And her name. She didn't know her name.

Shanti looked back at the swirling art, feeling mildly irritated but also like she owed the art something. "I like…where my mind goes when I'm here."

"Where does it go?"

Shanti looked back at the girl, whose face was serious. A slight frown. No hint of a smile.

"It goes…into the curves." How dumb she must sound. How weird. "I mean…it slips in for a rest," she said, making it worse.

The girl's frown remained, but she smiled now. "Come sit here. Tell me more."

This was troubling. How could she sit? Here? With this girl?

But the girl shuffled her bum back a bit, making room for Shanti.

"I can't. I have to…"

After a few seconds, the girl asked, "Have to what?"

"Have to…keep moving."

"Oh." She cocked her head like she was going to ask the

question everyone asked. *But why? Why can't you just stay still?* But then she said, "Can I come with you?"

No one had asked this before. Shanti wasn't sure she wanted to be asked this. How could she wander with someone else so close to her? Where could her thoughts go if she was thinking about this other person?

"I...no." Shanti could feel her feet wriggling in her shoes, her fingers twitching at her sides.

"Oh," the girl said again. Her lips squished to the left. She was thinking. Shanti wanted to move. But she wanted to know what the girl was thinking. Her mind curled up behind the girl's ear.

"Who are you?" she asked, before she could stop herself.

The girl laughed. "Essie. You're Shanti, right?"

Essie knew her name? Shanti's mind trembled with delight from its soft spot against the girl's neck. "Yes...yes." Shanti's knees started to ache. They weren't used to standing in one spot for this long, locked into place.

"Okay, well, Shanti—don't let me keep you. Maybe the next time you travel this way, there'll be more swirls for you to wander into." She smiled broadly.

Shanti attempted a smile in return, but wasn't sure she succeeded. As she unlocked her knees and gathered her thoughts back into her head, a mixture of relief and disappointment trickled through her.

"Hi, Shanti," Elena said. Elena was Shanti's nanny.

Shanti didn't think she needed a nanny. She was in the ninth grade, after all. She wished, at the very least, she could call Elena something other than "the nanny." Maybe "Substitute Caretaker" or "Person in Place of Parent" instead. "Nanny" made Shanti sound like a child. She didn't feel like a child.

"Hello, Elena," Shanti conceded, climbing into the back of the van. She never sat in the passenger seat. The one time she did, Elena had asked her all about her day—what she learned, who she spent time with, what her favorite class was. Shanti's mind had wanted so badly to push itself out the window and let the wind blow through it, but this was difficult to do when bombarded with question after question.

So she sat in the back. Not just behind Elena, but two rows back. She would pull out a book and stare into it, discouraging any further inquiries.

As Shanti's eyes blurred into the letters and words in her book, her mind stumbled upon a pair of lips slipping into a smile. Shanti closed her eyes so all she could see was the smile. The slightly chapped lips parting to reveal a tiny glimpse of teeth. A crinkle at one end of the lips pointing to a faint dimple.

She tried to keep her mind focused, and even succeeded for a few moments, but then a horn honked and her mind jumped and tumbled around the van for at least six blocks.

At the house, Shanti dropped her backpack beside her bed and changed out of her uniform. She opened the door to her bedroom closet and crept into the back corner where she had cleared a space. She reached up to pull the door closed and then folded into the dark.

The silent blackness helped her gather herself at the end of the school day. Her mind settled, her body stilled. Today, though, as she allowed the rest of her body to calm, she could feel her heart tiptoeing around in the darkness, searching for something.

She decided to let it.

At dinner, Shanti carefully divided her mashed potatoes into bite-sized sections and shifted her chicken over so it wasn't touching anything else on her plate. She arranged her broccoli into a small pile between the potato mounds and the chicken.

Her heart was still tap-tapping inside her chest and Shanti felt if she ate anything now, her heart might become too distracted to continue its unfamiliar beat. She didn't want the beat to stop.

"That's enough," Shanti's father said in his serious voice as he sat down at the kitchen table. He had just walked in, business attire and business face still on. "Eat your dinner, Shanti."

Shanti closed her eyes for a moment, trying to memorize the beat before taking her first bite.

As Shanti crawled under her covers that night, her bedroom door opened a crack and her mother poked her head in. It was the first time Shanti had seen her mother in four days. Sometimes Shanti thought she got her need to float from her mom, who seemed to bob in and out of their lives like driftwood—so many trips, so many responsibilities. And yet, they couldn't connect, even over this shared tendency. Maybe because of it.

"Hi, kiddo." Her mother's face hesitated between greeting and concern. She was often uncertain around Shanti. Shanti rarely made herself easy to understand. "I know it's almost lights out. I just wanted to say good-night."

Wrapped up in her own thoughts, Shanti failed to reply to her mother. Seeing this, her mother smiled awkwardly and began to close the door.

But Shanti's mind shook itself and prompted Shanti to call out, "Mom?"

The door paused and her mom's head nudged back into the room. "Yes, sweetheart?" Surprise and eagerness rose across her brow.

But now Shanti wasn't sure what her mind was trying to say. Or if it was her heart that was trying to say something. So instead, she just echoed, "Good night," and turned off her lamp.

Passing through the front doors of the school the next morning, Shanti's mind was already several feet to the left, skipping across the keys of the grand piano that stood extravagantly in the foyer.

She followed it and slipped her fingers over the keys. She didn't often feel the need to touch the spaces through which she moved—allowing her mind to roam in and out of them seemed enough—but the piano demanded something different. Its cool surfaces appealed to Shanti's fingertips.

While her mind darted across the strings inside, she would let her fingers travel over the smooth, dark surfaces and ivory keys. Until she was done. Then she would move on to the next space. But the piano was often her first stop after entering the school each morning.

Today, when her thoughts assembled once again, she found

herself gravitating toward the spiraling window. She ignored the niggling sense of hope and unease in her chest.

As she passed reception and then the bulletin boards on the way to the window, she heard, "Good morning!" She paused, and her mind had to reorient itself. It had been gliding closely beside Shanti, but the sudden stop sent it toppling forward, skidding to a stop in front of the girl.

The girl from the day before. Essie. She was sitting across from the window. So close. Again.

Shanti tried to reel her mind back. But it wouldn't come. It stayed, hovering, just in front of Essie.

A tiny sigh escaped Shanti's lips.

"Did I scare you?" Essie asked, her brow crinkling.

Shanti took a step forward—a half step. "No. Yes. A little." So many things scared her. Crowds. Teachers. Herself. But somehow, not this.

Essie smiled. "Sorry. I don't usually get here this early. But my sister has track practice, so I had to come with her."

Shanti didn't know what to say to that, so she said nothing.

Essie nodded toward the window with Shanti's curls and loops in it. "Coming to give your brain a rest?"

Shanti stared at Essie. This was tricky. Her mind seemed to have dipped behind Essie's shoulder and was peeking back at her. Shanti could see its cheeky grin. "I thought so. But I'm not sure my brain wants it."

Essie's eyebrows popped up. Her eyes hinted amusement. "Oh? What does it want instead?"

Half step. "I'm…not sure."

"Maybe a new curve?" Essie offered, getting up and walking to the window. Only then did Shanti notice the scissors and tape and paper, bunched in a pile on the bench where Essie had been sitting. "Come see." She held a hand out to her.

In no universe could Shanti imagine herself taking that hand. But she did want to "come see." Her mind slipped over to Essie's other shoulder and perched there, admiring the window. Shanti floated over to join it, carefully avoiding the outstretched hand but offering to Essie a bashful smile instead.

Essie accepted the smile, then used her extended hand to point to two new swirls—one bouncing atop the mass at the bottom of the window, one reaching toward the top. "See?"

Shanti looked. Her mind climbed back into her body and they both looked.

"I see." Shanti found herself wanting to explore these new twists and turns, but that would be difficult, given this person standing so close to her. Her mind couldn't focus on both. "Did you do this?" she asked, not looking at Essie.

"Depends. Do you like them?"

Shanti could feel—actually *feel*—Essie smiling beside her. How was that possible? Shanti said, "I like them."

"Then...I made them."

Shanti glanced sideways to see if Essie was, in fact, smiling. She was. This confirmation made Shanti smile a little too. "Thank you," Shanti said, without really knowing why.

"My pleasure," Essie said, as though she knew exactly why.

Shanti thought back to that moment as she tried to form numbers with her pencil. It had only been that morning, but it felt like a dreamy blur—a practical joke played on her by an increasingly impertinent mind.

Shanti's heart also felt a little blurry. Her close physical proximity to Essie had created something like comfort and confusion—both a rest and an invitation to move. To float.

When she'd realized this pull in two directions, her feet had shuffled backwards, away from Essie and the window with its two new whirlpools. Her confusion had been compounded when Essie's face filled with a look not of surprise or disappointment, but knowing instead—as though she'd expected Shanti to move away. As Shanti withdrew from Essie and the twists and turns, Essie had called out, "See you tomorrow, Shanti."

And Shanti knew that was true.

"Shanti—focus, please!" her teacher called out over the tops of her classmates' heads, and Shanti's pencil tip broke under the sound.

The next day, instead of passing along the piano and finding her way to the window, Shanti ignored her mind and allowed her feet to carry her toward the library. It wouldn't be open yet, but a space in front of the entrance had been furnished with a bookcase and two chairs, a kettle and a box of tea. An extension of the library, an attempt to gather people in with comfort and books. It worked.

Shanti's feet circled the area—it wasn't very big. In a matter of seconds she'd traveled around it at least six times. She was getting dizzy, but couldn't stop herself. Her mind was tugging her elsewhere, but she placed her hands over her ears and just kept circling.

Until.

Essie was suddenly in her path.

Shanti almost ran into her. But didn't. Managed to avoid contact. Barely.

"Sorry," Essie said, almost bashfully.

"For?" Shanti knew for what. But wanted to know if Essie knew.

"For stopping you."

She knew.

Essie continued. "I—can leave. I just wondered where you were roaming today."

Shanti wanted her to stay. And leave. How to say that?

She took Essie's hand and continued in her circle.

They spiraled in silence for a while. Shanti set the pace, but noticed her feet moving more slowly with Essie at her side. Maybe it was because her mind was curled inside Essie's hand—lingering between her own palm and Essie's. Maybe because it was harder to move privately and freely with another person beside you.

It was Essie who spoke first.

"I think I'm getting a little dizzy," she said, followed by a chuckle.

"Me too," Shanti replied. But kept walking. Because what else could she do?

"Could we walk elsewhere? I'll go wherever you lead me."

Shanti searched Essie's face with what she hoped were sneaky side glances. But she got caught. Essie was looking right at her, face full and open.

Shanti averted her gaze and avoided certain disaster by breaking the circle and walking forward, out of the library space and into the hallway leading off of it.

Her mind turned around in their hands, like a cat circling its resting spot.

As her feet led them to the first floor, Shanti thought of all the places she could go, but knew exactly where her feet were leading them. She had little control over them at this point, given her mind had contentedly situated itself between her and Essie's hands.

As they approached the window, Essie's hand squeezed Shanti's and then Essie's feet slowed. Their arms stretched between them as Shanti continued forward.

"Wait," Essie said.

Shanti looked at the window, a few feet ahead of them, then back to her hand in Essie's. Then to Essie, whose eyes flashed with concern.

"I just—you don't have to take me here. If it's not really where you want to go."

"It's where I want to go." Shanti realized it as she said it.

"Are you sure?"

Shanti replied with a tug of her hand.

They stood opposite the window. One of the spirals had started to unravel. Essie moved to fix it, pulling her hand away. Shanti's mind unfurled from its cozy spot, but found another, easily. Shanti caught Essie's hand, holding her firm. "No. Leave it like that."

When Essie turned to her, a question in her eyes, Shanti smiled, shy, but sure.

★ ★ ★ ★ ★

THE SOFT PLACE

by
Hillary Monahan

THE SOFT PLACE IS KIMBER'S WORLD, ONLY

better.

She sprawls across the floor, eyes fixed on the ceiling, pupils devouring the blue irises surrounding them. They are galaxies without stars. They are black holes absorbing everything and offering nothing in return.

They are empty and swallowing and will be for hours yet. Longer if she takes another tab.

I miss you, Shyanna.

Kimber's hand flexes around her phone. On the screen is a picture of them from the spring. They're smiling, arms slung across each other's shoulders. Shyanna's box braids are a deep wine that complement the flush in her brown cheeks. Her eyes are big and fringed with thick lashes. Wild freckles speckle her face, her brow, down her neck and over her chest. She's beautiful, and Kimber's face reflects that. Instead of looking at the camera lens, she's looking at Shyanna.

She *always* wants to be looking at Shyanna.

But parents. Hers. My mom. I just...

"The summer's coming," Shyanna said. "We'll have time then. They work. I can take the bus."

It was soonish, but not soon enough. Two months is a long time to pine. Two months is a long time to know your girl is out there, missing you, too, but you both have to wait and you both have to hide because not doing those things means you've got no place to live.

Kimber breathes deep so she won't cry.

You paid good money for this ticket to ride. Go with it. Go with the flow.

The chemical is pungent on her tongue—as pungent as the bone-deep longing she lives with every day. But that's what the soft place is for. To dull the pain. To leave it and the worry about the future behind. Kimber gleefully abandons reality. She follows Alice into the rabbit hole and plummets her way into Wonderland.

Maybe the March Hare has made her a place setting.

Her muscles clench and unfurl. Her mouth is dry.

She's floating.

Aaaaaaand...

Arrival.

The soft place welcomes her back. The cold seeping through the floorboards doesn't bite so hard here. It doesn't send shudders down her spine or set the hairs on her arms prickling. It's comfortable, not too hot, not too cold. She is swaddled in a cozy cocoon that pays no heed to the scratchy, threadbare rug below her body.

She doesn't care the heat was turned off last week. Or that

drafts gust in through the window frames because winter in New England is brutal no matter where you live, but especially in a tiny basement apartment in a run-down building.

In her soft place, there's no sound beyond the heavy thud of her heartbeat in her ears. The slow pounding of blood rising and falling is a metronome, a steady ticktock she lets echo through her head. There is no shouting in the upstairs apartment—no hurtful words followed by bodies striking walls or floors or tables. Mama isn't always yelling, either, or calling Kimber names Kimber would punch anyone else for using.

"Can't punch your mother, baby," Shyanna said. "It's a rule."

Shyanna is the better person of the two of them. It's one of the reasons Kimber loves her so much.

Kimber stretches, her fingers and toes tickling the edges of the soft place. She no longer smells Mama's cigarettes, nor the stink of the apartment's antiquated septic system. Instead there are flowers. Fake flowers, yes, because it's her deodorant, but that's alright. It's pleasant. Lavender, the bottle reads.

Lavender.

She played in a field of it once, when her grandmother took her away for a summer so Mama could "get better." Mama would never recover, not then, not any of the times she went into programs, but Kimber was too young to understand.

Eight years old. Carefree. She'd rushed through acres of knee-high lavender, laughing as velvety leaves tickled her bare calves. Her grandmother called for her to come back, she'd burn in the hot sun, but Kimber just kept running until she collapsed in a pile of giggles, a girl bathed in purple flowers and sunshine, not caring about the redness creeping over her pale skin.

Somewhere, past her horizon of violet, her grandmother muttered about Aloe.

Kimber flinches. She doesn't want to think about her grandmother. Not so early in her flight. If Kimber sails just a little closer to the sun, damn her wax wings, she can pretend her grandmother lives in the soft place, arms ever open to deliver one of her killer hugs. But the recesses of Kimber's mind are still freshly dipped, still *present*, and they're screaming the reality Kimber can't yet handle.

She's a ghost. She's a ghost. She's a ghost, ghost, ghost!

And ghosts.

Aren't.

Real.

Kimber grits her teeth. She feels so old right now. Seventy, maybe. Or seven hundred. Gram's been gone a year. A long, miserable, terrible year. She'd been Kimber's rock. She'd been Kimber's safety. Without her, so much is bad, and so Kimber finds escape in sheets of cartoon elephants she buys from Ricky Sheldon in the high school parking lot after school.

It's something, though, right?

Don't turn a good trip bad.

Five minutes pass, or maybe it's fifty. Time works differently here. All Kimber knows is the soft place is nearing its softest. Her fingers and toes tingle. She's unraveling from the bottom up, like a sweater, her tight stitches becoming loose and sloppy. She closes her forever-seeing eyes. The brush of her lashes against her cheeks feels exaggerated, like someone raking ostrich feathers over her face.

The walls are built, reality on one side, Kimber on the

other. Her heartbeat is a timpani drum, each steady thud an affirmation that she's still alive.

"Hey."

What?

How?

The voice is big, deep. It startles because how could it not when Kimber's Wonderland is so quiet?

"Yes, hi. I'm here. Helllllllooooooo," the voice says. "Eyes. You have them. Open Sesame."

Right, she has eyes. In her face.

She does as she's told.

There, looming above her like a mountain, is a woman with pale skin and ruddy cheeks. Her chestnut hair is short, shaved at the sides, the top spiky thanks to hair shellac that gleams in the dim lighting. She's heavy, round all over, a double chin, broad shoulders. She stands with her legs braced apart, her hands stuffed into the pockets of her acid-washed jeans. High-top sneakers with a logo Kimber doesn't recognize. A navy blue tank top beneath one of those retro satin jackets. This one has a logo of a pizza joint on the left breast, a pizza thumbs-upping and cheesing a smile.

It's aggressively cheerful.

The stranger smirks.

"Telling you to focus is probably not gonna work, huh?"

"I...who?" It's all Kimber can manage. The soft place has inflated her tongue. *Is* inflating her tongue. It's cartoonishly huge, filling her cheeks, ballooning her head as it grows and grows. Words are impossible to make because they're trapped inside by the enormous, rapidly expanding slab of flesh inside her mouth.

This is alarming.

"Renee, but Rey, please. Always been my thing." The large woman shakes her head and looks around the eight-hundred-square-foot apartment. The furnishings are sparse: a faded plaid couch, a tiny box TV set up on stacked milk crates, a cheap, corkboard decorator's table they used as a dining table, and some folding chairs. Rey grabs a chair, swings it around, and straddles it, her arms stretching across the top, metal rim. Her chin drops to rest upon them.

She peers at Kimber on the floor.

"How?" Kimber's words remain strangled. Annoyed, she reaches into her mouth to wrestle her tongue, trying to shove it out of the way so her voice can be free. Immediately she regrets this; there's something bitter on her skin. She smacks her lips, the sour taste lingering after she removes her fingers.

Hand sanitizer from the school bathroom. Chemical lemon. Yum.

"How's less important than why, kiddo, and only you can answer that. You're the one who brought me here." Rey pauses. "Maybe I'm like a Fairy Butchmother. You kids still use that word?"

Kimber tries to articulate that some do, some don't, but she can't because POP! goes the tongue. The balloon has expanded past its limits and only flesh tatters remain. She slaps her hand over her mouth, eyes wide, staring at Rey.

She's a miasma of feeling: fear, confusion, curiosity. Not only is she lacking a tongue, but she's grappling with the notion of an invader in the soft place. Sure, there have been glimpses of Gram or Shyanna, but she knows those are hallucinations, her mind giving her what she wants most but usually in ways she doesn't want them.

Rey is new.

Her mind has expanded its repertoire.

"You're fine, Kimber," Rey says. "Intact."

Kimber's eyes narrow as if to say, *Are you sure?*

Rey grins, revealing yellowish-brown teeth with a zillion silver fillings.

"Promise."

Gingerly, Kimber pokes a finger between her lips. The sour taste is a small price to pay for the reassurance that your tongue is still part of your face. And it is. It's there, slimy and wiggly and immediately retreating from the prodding digit.

We're good.

"Thanks," Kimber whispers.

"You bet." Rey looks around the apartment and shakes her head. "Hasn't changed much, has it? That blue wall in the kitchen? I did that. Meant to do the whole place but got busy. Then got lazy. Figured the landlord would cover it up at the very least, but he was a piece of shit. Harold? Graves or something. Greeves. No, it's Greeves. He still here?"

"Yeah. Barely. It's just tha—hold on." Kimber realizes her heart is no longer pounding in her ears. Her fingers creep to her chest, still slimy with her own spit. She wants to be sure she's alive, that she hasn't died and gone to Bizarro Heaven. It probably looks like she's fondling her own boob, but she doesn't care. She's located the thrum deep in her chest, pounding hard as it pumps life through her veins. Satisfied, she sucks in another deep breath.

"He's got cancer. His son has kinda taken over," she says.

"He always did smoke like a chimney, but who am I to judge? Didn't get these bad boys by being good to myself."

Rey taps her stained teeth. "Anyway, don't smoke, it's bad for you. Drugs are, too, but Nancy's 'Just Say No,' yeah?"

Kimber has no idea who Nancy is. Rey figures that out real quick. She grunts and streaks her hand over her hair.

"Never mind. Just be careful with that stuff. I get it, though—the why. You're missing your girl real bad."

Kimber wants to know how she knows that, but then she remembers the picture on the phone. It'd been in her palm, but at some point during her high, she must have dropped it. She cranes her neck. The phone is close by still—*but far, but close, but far, but close*—and she stretches her arm both inches (miles?) to retrieve it. There she is. Shyanna and her bright white smile.

The freckles *still* kill her every time.

"May I?" Rey reaches out her hand. Kimber doesn't think twice, though she knows she probably should. That phone was her last Christmas gift from her grandmother. It's the only one she's got or will ever get 'til she's on her own, and she babysits three times a week for some of the most obnoxious kids on the planet to pay for the service.

Rey runs a calloused finger over Shyanna's face on the screen. "She's gorgeous. Good for you. You happy?"

"No." Kimber's answer is immediate. When Rey glances at her, cocking her head to the side with expectation, Kimber reaches for words that again refuse to come. Her tongue is fine, she's fairly certain. It's just that the feelings are so big. "We can't. Our parents. My mom's a mess. Her parents are religious. I miss her so much."

"Okay. Yeah, I get you. That's probably why I'm back here."

It's this phrasing that clues Kimber into something her addled mind glossed over before: this is not Rey's first time in this apartment.

"That blue wall in the kitchen? I did that."

"Back," Kimber repeats, more to herself than to Rey.

"Yep. I dunno how long it's been, but probably a long time." She returns Kimber's phone. Kimber expects a smear of oil from Rey's finger to mar the screen over Shyanna's face, but no, it's pristine save for Kimber's own thumbprint on the bottom button.

"I've never seen you before, though." Kimber pushes herself up so she can sit. The world spins. She feels like Wile E. Coyote right after he's crushed beneath his own Acme anvil. No tiny birds dance around her head yet, but in the soft place, anything can appear without a moment's hesitation.

She blinks and narrows her eyes. It's helped mitigate the illusions in the past. Perhaps it'll prevent them altogether now.

"Like I said, you brought me here," Rey says.

"Are you a ghost then?"

Rey hesitates. "What's a ghost, really? Casper, sure. A spook in an attic, okay. Or, maybe it's bigger than that. A concept— something from the past we don't want to look at but should. A reminder given shape."

That's deep, deeper than Kimber is prepared to handle in the soft place, and so she points at the blue wall instead, letting the gesture say what she cannot.

Rey shrugs her shoulders.

"I don't have the answer you're looking for, kid. All I know is I'm here because of you. I'm kinda liking my Fairy Butch-mother theory. How many others you think can claim that one?" Rey's thick fingers swipe at the corners of her mouth. "Or, maybe you're just on drugs and this is where your brain went. Id gone wild. Damn, I want a cigarette. Should have never brought it up earlier."

"Don't have one, sorry."

Kimber is comfortable with her almost lie. Mama has cigarettes, a carton in the kitchen, but Kimber hates the smell and so she won't give away what doesn't belong to her. It's like Rey knows, though; her eyes drift to the stove. To the cheap, white cabinet above with the old brown splatters across the front.

"Don't worry about it. I get it," she says.

Kimber frowns.

I don't get anything right now.

I don't like being confused.

"It's okay, Kimber. You're going to be fine. I'm not here to hurt you."

Again, Rey looks like she understands things she shouldn't—like she can read Kimber's mind, and maybe in the soft place she can. There are no rules here, only that anything is possible and that the good stuff is ecstatic and the bad stuff is excruciating. Kimber's been lucky to this point. There's been far more good than bad in Wonderland.

But is Rey bad?

Or is Rey just Rey, a thing, neither good nor bad?

Is she just a ghost?

A reminder given shape.

Who badly wants a smoke.

"Yeah, that. Now you're getting it," Rey says.

"I am?"

"Sure, as much as anyone can get anything when they're tripping balls." Rey shakes her head. "It's about the girl, though. Isn't it always about the girl?"

Shyanna.

Kimber hugs the phone to her chest, the flat screen touching the sweatshirt fabric above her heart. Seeing this, a flash of pain distorts Rey's face, worry lines creasing her brow, her mouth pinched. She smacks her lips and motions vaguely over her shoulder, though at what exactly, Kimber can't say.

"My girl was Tammy. Met her in the club. See, back then— I don't know when, really, just…in my time—" Rey pauses "—we were club scene kids. We had to be. No one else wanted us around, so we made our own spaces. She worked there."

Rey takes a moment, looking like she's sorting her memories, before she speaks again. "I liked her immediately. She talked so much shit, you know? Made me laugh. We hooked up quick, were living together in a month. Had a cat 'cause clichés sometimes exist for a reason. It wasn't easy, but we made it. She waitressed in three places, I drove a taxi. Things were good for a couple of years, but back then people were getting sick. *Our* people were getting sick. You get what I'm saying?"

Not at first she doesn't, no. Kimber stares at Rey, wanting the answer fed to her, but Rey's quiet forces Kimber to do those mental calisthenics. Kimber thinks about the story, thinks about the things Rey's said. She grunts, frustrated, still not grokking it, her drug-laced mind building bridges that go nowhere and venturing off onto paths totally unrelated, but then Rey's fingers glide over the cartoon face of the pizza guy on the jacket.

The gear's thirty, maybe forty, years out of date.

The eighties.

Rey nods slowly. "There you go. Now you're with me." She reaches out like she'll clap Kimber on the shoulder, but just before contact, she recoils, peeling away and running her fingers over those too-glossy spikes on top of her head.

Kimber is fascinated by how quickly they spring back into shape.

"Come to find out, Tammy had it when I met her. Got it from her ex-boyfriend who got it from his ex-boyfriend. By the time she was diagnosed, most of our friends were already half-dead and no one outside of the folks in our scene seemed to care." Rey is looking not at Kimber, but through her. Her eyes are fixed, intense, and she is very much elsewhere when she talks.

"It's strange. You complain your whole life about no one seeing you, and when they finally do, it's almost worse, because they accuse you of killing them. It wasn't just our problem anymore, but theirs, too, and they were mad about it. You won't have to contend with that, thank God, but in my time...wow. Wow. I sound like my parents. Look at me with this, 'In my time' shit. Sorry. I just—sorry."

Rey chuckles, but it's humorless and dry and devolves into a cough.

Rey is so apparently sad, and Kimber is sad for her, too. She doesn't know Rey, doesn't know if Rey is even real, and if she is real, is she a Casper ghost or a memory given form or a manifestation of Kimber's high, but does that matter? Kimber cares about her and her story. It's also familiar—Kimber feels it every day when she thinks about Shyanna. People call loss poignant but Kimber calls it bullshit.

No one should have to feel that way. She shouldn't, nor should her Fairy Butchmother-ghost-hallucination person.

"I'm super sorry," she says, wincing at how inadequate that sounds in the wake of Rey's confession.

Rey rolls her head around on her shoulders. "Thanks. It's old news now, but grief doesn't go away. Not really. It's just that the world we live in gets bigger as we gain more experiences so the grief seems smaller by comparison. Sometimes, something will hit it right on the bull's-eye, though, and you get walloped like it's fresh. I feel like I just punched myself in the face."

Kimber knows this feeling, too, as it's the one that sends her seeking the soft place knowing it's not good for her. She extends a comforting hand to pat Rey on the knee, but Rey's too far. It's that inches and miles problem she had with the phone, where all space is the same space, but unlike the phone, no matter how hard she stretches, she's never quite close enough. She is lunging and grasping at nothing.

If Rey finds her futile maneuverings ridiculous, she's good enough not to say so.

"Thanks, Kimber."

Kimber acknowledges her with a nod.

Silence.

Forever silence.

Until it's too much to take.

Kimber looks down at her picture of Shyanna, her chin touching her chest.

"You don't have to answer if you don't want to, but what happened with you and Tammy?" Her voice is soft. Reverent. She's asking a lot and she knows it. It's not Rey's duty to perform her pain for her, but if she's willing to finish the story, Kimber is an active audience.

Rey's brow arches up, high enough it nearly kisses the deep V of her hairline. "Exactly what you think happened. Because people who should care didn't, until they absolutely had to. Until their inhumanity was so big, they crumbled under its weight. And the sad truth is, some folks still didn't care after that, but enough did that things got done eventually."

Kimber is tempted to ask if Rey got sick, too, but even drugged to high heaven, she knows it's inappropriate. Rey's sharp side-eye suggests the same, and so she silently considers Tammy and Rey, drawing her own, sad conclusions that do little to alleviate her loneliness about Shyanna.

More quiet. Too much quiet. Kimber is wistful for the trumpeting pulse from earlier. She rocks on the floor, back and forth, to soothe herself. Her fingers fidget with the phone. The soft place is a little less soft now, and the cold has begun to seep in from below. She shudders and pulls her hoodie sweatshirt until it covers her knees.

Rey stands from her seat and stretches. Her arms extend so far out, she looks like she'll take flight.

"It's time for me to go, kiddo, but—hey, look. It's not all bad. It sometimes looks that way, and it sometimes *is* that way, but—" Rey rubs her chin, thoughtful. She glances from Kimber on the floor back to the kitchen cabinet.

Without asking permission, she crosses to the cupboard and reaches inside for a pack of Mama's smokes. She pulls off the cellophane and tosses it aside before helping herself. One coveted cigarette is tucked behind her ear. The other is slipped between her lips. The rest of the pack is returned to its rightful place.

"—the thing is, us club kids always had each other, even on the worst days of our lives, sometimes on the last days of our lives. The world is full of people like your mom. It's the same brand of person who ignored sick queers til our bones littered their doorsteps. But the world's also full of good people—folks who just want to live and let live. Like your grandmother. They're out there, I promise.

"And the beautiful part about you being so young is you can blow this fish fry soon. You can get out in the world and form your own family just like me and Tammy did, with Shyanna at your side. You're separated now, but not forever. It'll seem that way awhile, but you just gotta hold out a little longer, 'cause soon your doors will burst open and you can fly high, kiddo. And I don't mean literally. You do what you gotta do, but everything in moderation. Don't break your brain with that bad candy, you hear?"

"Yeah, yeah, I know," Kimber replies. "It just helps when I'm so down, you know?"

"I said what I said. That shit ain't good for you."

Kimber peers up at Rey's face, the big woman standing before her with her contraband cigarette clenched between her teeth, she blinks, and Rey isn't there anymore. The space she'd filled so clearly in Kimber's mind is empty. Behind that space is a robin's-egg blue wall with a crack near the cheap molding. Kimber whispers Rey's name, but there is no answer beyond the baleful winter wind rattling her windowpanes.

Kimber forces herself onto her feet. She's wobbly, like a colt on new legs, but that doesn't stop her from walking to the wall and touching it, her fingers tracing over the textured bumps in the paint. It was real before and it's real now, and the cold beneath her finger pads lets her know it's not part of a grand hallucination. Kimber glances behind her at the dining table with the chair Rey sat in. It's no longer propped mid floor and turned around, but back in its rightful place.

Maybe it's all fake. Maybe I made it all up, she thinks, but that thought is quickly followed by, *does that mean it has no value then?*

No, that's not what it means at all and she knows it.

To drive that point home, when her phone buzzes with a text from Shyanna, two simple emojis of a smiley face followed by a red heart, she feels…eager. Anticipatory. The dread of separation is still there, but also there is a glimmer of hope that one day, not too far away, they can be free.

Together.

She answers the text in kind before staggering into the kitchen, the countertop the only thing keeping her from succumbing to jelly knees. She's painfully thirsty. The drug always dehydrates her, like she's lined her insides with cotton. She turns on the faucet to get herself a drink. It whooshes to life, her own personal Niagara, and she fills her glass, taking no time at all to guzzle it down. It's not enough because it's never enough, and so she has a second, and a third, the thirst inside of her finally sated at the cost of her poor bladder.

Another blast of cold air. Another shiver. Kimber deposits her glass next to the sink.

Right beside a piece of recently discarded cellophane.

★ ★ ★ ★ ★

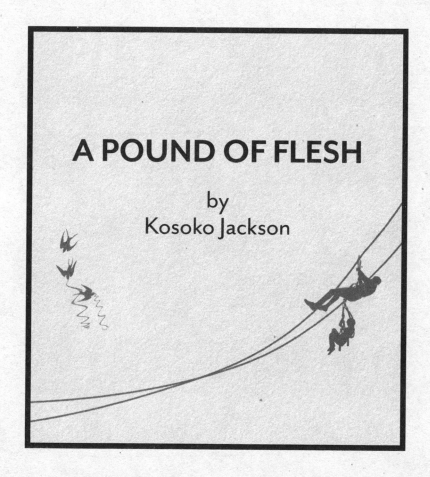

A POUND OF FLESH

by
Kosoko Jackson

I

WHEN MY LOVE IS NEAR, THE AIR ALWAYS
smells like sharpened steel.

You know the smell, like metal recently folded and burned. The edges glowing bright red. That sharp, almost sweet smell, that tickles your nose and makes your eyes water.

Yeah, that smell.

I've smelled it twenty-f—no, twenty-seven times. And still, each time, I want to vomit in disgust. At first. I know that'll change. It always does.

Today is no different. Today will be no different.

I feel him and his suffocating presence behind me. Like when you're light-headed from panic and filled with an all-consuming amount of dark fear? All at once and multiplied tenfold? Yeah.

His steps are quiet, but each one pulses in a way that sends my soul off-kilter. Each step closer makes me dizzy. The corners of my eyes turn black. The tips of my fingers and toes turn cold.

And then he's next to me, sitting on the edge of the rooftop. We don't make contact. He's looking down. I'm looking into the distance, studying the horizon, as if my will could command the golden curvature to bend.

"You always had a penchant for rooftops. Just don't fall off this one, please."

Giving him a side-eye, I take in a quick look at his features. Quick enough to paint me a picture. Not enough to give him any satisfaction.

"Scottish this time?"

"Irish," he replies, not looking at me either. "Can't you tell by the accent?"

"I have more pressing things on my mind right now."

"Don't you always? What makes this time any different?"

I shrug in response, settling back into the silence. At least, that's my intention.

He has other thoughts.

"Do you like it? Me, I mean." A beat passes. "I can change, if you want."

"Can you leave me alone?"

"You know I can't do that. Even if I wanted to. We're bound, or did you forget the gift Aphrodite left you?"

"Then answer something for me. What do you think happens if I jump? Not fall. Jump."

He shrugs, his skintight leather jacket squealing in protest. He then leans back, resting the palms of his hands against the roof, crossing his booted feet at the ankles. The wind whistles, his brown hair fluttering in the soft breeze.

"That's not an answer."

"I'll catch you," he then adds. "I'll always catch you. Th—"

"Carson. My name is Carson."

"Carson, right, my bad." The right corner of his mouth turns up in a smirk. It's a subtle one. The type of smile that says he doesn't truly believe me, and he knows I know it.

But I've lived with the name Carson for seventeen years. The name Theo feels foreign. Like all my other names in my past lives. Each one is just a sour reminder of this stupid curse. And that stupid pact I made with that stupid goddess years ago.

We sit in silence, watching the darkness snuff out the light in the distance. It's a painful death, the chill of night creeping in and tapping Morse code against my skin as it wraps me in a slow embrace. Boston is calm tonight. Calmer than usual. The streets, on a Wednesday, aren't a hustle or a bustle, more a low, constant hum. You can tell the city is breathing; inhaling and exhaling—steeling itself.

The calm before the storm.

Without a warning, my unwelcomed guest takes off his leather jacket and drapes it over my shoulders. I want to shrug it off. I should shrug it off. But the leather radiates a familiar warmth and reminds me of memories with heavy scents of oak and summer. My shoulders slouch, and I notice for the first time how tense I am. My mouth turns slack, and a soft exhale escapes. One by one, defense by defense, I can feel the fortress crumbling around me.

All from a simple leather jacket.

Reluctantly, I wrap it around my body, making the leather purr this time.

We sit there, in silence, for I don't know how long, but it's not as calm as *he* thinks it is. The tension in the air is like something I can see, but can't make out. I know it's there. He knows it's there. And it's just a matter of time before one of us speaks first, showing weakness. Usually it's me. I expected it to be me.

But I'm surprised.

"Carson, you know you can't stop this, right? You've tried before. *We've* tried before and it always ends the same way."

The words are right on the tip of my tongue, fully formed and ready to burst from my mouth. But instead, my voice vanishes and the situation: sitting on the roof, with him, doesn't feel so foreign. In fact, there is comfort—terrifying comfort—in the repetitive familiarity.

"You don't know that," I reply. Not what I wanted to say. Not as strong, as firm, or nearly as convincing as I want—*need*—it to be. But it'll do. "If I can stop what's about to happen down there…"

"What, you think if you keep humans from fighting, that'll change things?" He shakes his head, moving his leg so the left ankle is now over the right. "Humans are bloodthirsty creates. It's why I exist. The conflict in the city isn't yours to stop. Only me and my sister can do that. It'll end when one of us delivers a killing blow and the victor is decided. You know this."

Ares sighs, and frustratedly runs his fingers through his hair. "You shouldn't even *be* here. Last time I saw you…"

"I was in Seattle. I know. I knew you'd be here."

"So, you just came running? Throwing yourself into harm's way? Making thoughtless choices? Disregarding consequences? You haven't changed or learned anything in your past twenty-eight lives."

"Twenty-seven."

"Twenty-eight."

"I think I'd remember how many times I've been reborn, Ares."

"And I think I'd remember how many times I've failed to save you, Theo."

I whip my head toward the God of War, glaring at him. The name—my name, from my first life years and years ago, is a comfort akin to seeing an old friend from years ago. A name I've told him not to use.

Staring now, I get a good look at him, unlike before, and his features make me softly gasp. He's not much older than me. This time. Nineteen, maybe twenty. The black, loose Henley he wears now has the sleeves rolled up, showing his leather bracers on both arms. His hair is perfectly styled, not a single brown blade out of place.

He still stares into the city's distance, but my reaction is all he needs to stroke his massive ego.

A police cruiser's sirens warble through the air in the distance. One echo turns to three, three turn into six. On the other side of town, smoke rises. An apartment building, I think.

I lean forward, resting my arms on my knees. The wind up here is temperamental: a soft gust here, a stronger one there, but I keep balance as I focus on the apartment fire. As if moving a few inches closer will give me a vantage I don't have.

"You said it best yourself," I say. "You could stop this."

Ares shakes his head. "What's been set in motion..."

"I know, I know. Can't be stopped, only seen through. You sound like your sister."

"I sound nothing like Athena," he snaps.

"You do now. She'd abide by the rules. You'd bend them to be your own."

"You want me to sound like my sister? Fine, *Carson*. This, your curse? Living your lives over and over again? Being forced to be reborn after each death, never finding solace? That's your fault. No one but yours."

I purse my lips together in a thin line, looking back out at the city, focusing on the billows of smoke. I pretend they're different shapes—Spartans engaged in combat, Trojan horses, golden apples—anything to distract me from Ares.

"If you hadn't made that deal with Aphrodite, you wouldn't be here. If you hadn't let love get in the way, you could have lived and died a happy human life and that would be that. But look." He gestures wildly and angrily. "Here you are, in the middle of a mortal conflict, like always. You think that's a coincidence, Carson? No. The fact we can't keep ourselves apart is just another example of gods doing what gods do best—toying with humans for our pleasure."

"*I'm* a human," I remind him.

He scoffs. "Barely."

I grit my teeth, but push past that comment. This isn't the first time we've done this dance. It won't be the last.

"I made the deal for you, Ares," I seethe. "For us."

"But that's the thing! I never asked you to do that!" he roars, loud enough that the air vibrated and burned. "I would have been happy with having just one life with you! One good life! This never-ending cycle of us finding each other and losing each other life after life? No one, not a god or human, should have to put up with this!"

Turning away, I grip the edge of the rooftop hard. I don't look at him, I can't, and instead watch the roadways below shift in response to the apartment fire. I see squad cars and fire engines slicing through the streets like a knife, hurrying toward their destination. Hurrying to be a hero.

I wanted to be a hero and look where it left me.

After a minute or two of silence, I speak.

"I'm going to change it."

"For the love of Zeus. You can't stop this, Carson. Like you said, you made a choice, and a bond with a god is unbreakable. *Unfixable*. No matter how unfair the bond proves to be years later."

"Not going to stop it. Fix it. I'm going to reclaim my life, Ares."

He shakes his head and extends his right hand. With a twirl of his wrist, the air around it ripples and a dagger, with a blade six inches in length and a golden hilt, appears. He casually tosses it up and down; each time it flips twice before settling, hilt first, in his hand.

I've seen that action enough times to know what it means: Ares, for once in this life, is thinking carefully about what to say.

And still, his words miss the mark.

"You're going to fail and you're going to die and then you're going to end up right back where you are, Carson. Forgetting *me*. Forcing *me* to find *you*. Like all the times before."

The words hurt. But that's the spark in my pilot light I need.

I'm not sure if it's anger, or the desire to simply get away from Ares as quickly as possible, but I stand, carelessly, and stumble. He moves to grab me, but I've righted myself, and step back, pulling his jacket off. I extend it to him, keeping an arms-length distance between the two of us.

"This time will be different," I say, almost confident enough to convince myself. "I'm going to do whatever it takes to *make sure* it is."

Ares doesn't move from his half-kneeling position. Not at first, at least. But slowly, he rises, now-golden eyes focused on my own. At his full height, he's still taller than me; this time by about three inches. When he grabs his jacket, our hands touch.

The world around me melts away. Memories from all my past lives threaten to send me down a spiral, but I keep them at bay. It feels like a deluge of cold rapids mixing with the scald of a geyser, and it's enough to make a physical reaction; a scrunch of my brow. A tenseness in my body. The softest of whimpers.

I push Ares back in response, just a soft nudge, but he gets the message.

"You're a human with the memories of twenty-seven humans, Carson," he whispers softly. "And like humans, you think you can do anything, no matter how foolish it is. *Perhaps* you can best this curse, *maybe* you're the one human in history who can truly beat a god's plans, but there is always a price to pay, especially when dealing with the gods, Carson. Is tempting some of the most vindictive creatures in the universe worth it?

"Maybe," Ares says, throwing his jacket on in one smooth

motion, "maybe this life, these lives, no matter how twisted and cursed they are, are something to hold close, to make your own. To do with what you want, to learn from your mistakes, to repeat your successes. You have a gift, and a curse, that no one else has: the gift of awareness. I don't even have that. This—" he gestures "—is me. This conflict that's in motion? I feed off of it, it's a hunger—an addiction, your human counterparts might call it. And I love it, I fuckin' love it, Carson. But I can't choose who I am. I can't change my purpose. You can mold your existence into anything you want. Is that so bad? Is knowing us, the gods, such a bad thing?"

He takes a step forward, and another, and another. Before I know it, my back is against the leg of the water tower. Ares is encompassing, but not touching me. Close enough that his breath, sweet smelling, skips against my lips. He leans down, brushing his lips against my right ear, and whispers.

"Aphrodite may have given you a curse, but it's up to you to decide what you do with it. That's what a hero does, Carson. They make a choice, they understand the consequences of all their actions, and they go forward, trying to do the best they can. You want to be a hero? Then be a hero."

His right hand strokes my cheek, just a light touch, barely tactile enough to get a response. There's a soft spark between us, and I shiver, not from cold or pain, but from something deeper.

"But know there is always a price to pay, and it's never what you think it will be."

And just like that, the God of War, he who has killed thousands—if not millions—of men, in the name of fighting for my love over dozens of lives, is gone. As quickly as he appeared but not without a parting gift:

An explosion in the distance.

II

Athena, the Goddess of Wisdom, waits for me in the local indie coffee shop, with a pumpkin spice latte in one hand, and a white chocolate mocha in the other.

It's our tradition, in times like these. If Ares is here, then his sister will be here, too.

Her dirty-blond ponytail is high, her dark-rimmed, square-with-rounded-edges glasses are perfectly clean, and the business-casual power suit she wears makes her look like a Type-A, already-written-in-stone CEO of a Fortune 500 Company.

Which, in the grander scheme of things, isn't entirely inaccurate.

When I sit—no, collapse—in the booth in the back corner, she doesn't react. Her eyes are methodically scanning the book in front of her. She carries herself like she doesn't notice the world around her. She's purposely ignoring all the sensations in the shop: the sharp smells of artisanal coffee, the news report on the fuzzy TV discussing the growing riots that are spreading through Boston like cancerous tendrils spreading through the body. It seems the only thing that matters to her, is the book in her hand.

Until I sit down across.

I take the pumpkin spice—my drink—and give it a small sip, looking upside down at the book.

"What is that?" I ask, leaning forward for a better look. "Latin?"

"Greek."

"You know you can listen to an audiobook of *Moby Dick*, right? That's still reading."

"This keeps my brain sharp."

"You're a god. Your brain doesn't dull."

"You're too smart, and not pretty enough, to be that stupid, Carson."

The cut is precise, but expected from Athena. Our relationship has never been great. Antagonizing at worst, standoffish and cautious at best. But just like with Ares, my fate and Athena's are bound together.

"I ordered you a turkey club," she says, licking her index finger and dragging it across the page to turn it.

"I'm a vegetarian."

"You weren't in your last life."

"You weren't blonde the last time I saw you either. Tired of the brown hair?"

She shrugs. "I needed a change. The benefit of being a god." She snaps her fingers, and her eyes shift colors, only for a fraction of a second, before reverting back.

"Must be nice. To be able to pick and choose your traits. What you look like, your strengths and weaknesses, if they see you at all. Speaking of which, can anyone see you now, or do they think I'm talking to myself?"

She laughs, a shrill, patronizing chuckle meant to grind my gears. "Boston is folding in on itself, consumed in hatred, violence, and flames, and you're worried about looking crazy?"

Before I can answer, she waves the waitress over, her way

of answering my question, and changes the turkey club to a Caesar salad. The waitress nods and smiles at me with a grin that lingers a few seconds too long, before she disappears into the kitchen.

Athena rolls her eyes. "Always the flirt."

"I don't do it on purpose," I say defensively.

"It's in your nature, I know." She finally closes her book and stuffs it into her black leather shoulder bag. "How is my brother doing?"

"You could talk to him and ask."

"I believe approaching someone who wants nothing more than to kill you would be the human definition of insanity."

"And thinking that I don't know how you love to get under your brother's skin would be the definition of stupid, on your part."

"It's just so easy."

Athena's brightly-painted, silvery-pink lips curl upwards. Her eyes are the same vibrant gold Ares' are, whenever the bloodlust of war prickles at his soul. For Athena, it's a verbal spar that sparks her engine. Or a physical one. Any form of honorable combat with an equal, really.

And maybe, just maybe, after twenty plus years, she's starting to find me her equal.

But really, would anyone be Athena's intellectual equal?

"You're different," she says, cupping her drink with both hands, looking over the rim of the porcelain mug.

"Is that a good thing or a bad thing?"

"Neither. Both. I've never seen you so…outwardly brazen before. And I was your best friend during the French Revolution."

"You left me to die then."

She shrugs. "I couldn't stop what was happening then. Just like you, no matter what you do, cannot stop what's going to happen now. Driving a new model of car doesn't matter if you take the same road, Carson. It just changes how long it takes to get there."

The waitress returns, dropping our food in front of us. This time, she doesn't even hide her favor for me, never turning to look at Athena. "Can I get *you* anything else?"

Athena snorts, and I shake my head. "I think that's everything, thank you."

The waitress slumps slightly as she walks away, leaving us to a meal Athena doesn't need, and I don't really want.

"Just so you know," I tell Athena, chewing slowly, "you lost me with that car metaphor."

The sharp Caesar dressing tap-dances against my senses. In this life, I enjoy it. In my last one, it made me want to vomit. There's still a twitch of that gag reflex each time I eat it. No matter how much I like it.

I stab a crouton and a curl of lettuce, and lift them halfway to my mouth before Athena's French-manicured hand grabs my wrist, stopping me.

"Then let me be clearer. Associating with my brother will lead to your death. *Faster.*"

Her grip is strong, stronger than my human grip. There's a moment of push and pull, my arm moving an inch or two in each direction, but I can't break her grasp, nor her gaze. Even as I push a command out with my mind, a gift I've developed over my lives, and feel my will wrap around hers, she resists, shredding my influence with ease.

"Don't insult me, Carson," she whispers coldly. "Your tricks won't work on me. You may be able to make men and women bend to your will, but that doesn't apply to gods."

"It works on your brother," I snap without thinking.

Athena's brow twitches. A successful blow. One point for me. But that's the only success I get. "Again. You're smart enough to know better. My brother loves you, in spite of how foolish it is. You should have stayed in Seattle instead of coming here."

"Then you're smart enough to know, eventually, we all would have been brought together anyway. Aphrodite would have made it happen once she got bored. At least now I'm taking a proactive stance when it comes to my own future."

Athena and I sit in silence, me eliminating half of my salad, and her looking out the window. Police cruisers zoom by, heading south. Men and women in masks, painted with rainbow glitter pass by, chanting an energizing call to arms that would surely make the news and social media rounds before the day was up.

"Do you think he did it?" I ask, breaking the silence once I'm done eating. When she doesn't answer, I clarify. "The cop."

"Does it matter?" Athena still doesn't look at me, but she taps her middle fingernail against the table with a four count.

"It should. You're the Goddess of Wisdom."

"And I have the wisdom to know some questions don't have answers. Some conflicts might be born from a specific event, but that's not the reason they continue.

"Take the apartment fire, for instance. That's not an isolated event—it's a byproduct of a group of people fed up of being viewed as nothing. It's the manifestation of hurt and pain when a cop, the cop is question, is found guilty of a hate crime, but the sentencing—time served and community service—doesn't fit the crime. What about the family who lost their son? About the community who has dealt with being under the oppressive thumb of those who have sworn to protect them? What about the people who, time and time again, are the ones left to pick up the pieces of themselves and put themselves back together when justice is not served in the way they deem it should be? What happens when enough is enough?"

Athena sighs, and leans back, pausing for only a moment. "Chaos. That's what happens. Right or wrong, just or fallible, driven by greed or justice, chaos is the product of pain and sometimes, like this time, chaos gives birth to war, Carson. A war that is already set in motion and cannot be stopped. Not by you. Not by me. Not by my brother. The only way it can stop, is if one of us…"

"Has to be victorious," I finish for her. "Ares told me that already."

"Well, he's immature, not stupid."

A twinge of white-hot fire bubbles in my stomach at her jab at Ares, but I choose to ignore it in favor of another question. "Whose side are you on this time?"

Athena doesn't hesitate. "The side of justice and law and reason," she says. "The courts. The justice system. The lawyers, on both sides, who did their jobs to discover guilt and innocence."

"And you're okay with this?"

She shrugs. "He'll live with the shroud of public shame, a record, and loss of his job for the rest of his life. I'd argue he's received his due. More than other officers in this generation have. Ares doesn't want justice, of any sort. He feeds off the vitriol of people. Stirs it. Churns it. He doesn't care who is right or wrong. Only who is the angriest and most filled with bloodlust. In this iteration, it's the rioters."

She takes a sip of her drink. "Have you thought of what might happen if Ares wins this little scuffle between the two of us?"

"He represents the protesters, he should win. When something wrong happens…"

"Justice decides the outcome, not the bloodlust of humanity, Carson," Athena sighs. "My brother has always represented the primal rage inside of people. I've always represented the law and fairness of the judicial system. When there is conflict, we appear, and our presences help determine which side will win. It's been like that for centuries, a cyclical event. And you ignoring the societal ramifications of what happens if Ares wins this scuffle, is just as repetitive. You know what happens when people get a taste of victory by the hands of violence. You've lived through half a dozen of those simulations."

"I'm not stupid either, Athena," I say through gritted teeth. "I know—"

"Then stop acting like you are," she interrupts with a cold tone I'd expect from someone like Hades. "Some things, Carson, are out of our hands. How many times do you have to die prematurely before you realize that? How many times must you try and stop Ares—*The God of War*—from being who he is? How many times must you meddle, and manipulate, poorly, I might add, for something as foolish as love, when the man you're fighting to be with doesn't even care about you?"

"He cares about me," I object. "You even said before…"

"Yes, yes. My brother loves you. But caring about someone and loving someone are two very different things. Love is a powerful emotion. Just like hate, or bloodlust, or valor. My brother feels all those things. But he *cares* only about war. And winning. Caring about another person requires sacrifice and asks all of you. My brother will only give all of him to one thing: war.

"And besides, look at where loving someone like him has gotten you. You were an idiot to fall for him back then, and you're an idiot to keep loving him. If you were smart, you'd put that brain of yours to work thinking how to avoid him and I, not flocking toward him like a lovesick child."

"That's what Ares said."

"Even a broken clock is right twice a day."

I swallow thickly, digging my nails into the palm of my hand. I know where this is going. Every few lives, Athena tries this same song-and-dance.

"Are you saying you're any different?"

"Very. Not because I care about people. But because I know that I don't. You make him weak, Carson. That scares him, and emboldens him. Why do you think he'll go to the end of the Earth for you, but also pushes you away?"

"Because he *loves* me," I correct and repeat. *Like I, despite everything, love him.* I don't care about Athena and Ares' endless tit-for-tat. It'll never end. But these riots outside? The violence that's threatening to bubble over? That needs to end. Now.

"How do I stop this, Athena?"

"This conflict?"

I nod. "Do I need to kill Pandora? Find the Box again? Make a pact with another god?"

"That's what got you into this mess."

"A witch? What has to be done? I met you here because I want this to end. Every problem has a solution, so what's this one's?"

Athena laughs again. She stands and her clothing ripples like gold flecks on the surface of a pristine lake. Her power suit changes into a white tunic, fit perfectly with a gold-and-leather breastplate. Golden-plated boots appear as sandals and a matching helmet and wrist guards adorn her. Her shoulder bag is replaced with a circular shield. Her copy of *Moby Dick* with her signature gladius.

"This will stop, like everything else horrible in this world will stop, when I kill Ares. For good."

III

For most, the sound of thunder is a (familiar) omen of an ongoing New England summer storm.

For me, it is the familiar sound of two gods exchanging metallic blows during a fight to the death.

The streets of Boston are overrun with protesters and cops—a sea of rainbow flags bleeding into waves of dark blue. News crews report from the sidelines as demonstrators chant so loudly it's one homogeneous roar of live-wire energy.

Citizen journalists weave in and out of the groups, taking pictures with their phones and inserting themselves into conversations, trying to balance the truth with sensationalism. Everyone knew this was going to be big—the cop who bashed a gay kid's face in only got community service? It was a huge national news story.

But no one thought it would turn into a full-on mass riot in the city, fueled by opinions, social exhaustion, and most of all, anger. No one knew how this incident was filled with so much human…*pain*, that the gods themselves would insert themselves into the narrative. No one knew how out of control their lives truly were.

But that isn't my concern. Not now at least.

My attention is focused on the two gods on a rooftop locked in combat.

After Athena left, I knew exactly where she was going to go. Finding Ares has never been a problem. We can always find each other; a parting gift Aphrodite gave me along with this curse so many years ago.

The closer I get to his location, a roof, the more the sizzling and crackling air pushes me away. But I fight through it, kicking the door to the rooftop open, just in time to see Athena's shield block Ares' foot.

The impact forces her to slide back. She keeps her ground, her toes digging deep into the concrete roof. Ares brandishes his broadsword in a wide arc. He swings, but she blocks with her gladius. With her knee, she drives a sharp blow into his abs.

His feet leave the ground, and Athena strikes again. Using her strength and speed, she hits the side of his face—hard—with her shield. He flies for a meter or two, then lands on his side, with a heavy thump.

"Ares!" I yell. He only holds up his hand, a silent command to *stay back*. In typical Ares fashion, he laughs and spits out blood in Athena's direction.

"You've gotten better." He smirks.

"And you've gotten worse," she replies, taunting him with three taps on her shield with her sword.

This isn't the first—or second or third—time Athena and Ares have fought. In fact, much of this life reminds me of our times together through history. France in the nineteen forties. The Civil War. Major events that shaped world history, where right and wrong were blurred.

Where there is war, there is Ares.

Where there is justice, there is Athena.

One will always win, one side will be proclaimed in history books as being victor.

And this fight, right here? Is the true deciding factor. Not politicians, not weapons of mass destruction or wise empathetic spokesmen. This.

And the pattern repeats.

Always.

How can they not see this? How can they not understand that this endless war they have, this fight for control, is accomplishing nothing? Don't they see this cycle will never stop? That they'll be back to exchanging blows ten, twenty, thirty years from now?

Or maybe they just don't care?

"Stop!" I beg, pushing away from the door and running toward them.

Ares and Athena are less than fifteen feet away from me. Within the time it takes to travel the steps, they've exchanged more than three dozen blows. Their battle is a golden and white blur, much like what a highway looks like at night when a photographer takes a long-exposure shot. The only time I can make them out is when they pause, in different battle positions, before resuming their dance.

Athena on top of Ares with her blade at his neck.

Ares with Athena in a choke hold.

Athena and Ares, blades shaking as they push against one another.

"Why?" I whisper to myself. Why was I given this curse by Aphrodite? What does living forever and loving someone who can never die mean if this is how we spend our lives? Who deserves that?

Me. The human who thought loving and being loved by a god would be a cakewalk. The boy who thought calling upon Ares, the God of War to help avenge the loss of his fallen lover was a smart idea. Who assumed our passionate and all-encompassing love that came to be wouldn't cause ripples in the Pantheon? Me, who thought the Goddess of Love herself wouldn't be intrigued by our romance.

I'm not certain why Aphrodite picked me for this curse. Was it because she saw the love Ares and I had and was jealous? Or was it because she was rooting for us and knew we'd need more than one human life to succeed? All I know is the gods are known for meddling in human lives, and Aphrodite is no exception.

Was she proud of me? Proud of us? How we kept coming back to one another, no matter how many times or how far apart we were? Did she revel in the pain she caused? In revealing that true love always ends in pain?

And most importantly, was it worth it? The fleeting moments where we both know the allure of war and winning will pull him away from me? The wars Ares has caused to find me? The people he's hurt? The situations I've put him through? The sacrifices we've made? It's a dysfunctional love. A tragic love. A horrible love.

But it's ours, even if it won't end any differently. Even if he wins this fight with Athena, or Athena beats him, the by-product will always be the same. I'll die. Maybe not right now. Maybe in a minute, or in a day, or a week, but death *will* come for me. Aphrodite will see to that, and her secret experiment will start again.

An experiment with one simple hypothesis: is it truly possible for a human and a god to love one another?

This time, when Ares and Athena pause their dance, Athena's back is against the wall, her impression imprinted on the brick. Sweat is on her brow—something you rarely see on a god—and her shield is off to the side, out of reach.

It's clear, even on her usually poised, always in-control face, that she's on the defensive. It's a reflection of the battle below. Just like her, the cops are outnumbered. Outmanned. The hate crime had spilled outside of Boston proper. The news and social media had stoked the flames and the whole USA was talking about it.

Athena, and the cops, had lost before this riot had even begun. And Ares, with the hungry, almost crazed, look in his eyes, lunged forward to make a—*the*—blow.

The blow that would kill a god.

The same blow that I leap in front of, causing Ares' broadsword to sink deep into my abdomen, and gives Aphrodite an answer:

None of your fucking business.

IV

When my love is near, the air usually smells of sharpened steel, but this time, it smells faintly of roses.

I can hear the sounds of Ares and Athena arguing over me, but their words are muddled. The tips of my fingers and toes feel cold—and once again, the corners of my eyes are dark. I can't move, despite how many times I tell myself to, the request is denied. My body feels like an engine trying to rev itself back to life, and each growl is weaker than the last.

I try to focus on the words the two gods above me say, to force my mind to remain alert, but the growing scent of flowers distracts me. For a moment, none of it makes sense—we're on a rooftop, not in a forest. Until I feel time stand still, the pain is replaced with warmth, and something tickles my nose.

A woman looks down at me, her long hair brushing against me. She's smiling, her demure, heart-shaped face and warm eyes make it clear who she is.

"Hades doesn't usually send you to deal with my passing," I note. "We usually use this time to play a game of chess."

Persephone smiles, stroking her fingers through my hair. Her nails scratch against my scalp and my eyes close slowly. I feel my lips curl into a small, stupor-like grin, my stiff joints relaxing with each touch.

"Something has come up in Africa. He sends his regards," she whispers.

We lay in silence for a moment, somewhere between life and death.

"How long do I have?"

"A minute," she whispers. "Maybe two. The wound is

291

deep. And it was made by Ares. Wounds from his weapons don't heal."

"Will it hurt?"

"No more than usual. I suppose that's a benefit of this curse of yours. You may experience death, over and over, with no rest like most humans are gifted, but at least you also build up an immunity to the pain."

She says it more like a question as if she isn't sure if her deduction is right.

It's not.

"Why can't you just take me?" I ask. "Why do I have to wake up?"

Her fingers pause, for just a moment, long enough to tell me she's hesitating. Does Persephone, of all the gods, feel sorry for me?

"I wish I could," she whispers softly, pressing her lips against my forehead. "But your soul is not for us to take. Not yet. Just rest. Let the feeling take you away. It'll be over soon."

"I'll just come right back. The curse…"

"Oh, my love. You don't know your power, do you?"

Time may be still but I'm still dying, and I can feel myself slipping away. Each death may be different, but at the same time, they all come down to one central point.

I just want to get it over with.

"I suspect you'll learn it very soon," she whispers, her voice so far away I almost think I imagine it. But Ares' familiar aura, that feels like pressure against my chest, is there. Time returns. And Persephone's warmth is gone.

And so is the pain.

Everything happens in reverse. My vision returns. The

coldness of my fingers is gone. And the bleeding? That slows down, too. The world is more vibrant and bursting with color. Sounds are like electric pops right against my ears.

And Ares is holding me. My back against his chest, laying between his outstretched legs, Athena nowhere to be seen.

"She's gone," he said, answering my question. "Athena. She isn't worth it. Not if it means losing you."

I flex my fingers, looking at the palm and then the back of my hand. My digits shake, just slightly, and my vision is still blurry around the edges.

"Valor," he says. "Adrenaline is pumping through your body. I can't stop what's happening, but I can slow it down. Give you—give us—a few more seconds."

He's right. Just a few more seconds. The corners of my eyes are already starting to darken again and the pain, though distant, is there. And growing.

"Why?"

"Because of love," a new voice says.

Both Ares and I look toward the voice, which belongs to a woman with skin as dark as my own and beautiful braids. She's wearing jeans and a leather jacket on top of a white shirt with graffiti lettering that says, *All you need is love.*

Ares grips me tighter, and snarls. "You did this."

"I would argue your sword is what did it, Ares, not my gift," Aphrodite says, approaching us both. She kneels down next to me, her brown-tinted hand stroking my cheek. Her touch is warm and her body smells of vanilla, my favorite. Her lips curl into a warm, almost sad smile.

"You proved me wrong, Carson," she speaks softly. "A boy who is willing to end his life for a god. A god willing to ignore his purpose for a human. I didn't think it was possible for a god to love a human, and vice versa, as much as you two love each other.

"So, I have a proposition for you two. If you're interested."

The coldness, darkness and pain return, along with the bleeding. Ares puts both hands on my wound, as if his hands could push the blood back in. He adds pressure, which makes me whimper loudly, and does the opposite, only pushing more blood out of the gaping hole. For the first time in his eyes, I see panic. Pain. Fear.

"One more time. One more life. I'll wipe your memories of each other, even yours, Ares, and we'll work with the Fates to orchestrate a situation to make your threads intertwine. Prove to me this isn't an anomaly. Prove that love truly always wins."

"And if we do?" I ask.

"Immortality. No new lives. No rebirth. You'll get the status of a demi-god with no allegiance to anyone but yourself."

"And if we fail?" Ares asks.

"Since when you do fail a challenge, Ares?"

This time, instead of words leaving my mouth, a gurgling sound of blood and a whimper mix together. Ares looks down, using his sleeve to wipe my lips. He is looking only at me, not her anymore.

"So, what do you say?" Aphrodite asks.

I ignore the question and focus on nodding, showing her I accept the terms.

Aphrodite says something that sounds like confirmation. Ares squeezes me tighter, so tight I think my bones might break, but I can't feel any more pain. I can barely feel him. Or see him. Or hear him.

But I do hear the last three things he says:

"I need you."

"I'll find you."

"I love you, Theo."

Before it all goes dark and I awake, with a gasp.

To the strange, almost nauseatingly strong smell of sharpened steel.

★ ★ ★ ★ ★

ONE SPELL TOO MANY

by
Tara Sim

ANNA TASTED HER BUTTERCREAM FROSTING

and decided it needed a pinch more spite.

Opening the cabinet above her head, she rooted through the mason jars and spice shakers until she found it: a jar of marjoram. She took out a sprig and placed it carefully into her stone mortar.

"Antithesis," she muttered to herself, snapping her fingers as she tried to remember what to add to the spell. "Ah, right."

She grabbed the pepper mill and twisted it once over the herb. The final touch was a single leaf from a bitter melon. With everything properly gathered, she began to smash the ingredients together with the pestle.

"A taste of revenge most bitter and sweet," she recited as she ground up the marjoram, "let one bite lead to where dreams and dismay meet."

Once the herb was finely ground, she sprinkled the spell into her red velvet batter. It was much harder to identify a spell in batter than it was to taste it in the frosting, so that was where she always put it. The flavor was more subtle once baked, and there were others out there who, like Anna, lived for the moment they could lick all the frosting off their forks. Anna hummed as she stirred in the spell, a small smile on her face. Revenge cakes were one of her favorite things to bake.

Carlin popped their head into the kitchen while Anna poured the batter into springform pans. "You getting the Scarlet order ready?"

Some customers liked to keep their orders confidential, so she and Carlin used codenames. "About to go in the oven."

"Great. I need to step out for fifteen, can you cover the front?"

Anna gently tapped the pans against the counter to get rid of air bubbles. "As long as I get to check on the cakes."

"No, I want my customers to get burned baked goods," Carlin said while rolling their eyes. "Whatever you need to do."

Anna slid the pans into the oven and took off her apron. She patted her bun of black hair to make sure it was still doing its job and followed Carlin to the front of the shop.

Sorcerous Sweets was Carlin's pride and joy; the bakery had been around for at least a decade, and was regularly voted the best in the county. Business had always been good, but it had exploded two years ago when Carlin had competed on *Cake Combat*, a television baking competition, and won.

That was when they had hired Anna to help out. She had been a sophomore in high school without any previous experience other than helping her kitchen witch father with recipes and spells. But she had proven herself to Carlin with an exceptionally made plate of macarons, each infused with a different spell and flavor.

Now in her senior year, Anna was well on her way to getting into her dream school: Gramoire, a college devoted to kitchen witches of all sorts, which had the best bakery program in North America. All she needed was a letter of recommendation from Carlin, and she was sure to get accepted.

She hadn't gotten around to asking them, though, on account of how busy they had been. Her deadline wasn't for a couple more months, anyway—she could wait.

Anna smoothed out her skirt and situated herself behind the display case. Under the spotless glass was an impressive array of cakes, cream puffs, macarons (and –roons, for that matter), cookies, and Carlin's specialty: cinnamon rolls as big as her head.

"I'll be back in a bit," Carlin said as they shrugged on their coat. "Don't let the place burn down."

She saluted. "I will do my best."

Once they were gone, Anna sighed and leaned against the counter. It was the beginning of their slow period of the day, the strange sludge between 10:00 and 11:30 AM that carried over even into the weekends. Anna had no idea where people were supposed to be during that time—work? At the movies? An interdimensional rift in the multiverse?

As she was about to reach for a magazine, the bell on the door chimed. Emma shuffled in, her silver-and-purple hair gleaming under the fluorescent lighting of the shop.

"Ugh, this place always gives me a migraine," Emma muttered, squinting at the cheerful, lime green walls and white-washed chandelier hanging from the ceiling. Dressed in black leggings, boots, and leather jacket, Emma was like a walking, talking black hole about to devour the brightness of the shop. "How can you stand working here?"

Anna grinned. "Free desserts, obviously."

"Oh. Good point." Emma leaned her elbows on the counter, leaning in with a grin. "Heeey, Anna. You love me, right?"

Anna raised an eyebrow at her best friend. They had gone through a lot together; both of their parents were immigrants—Emma's from Taiwan and Anna's from Pakistan—and both of them were bi. Anna had once jokingly referred to them as Bi Besties, which Emma had promptly shut down with a swift pillow to the face.

So Anna knew that Emma's tone meant trouble on the horizon.

"Depends," Anna drawled. "What do you want?"

Emma pouted. "You sound like my mom when you say that." She sighed and hopped up on the counter. "You know Riley, right?"

Anna couldn't help but know a *lot* about Riley, considering how often Emma spoke about him. He was a senior at Preston High, like them, and was often cast in starring roles in their drama productions. Emma had been pining after him for months, even going so far as to drag Anna to every. Single. Performance. Of. *The Crucible.*

"You may have mentioned him once or twice," Anna said.

"Okay, so…don't be mad, but…I was wondering if I could call in a favor. You know, from the time I totally saved your ass from getting detention when you were selling daydream cupcakes at school?"

Anna groaned and almost rubbed her hands against her

face, then remembered the amazing job she'd done on her winged eyeliner this morning. "Emma, *what do you want?*"

Emma clasped her hands before her. "Please make me a love spell? Please? Pretty please?"

"A *what?*" She suddenly got flashbacks of her father lecturing her on the evils of certain spells, and how they could range from harmless to harmful with just the slightest error. "Do you have *any* idea how tricky those are?"

"I mean…I'm not a witch, so no?" Emma shrugged. "I don't need a big cake or anything, just *one* cupcake. Or even a mini cupcake!"

"Emma—"

"I know what you're thinking: this is so creepy, making a guy eat a love potion. But they're only temporary, right? I just want him to ask me to Homecoming, and that's it, I swear."

She made it sound so simple, but it was anything but. Anna had read all about love potions—how, depending on the witch and the intent with which they baked the spell, it could end up being one of the most sinister concoctions you could feed to someone.

But there were ways to counter that, of course. Adding fewer ingredients, keeping your thoughts pure as you mixed them… And, of course, making sure that the person who ate the spell *accepted* the baked good without being coerced. If they didn't, or if the person giving the spell tried to force anything intimate without consent, the spell would immediately reverse.

Anna glared at her. Emma glared back. Anna had known her forever, knew full well that her best friend would never do anything…villainous. Besides, Emma had clearly said she wanted *Riley* to ask *her*, to have it be his idea. But while it was true that Emma had saved her from that daydream cupcake fiasco, to make something as questionable and complicated as a love potion…

Anna sighed. "Fine. But I'm mostly doing it for the challenge, understand? And I won't be responsible for whatever happens."

Emma leapt over the counter to hug her. "Thank you thank you thank you!"

"Okay, okay. Now let me get back to work before I change my mind."

Once Emma was gone, the idea of the love potion teased her brain while she worked on constructing the revenge cake in the back. She frosted the layers, lost in thought while muscle memory took over. She would need to make the potion weak enough to last only a little while, enough of a time window for Riley to ask Emma to Homecoming.

Anna came back to the front with the cake box in her arms just as a woman wearing sunglasses walked in.

"Are you…Scarlet?" Anna guessed. The woman nodded. "I have your order right here."

The woman paid in cash. While Anna counted out her change, she couldn't help but ask, "May I know what it's for?" She was always curious about what people intended to do with their spells.

The woman pressed her lips together, and Anna thought she wouldn't respond. Then she whispered, "It's for a company potluck. I hate everyone at the office. Pretty sure they're going to fire me anyway."

Anna choked over a snort. "I approve. Have fun."

She waved to the woman as she hurried out of the store with her revenge cake. A boy held the door open for her before walking inside and taking a deep breath, the corners of his mouth turned up in a smile at the smell of sugar all around him.

Anna's heart thudded painfully in her chest. *Noah.*

He was in her grade at Preston. The two of them had often had classes together, making the leap from *strangers* to *acquaintances.* They exchanged smiles in the hallways, and sometimes even made small talk before class started.

Noah had no idea that Anna had had a crush on him since freshman year, back when he'd felt pressured to keep his hair long and wear skirts. Now that he was transitioning, Anna was blown away by how much more confident he was, how... how *Noah* he was.

Seeing her, he broke into a full grin. Even though her chest fluttered hopefully, she knew it was just a Noah grin; the smile he flashed at people whether he knew them or not. That was the kind of guy he was.

"Hey, Anna," he said as he came up to the counter. "What's new?"

She stared up at him, lips parted. What *was* new? Her mind was blank. Nothing was new. She had done absolutely nothing and was officially the most boring person on earth.

"I..." She cleared her throat. "I made a revenge cake?"

It blurted out of her, even though the order was supposed to remain confidential. She cringed as Noah laughed in surprise.

"A *revenge* cake?" he repeated. "How does that work, exactly?"

Anna rubbed the back of her neck, feeling some stray locks

of hair that had fallen out of her bun. She probably looked like one of those witches who got a little *too* into their craft and became raving hermits in the woods.

"Just, you know, a spell," she said, her voice unnaturally high. "It sorta brings bad luck to whoever eats it."

"Oh. Dang." Noah eyed the display case beside them. "None of these are bad luck, are they?"

Anna breathed out a faint laugh. "No, none of the display goods are spelled."

"Cool. Remind me not to get on your bad side." He flashed her another smile, and she had to lean against the counter as her knees weakened.

"Are you… You're a witch, right?" she asked. She already knew, of course, that he was a tailor witch—the benefits of social media—but it seemed a good place to start. Even witches aren't immune to a social media deep-dive.

He shrugged. "Yeah. My whole family has an affinity for fabrics and whatnot."

"You sound like you're not a fan."

Noah raked a hand through his blond hair. It was thick and luxurious, and fell in a wheat-yellow wave as his fingers passed through. "It's cool, but it's not really what I want to do. I think witches like you are really lucky—you love what you're attuned to." He gestured at the shop around them.

"So…what *do* you want to do?"

He bit his lower lip, studying a nearby cinnamon bun. Shoving his hands in his pockets, he murmured, "I wanna go to school for music. To be a professional piano player."

Anna didn't realize there was a way to be *more* attracted to

Noah, and yet here she was, weak at the thought of Noah's perfect hands gliding over piano keys.

"That's amazing," she said. "You should absolutely do it, if it's what you want."

"Yeah, well, we'll see what my parents say when they see which schools I'm applying to." He winked at her, and she blushed. "Anyway, I'm stopping by because I wanted to place an order. A…special order."

She perked up. Noah wanted a spell? "Oh, okay! Um…" She hunted for paper and a pen. "What's the… I mean, what do you…what is it?"

Another patron walked in. While they browsed the breads along the back wall, Noah leaned in and lowered his voice.

"A confidence spell," he whispered.

Anna ducked her head to hide the widening of her eyes as she wrote the order down. *What does Noah want with a confidence spell…?*

"Any preference for what it's baked into?" she asked.

"Could you do a whoopie pie?"

"I think I can manage that."

He handed her a credit card. Once she'd rung him up, he shifted on his feet and raked his fingers through his hair again.

"Hey, um, thanks," he said. "I'll be by to pick it up tomorrow?"

"Yup! See you then!" She winced at the fake cheeriness of her voice.

He smiled, waved, and walked out the door with a jingle of the bell. Anna slumped against the counter and groaned.

A love spell and a confidence spell. She could do that—if she didn't die of embarrassment before then.

★ ★ ★

Anna muttered to herself as she scoured the list of ingredients laid out on the counter before her.

A love spell for Emma, and a confidence spell for Noah. A cupcake and a whoopie pie.

"I can do this," she muttered, opening the flour bin. "I can totally do this."

But the thought of handing Noah something she had baked—and beyond that, a *spell*—was making her stomach twist into knots. What if he hated how it tasted? What if it didn't work? Or worse—what if it *did* work, and he asked out Caty Sutherland? Anna had seen him flirt with her more than once.

Growling at herself, she patted her cheeks. *Focus, Anna.*

She did the love potion first. She had to make some chocolate cupcakes for Carlin anyway, so she used her favorite recipe, adding in a cup of strong-brewed coffee to enhance the natural chocolate flavors. Then she scooped some of the batter into a smaller bowl.

She grated a bit of nutmeg into the batter, and then crushed up a couple leaves of sweet basil, double and triple checking her ratios to be on the safe side.

"Bleeding heart to bleeding heart will bind," she whispered as she mixed, "let the sweetness of love overcome the bitterness of the mind."

Once those were in the oven, she turned to the whoopie pie. She'd decided on a pumpkin spice cake with cream cheese buttercream in the middle—which would nicely cover up the added ingredients of the spell. Into the pumpkin spice batter, she added some ground pink peppercorn, for heat and ambition, and finely chopped dill, for courage.

"What once was out of reach is now yours for the taking, let thought become action become success in the making."

Once everything was baked, Anna put the cupcake and the whoopie pie in small carry-out boxes and tied them with ribbon. Then she switched places with Carlin, situating herself at the counter in front and trying not to bite off all her fingernails as she waited.

Emma arrived first. She bounded up to Anna, eyes wide and pleading.

"Did you make it?" she panted.

"Yeah—wait, have you been *running*?"

"Riley's rehearsal ends in like twenty minutes!" she gasped, holding a stitch in her side. "I wanna be there to give it to him!"

"All right, jeez." Anna slid the box containing the cupcake across the counter. "You're welcome."

"Aw, don't be like that." Emma leaned over the counter and kissed her messily on the cheek. "Thanks, babe! I'll make it up to you."

"Mmhm," Anna hummed as Emma grabbed the cupcake and ran back out. Sighing, she began to wipe down the counters and rearrange the display case, her nerves too frazzled for her to sit still.

The bell chiming above the door made her start and bang her head against the display window.

"Whoa, you okay?"

She turned and rubbed her head, gaping at Noah. "Oh, hi! I—me? Yes!"

He eyed her. There was a blue and silver scarf wrapped around his neck, his hair windswept.

He's a Ravenclaw, she thought with a pounding heart. *Called it.*

"I…" She cleared her throat and shuffled to the counter. "I have your order."

"Great!" Noah smiled and walked over. Anna was distinctly aware that there was no counter between them right now. What was she supposed to do with her legs? How did people usually stand? Should she put a hand on her hip?

Flushing, Anna handed him the box with the whoopie pie. Noah's smile widened.

"Thanks for this," he said. Their fingertips brushed as he took it, and Anna thought this was surely, without a doubt, the day she was destined to die. "I really appreciate it."

"N–no problem," she said. "Come back any time."

And then he was gone, taking her whoopie pie with him. Anna breathed out a sigh and held her head in her hands, wondering if she had just completely missed her one and only opening.

She spent the rest of the day cleaning up and helping Carlin in the back to prep for tomorrow's bakes. When she finally closed up the bakery and locked the door behind her, her phone began to buzz in her pocket. It was Emma.

"Hey!" Anna said brightly. "Did it work? Did you ask him?"

There was silence for a beat. Then Emma started screaming.

"What the *hell* did you put in that love potion?"

Anna held the phone away from her ear. "What the hell, Emma? It's a love spell! I put in all the usual love spell things!"

"Yeah, well, it didn't work! Or rather, it didn't work the way it was supposed to!"

Anna's heart sank to her stomach. "What do you mean?"

"Before I could even ask him to Homecoming, he ran up to Vivian Huang and asked *her* to Homecoming!" Emma burst into tears. "So, what the hell, Anna?"

She leaned against the door of Sorcerous Sweets, mind whirling. The love spell was supposed to make the eater of the spell fall momentarily in love with the person who had given it to them…so then why would Riley ask *Vivian Huang* to Homecoming before Emma could make her move? Did he like Vivian so much that the spell had bent to his desire? It was possible…

"And you didn't even make it into a cupcake!" Emma went on. "Who the hell eats *whoopie pies* anymore?"

Anna's eyes widened as her stomach sank. If Emma had taken the confidence spell…

Then Noah had taken the love spell.

And Anna had been the one to give it to him.

Her phone slipped out of her hand, Emma still ranting on her end, as horror sank its claws into her gut.

What have I done?

Anna raced her bike to Noah's house. She remembered where it was, because he had hosted a cast party after last year's musical, which she had worked sound for. She *might* have signed up because Noah had been the stage director at the time.

She practically leapt off her bike and stumbled up the stairs to the front door, ringing the bell as she caught her breath.

When the door whisked open, she was leaning on her knees and panting heavily.

"Anna!" Noah stood there, looking stricken. He was dressed in a pair of skinny jeans and a loose white shirt that showed off his collarbones. "Are you all right?"

She straightened and looked him in the eye. His worry was quickly being replaced with a dreamy expression, and the corners of his lips began to curl upward.

"Do… Do you want to come in?" he asked, sounding shy.

The spell's already taking effect, she thought, panicked. "No! I mean, uh…thank you, but no. I was just, um…coming by to see if…if everything was okay?"

His smile grew into a dopey grin. "Yeah…yeah, everything is perfect."

Her mind reeled. She wasn't particularly experienced when it came to love spells, and had no idea what to do—and, for that matter, realized she had probably made everything worse by coming here.

"I—I have to go!" she wailed, running back to her bike. "I'm sorry!"

"Wait, what? Why are you sorry? Anna!"

But she was already pedaling down the street, cursing at herself for being so foolish. When she got to her house minutes later, she stormed into the kitchen and rooted through her dad's spellbooks and recipe cards.

"Something the matter?" her dad asked, leaning against the kitchen doorway with a mug of tea in his hand.

"Nope," she squeaked. "Everything is fine."

"Beti, come here."

She sighed and closed her eyes, then turned to face him.

He pushed up his glasses and raised an eyebrow. From the garage, she could hear the familiar whining of a saw as her metal witch mother crafted her latest sculpture.

"I messed up," she whispered. As she explained, her dad's expression grew stony, but he didn't reprimand her. Instead, he nodded and took a sip of tea.

"Love spells are tricky," he said. "But one that small shouldn't last for too long. A couple days, at most."

"A couple *days*?" She groaned and rubbed her face. How was she supposed to avoid Noah until the spell wore off?

"You should also apologize to Emma and that boy you spelled without his consent," he continued with that patented Dad Voice. "And you need to tell Carlin what happened."

"*What?* I can't do that! They'll be so mad!"

"You need to tell the truth, beti. It is the right thing to do."

Anna spent that night tossing and turning in her bed, occasionally texting Emma only to be left on Read. Finally, she sat up and dragged her laptop over.

How to counteract a love spell, she typed into the search engine.

She didn't tell Carlin what had happened, and her apologetic voicemails to Emma went unanswered.

She had no choice but to go to school the next day. Her shoulders were tight throughout first period, and she could barely concentrate on the lesson that was sure to be on Friday's quiz.

There were two shortbread cookies in her pocket that she had to get to Noah and Riley. She had spent hours researching how to properly negate a spell, and then had gotten up early to make the cookies.

When she spotted Emma in the hall between periods, she hurried over to her.

"Look, I'm so, so sorry," Anna said in a rush, fishing a wrapped cookie from her pocket. "Give this to Riley and the spell will wear off. You can ask him to homecoming after that."

Emma sighed and crossed her arms. She didn't look angry, just...sad.

"Don't bother," she said. "Vivian Huang turned him down anyway. He's still making pathetic puppy dog eyes at her. What's the point?"

Anna winced. "Em...really, I'm so sorry. I messed up."

Her best friend stared at the ceiling, as if pleading with some higher being. "I know. I'm still kinda upset, so just... I dunno, can we hash things out later?"

Anna wilted, nodding. "Yeah, okay..."

She sat in her usual desk for second period, trying not to cry. Why hadn't she just used different boxes for the orders? Or even written their names on the side of them? She was still kicking herself when Noah sat in the desk in front of her, making her start.

"Hey," he said breathlessly. He looked a bit stunned, as if surprised to see her. "Um, about yesterday—"

"Sit in your own seat, Noah," Mrs. Garcia said without bothering to look up from her desk.

Anna took out a cookie and handed it to him. "Sorry for being weird before," she whispered. "I made this for you, as an apology. Promise you'll eat it?"

Noah grinned, nodding. "Of course."

All throughout class she could feel him sneaking glances at her, making her flush and fidget.

Finally, at lunch she spotted him eating the cookie. He smiled as he ate it, chatting with his friends and being the good-natured, carefree Noah she admired so much. She watched him like a hawk, picking at her sandwich, watching for any difference.

He noticed her staring at him and grinned wide, blushing. He waved, and she swallowed a curse as she waved back.

That love spell must have been stronger than she'd thought. She'd once thought she would do anything to have him look that way at her, but it just wasn't the same. This was a lie. A forced crush.

She would just have to continue avoiding him until it wore off.

If it wore off.

A couple days passed, and still the spell had its clutches on Noah. He continued to give her dopey smiles, tried to talk to her in the halls of Preston, but she made up excuses and ran away as fast as she could.

She also hadn't been able to muster up the courage to admit what she'd done to Carlin. Anna worked a shift at Sorcerous Sweets and couldn't even look at them, she was so full of shame and guilt. She could practically hear her dad *tsk*ing her in her mind.

When Friday afternoon rolled around, Anna was on her way upstairs to play mindless video games—her favorite form of distraction—when there was a knock on the front door.

She opened it to reveal Emma, dressed all in black and holding a small bakery box in her hands.

"All right, let's get this over this," Emma said, shouldering her way inside. "You're so sorry, I forgive you, of course we're still best friends, blah blah blah."

Anna was so relieved that she hugged Emma tight, making her grunt.

"Okay, enough of that," Emma said, shoving the box at her. "I *hate* all that mushy stuff."

Anna took the box and frowned at the label on the side. "Sweet Cream? You do know this is our rival bakery, yes?"

"You deserve it," Emma said, plopping down on the couch. Anna couldn't help but laugh and join her, opening the box and revealing a cupcake inside.

"It's not spelled, is it?"

"You deserve that too, but no."

Still, Anna took a small bite, searching for extra flavors that would point out a spell. But it was just a simple chocolate cupcake with vanilla frosting. And ultimately inferior to hers, of course.

"So," Emma said, crossing her legs, "tell me what happened."

Anna sighed and gave her the whole story. When she explained about Noah, Emma's eyes widened.

"What are you going to do?" Emma asked. "How does this get fixed?"

"I don't think it *can* get fixed," Anna mumbled. She scooped up some frosting with her finger and shoved it in her mouth. "I just have to wait out the spell."

Emma hummed, then snapped her fingers. "Let's go to the

theater tonight. Take your mind off things. They have that new horror movie—have you seen the trailer? It looks *wild*."

So Anna let herself be dragged to the theater, even though she wasn't the biggest fan of horror movies. It was busy, even for a Friday night, but Anna found that being around so many people actually helped to lift her mood.

They were waiting in the popcorn line when Emma choked.

"Great, Vivian Huang is here," she muttered. "Thankfully, I don't see Riley…"

Vivian, hearing her name, turned and spotted Emma. She waved with a bright smile. Startled, Emma waved back.

"Looks like there's no hard feelings," Anna said. She looked around to see if anyone else from Preston was here.

There was. Specifically, the one person she didn't want to see right now.

"Crap!" Anna ducked down behind Emma. "Noah's here!"

He was buying tickets at the counter, two middle-school-age boys beside him. She recognized one as Noah's brother; they had the same blond hair and sharp chin. He was holding the hand of another boy his age. When Noah handed them their tickets, they ran off without him.

"Hey, not too far!" he called after them.

Then, as if feeling Anna's stare, he turned and saw her. Anna squeaked in Emma's ear.

"Oh my god, just go talk to him," Emma hissed. "Explain what happened. Maybe that'll break the spell."

"I can't do that!" Anna whispered back, even as Noah started to make his way toward them.

"Hey," he said. "Didn't expect to see you here, Anna."

"Oh…yeah, I love horror movies!" she said a little too loudly. Emma winced.

"Same. My brother does too, unfortunately." He jerked a thumb in the direction the two boys had run off. "He's here on a *date*, can you believe that? I'm supervising them." He looked at her with that dopey smile, and Anna's chest heated.

"So you have no one to sit with?" Emma ventured. "I'm sure Anna would like to sit with you."

Anna looked at her in horror, but Emma gave her a cutting glare that said, *Tell him the truth!*

Noah blushed. "Oh! Yeah, I…that is, if you want to, Anna?"

With a sinking feeling in her gut, Anna nodded, her mouth paper dry.

Ten minutes later, she was somehow, impossibly, sitting next to Noah in the theater, sharing a medium sized popcorn. She was far too nervous to eat any of it, though—especially with the risk of their hands bumping into each other.

"So," she said before the movie started, "your brother is on a date? Isn't he a bit young?"

Noah shrugged. "He'll be a freshman next year. As long as they don't try anything, I'm fine with it." At the reminder, he frowned and looked around for them. Anna saw the two boys huddled close, whispering and giggling. "They're adorable, but if they start making out, I'm calling the cops."

Anna laughed as the theater went dark and the movie started. Then she was tense in a whole other manner, gripping the armrests of her seat and gasping at all the jump scares. One got her so bad that she screamed and clutched the nearest available thing—Noah's arm. But Noah didn't seem to mind, and actually laughed at her reaction.

She turned to glare at him, then realized just how close their faces were. Heart pounding, she looked at Noah's lips, wondering not for the first time if they were as soft as they looked.

In a moment, she found out. Noah bridged the small gap between them, kissing her gently on the mouth as one of the serial killer's victims screamed on screen. Everything turned hot and liquid as he kissed her, as his piano-callused fingers brushed her jaw and wove into her hair. She shivered at his touch, at the way his mouth brushed reverently against hers.

And then she remembered—he was under the influence of a spell.

This kiss was a lie.

Anna broke away. Brimming with shame, she got up and tripped over other moviegoers' legs on her way out, needing to get away as fast as she could.

She was halfway across the parking lot when Noah caught up with her, calling her name. She stopped and closed her eyes, her breath fogging in the chill night air.

"Anna! I'm—I'm so sorry, I didn't mean to make you feel uncomfortable—"

She laughed harshly and turned back to him, tears building in her eyes. "No, that's not it. This… This is all fake. I can't do this with you."

Noah frowned. "What are you talking about?"

"That spell I baked for you? It wasn't a confidence spell. I accidentally gave you a love spell." She swallowed as her throat burned, the shame choking her. "It was an accident, and I tried to give you a counter spell, but it didn't work. So then I tried to avoid you until it wore off, but…"

He stared at her, uncomprehending. His pale face was flushed from the cold, or maybe from the kiss, or maybe with anger.

"I'm so sorry," she whispered. "I… I wanted to kiss you, I really did, but not like this."

He looked around, at a loss, and ran his fingers through his hair. "So…that's why it was a cupcake instead of a whoopie pie."

"Yes," she whispered, staring at the ground.

"I guess now I know why my brother was acting so weird for a couple days."

Anna frowned and looked back up. "What?"

Noah put his hands in his pockets. "The spell wasn't for me. It was for my brother. I've known he has a crush on one of his friends for a while, now. We've talked about it, but he could never get up the courage to ask him out. So I wanted to give him a confidence spell to finally make the leap."

He ruffled his hair again, frowning. "I gave the box to his friend, who brought it up to him. I guess since it was a love spell, it did work, in a way. But my brother was already half in love with the guy, so…" He shrugged. "He was acting pretty goofy for a couple days, like I said. Drawing hearts. *Giggling.*"

Anna could hear her heartbeat in her ears. "So…you didn't eat any of it. You weren't spelled."

"No. I kissed you because I *wanted* to." He sighed, shaking his head. "Why didn't you just tell me this earlier?"

"I... I didn't know how." She crossed her arms, shivering. "I'm sorry, Noah."

He looked at her a moment, then turned back to the theater.

"Well, I still gotta chaperone those dorks, so I guess I'll see you later."

He left her in the parking lot as her tears finally fell, stinging in the cold.

The next day, she told Carlin the truth. They sat across from her, listening silently, their brows furrowed.

"It's completely my fault, and I would hate for this to reflect badly on the shop," Anna finished. "I promise I'll never do anything like this again."

Carlin took a deep breath. "Anna, you *know* you're supposed to run all spelled orders by me. Even if it's a favor for a friend."

"I know. I'm sorry."

Carlin shook their head, eyes filled with regret. "I'm sorry too, Anna. I've got to fire you."

Her stomach clenched. "Wh... What?"

"The shop can't be linked to stuff like this—stuff that can endanger others. I know you meant no harm, but I have to set an example. I have to let you go."

Anna nodded numbly, getting up from her stool. She could barely feel her body as she took off her apron, as Carlin handed her an envelope containing her last paycheck.

"You're a great baker, Anna," they said. "You're going to go on to do amazing things. Don't let this setback cost you a promising future, all right?"

She couldn't tell them that she likely wouldn't have that

future without a letter of recommendation from them—the surefire way she could get accepted to Gramoire. Shaking, she nodded again and left, saving her sobs until the bakery was out of sight.

Her father took pity on her and made her some laddu while her mother lectured her, barely pausing for breath.

"You were foolish to do such a thing!" she said for the tenth time while her dad set a fresh cup of chai before her. "You could have ruined someone's life!"

"I did," Anna mumbled into her chai. "Mine."

"Nahi, beti," her dad said. "You did the right thing, in the end. People learn from their mistakes and become better people for it."

Her mom fiddled with her welding goggles as she muttered. Anna slunk away from the kitchen to curl up in her room, deciding to call Emma.

"This sucks worse than the tentacle monster in *The Revenge of the Space Kraken*," Emma said. "But you'll get through this, babe. I know you will."

"Just tell me something good."

"Well…you'll never believe this, but guessed who asked me to Homecoming?"

"Riley?"

"Nope. Vivian Huang."

"Wait, what? Seriously?"

"Yeah! Apparently, girl's had a crush on me like, all semester. Go figure."

"You sound pretty happy about it."

"Um, yeah, because Vivian is *hot*. And like, really funny?

I sat next to her during the movie and she kept making me laugh."

Anna winced at the mention of that night. "That's great, Em. I'm happy for you."

"You sound all emo when you say it like that."

"Sorry, I just..." She sighed and rubbed her eyes. "Still trying to process things."

The doorbell rang, and her dad called for her. Frowning, Anna sat up.

"I'll call you back."

She crept down the stairs, then nearly ran back up in mortification. Noah was standing in the front room with her dad.

And she was wearing her pajamas. Specifically, her Harry Potter pajamas.

"Hey," Noah said.

It took her a minute to breathe out the word. "Hey..."

Her dad, getting the hint, went back to the kitchen. Anna flushed and grabbed her peacoat from the hook by the door. "Let's go outside."

They sat on the front step. Anna burrowed her hands in her pockets, biting her lower lip as her stomach writhed anxiously.

"So," Noah said, nodding to her pajamas. "I didn't take you for a Slytherin."

She blinked, then laughed weakly. "Yeah, everyone assumes I'm a Hufflepuff, but I'm not nearly nice enough for that." She shifted and cleared her throat. "As you probably know by now."

Noah shook his head. "You're being too hard on yourself. I've been thinking about what happened. It's like you said—it was an honest mistake. You weren't trying to hurt anybody."

"I hurt my best friend, though. I hurt *you*."

"I understand why you kept it from me. Honestly, I'd have probably done the same thing." He sighed, and a long plume of fog drifted from his mouth into the air. "And you know what? It worked—my brother and his friend are happy. To me, that's what matters."

Anna shifted again. "So you…you forgive me?"

He smiled. "Yeah. And that's not some weird spell talking."

She laughed, then realized how close they'd gotten. She sucked in a breath, remembering all the times he had looked at her this week, the silly smiles he'd given her.

Noah *liked* her. Really, truly liked her.

When he kissed her, she melted against him. For a half second, she wondered if maybe *she* was under a spell, wondering how this boy could do this to her.

After a minute, Noah pulled back, flushed and grinning. "I uh… I have to get back home, but I'm glad we talked."

"Yeah," she breathed, too light-headed to think of anything else.

She walked him to the curb, where they kissed again before Noah took off. She watched him with her own goofy smile, not even caring that the whole street could see her Slytherin pajamas.

She grabbed the mail before heading back in. Plopping the stack down on the table beside the door, she did a double take. The top envelope was addressed to her, and it was written in Carlin's hand.

Anna ripped it open and read the letter inside.

It was a recommendation. One she could send to Gramoire with her application.

Her eyes stung as she hugged the letter to her chest. Maybe her dad was right—admitting you'd messed up was hard, but ultimately, it forced you to grow and become a better person. Or at least, she hoped to become a better person, a better baker, a better witch.

One spell at a time, she told herself.

★ ★ ★ ★ ★

FAR FROM HOME

by
Saundra Mitchell

"I *KNEW* YOU WERE HIDING SOMETHING FROM me," River says through gritted teeth. His grip on the line above us hasn't wavered, but every time the wind blows, we dip a little lower over the ravine.

Actually, looking down, with my sweaty hands threatening to slip at any moment, I have to revise that. It's not a ravine. It's a chasm. A canyon. Maybe even an abyss. A waterfall of loose stone showers over us, and I can't get my stupid, alien brain to focus. "Can we fight about this later?"

"I hope so," he retorts. "Can't you do something about this?"

Incredulous, I say, "Like what?! I can't *fly*."

"That's your yearbook quote, right there," River says, sarcastic to the end.

Sweat softens the angles of his panicked face, and sunlight slants into his dark eyes. Usually, those eyes are so dark, his pupils disappear into the irises—every look is dark and deep. His eyes brood for him, no attitude required.

What the hell? We're about to *die*, for real *die*, fall—no, *plummet* to our deaths, our permanent, very messy, very painful deaths, but here I am, dazzled by the secret bronze in his eyes. It's on brand for me; I've always been distracted by River's details. From the moment we met, and now, apparently, until the moment we die.

A thin *twang* cuts the air.

We drop. Hard.

The rope gives another groan and bows with our weight. Pebbles fly through the air like confetti; my shoulders wrench almost to snapping. River's must, too. We both hiss in pain. Our hearts stop, skip, then crash back into rhythm. I can say that with authority; I can feel River's pulse inside mine.

That's what being in love is like when you're from a galaxy far, far away. I don't remember my home planet; hell, I don't even know the name of it. But I've read a *lot* of books, watched even *more* movies, and not one human has mentioned the surge of another heartbeat in their blood. It's like having River inside of me, 24/7. No matter where he is, I feel a trace of him in my veins. Most of the time, I find that comforting.

Our linked beat started in elementary school, when Mrs. Bakker put me next to him in her class. River was a good student; I was a juvenile delinquent. Teachers murmured about me sometimes; I heard them in the lounge, where secret teacher meetings happen.

Sorry, you're going to have him for art and music this week.

Lucky, lucky me. Guess I'd better spike my coffee.

Ha, or jump off the roof!

Maybe they wouldn't have said it, if they realized I could hear them, even across a football field. Or maybe they would have. In any case, their brilliant plan to reform me went exactly as far as changing the seating chart so that Dumaresq, Wade fell next to Hart, River.

Second-grade social engineering. He was supposed to be my good influence, and I guess he was.

He took the job seriously, helping me with my cursive, and sharing whatever dessert showed up in his lunch with me. (I got free lunch, so I had to stand at the end of the line. Free lunch kids got whatever was left over after the paying customers filled their trays.) When my test scores ticked out of the basement into gentleman's Cs, River acted like I was Einstein.

The static in my head settled when I was near River. He was my reason to do my spelling test instead of folding it into progressively smaller stars to flick across the room. River, just River, his warmth and spotlight attention—his freckles and his too-long hair...they felt like home, to me. A real one; not the group home where I had my bed and nothing much else.

In River, I found peace that kept me from tipping my chair back, breaking my pencil, drawing in my books, sneaking games on the Leapfrog Pad...but I still got in fights.

I just got in fights over him. For him. In his honor, to right the injustices against him. Basically, I was his rabid dog, bigger inside than my scrawny frame at the time justified. All anybody had to do was give him a look I didn't like, and I rushed in, fists first.

(It's worth mentioning River came out in eighth grade, when he was the star hitter for our baseball team. He took us to junior State, so nobody at our school gave a shit if he wanted to wear eyeliner and kiss guys. A lot of Visiting jack-asses had a problem, however, so that meant I had plenty of lips to split and eyes to dot over River Hart.)

"Superman couldn't fly in the beginning."

I blink at River as I try to pull myself up on the rope. If I can get an elbow over it, I can get my waist over it. Pull River up and then…nope, still no good plan. And now River's dangling with his unlaced Converse slowly slipping off his feet. Sharing comic book facts. For no reason at all.

Finally throwing an arm over, I wince as the rope burns against my skin. "What does Superman have to do with anything?"

River watches me, his dark eyes running over me like I'm a map to salvation. "All he could do in the beginning was jump over stuff."

With a grunt, I finally drape myself over the line by the waist. My hair falls in my face, because of course it does. It's wet with a flop sweat, and I can smell myself when the wind shifts directions. Ripe. Groaning, I try to lay out a plan in my head. River keeps me on the narrow, and I keep him out of danger.

Usually.

How we got here isn't important—it will be later, if we survive. Suffice it to say that Area 51 got a bad rap for alien autopsies, but it was only testing experimental aircraft. Fort Carter Research Center, on the other hand, had a morgue full of starbois like me and a staff of scientists that had recently developed an interest in adding me to the collection.

Yeah, I gave myself away when I flipped that jackknifing semi over our school bus with a psychokinetic blast. It's not like I was gonna let a bunch of people die, just to keep this secret.

And come on! I'm a high school senior with just enough credits to get my diploma and squeak into a community college. It's not like I'm on an Ivy League path to world domination.

I work construction all summer to cover my studio apartment (got emancipated right out of the group home at 16; River helped me file the paperwork with the court). I eat cold hot dogs from the fridge because I'm too lazy to boil them, and I'd probably have to carbon date my jeans to figure out when I washed them last. All I care about is River Hart and paying my rent on time, in that order.

Well, and now, not *dying*.

River and I are about equally athletic, but his is from sports and mine's from framing walls and putting on roofs. Dexterity versus brute force, you know? Once River sees how I alienhandle my way up, he follows deftly. That crazy bastard even does a kind of flip that stops my heart completely, but ends with him sitting on *top* of the rope.

Slinging my leg over, I manage to straddle the thing. Hauling myself up, I find myself staring into River's eyes, and they've gone all dark again. Rich, like a night sky with a full moon. There's light and depth and stars in there, if I stare too long. I stare, but I also tell him, "There's a little ledge over there, if we can get to it."

Holding on to the rope, River turns slowly to look. The wind kicks up his hair, baring the shaved nape of his neck. It's one shade paler than the regular, deeply-tanned copper of the rest of his skin. My heartbeat twines around him; I love that spot on his neck. It's always so sensitive. All I have to do is rasp my nails against it to get him worked up.

And if I wanna live to do that again, I need to *focus*. Assess the damned situation. Down—definitely still too far down. Up...well, that's impossible, unless a helicopter decides to come to the rescue. But my eyes burn as I look to the sky. It's so blue that everything seems to stand out in relief to it. A natural, magic outline. I look around again—we can't go back, but maybe we can go forward.

The rope is piked into the rock on the far side of the ravine, tied in bright, complicated knots. Best as I can tell, somebody was using it as a zip line. There's elevation over there. I don't think we can just head that way, not together. We'd be sliding uphill on a line that's already coming loose.

Turning back, I can't see the spike on this side anymore. It's overhead, over the ledge, and just out of sight.

"So," River says, "I'm thinking that Superman could always fly, he just didn't know how to stay up in the beginning."

"Do I look like Clark Kent to you?" I snap at River. This is still a bad time to bicker, but a slightly better time than twenty seconds ago. "I can move stuff. I can hear stuff. That's it."

Stubborn and patient, River raised one of his Peter Pan eyebrows at me. "You threw a semi. Throw me."

"Are you out of your *mind*?"

"What's the worst that could happen?"

There, hundreds of feet from the ground, clinging to a rope that ominously groans and sags, River Hart is asking me what's the worst that could happen if I yeet him with an ability I can barely control.

Answering him, gravely, I say, "I could *kill* you."

River's shoulders, his just wide-enough shoulders, roll carelessly. "And I'm not gonna die if I fall?"

It's infuriating that he's right. And infuriating that he's in this position. All he was trying to do was protect me. He got to my place early—we were going to drive into the next town to hit the movies—when he saw someone waiting inside for me.

Raised on one too many of his mom's Investigation Discovery documentaries, River started poking around downstairs. He's the one who found the federal ID in the unfamiliar car parked in front of my place. He's the one who said we had to run.

He didn't even know why the guy was there! He just took it for granted that whatever the federal government wanted from me, it wasn't good, and he planned our getaway.

When I rolled up, he practically dragged me into his truck and took off at top speed. I guess peeling tires got the alien-catcher's attention, because after a few minutes, his black car appeared in the rearview mirror.

"We're going to the caves," River informed me as he dropped the gas pedal to the floor. Dust rose around us in volcanic plumes, escorting us on our mad race out of town. At some mark River alone recognized, he veered suddenly off the road and into the desert.

Bouncing like a dune buggy, the truck (affectionately known as Carnivale, because "it's a party on wheels") bounded through the sagebrush like a boss. The shocks rattled like cans full of coins. More than once, the exhaust met the geology at top speed, but River never slowed. Eventually, he just slammed on the brakes. Miraculously, we stayed on all four tires.

The next thing I knew, we were out of the truck and running as fast as our legs would take us. Grit stuck to our sweaty skins and the taste of earth coated our tongues. Heat licked at us, spilling down from the sun, reflected up from the desert floor.

River skidded down a cleft in the rocks, disappearing into an opening, and I followed.

We got away! I didn't whoop, because we were still running. But I couldn't hear anybody behind us. Or anywhere around us, for that matter. My lungs burned from exertion, but I felt like I could jump the Grand Canyon. Me and River, the two of us against the world. We ran from the law and the law—

Shot at us.

It was comical; when he fired at us, it wasn't a *boom*. It sounded like the faint snap of smashing caps on rocks, or those snap'em pops that turn up around the Fourth of July. But the blaze of hot lead ricocheting around us—that was real damn real.

River and I cussed in two-part harmony, and slithered through cracks barely big enough to fit through. Reckless, we dropped through holes and scrambled as fast as our feet found purchase.

There was one part of the cavern where we had to get flat on our backs on the ground and slide through. River got through quick. He's wiry strong, and fast as hell. I'm...not. My nose rasped against the stone. For a second, it looked like me and my big head were gonna get stuck.

Just then, River grabbed my ankles and pulled me through. A sear of pain lit up my face, because it got grated good and deep by the sharp rock. But it was fine—it was a relief to sit up on the other side of it.

In this little hollow, River stood, hunched over me, and searched my face. "Wade, what are you into?"

"Nothing," I swore, pressing my shirt against my face to soak up the blood.

"Hey, look. We're gonna fix it, but I have to know what we're dealing with."

For a second, I thought about playing it off again. Somebody's stealing copper from the construction site, and probably they want to finger me for it. Or, they found out that sometimes, I like to go out into the desert by myself, and commune with some peyote and the universe.

Instead, for the first time in my whole life (what I remember of it,) I told the truth. That the 2005 meteor, that took out the water tower on the north side of town—that was me. Me, my ship and a crash landing.

It all spilled out. I told him that my first memory is a beautiful black woman with silver hair, and gems glimmering in a floating crown, kissing me goodbye and shutting the hatch above me. I think the word for her on my lips is *mother*, but it's not in English. It's in a language I don't know, and I don't speak, but sometimes, I dream about.

Then I tell him my second memory is a county sheriff, carrying me away from the crash and wrapping me in a blue blanket he kept in his trunk.

It was a little much, all at once.

At first, River said nothing. Then he kicked at the floor

and clapped a hand against the stone wall. "You want me to believe—" He slapped the wall again, furious. "Damn it, I'm trying to help you!"

So instead of arguing with him, I demonstrated.

I raised my hands, mostly for effect (it feels good, but I don't have to wave my hands around to move stuff with my mind,) and he slowly lifted off the floor. So did every bit of debris on the ground, stones and pebbles floating up silently, starting to orbit his feet. It took only a second for him to look down, to realize—

The blood drained from his face. And River? He's smart. So smart that he could be a detective or a nuclear physicist or anything between. He did the math, alien plus floating, plus an impossible close call driving back from a game at Barstow... Through his graying lips, River pushed a whisper—one full of realization. "The bus. The bus crash. That was you."

Slowly bringing him back to his feet, I nodded. "I've had a couple of other run-ins, but I mostly stayed off their radar until that. What was I gonna do? Let everybody die?"

The funny thing about the way River reacts is that it's nothing like the ways I played it through my head over the years. He's not afraid of me. Not fascinated, either. He doesn't call bullshit, or ask for more proof, or anything like that. He gets *mad*.

"Why didn't you tell me?!"

Awesome question. Because I figure there's two ways to play this: the Tony Stark way, and the Peter Parker way. Stark says you own it and flaunt it and count on having so many eyes on you that nobody could get away with giving you hell... Or it's Spidey all the way: secret identity. Hide. That's how to protect yourself, and everybody you care about.

For me? "Everybody" was exactly one River Hart, end of list. Since I wasn't rich enough to pull off a Stark, I'd stuck to the Parker.

Impatient, River says, "Well?"

"I don't know," I replied, flippantly. "I was afraid you'd lose your shit when you found out you've been sleeping with a space man."

River pointed at me. "That's one reason why you shoulda told me!"

But before we could get much deeper into our feelings, Agent Dickheel found the opening above us. The rasp of his chinos on exposed stone whispered like the slide of a snake. His hard-soled shoes crunched on rubbled stone when he landed. Walking. A flashlight flickering along the seam we slid through.

Grabbing River, I dragged him with me this time. I'd spilled my biggest secret, but we were still in danger.

Running again, we slid across rough floors and banged into stone alcoves. The bright stink of bats puffed up in our faces as we bolted. We followed the cavern until a streak of sunlight beckoned to an escape. We'd gotten turned around though, because instead of bursting onto the desert floor, well. River stepped into empty space. I ran right after him.

We got *lucky*. We got so damned lucky that some rock climber had left a line in place. Our end was one more step into nothing, and we both almost took it. Instead we jounced, bending the pike that held the rope on one end. We slid, burning our hands on the line. When we came toward the stop, we hung halfway to the other side, and a couple hundred feet in the air.

Captain Jackhole almost went over the side too. He exploded out of the cavern, but caught himself at the last minute. He wore his mortality on his face, his average, symmetrical face—ordinary to blend in while he hunted aliens. While he tracked us down to torture us, or worse. In a flash, he raised his arm. Silver glinted in his hand.

Twisting on the rope, I did my best to block River's body with mine.

In jolting response, the pike bent more and we plunged down. This time, River only stayed on the line because I grabbed him. It happened too fast to think, and River was quick to climb back up over my arm. It wasn't until he was safe-enough again that I started to shake.

Damn. Damn! I just almost lost him. I nearly lost my twin heartbeat, and it would have all been my fault.

I guess because it looked like we were done for, or because he didn't have the stomach to shoot us in the face instead of the back, the government plebe hesitated. Then he holstered his gun, and backed into the cavern. Shadows swallowed him, followed by silence.

Which is when River started in on knowing I'd been hiding something, and also Superman, etcetera, etcetera. That's how we got here—at the mercy of gravity, by the grace of the wind. And neither one of those forces had a reputation for kindness.

"Wade," River says, tossing his head to get his hair out of his eyes. His voice is low, reassuring. His gaze falls on me, physical in its weight.

I've spent years pressed to his side, making a home in his company, falling in lust into his bed, and love in between all of that. Always, always his voice slips into me—it's okay if I don't know fractions; it's all good with him that I'm not a guy or a girl, no matter what my body looks like. And hey, who cares if I live by myself in high school—do I know how many people wish they could?

River has always made everything okay. And now…he's going to try to make this okay.

Reaching out, he catches my hand. And even though we should hold on with both, we hold on to each other instead. He finds a smile, a smile like sunrise, that wakes me up like nothing else. "Just pick us up. Like you picked me up in the cave. Step one. Pick us up."

Even though I don't need my hands to make this work, I usually have a frame of reference. I'm not waving force around in the air—I'm pushing against the ground, pulling toward the ceiling. But River thinks I can do this. He believes it. I see it in him—his face is certainty, not fear. Encouraging, not pleading.

Twang!

We drop again. This time, the rope doesn't stabilize. It keeps slipping. The spike behind us grinds in the stone, rock disintegrating, steel ringing as it gives way. We're falling in slow motion. I see everything, I hear everything, I feel everything. My only thought is, *not River.* Not him. If only one of us survives today, it has to be him.

Another jolt. Another drop. We're gonna die.

River looks like those saints in churches, his face smooth and beautiful even though agony's coming. Lifting my hand to his mouth, he kisses one knuckle and nods encouragingly. "Step one, baby. You can do it."

There's nothing physical inside me where the psychokinesis comes from. It's just like knowing I have the strength to pick up a glass without testing it. I don't have to tell my hand to do it; it just does. So I forget push and pull. I forget everything except River needs me, and I need him, and today's not gonna be our last day. It's not.

I was made for River Hart. Maybe we were even made out of the same star when the universe was born. I have his heartbeat inside my heart, and his heart *knows* I can do this. I can do this. I can—

I don't push. I don't pull.

I rise.

And River rises with me. I feel the rope drop from beneath us, and it just doesn't matter anymore. It's a strip of ribbon, fluttering toward the canyon floor. Slipping the earth, we stretch out, we reach out—like treading through the sea of the sky to get to each other. With gentle caresses, the wind fingers through our hair and streaks cool fingers through our clothes.

I open my eyes to River's, wide and full of wonder. We drift in a lazy spiral above the canyon, untroubled by gravity. We are, at once, weightless and impossibly tethered to each other. For the first time since we started running, I hear his breath again. I taste a distant storm in the air. I bathe in River's warmth, and I close the space between us to claim his mouth.

Galaxies separate the places where our bodies were made, but we harden the same way. We're daredevil geminis, drunk on adrenaline and rushing with the kind of thrill that comes with fast cars, sure hands and cheating death. Our tongues tangle, and I shiver at the cut of his teeth against my flesh. My thoughts streak ahead to *what if what if what if,* what if I peeled away his clothes right here and—

A bullet whizzes past our heads. Two more follow it quick. On the cliff below us, the agent runs for higher ground to take aim again.

Damn it, River just taught me to fly. I hope to hell he can figure out how to turn on my laser vision or something, because this chase? It's far from over.

But at least I know that when River runs with me, I'm never far from home.

★ ★ ★ ★ ★

THE CORONATION

by
Meredith Russo

WHAT HAPPENED WAS THIS: THE LIGHTS WENT out. The generators stopped. The radios fell silent. The wheels of the world ceased to turn in the span of a single night. There were seven nights of darkness, of cold and confusion and terror, of prayers and desperate begging and combinations of the two.

Then, as suddenly as the electric lights had gone out, a new yet ancient kind of light flickered into existence. The gods awakened, making themselves known once more in the hearts and dreams of especially sensitive individuals.

The gods followed where their flocks had gone since they last went to sleep, and if the Orisha, the Aesir, the Tuatha De, and the rest were surprised to hear voices calling out thousands of miles from where they expected, they showed no sign.

Legendary creatures crawled out of the shadows and made themselves known—horned serpents, thunderbirds, the Fair

Folk, Yōkai and creatures for whom no name yet existed. Civilization contracted.

People lamented the sudden chaos, but, as people have always done, they eventually came to terms with the new shape of things. They returned to the land. Three generations passed under the decaying shadows of once magnificent cities, until only the exceptionally old could even remember the time of engines and lights.

Sixty years after the lights went out, on Samhain night, a red-robed druid with gray-streaked hair led a pious crowd into the ruins of what had once been a garden district overlooking a river, the rusted statuary looking more like spirits frozen in revelry than anything man-made.

Their village was cursed, but they knew that a tribulation is often an opportunity to demonstrate devotion, and so they lifted their voices in song. A wicker man loomed above the scene, its featureless face pointed back toward the faint lights of their village nestled in the city's skeleton.

Beyond the hill and the swift, cold river, crouching low and dark like a hunting cat, the cursed forest waited, and no matter how badly the two young people at the rear of the procession wanted not to, they could not help stealing glances at their fate.

Tall, gangly McKenna pulled her hood back and shook her unbraided black curls loose. Her hands shook despite her high chin and square shoulders. She looked where she imagined the moon rose behind the low clouds and whispered soft, urgent prayers to Cerridwen and Mawu—her village formally paid homage to the Tuatha De, but McKenna kept private shrines to the Orisha to hedge her bets and honor her grandmother. As always during her waking hours, the goddess and the Orisha remained silent, but the habit of prayer still brought comfort.

Diminutive, wild-haired Tiwa hunched his shoulders and glowered at McKenna, his betrothed in the play-act of this ritual, at the sacred spear Summer clutched in the boy's shivering hands. It served only to make him seem that much scrawnier. Tiwa thought of the damage *he* could do with such a weapon—his knuckles were rough and scarred from countless fights, and despite his size he knew that, with the element of surprise, he could unleash bloodshed glorious enough to earn the spear a better name than a stupid season.

"Give it to me," he hissed. His gaze darted to the adults marching before them, but they were too absorbed in the ritual to hear.

McKenna blanched and held Summer closer. She was so like a woman in every way Tiwa hated, and besides piety, cowardice was what he hated *most* in women. As McKenna's face twisted in indignation the knot of disgust grew in Tiwa's stomach. How could fate have wasted manhood on this coward?

"No," McKenna said. "It's my responsibility."

"You don't know how to use it." Tiwa sidled close and grasped McKenna's elbow with startlingly strong fingers. "I do. None of the adults are armed and Brandan's guards must be further ahead. We can escape."

"We could..." Uncertainty flickered on McKenna's slender face, but then she scowled and tried to yank her arm away. It was a show of *respect* that they weren't being led in chains—respect for McKenna's sense of duty, at least, and so long as she had the spear Tiwa couldn't do much harm or run too far. She knew Tiwa too well—everyone knew everyone in a village this size, and McKenna knew Tiwa was a vicious little monster, nothing like the other girls. Why the gods would waste a woman's body on *Tiwa* was a mystery McKenna supposed she would only understand once her spirit floated across the western sea.

"No. Where would we even go? Druids spread news faster than we could run."

"Stupid!" Tiwa hissed. "There are places druids don't go. I heard in Atlanta they worship the Orisha *first*, and out west they haven't heard of the Tuatha De *or* the Orisha, but something called an 'Odin' and the Wakan Tanka."

"*That* far?" McKenna balked. "Do you know how to cross the Great River? Can you traverse the Smoking Mountains? I suppose you've got a boat and climbing gear and food hidden in your robes?"

"We can figure it out as we go," Tiwa said. He grabbed Summer and tugged, but McKenna found her strength and snatched it back so hard she nearly fell over.

"It's the will of the gods," McKenna hissed. "I know *you're* an impious little shit, but *I* won't be cursed because you decided to run from your first responsibility."

"What gods?" Tiwa said. He made a mocking face and looked all around. "Where are they? *I've* never seen one and neither have you—nobody even believed in the gods when the world was electric, and they did fine!"

McKenna's face paled and her eyes grew wide as Tiwa spoke. He took small pride in scandalizing the weakling, but then a rough hand fell on his shoulder.

"Until they didn't," Brandan's deep voice rumbled. "You shame yourself, Tiwa."

Tiwa looked up into the druid's weathered, tawny face

with a suddenly dry throat. The adults were all staring at him, and the hill rose horribly behind them, and beyond that the forest waited closer than Tiwa ever liked to see at night. A stark white cow lowed sleepily between the wicker man's legs, blissfully unaware of what this ritual would mean for her. Tiwa envied her.

"It's time," Brandan said. "Come."

McKenna followed, shoulders hunched and hood pulled forward to avoid the eyes of everyone she had ever known. Tiwa clenched his fists and ground his teeth but followed all the same. The crowd parted, whispering as the winter prince and winter princess crested the hill.

Tiwa and McKenna took their places at the right and left hand of the wicker man. The tumbled brick, shattered glass and twisted, vine-strangled metal of the dead River City glistened in the moonlight in the valley below. Brandan's assistant handed him a bone-white knife and stood aside. Brandan stroked the white cow's velvet snout, then turned to the people and raised his knife.

"The gods demand sacrifice," he called, in a voice clear and bright as the moon above. They chanted his words back like the tide. "And we give gladly, dreaming of spring."

McKenna and Tiwa knew their part. No sense in defiance now. Tiwa lifted his voice.

"Our forebears forgot their duty under the electric glow," Brandan said. The people called back.

"They forgot that prosperity and life have a price," McKenna said. The people called back.

"We do not forget," Tiwa said, though his face twisted in disgust. Secretly he'd always suspected the world going dark was just a thing that happened with no moral dimension one way or the other, like a thunderstorm or getting kicked in the head by a donkey. Even if the gods *did* exist, who could say what they wanted or why? "We hear the voices of the gods, and we gladly pay our debts."

"When will winter end?" the people called.

"When we have proven our devotion," Brandan said, "or never, whichever comes first." He slashed the cow's neck. Blood gushed forth, black as rich earth in the moonlight, and ran through the wet, slick grass.

She did not struggle or cry out, but merely lay on her stomach and blinked at the incomprehensible world as her life faded. The people took her calm as a sign the gods watched and approved.

Brandan knelt in the tide of blood and kissed the cow on her forehead, then rose again. "All rests on the resolve of our king and queen." He held out a hand and another assistant approached and passed him a torch. "A boy will never know manhood. A girl will never know womanhood. We thank them for their blessed sacrifice."

"We thank them for their blessed sacrifice," the crowd called.

Tiwa did not *feel* blessed, and even McKenna felt a shadow of doubt.

Brandan touched the torch to the wicker. Flame crawled up the leg, casting the faces below in otherworldly light. The sounds and smells of roasting beef washed along the wind. All voices rose in song.

A roar washed down the hill into dilapidated streets as the

fire blazed unnaturally high. McKenna and Tiwa covered their eyes, and the people gasped, and Brandan stood calmly.

"The veil thins," Brandan said. He wrapped the knife in a rag and slipped it into his belt. "The dead walk. The crown passes. Go now. Find comfort. Mourn the passing of McKenna and Tiwa. Pray that winter is short."

The crowd dispersed. Brandan turned to address the children while his attendants set about cleaning.

"I know you think I'm a monster," he said.

Tiwa crossed his arms and spit in the grass. McKenna squeezed Summer's haft and shook her head.

"You speak for the gods!" she said, but her voice shook with fear and sadness. "Who would I be to...to—"

"A human who wishes to stay alive," Brandan said. He rested a hand on her shoulder. "No shame in that."

"How kind," Tiwa spat. "I suppose this exchange will warm your heart while you sleep by your fire and we freeze in the woods. Can we go?"

"Not yet," Brandan said. His eyes drifted between them. "Heed me," he said. "Do you know what happens when girlhood is burned out of a girl?"

"She withers and dies," Tiwa said flatly. All the children had been raised on stories of this ritual, on the off chance that they might be chosen. It was meant to be an honor, or at least the adults said so, and no parent wanted their child to shame them or, worse yet, fail in their duty.

"And what happens when boyhood is burned out of a boy?"

"The same," McKenna said in a small voice.

"You should know," Brandan said, "that you will not be escorted to the thrones."

McKenna and Tiwa scanned the bridge spanning the river and, beyond it, the path leading to the forest, with narrowed eyes. They'd assumed an escort waited in the darkness. It was how things were done—a dutiful young person might walk this far on their own, but in the forest alone? In the dark? It would only be human to break and run. Still, from this high vantage, with light from the fire pouring down, where would they even hide?

"Wait," Tiwa said. He leaned in and smiled conspiratorially. "So we can leave? You're just letting us go?"

Brandan cuffed the side of his head. Tiwa stomped and issued a stream of curses.

"I'm telling you I *trust* you!" Brandan said. "And I need you to trust me. Attend closely, because this is the last thing I will say before you must go: I am not blind. I know your lives have been…hard. Disappointing. But no matter what you have endured, there are people in this village you love. Who love you, in the only way they know how. Picture their faces while I speak. The stakes are very real, I promise you, and if you fail to do your part tonight, a five-year winter will kill or drive into exile everyone you have ever known."

"But—" Tiwa said.

"And if I'm wrong?" Brandan said. "If there is no curse, and the thrones in the forest are little more than dead stone?"

He snapped, and an attendant brought two packs heavy with gear and provisions and dropped them at McKenna's and Tiwa's feet. "No guards. No threats. You've done your part and you're free to go. Strike out for a place where you can be what your spirits say you are, and no druid will bar your path." He jabbed a finger first at McKenna, who flinched, and then at Tiwa, who blinked and huffed. "But know that if the curse is real, as I say, and you resolve to do what you must, that there is a way to survive the sacrifice. Only you two can do this."

"Isn't that cheating?" McKenna said.

"How do we survive?" Tiwa said. "Tell us!"

"I will say no more," Brandan said. He embraced the children, wished them good luck, bade them to keep faith, and set off for the village with his attendants following on his heels.

The clouds parted. Mingled silver and orange light bathed the crumbling bridge and the trees at the edge of the forest. McKenna and Tiwa watched the old druid walk down the westward path until he disappeared behind a pile of bricks that had once been a cafe, both feeling naked despite their heavy clothes as they put together what he'd said about their lives thus far.

Up to this moment the king and queen had imagined themselves quite subtle, had convinced themselves that they might fail to be a *perfect* son or daughter, but that the secret in their heart was perfectly safe. Not so apparently. And then, almost as one, they put the pieces together.

"Oh," Tiwa said. "You too?"

"Yes," McKenna said. She shouldered her pack and strode toward the bridge.

"Hey," Tiwa said. "Wait!" He grabbed his pack and trotted after her, cursing the length of her legs almost as much, he realized, as she probably did. As much as he hated being short, someone with the heart of a girl must have despised the idea of towering over her peers.

But she did not wait, nor did she look back.

"Slow down!" He pouted once he caught up to her. She

kept her eyes straight ahead. "Why so cross? At least we finally know we're the same."

"We are *not* the same," McKenna said. She stopped at the end of the bridge, squatted, and set about lighting a torch.

"But Brandan said…" Tiwa mumbled. "I thought… I'm a boy, in my heart anyway, and…" He swallowed and squared his shoulders. "Aren't you as well? Not a boy, I mean, but—"

"A girl?" McKenna said. "I am."

After the third strike of flint against stone the torch lit and she rose to walk further down a narrow game trail. From a distance the forest seemed to be nothing but trees climbing the mountainside, but once you got close to it, once you got *inside* it, it became clear that this forest was the destiny of all the dead, electric cities without people to clear and cultivate them.

Oaks and peach trees in their fall colors erupted through pharmacies long ago cleaned of every useful medicine. White pines and Fraser firs twisted their way out of banks, withering kudzu on the crosses from old churches. The trees seemed to rise forever into the sky and the darkness seemed to move, but if McKenna was afraid, she did not show it. "Still, I'm not like you."

"But—" Tiwa started.

McKenna turned, the torchlight glittering in her narrowed eyes, and Tiwa wilted.

"*I* never laughed while my friends threw cow shit at *you*," she hissed.

"I…"

"*I* never drove livestock into the hills with my games. *I* never broke the scavver's son's thumb and called him a weakling when he ran home sobbing. I *also* never stole old world tools from my neighbors when the scavver justifiably stopped selling to me because I brutalized his son. *I* never smashed the fence Widow Yadira's husband built for her before he died!"

"Come on!" Tiwa said. He struggled to light his own torch under her withering gaze. "It was just a bit of fun, and that last one was an *accident*. We never—"

"Did your 'friend' Beli tell you he spied me kissing the bard who came through last summer?"

Tiwa's face went slack. He remembered the bard, yes, and Beli snickering about something, but he hadn't heard…he'd never imagined…and didn't he remember the man saying he was nineteen or twenty?

Under all the confusion, a little spark of indignation burned in Tiwa's chest that a man that old would kiss McKenna when she'd only been fourteen. The spark faded to guilt as Tiwa recalled all the *other* bad things he had allowed to happen to her.

"You've laughed at the things Beli's yelled at me since then," she said. "Did he tell you he told my father and brothers?" She leaned closer to Tiwa with each sentence until their noses almost touched, and had the dense woods not been to his back Tiwa thought he very well might run away. "How do you think they felt, knowing their 'son' and their 'brother' had kissed a man? Did he tell you they *beat* me?"

"*I* never meant anything by it," Tiwa said in a small voice. His torch finally caught and he did his best to stand with dignity.

"I know boys think so, but girls aren't stupid," McKenna said. "Whatever I am, I'm not stupid either. I always *suspected* things about you, and when we were small, I even thought

357

you handsome. I almost considered broaching the subject with you, trying to be your *friend*." She turned and continued down the trail. "But then I realized that whatever else you are, you're a nasty, cruel little brute. So, no, we are nothing alike, despite what we might have in common."

Tiwa ground his teeth, his face hot with the directionless anger and resentment of a young man who doesn't want to feel shame. They walked in thunderous silence. Time passed, though neither could say how much with the overgrown ruins hiding the heavens.

The darkness to either side of the trail seemed to twitch and rattle with a thousand growls and chirps and hisses. Fear flashed on the king's and queen's faces, but neither was willing to let the other see.

"Why didn't you hate me for—" Tiwa said eventually.

"For being a beast?" McKenna said. Relief flashed in her eyes at the sound of another human voice, but she hid it with a flip of her hair. "I did. I do. Here I thought I'd made that clear."

"No," Tiwa said. "Why didn't you hate me for having what you wanted?" He held his arms out as if to encompass his entire body, seeming shorter and less comfortably shaped every day, and a look of disgust spread across his face so thoroughly that McKenna's glare couldn't help softening. "And wasting it."

"Audrinahae sets souls in motion as she will," McKenna muttered, though a guilty twinge plucked the corners of her eyes. "It is not my place to—"

"Don't use the gods as an excuse!" Tiwa said, and the forest seemed to go quiet.

"Don't raise your voice at me!" McKenna said.

Tiwa opened his mouth to yell again despite her protest, but a sound froze him in place. It started with a loud snap and a snuffling like a bear, then grew into the groaning of trees being pushed aside and a rumble like a landslide somehow slowed down.

"Be quiet," Tiwa said.

"*You* be quiet," McKenna hissed. She grabbed him and pulled. "Come on, it's probably just a deer."

"Bigger than a deer," Tiwa whispered. He saw an eye open through the trees, and it seemed almost to glow with an inner fire. "We need to get off the trail. Hide."

"Don't be a fool," McKenna said. "The gods wouldn't let—"

A twisted giant lurched into the light, half again as tall as McKenna, with skin the color of stone, long, spindly limbs, the face of a horrible old woman, and a right hand with an index finger like a long obsidian knife. The thing kept this appearance for only an instant.

In a blink its stone form warped into a towering copy of McKenna's father, with his heavy brows and arms just a little too long and heavy for his frame. The stone face sneered, and one over-long limb reached out faster than should have been possible, snatching McKenna by the neck and driving her into the mud.

Summer clattered to the ground. The stone giant leaned in close to the lanky girl, its face especially horrible for all the ways it resembled her own, but somehow gone wrong.

Gibberish billowed over its tongue, and its gaze bored hungrily into her. McKenna kicked and scratched and pried at the hand, but it fixed her to the earth like a tree grown overnight.

Tiwa willed himself to move, but with every moment the

giant seemed to grow larger and more grotesque, its back bulging and its stone skin rippling as muscles warped impossibly.

"*Run*," McKenna rasped with what little breath she had left.

Tiwa took one step back, and then another, his head rattling with visions of the life he could make if he ran. His gaze darted from the salivating, monstrous face back to McKenna's struggling features growing paler by the second. One more step away.

But then, in a flash, he saw himself from the outside, and he thought: *The boy McKenna thinks I am would have run away without being told.*

He clenched his fists. He willed his right foot to slide forward through the mud. The giant laughed and bared more of its awful teeth. McKenna's gaze darted to Tiwa, wild and desperate. He kicked Summer up and into his outstretched hand as easy as slipping into a shoe and lunged forward with a jab worthy of Cú Chulainn.

The giant batted the blow aside but left room for McKenna to wriggle free. She scrambled to her feet, coughing and clutching her throat as her heels slid and sent her crashing into a tree trunk.

The giant wheeled on Tiwa, its form shifting to a new horror, the undulating mass blocking the path, its burning eye singing like rock heated to the breaking point. Tiwa dropped into a low stance and licked his lips.

A golden light began to grow in the core of Summer's haft, brighter and brighter in tune with the beat of Tiwa's heart.

"Tiwa…" McKenna coughed.

"*You* run!" Tiwa growled.

The giant's eyes flared and it lashed out. Tiwa dodged and jumped higher than he'd known he could. The giant over-extended, stumbled forward, and howled as Summer bit into its shoulder, chipping away bits of stone.

Its shape solidified into Tiwa's grandmother Athas, whose blind right eye had frightened him when he was small and who used to cuff him in the head and whip him with switches when he refused to wear dresses and dance in ceremony with "other girls."

When Tiwa landed McKenna was gone, but a kick from the giant's prone form robbed him of the chance to dwell on it.

Shame and fear tore through McKenna like a fever as she sprinted away, her torch guttering in time with the tears streaming down her cheeks. She shut her burning eyes and let her feet carry her blind down a straight section of the trail dotted here and there with chunks of asphalt. She snapped her eyes open as hoofbeats pounded just off the trail.

She looked out through hazy eyes and just made out a black coat highlighted orange by slivers of torchlight, black hooves tearing through the underbrush as if over an open plain, and a single golden eye casting its own eerie light.

Lacking other options and quickly growing exhausted, she came to a slow, gasping stop.

The creature stopped beside her and kept its golden eye pinned to her, though a wall of trees and rusted iron light fixtures remained between them.

"Friend or foe?" McKenna asked.

"Changes as often as the weather," an impossibly familiar voice called out, seeming to originate from inside the horse's body. The darkness thickened and in it there was a shifting and cracking of bone, and when the veil lifted again, McKenna's skin went cold.

The bard—Taliesin, his name had been—strode into her light, his eyes the same vibrant gold as the horse's, his tunic fine and velvety black, and his face as handsome as ever. She could not help but notice the horse ears poking out from under his fine cap, and how his belt seemed to be made of horsehair. He clicked his teeth and smiled. "But on a night like this, alone with a pretty girl? Let's say friend."

An ash tree fell in two under the giant's razor-sharp finger. Tiwa swung from a low branch and flew under the beast's dipped shoulder, then pivoted above its lunging body already chipped and cracked from a dozen wounds.

Tiwa was battered, certainly, and he guessed his right eye would be swollen shut soon and probably his left ankle wouldn't want to support his weight for a while, but these concerns were small compared to the thrill in his heart as he landed behind the beast and skidded through the mud, sunlight spear whipping into position like a raptor's open talon.

He watched the giant realize its mistake, groan and start to turn, but it was too late: Tiwa pivoted his hip, pushed his shoulder forward and drove Summer through the back of the thing's elbow and out through the palm of its left hand.

It coughed, once, a tremendous rumbling wetness, and fell to the earth with an impact that shook the branches.

Tiwa tried to catch his breath. His cheeks hurt, and only after he touched them with shaking hands did he realize he was smiling. He yanked Summer free, flicked foul-smelling blood away into the darkness, and, wincing with every other step, limped after McKenna.

"Hold, child," a wheezing, earth-deep voice called, so like Tiwa's grandmother that he couldn't help flinching.

Tiwa turned to find the giant lying on its side, its single good eye dimming as more and more reeking blood pooled around it. His gut screamed to put the creature down for good, but his heart told him that if it was capable of speech then, being helpless, it probably deserved certain honors.

What those were, he couldn't say, but he imagined that last words were probably important. He made a show of leaning against Summer and motioned for the creature to continue, and to his surprise it actually laughed.

"My heart," the creature muttered. It lifted its mangled left hand. "My heart...how did you...?"

"The one in your palm?" Tiwa said. "Every child has heard of you, Spearfinger."

"As you say," the giant said. "Still. You have...proven yourself...a worthy warrior," it rumbled. "And...honorable enough at least...to hear me out. I keep...medicine...in my home. Not...too...far. Retrieve it...and I can...grant you any boon... in my power."

"What kind of boon?" Tiwa said.

"Medicine to...make you...stronger. Faster. Larger. Medicine to...change your shape."

Tiwa's eyes widened.

"Change my shape *how*, wretched creature?"

The stone woman's eye flared and it smiled weakly.

"I have...seen...your heart...*boy*. I know...what you...want. I can...make you...a man."

Farther down the trail, the bard Taliesin stroked McKenna's hair as he led her to a rusted bench in the shallow darkness by the trail. McKenna leaned into the touch and sniffled, fear and confusion and heartbreak mingling on her young face.

"You are not Taliesin," she said as she sat. He looked down at her and smiled. She felt her cheeks flush despite her fear, despair and exhaustion. "You are a púca. A shapeshifter."

"What's the difference?" Taliesin said. He knelt before her and took her right hand in both of his.

McKenna's heart remembered those calluses and the smell of resin, pine and a hint of road dust on his clothes. Tears flowed more freely than ever as she sat helpless, caught between the urge to run and the urge to leap into his arms.

"Perhaps I kept my ears tied back," Taliesin said. "Did you check?"

Had she checked? She couldn't remember, and she was so tired, and her thoughts felt slow like fingers in winter. Her shoulders sagged, her breathing slowed and her pupils dilated in the soft light. Taliesin's smile widened at this.

"Where *were* you?" McKenna said. She hung her head to hide behind her hair.

Taliesin wiped a tear from her cheek and stroked the nape of her neck.

"Everything got so bad," she said. "My voice dropped and now the other girls avoid me, and they sent me into the woods to die, and after you left, my family—"

Taliesin placed a finger over her lips, shushed her, and winked.

"I was out searching, beautiful."

"Searching for *what*?" McKenna said, her head so full of grief she sounded as if she had a cold.

"For a way to fix you," he said.

Her eyes went wide and the tears nearly stopped.

"I didn't want to get your hopes up in case the search was

fruitless, and I couldn't stand to see your face when I told you I was leaving."

"*Fix* me?" McKenna said.

"Make you a woman," he said. "In flesh as well as spirit."

"Is that possible?"

"Only a matter of technique," Taliesin said. He rolled back onto his heels and unslung a black guitar from his shoulder. "With the right song, the right rhyme? Even human bards can change the winds of fate or curse a king's skin with boils. Honestly, when I found the trick to it, I felt a fool for not already knowing."

McKenna's tears were dry now, and her eyes distant. She sniffled and giggled, there in the dark on the cusp of winter.

"I prayed you'd come back," she whispered. "I was so sad, but I never gave up. Never. And now you're here, and…is it true? Your song can really…?"

He nodded.

"So I…won't grow a beard? And I can have a baby of my own someday?"

"With me, if you'd like."

Taliesin favored her with a rakish grin. Her cheeks darkened and her gaze darted away.

"There's only one problem," he said. "The magic won't work here, but there's a standing stone a ways south that should do the trick. We'll need to leave now if we wish to get there before the season ends."

"But…" She shook her head and swayed like a drunk, her eyes momentarily coming into focus. "But Tiwa is back there, fighting for his life."

"Against the giant I saw when I caught up to you? Dearest, he's already dead, and if we don't leave soon, we will be too."

"If he's dead, he needs a burial," McKenna muttered.

"Does he?" Taliesin said, his tone incredulous. "This *is* the same Tiwa you told me of, yes? The 'dreadful little monster'?"

"Well, yes, but…" *Had* she told Taliesin about him? It was hard to think, but she remembered he'd done most of the talking, and she hadn't wanted to make a fuss about herself. "I have responsibilities to the village. I can't just leave."

"Right, the curse," Taliesin said. He scratched his chin and shrugged. "Have they *earned* a sacrifice like this from you though?"

"I. Well. I think. I mean. Brandan said it's possible that I won't die. So…but…" The fog returned to her eyes. She glanced down the trail and sucked her lip, distantly remembering the teasing, and the alienation, and the beatings. Her slack expression hardened. "No. I suppose not."

"The answer seems obvious then."

Tiwa heard distant voices and limped faster, bracing himself on Summer's haft. A few steps farther and one of the voices resolved into McKenna's, so he gritted his teeth and hustled with Summer raised, only to halt when he rounded a bend and saw her talking with a man dressed all in black.

Tiwa thought about calling out, but then the man's face tilted in his direction and he saw the otherworldly golden flash of his eyes. Tiwa hid behind the low branches of a yew tree, concealing Summer's glow in his cloak and testing his injuries with his fingers.

His breath froze as the light from McKenna's torch caught a black guitar Tiwa remembered from the previous summer— so not a stranger at all then, though certainly *strange* enough.

Tiwa ground his teeth as he wrapped shaking hands around Summer and twisted as if strangling an imagined foe.

"Come on, love," Taliesin said. He took McKenna's hand and she rose slowly, almost as if she were in a dream. "I swear to you, you're going to be the most beautiful woman this side of the mountains."

"I'm so glad," McKenna said.

"Wait!" Tiwa said. He limped out from behind his tree and brandished Summer's full brilliance, bathing the path in summer light.

Taliesin's eyes flared and his expression shifted to an almost animal fury as he moved McKenna behind him. She craned her neck and gasped to see Tiwa, clothes torn, face bruised, hair matted with blood, and yet with his shoulders wide and feet planted apart like a proper warrior. Tiwa spun Summer and took a purposeful step forward, his good eye twitching at the pain in his ankle.

"Tiwa!" McKenna said. The light caught in her eyes and they went wide. "You're alive? And the spear...!"

"Tell him no," Tiwa said.

"What?"

"Leave, boy," Taliesin said, and behind his words was a braying as of a furious animal.

"Or what?" Tiwa said. He took another step forward. McKenna tried to run to him, but Taliesin held an arm out. Tiwa growled. "You'll kill me? Friend, I just sent an eight-foot tall stone woman with a sword for a hand back to her maker. What can *you* do? I'll warn you, I don't like music, and I'm not in the habit of letting old perverts sweep me off my feet."

"I wield powers you can't imagine," Taliesin said. His mask of fury twisted into a smile. "The girl's affection among them. Come, McKenna. We're leaving."

McKenna looked from Taliesin to Tiwa, her breath speeding up again.

"Tell him no," Tiwa said. Another step. Taliesin narrowed his eyes. McKenna bit her thumbnail.

"He said he can make me how I'm supposed to be," McKenna said. "And…and maybe if you put your weapon away, Taliesin will—"

"The spearfinger offered the same thing," Tiwa said. Another step, and he was almost close enough to throw Summer. He spit into the mud. "I put out her eye with my spear. We *are* the way we're supposed to be."

"Idiot," Taliesin sneered. "You could have had everything you ever wanted."

"A body doesn't make a man!" Tiwa bellowed, and Summer shined brighter. "*Choices* make a man. Whatever shape I might take, if I run from this challenge, I am no man worth the name." He let out a long breath, eyes closing against the pain in his ribs. Summer fell at his side and he held out his empty hands, his face hard yet pleading. "McKenna, don't you see? We already *are* what we're supposed to be in the way that matters. Is a woman her body, or is she her heart? If you run now, I promise you one day you will look back on our frozen home and hate yourself."

"Tiwa…"

"Come with me when this is over," Tiwa said. Two steps now. His shaking hands belied the steel in his voice. "*When* we live, because we *will*. We can find a new home. We can get to know one another properly. And…and if one day you decide I deserve you, I would be happy to call you my wife, no matter your shape. You probably want a baby as much as I dread the thought, but there are enough forsaken children who might need us that we could—"

The word *wife* hit McKenna as if she'd fallen into a warm bath on a frigid day. She blinked and swore under her breath. Then Tiwa brought up children and McKenna shook herself awake. She wrenched her arm free from Taliesin's grip and leapt aside before he could grab her again, then ran into Tiwa's arms.

There was a sound of hoofbeats, and when they turned their attention back to the path, they found Taliesin gone. Tiwa retrieved Summer, its glow now dimmed, and despite the wounds to his body and McKenna's heart, they clasped hands and resumed their journey.

"Was that really him?" Tiwa said.

McKenna shrugged and cast a last, anxious gaze in the direction she thought he might have gone.

"What was he?"

"A púca," she said. "A faerie who likes to take on the shapes of animals and cause mischief."

"So…not terribly dangerous, then?"

She cast him a withering look.

"In the *physical* sense, I mean?" He made a show of limping and wiped blood from his forehead. "Because if he finds his courage and a weapon deadlier than a guitar, I'm not really in any shape to fight him off."

"We should be fine," McKenna said in a low voice, "so long as we don't sleep."

They grew quiet as the forest closed in around them. Occasionally one would open their mouth or take a breath as if to speak, but the other's gaze would shift to them and they would wilt. The night wore on. Miles passed beneath their feet. The air grew chill, and a mist thick as milk rolled in through the trees, until all they could be sure of was the next step and the other's fingers laced in their own.

A wild dog howled somewhere, the sound lonely and soft in the muffled air. Time slipped into a blur and worry troubled their faces as their walk seemed to stretch forever.

Then the path widened into a clearing. The mist lifted and the moon shone its silver light, slowly unveiling the crumbling metal and glass walls of a building they had heard of only in stories.

A vine-choked sign near the entrance named the place in the old dialect, though even if they'd known how to read the words neither child would have understood what a "university center" was. To them it was simply the secluded temple, the place of sacrifice, and they felt the footprints of their forebears as they took their first steps toward it.

They approached with the slow caution of lowborn petitioners to a royal court, shoulders tense and hoods pulled forward. Cracked glass doors slid open when they neared, and moonlight poured into the great, white tiled hall through fissures in the ceiling, somehow even brighter than outside.

Two thrones stood at the end of the hall, pristine and shining silver despite their surroundings. The crest of the right throne bore the likeness of a man in golden filament, while the crest of the left bore a woman in silver. The king and queen stared at the thrones for a long moment, their heartbeats nearly audible.

"Where are the two from last time?" Tiwa said. A bird

alighted from some distant corner and both of them flinched. "Even if animals made off with their bones there should be stains or something."

McKenna frowned and shrugged. All that sat on either throne was a slim diadem.

"Perhaps the gods took them," McKenna said eventually. She pulled her cloak tight and stood up straight, chin high. "But…suppose nothing happened and they ran off?"

"No," Tiwa said. He squeezed her hand and smiled ruefully. "In all the long years one of them would have come back to the village or at least been spotted nearby. I doubt we'll be so lucky. Though…" He pulled her gently over the treacherous fallen pipes and support beams of the hall, holding Summer up to light the darker recesses.

"What?"

"Seems odd," Tiwa said, "that a monster and a spirit should appear together and offer us the same thing."

McKenna remembered her prayers and glanced at the sky through one of the bigger cracks, then back to the thrones with a thoughtful expression.

"Tiwa?" McKenna said.

"Hmm?" Tiwa shoved a moss-covered stone away and tested the floor with a hop.

"Which throne should I take?"

"The queen's," he grunted as he vaulted over an upturned feast table. He turned to help her with an impatient look. "*Obviously*. In the ways that count most—put your foot there—you're already a woman and I'm already a man."

"Yes," McKenna said as she landed on the other side of the table, "but does the curse know that?"

There was nothing but dirty tile floor between them and the thrones. They paused again to stare.

"Bit of an oversight," Tiwa said with a laugh.

McKenna's eyes went wide and she touched her lip.

"What?" Tiwa said. He squeezed her hand tighter than before, until she winced and slapped him away.

"Ow! Oaf." She rubbed her hand, frowned, and then laughed despite herself. "I just realized why Brandan picked us." She strode up to the king's throne and placed her hand on the armrest, its subtle radiance rippling in her eyes. She held out a hand. "Give me Summer."

"Why?"

"It's a symbol of office," she said with a note of impatience. "The king has to hold it."

Tiwa held the weapon out to her, but when she grasped it, he found he didn't want to let go. She pulled, once, then gave him a tender look and placed her other hand over his.

"I understand," she said. "I hate holding it as much as you hate giving it up. Just for a moment, all right? Then you can have it back."

"If we're still alive," Tiwa muttered, though he did let go.

"If we're still alive," McKenna agreed.

She blew out a breath, took the diadem in her free hand, and climbed the dais to sit on the king's throne. Tiwa closed one eye and hunched his shoulders, then relaxed when nothing happened.

"It has to be both of us I think," McKenna said. Her voice shook like an autumn leaf and her face had gone pale. "And we need to wear the crowns."

Tiwa mounted the dais and made his way to the queen's throne, his stomach churning every time his eyes fell on the feminine figure atop it. He sat easily enough, but his hands shook more than exhaustion could explain once he held the diadem.

McKenna swallowed, lifted her diadem, and smiled at him. "Hey…were you serious? About being companions and…everything else?"

"Absolutely," Tiwa said in a dry, raspy voice.

"Then I accept," McKenna said. She poised the diadem above her head and nodded. "Now or never."

Tiwa blushed despite his fear and nodded back. They crowned themselves together. Light filled the hall and then their minds, and there was a distant sounding of chimes and horns, and then darkness.

McKenna awoke first, and she gasped to find that the hall and the clearing beyond were even lovelier in the crisp morning light.

The fog was beginning to burn off, and the cardinals to sing, and she could just make out the silhouettes of turkeys and of deer weaving through the tree line.

In the foggy dimness of an as-yet half-conscious mind she touched her fingers together to see if she still existed in a way she understood, if she was still a creature of flesh or some kind of spirit. Her hands felt normal, and before she could guard against it a second thought entered her head: she was still alive, but after all this the gods must have transformed her somehow, right? Or else what was the point?

She brought her fingers to her jaw, praying for smoothness, only to have her heart break when the same sparse hairs that had tormented her for a year bristled under her touch.

"We're alive!" Tiwa said.

McKenna only realized she was crying when she looked to

the other throne and saw her vision distorted through tears. A tan shape moved toward her and squeezed her hand.

"What's the matter?" Tiwa said, closer now. "We're alive. We're *alive*."

"I'd just hoped…" She shook her head, sniffled, and wiped her nose. "It was so stupid."

"I don't think it's stupid to hope," Tiwa said. He wrapped his arms around McKenna's shoulders and held her tight. Her eyes cleared in time to see a pair of cranes alight on an exposed beam. "We've got our whole lives to hope, and the world's bigger than we could ever see."

"I guess," McKenna said. She took a deep, shuddering breath, stood up, and kissed the top of Tiwa's head, most of her sadness evaporating when she noticed how he laughed and rubbed his nose. "So where should we go first?"

"I've always dreamed of seeing the ocean," Tiwa said. He plucked Summer from McKenna's lap and laid the spear between the two thrones, then stood and planted his hands on his hips. "And I heard from a traveler there's a village near a ruin called Savannah, where the Orisha grant people powers."

"Think it's true?" McKenna said. She shouldered her pack and smiled at Tiwa over her shoulder, a little redness around her eyes all that was left of her tears.

Tiwa laughed and shrugged. "After last night, who can say? But it's like my dad always says."

McKenna gave him a curious look, but he rubbed his nose and grinned as he left her waiting. Eventually she punched him in the shoulder and he snickered.

"*What* does your dad always say?"

"'No journey ends in disappointment if a woman walks five steps ahead of you.'"

She punched him again, and as they left the thrones and walked into the sunlight their laughter sent deer and turkey fleeing back into the trees.

What happened was this: Barnard received a dream praising him for his cleverness. The winter came, so mild and wet that bumper crops of spinach and asparagus filled the bellies of the faithful and the livestock barely lost a pound.

Winter ended. Cherry blossoms bloomed and a wave of kudzu hid the bones of the electric world for as long as the weather remained warm. The roads reopened and travelers came with trade and stories.

Between the usual tales of wolf men taking sheep and fair folk stealing daughters was the occasional mention of a young man and a young woman who wandered from village to village, the young man laying low brigands and bullies while the young woman sought after ever more spiritual mastery, ever deeper knowledge of the gods.

Some put two and two together and some did not, but as seasons and then years wore on the stories slowed, then stopped. Memories faded, and eventually all who might have remembered had passed on.

What happened was this: A very, very long time after the curse was broken, a mighty warrior and a potent sorceress, both stooped and gray with age, visited the village where they were born.

They paid their respects at the faded memorial of a long-dead druid and left as quietly as they had arrived. Only the gods know what happened before their return, or where their road eventually ended.

★ ★ ★ ★ ★

ONCE UPON A SEASTORM

by
Fox Benwell

ONCE UPON A BREWING STORM, A BOY—STILL a boy, whatever else—sat on the Northern Line trying to see the future. But like the tunnels that he rides, it forks, and there is darkness, and he cannot see at all.

Some days, he's not sure that he's human. And this isn't new. As far into the past as he remembers, there were stories. His mother traipsed them to the library every Friday afternoon. Maxed out their cards and took the spoils on home, where they'd drape the bedsheets over chairs and sit in caves and castles, telling tales.

Her favourites were the happy ending stories filled with love and riches.

His? His favourites were wilder, full of faerie folk and gnolls and trolls and magic, of moss and stone and sea. And his most-beloved of them all were the tales of seals and mermen and the Finn.

Oh, they scared him. Sometimes, he would lie awake and feel the cold lapping of seaweed at his toes, the stabbing of a trident, or watch the curled, beckoning finger of the Finn in shadows on the wall. Sometimes he would hear a lullaby sung by a voice made of waves, feel the snuffling of whiskers or the memory of thicker skin, and it felt *good*.

Sometimes, that was worse. Because belonging *there* meant that, perhaps, the cotton castles weren't his after all.

His mother loved him. Wove a net of happiness and wonder, fed and clothed him, taught him all she knew. But the shadow of the sea stayed with him as he grew, and all the while he wondered whether he might be a seal.

Theodora Hearn was definitely *something*.

The other children didn't like him. Didn't understand his need to *move*, the way his heart would race if the walls were too thick or air too dry. They poked at his love of wild things. Called him animal and changeling child, and marked him dangerous.

He had asked her once, expecting her to laugh and tell him that he's no more Phocidae than hedgehog, but all he got was silence and the smallest, saddest smile.

The next time seals were mentioned he was ten, and he was not expecting it.

He'd been psyching himself up for a Big Conversation for a week or two. Ready, but a thousand times not ready, too. He threw open the window for some air, but when his mother joined him he could barely breathe, even from the safety of their bedsheet cave.

"Mama," he said, his heart breaking, "I think I'm all

wrong." And he told her that he didn't fit this skin, that he wasn't ever who the world thought he should be and the words it used for him were misaligned.

"My poppet." She leaned closer. "There is nothing wrong with you, at all. I'm sorry if I got it wrong."

And by way of explanation, she told him a story.

"Everybody knows the story of the selkie wife whose anxious husband locked her skin away so she would stay. But once there was a woman—wild and sad and all alone—who wanted nothing more than to belong.

"One night it got so bad that she left the house and walked and walked and walked along the beach, willing for the sea to help her, or to take her in. And as she walked, she cried a storm, and seven of those tears fell right into the ocean. Seven wishes, all for the same thing.

"And the sea answered.

"As the sun broke red over the waves, she heard it. Crying. And at first she thought that it was *her*, so closely did the voice match hers, but there, nestled in a bed of seaweed on the rocks, there was an infant, and underneath the infant was a scrap of leatherskin: a blanket of a sort.

"She scooped the baby up, and warmed it up against her chest, and right there on the beach she knew where she belonged.

"You see…you are not wrong at all. You were a gift."

"But—"

"Whisht." She stopped him with a finger, for she still had more to say. "And I'm sorry if I got it wrong. It's hard to tell the gender of a seal."

He did not really know what she meant: whether she meant

he was a selkie in the actual, proper, see-it-with-your-own-eyes sense, or like a sort of *allegory*—a word that he knew because sometimes his mum would sit down with a mug of tea and tell him about different kinds of stories and the ways they work. But he supposed it didn't matter. Not then. He was loved, and she did not mind that he was different.

They switched pronouns that day, choosing he and him to better fit his form. And his mother took him for a haircut and did all the necessary adult cringey things like talk to doctors about puberty. And with those changes and with time his troubles eased.

With time and teenagehood the tales of seals were pushed aside, becoming more story than fact, more past than present. But still, Theodora Hearn always felt a little wild, and sometimes he would wonder what she'd meant that day and whether, if he went up to the attic, he would find a sealskin neatly folded, in a box with all his baby things.

He never looked. It scared him, and he didn't want to know.

But then...

Today Theodora Hearn sits on the Northern Line, his savings in his pocket and a hundred questions on his mind, and he is going home to find out who he is, and how to be.

King's Cross—home of young wizardling dreams—is commuter-busy, packed with people in a hurry. Good. There're fewer chances he'll be noticed.

Not that anyone would know. Not yet. He has—he looks at his watch—nine hours before his mum will find the note.

He packed sandwiches. Sardine. And his mother's chocolate chip banana bread, both neatly wrapped in silver parcels. But he stops to get a coffee just to kill the time, and then he sits, back to a pillar, and watches all the ordinary people trotting through their ordinary lives.

A small, Chinese Slytherin in wizard robes and flip-flops drags her dad towards the queue for pictures by the platform. Theo grins at her tenacity, but as she joins the line, he wonders whether he's the only person to have dreamt not of the castle but the lake.

It tempted him. The water. Always. And though he would not—could not—bear the chlorine and the stares and the way his body felt in Lycra at the pool, he longed for it, and that longing grew stronger until one day he could not stay still, could not bear to be confined by cotton castle walls, and when his mother was asleep he slipped out in the dark, and headed for the Thames.

The first time, he was terrified. Terrified of London's less-than-honest folk, and walking into trouble, terrified of getting lost, or being swept away to sea. But the thought of moonlit water in this summer heat was too delicious to ignore, and so he went.

That's where he met the boy. A beauty. He smiled like a lazy trickster god, and when he moved, he moved with all the loping ease of water. And for a moment, Theo wondered whether *whiskered kisses* weren't a memory but something in his future.

Theo ducked beneath the god-boy's boat to catch a breath, and the water raked his hair, and soothed him, and was everything he ever needed.

He rolled beneath the surface as he swam, relishing the way

the city river toyed with him, pushed and pulled and left its dirt-slick, greasy mark beneath his nails. He laughed. Right there underwater, great bubbles of joy. Then he dove deeper. Swam a little farther. And when he rose, lungs burning, he was being watched.

The boy laughed at the seal-boy bobbing out beside his narrowboat, and slipped out of his clothes to join him. And when they kissed, two heads just above the surface, and then under—fingers meshed like pennywort—Theo was as full as oceans.

It became a habit then. Every second Tuesday, Theodora's mother worked, and rather than stay home with all his schoolbooks, Theo headed for the water. Every second Tuesday, two boys would explore a little more, of the river and each other, each time going deeper, further, trying something new.

And they both were caught up in this new eddying love—which everybody knows makes you invincible—and neither one was careful.

And now… Theodora Hearn does not know who he is, for he has heard the stories.

You've been warned about him. Child-snatching temptress. Faker.

Nothing with the boy felt fake. Not while they were doing it. Theo loved him—the way his skin would smell of white soap and of sparks and wood smoke, and how his fingers gripped but never left a mark. He loved the way this wild boy talked of open skies, and travelling, and stars.

But after—as they sat upon his boat and stared at the pee-stick with its thin blue lines silently blaring POSITIVE—the loping sea-roll of the boy turned hard and sharp and angry.

That night, Theo heard names that he'd thought were locked inside his past.

Trickster. Changeling. Pervert. Freak.

There are stories, old as time, in every newspaper and mummy-blog across the country, policing what our bodies are and who they're for and what they're meant to do. You'll know them, sure as you know of the waterkind. That night, the god-boy threw them all into the open.

Halfway to Edinburgh, Theodora Hearn stares hard at his reflection, flecked with redbrick terraces and pylons as they fly along the track. He doesn't recognise it, but he's not sure what should be there looking back at him instead. And if he's honest he's not *really* looking, because all those words are in his head and warping everything before his eyes.

What are you, when you're not quite human?

What happens when you—

Nerves roil around his insides, and one hand wraps instinctively around his stomach, as though that'll protect them both from words he cannot even think.

That night—that dreaded awful night—Theodora ran all the way home and tore up to the attic looking for some answers as to *why*. Evidence that he was real and wanted, and nothing like the god-boy's tongue proclaimed.

He expected secrets stuffed into a box. He half expected sealskin. But his mother travelled light, and all there was up there were neat, dated and alphabetised boxes of paperwork and a chest of neatly folded sheets and blankets. He unfolded each of them, in case, and his mother's camphor-cinnamon-stick bundles rolled across the floor.

He tried under her bed—shoes, and baby pictures which Theo had asked her to take down on the day of the haircut because all those dresses made him feel too squirly on the inside. And he tried the backs of kitchen drawers, searching among long-forgotten keys and screwdrivers and cables.

He found nothing. Nor was there anything of use in the *dad* department. No spine-cracked Doctor Spock or *Fatherhood for Dummies*, or carefully clipped articles about unusual families who are in other ways exactly like your nuclear households: warm, striving and joyful, bringing up their kids as best they can.

He found nothing but remnants of blanket forts and stories, and although that was *everything*, it was not, in that moment, quite enough, and crying tears of rage and shame and Oh-Gods-how-am-I-supposed-to-do-this, Theodora hatched a plan to travel north, to the start of everything, the Once Upon a Time.

At Waverly, he unwraps a sandwich, wolfs it down, then flicks through magazines in Smiths to pass the time till he can board.

His pack is heavier than it had felt this morning. In it, he has everything a boy—a seal—a runaway could need. Socks and pants and his mother's old scrapbook of stories they had found and loved and told again. A pen. A sleeping bag, musty from the attic. A hat. And a ukulele, on which he knows how to play five chords, each of them as angst-filled as the last.

Once upon a seastorm, a woman stepped onto a beach and found a seal.

Once upon another…

But try as he might, he could not see the future.

He needs to know what happens next.

She'll be on her lunch break now. In the tiny room for nurses, with its strange coffee and cardboard smell and windows that won't open. For a moment, he wants to turn back, to find a bar of Chocolate Cream and take it to surprise her.

But—

"Mint, dear?" The old lady next to him stops knitting to offer him an open packet. "Fix what ails you."

"No, thanks." He tries not to sigh, but her voice is soft the way his mother's is, their accent far from most of London, and a hint of worry leaks out of his lungs.

She shifts her own mint to her cheek and sucks on it a moment, watching him intently. "Suit yourself." And he's going to go back to thinking when she says, "Where are you headed?"

"North."

"Och, aye?"

He nods, not quite trusting himself to say more.

"On your holidays?"

"I'm heading home."

He expects the usual probing questions—where is home? Was he away for school? What is he going to be?—and dreads them, but she merely flashes him a look, and nods, and goes back to her knitting—something small in a deep forest green.

Theodora's never seen somebody knit before. He watches as her fingers move all on their own, pushing, pulling, sliding. Her eyes close, but her fingers keep on going, and her lips move just a little, muttering intent. And he's sure that it's magic—an incantation to turn thread into a sheath of warmth and care.

He wonders what she's making. Who it's for. And he'd ask her if she seemed to be awake.

Somewhere around Perth she wakes, and fully concentrates, and the scrap of wool becomes a glove: the kind without fingers which wraps around your thumb.

It's beautiful.

She tucks an errant thread into the thumb and pulls another matching glove out of her bag. Turns them over. Fusses over this stitch and then that. Places them together.

And at Pitlochry the wizard-woman stands and gathers up her coat and bag of wool.

"Take 'em," she says, pushing the gloves towards Theodora. "You'll be needin' all the warmth o' extra skin for home."

And before he can protest, she's halfway down the carriage. Gone.

Theo blinks.

Reaches out to stroke the wool. They're soft and warm and solid-real and even though the train carriage is warm, he pulls them on.

At Inverness, he paces for the entire forty-seven-minute wait. His new, knitted pelt is warm and comforting and it reminds him of a sealskin from his past. He's restless.

Once, his mother told him of a man who walked seventy leagues to win his love. Others who set out into the road for fortunes and belonging. As a young boy Theo did not get it, but now, in this white-floored waiting room, he wanted nothing more than he wanted to walk.

She'll be leaving now. Nearly home. Getting his note.

Dear Mama,

Once upon a summer's day there was a boy who met another, and they swam together. It was...everything you'd hope from fairy tales, two boys tumbling through the Thames.

You'd have liked him, I think.

But they did something foolish, or rather, they did not do something sensible, and well, you know this story: boy meets boy and they...we...

We didn't use protection. ☹

I'm sorry.

And now I don't know who I am, or what this baby will be with a dad like me, and I'm going to find some answers. Please don't worry. I'll be back.

I love you.

Theodora

It wasn't...all the truth, not spelled out, because Theodora hadn't found the words. He wanted to tell her that he loved her. That whether this kid turns out to be Hominidae or Phocidae or something in between, everything would be all right. Somehow.

He wanted to ask her outright whether he was boy or seal, so that he didn't have to go. And to tear apart the stories which say boys like him—in all the ways—

But he had found his feet before he found the words, and here we are.

The last train is an anomaly of time, the journey short and long, the train hurtlingboltinggliding down the tracks and crawling, weightless, stuck unmoving. Beauly, Muir of

Ord and Conon Bridge pass by in a sort of nothingness. Time stops. But every second—every mile—that should have passed builds under Theo's skin until he hums with the anticipation.

The tannoy announces Garve, and Locluichart: old, familiar-sweet sounding places, each one more a comfort than the last—lullabies from his own story, pieces of his infant past—Achanalt, Achnasheen, Achnashellach.

And then home.

Almost.

At Strathcarron, he alights. Breathes. The air is different here. Salted. Wet and fresh and wild, and it sits heavy on the skin and clears the lungs, and for a moment Theodora stands there on the platform breathing long and deep until he's full of it.

Home.

When his mother spoke of it in tales of old, she spoke of earth and air and sea, and he knows what to expect down to the tributaries and the grain of gneiss and sandstone, but he had not expected this…this *feeling*.

Perhaps this was his answer. Maybe this is where he's meant to be.

And he'd planned to get a room in tonight, right here beside the station, but now that he's here with this new air in his lungs, and so close to the beaches that his mother walked, he can't imagine *inside* as a possibility. Instead, he hops down off the road towards the burbling of a river, and follows it towards the sea.

Theodora Hearn was not prepared for rain. In all his mother's tales, their Wester Ross was wild and full of magic, and of course the winter tales were cold, and the nights in summer long, but—excepting their one storm-story—she'd never told him that it rained.

And he had never met a rain like this before. In London, the rain spots a bit, or it falls hard and fast and then it's gone.

Scottish rain, it turns out, is as wild as stories.

And Theo's coat was built for London. By the time he's walked a mile along the river shore he's soaked, and somehow getting wetter, and it feels like there are two rains in the air at once—one lashing relentless, and the other *mist*— a rain that defies gravity and hangs mid-air and clings to everything.

Not that he minds. He walks, and marvels at the wetness of his skin, the bright green purple-freckled-white of everything, the bounce of moss and heather underfoot and the total, utter absence of the sound of cars.

Half an hour of following the river, and it opens wide, becoming less a river, more a loch, and suddenly he's on a beach, all salt and sea and lapping waves on stone, and all he wants to do is strip down to his skin and swim.

He almost does—gets as far as tugging his arms out of his coat sleeves—but he's already wet and cold without adding an ocean's chill, and besides, he is alone and he does not know the tides. Instead, he walks a little more, until the rain turns into drizzle, matching the crunch of his feet on shingle with each incoming wave.

He settles in a small cove as the sun sets, streaking heather-purple lines across the sky. Sits against a rock, unwraps his sandwiches and cake, and tells himself a story.

Once upon a seastorm, a woman, wild and sad and all alone, walked out onto this beach to have a conversation with the sea—

He stops.

Once upon a seastorm, a boy, wild and sad and terribly confused—

He stops again, not knowing how this version of the story goes.

Are there seals out in the water now?

He squints at far-off waves that might be bobbing heads, and wonders how he's never asked his mother where seals sleep at night or if they sleep at all.

It's probably different for selkies anyway.

Right?

Probably. But still he watches. And he falls asleep like that, back against a rock, trying not to shiver and staring out onto the beach where everything began.

He wakes several times that night, each time more surprised at the ice touch of his still-wet clothes, the bite of the wind and the sharp scratch-dig of shingle, each time turning over, hunching down or stretching out, trying to get comfortable.

Seal, he thinks. *Think seal, lying like a king out on the beach*, all blubber-warm, but as soon as the sun begins to rise, he rises with it, stiffly, and walks down to the sea. Here, he pulls off his gloves and crouches, lets the foam rush up over his fingers, splashes water on his face.

The water here is different from the Thames. More *alive*. And he watches it with interest. There's sand beneath the shingle, etched by waves and gulls and oystercatchers, scattered here and there with shells and weeds and driftwood. He could probably look at it for a lifetime and never see half of the life that's here.

It's…comforting, somehow.

What *isn't* comforting is the hunger gnawing at his core, and as soon as anything is open, it is time for supplies.

He finds the village store beside a café-gallery and church, right on the seafront and exactly as his mum described: white, salt-crusted walls and blue slate roofs and they look as though they've hunkered here forever, right where they belong.

There's even the perfect-village dinging bell as he opens the door.

"G'mornin'" someone calls from in the back. "I'll be right in."

"Take your time!" he answers, grabbing a basket and filling it with macaroni pies (weird, but he's here for it, he thinks) and Tunnock's Caramel bars. He adds a pint of milk, a can of peppered mackerel with a ring-pull on the lid and a bag of apples. Bear Grylls has nothing on a teenage boy for good survival food. And with that thought, he remembers that you cannot drink the sea, and adds a big bottle of water.

He considers midge repellent from a rack beside the till, but so far, despite the horror stories, he hasn't been bitten—maybe it's his sealskin, and they only go for softer human flesh.

"Hi."

"Hi." He blinks. He'd expected your quintessential village granny up behind the till, but instead a tall, messy blue-haired girl with Celtic knotwork inked into her neck is reaching for his basket.

"Find errything you need?"

"Yes, thanks," he says, adding a postcard featuring a beach of common seals.

She grins. "Quite a feast ye've go' there."

"Yep. I'm...seal watching."

"Ahh, a nature lover."

He nods.

"Well, be sure'n warm up at the café when ye've finished." And she smiles wider and warmer, and Theo's insides thaw a little. But no. No. He cannot have that. Not again. It is too dangerous.

He drops his things haphazardly into his rucksack, and runs from the shop back to the water, barely calling a goodbye-and-thanks over his shoulder.

He spends the next days on the beach, up against that semi-sheltered rock. Watching, mostly. Staring at the sea and willing his...what? Selkie dad? Mum? Sea master? Someone from his past, to rise up from the waves and welcome him back to his real life. Even to see seals, but while some of those glints of grey *could* be something swimming, he's pretty sure that it is just imaginings.

He writes his mum a postcard. Nothing much.

Dear Mum,
Doing okay up here. Looking for seals and answers. It's nice here: exactly like you said, but not at all. I love it. Theo. ♥

He does not post it right away; he waits, until the sea is ink-black and he has no chance of seeing seals. And although he does not want to miss the chance of someone visiting his dreams (such is the way of stories), Theo walks up to the post box by the store. He thinks of the blue-haired girl and how she'd smiled, and how unexpected it was that he cared.

Who had she seen: boy or girl or seal?

And he wanders back down to the water all confused.

It was...quite warm in the daytime, but as soon as the sun went to bed there was a chill. Damper than your city nights, and it got in your bones.

The next day, he tries to build a fire, but he's worried that he's done it wrong, and the whole beach could catch alight, and every chance he ever had of finding home would burn. So his neat pyramid of moss and twigs and driftwood stands untouched beside his pack.

He pulls on his new woolskin gloves and wonders how the wizard-woman knew how deeply *human* he'd feel wearing them against the cold. How much he would need them.

Time passes and stands still. He tries taking the ukulele to the water's edge and summoning his people with a song, but all he knows is "Hallelujah" and the "Skye Boat Song," and after a while, he reverts to stories. And he tells the sea the ones he knows, and then pulls out his mother's book and reads those, and remembers.

He pores over the selkie pages, lets his fingers pass over the words, stares at every line in turn and flips it over in his head in case there's hidden meaning.

No one comes.

How did his mother do it? All those years alone with a small scrap of a thing counting on her every day?

On the third night, the sea starts to call louder, and Theodora digs his nails into the shore to stop himself.

He mustn't swim.

He can't.

Because what if he has it all wrong and there is nothing

out there? Or he's right, but without his sealskin he must stay on land, an outcast?

What if—what if this wild water does not like him, does not let him be the way the river would?

What if—what if Theodora lacks the strength his mother had, and cannot find a way to stay and so the water claims him, carries him away?

He turns his face away from breaking waves that night, wishing himself in his own, comfortable bed. Wishing himself a new body, one that everyone would understand. Wishing that he knew the media was wrong, and there was somewhere he'd belong.

Theo wakes to whiskers, cold and wet and snuffling at his face. And weight upon his chest. He reaches up and finds slick, icy fur.

A seal?

And he knows that he should force open his eyes and follow it, because the seal's the reason that he's here. His summoning. But the sun is slowly baking Theo's bones, and it feels good, and he just...

can't.

help.

but.

sink—

"Oh geez, come on, wake up."

And there's something nuzzling-nipping at his neck.

Theodora groans. Stretches hard against the salt-and-sun-baked stiffness in his legs and lower back.

"Thank *Lyr*," the voice says, as Theodora blinks open his eyes. The blue-haired girl from the store hovers above him, all anxious. "Muckle. Muckle, ye can stop tryin' te rouse him, he's awake." And she pulls a purring, whiskered creature off of Theo's chest.

"Is that a cat?" he says, even though its catness was obvious, because he's not quite awake, and in his dream it wasn't, and *who brings their cat to the beach?*

"Yes."

"What's it...doing here?" he asks, sitting properly upright and rubbing at his elbow, where he'd lain on a particularly sharp rock.

"Could ask ye the same question. What kind o' fool sleeps out here wi'out any kind o' shelter?"

"I told you. I'm seal watching."

"In the dark though?" She shakes her head.

"It's not dark."

"It's early. And ye must be freezin'." He was going to deny it, but she kept on. "Let's go ge' a cuppa. Warm ye' insides."

"I—"

"C'mon. Muckle here's taken a shinin' te ye and I'd ne'er hear shut of it if I let you catch hypothermia." And she stands there, arms crossed, waiting while Theo picks himself up off the floor.

"Ah'm *Bran* by the way."

"Like Stoker?"

"Like, raven."

"Oh."

Bran doesn't press for conversation as they walk. Instead, their feet crunch stones in almost unison, and Muckle bounds ahead, sniffing at the rock pools.

"Ah call it 'Highlands Secrets,'" Bran says, noting Theo's wide eyes as she avoids a weaving Muckle and plonks two full cups and saucers on a table.

This café is not what he expected. Or, it half is. There's a cabinet of china and another full of fine, tall cakes. Tables decked in pink carnations. Seascapes hung over one wall. But Bran led Theo past this, up some narrow stairs, and up here is a leather sofa. Small black-and-white photographs of tired fishermen; of fire-lit dances and a ring of beer cans in the sand; a circled, annotated page from the jobs pages of a paper. On another wall there is bright graffiti, and another houses sculptures made of nets and rusted iron.

"You did this?"

"Most of it, aye. The idea for the fire-dance picture was my brother's, but I took the shot."

"They're *amazing*."

She stares hard at her teacup, turning pink. "So, what brings a city boy all the way up here alone?"

"The—"

"Seals. Sure. But *why*?"

And Theo doesn't want to share, and if he *did*, he does not quite know how. How do you tell someone that you're…not what they assume but that you also are? How do you explain that stories can be true? That seals are home and answers and identity and maybe you're not even human?

"I'm…have you ever heard of selkies?"

Bran raises an eyebrow. "Aye, o' course."

"Well… Once upon a seastorm." And that's that, he is telling her everything, right from the start.

That night—still light, in the way of summer—they're on the beach together, leaning up against a rock and staring out to sea, their hands entwined.

They have talked of *everything*: art and home and aspirations, and past loves and whether calamari is better than chips, and what story really means.

"Do you think it's real?" Theodora asks quietly.

"Does it matter?"

"Yes? No. I don't know."

"D'you want me to come wi' ye?"

"Where?" He says, confused.

"The sea."

Theo blinks in surprise that he's *never wanted anything so much*, but then—

No. Because that is how he met the boy; how he ruined everything.

Instead, he lets them sink into a silence. And in that silence, feelings grow, heavy-warm-excited. And air grows heavy too, and a storm-brown sky blows in, and rumbles.

"Uhhh," he says, as the first flash of lightning lights the sky. "Maybe we should move."

"Townie." She grins, nudging him. And then she stands and strips her shirt off with no warning. "Let's go for a swim!"

"What? No!"

"Wrong answer." And she's pulling him towards the water as the sky cracks open.

Theodora's heart thuds hard, because there's sea and seals and sky-fire, and a boy and so, so many questions, but his feet go with her, and they're knee-deep, waist-deep, two-heads bobbing in the waves, and the girl has not let go.

"You do know water is conductive, right?" he asks, terrified.

"Aye!" she shouts back, loud above a roll of thunder. "But dun' ye feel *alive*?"

"I'd like to stay that way!"

She laughs, and it sounds like water lullabies, and Theo breathes a little, but the sky flares again and Theo screams. "Okay, okay, staying alive," she mock-sighs, pulling him back to the shore. And then they're running for their clothes and shivering and laughing so hard that they cannot rightly tell where one starts and the other one begins.

The storm crashes behind them, overhead, and possibly below, for it feels as though the whole world shakes with it.

Inside—in Bran's tiny flat above the village store— Theodora thinks about his mother once upon a seastorm, and how she chose to stay. How she moved them south for opportunities and loved him in whatever skin he chose.

He thinks of stories, and of seals, and how nobody ever *really* knows who they are or who they might be. And he's still not sure what *dad* should look like, how he'll manage, whether everyone is right and a seal-boy who's with child will ruin everything. But maybe that's just life.

He thinks of the woman on the train, how sometimes a given skin can give you warmth and courage until you're okay with your own.

"Here." The blue-haired girl chucks him a dressing gown, lays their clothes out by the fire to dry.

And Theo settles, staring from her tiny window out across the shore, as he writes another letter:

Dear Mum,

I stood on the shore today and watched the waves. Just watched. And I missed you. I want to stand up here together one day, all three of us, you and me and baby. And I want this child to know the seals by markings and by name.

I love you. And I don't know how you did it just the two of us and I just—

I will see you soon.

I love you.

Theodora

He'll probably go home soon, but for now—just for a while—he wants to get to know a blue-haired girl and spend some time wild as a seal.

He sighs, content, one hand wrapped around his stomach as he thinks about the thousand thousand things that their futures might be.

Once upon a storm, a boy—still a boy, whatever else—sat and watched the roiling sea and listened to it call his name (a lullaby, a summoning) and made a conscious choice to stay.

THE EDITOR

Saundra Mitchell (she/they) has been a phone psychic, a car salesperson, a denture-deliverer, and a layout waxer. She's dodged trains, endured basic training, and hitchhiked from Montana to California. The author of twenty books for tweens and teens, Mitchell's work includes *Shadowed Summer*, *All the Things We Do in the Dark*, the nonfiction They Did What!? series, and two other anthologies for teens, *Defy the Dark* and *All Out*. She always picks truth; dares are too easy.

THE AUTHORS

Fox Benwell (he/him) is a YA author, creative writing mentor, and an advocate for diversity. He runs the Trowbridge Young Writers Squad, is the founder of The Variety Shelves, a series of events highlighting diversity in literature. He loves jungles and deserts and the dark, still corners where the stories live, but spends most of his time at his tiny desk in Bath, with his trusty feline sidekick.

Tanya Boteju (she/her) is an English teacher and writer living on unceded territories of the Musqueam, Squamish, and Tsleil-Waututh First Nations (Vancouver, Canada). Her writing life has mostly consisted of teaching writing for the past sixteen years at York House School, an all-girls independent school in Vancouver, where she has continually been inspired by the brilliant young people in her midst. Her novel, *Kings, Queens, and In-Betweens*, debuted in 2019. Tanya is grateful for her patient wife, supportive family and friends, committed educators, sassy students, and hot mugs of tea. She hopes to continue contributing to the ever-growing, positive representation of queer folks in literature and to that end, is delighted to be included in this collection of stories.

After studying Spanish and history at a small liberal arts school, **Kate Hart** (she/her) taught young people their ABCs, wrote grants for grown-ups with disabilities, and now builds tree houses for people of all ages. Her debut YA novel, *After the Fall*, was published January 2017 by Farrar, Straus & Giroux; she's also a contributor to the 2018 anthologies *Toil and Trouble* and *Hope Nation*. A former contributor to *YA Highway* and host of the *Badass Ladies You Should Know* series, Kate also sells woodworking and fiber arts at The Badasserie. She is a citizen of the Chickasaw Nation with Choctaw heritage and lives with her family in Northwest Arkansas.

Kosoko Jackson (he/him) is a vocal champion of diversity in YA literature, the author of YA novels featuring African American queer protagonists, and a sensitivity reader for Big Five Publishers. Professionally, he is a digital media manager for a major nonprofit organization, and a freelance political journalist. He has also recently taken the position as Social Media Manager for Foreshadow: A Serial YA Anthology, through 2019. Occasionally, his personal essays and short stories have been featured on *Medium*, *Thought Catalog*, *The Advocate*, and some literary magazines. When not writing YA novels that champion holistic representation of black queer youth across genres, he can be found obsessing over movies, drinking his (umpteenth) London Fog, or spending far too much time on Twitter. His debut #ownvoices *Yesterday Is History*, will be published in Spring 2020 by SourceBooks.

Will Kostakis (he/him) lives in Sydney, where he writes books for teens and the adults who like to read about them. In his native Australia, he's a critically acclaimed and award-winning author, having won the Gold Inky Award and been short-listed for both the Prime Minister's Literary Award and the CBCA Book of the Year Award for his sophomore novel, *The First Third*. You can find him on the web at www.will-kostakis.com or on Twitter, @willkostakis.

CB Lee (she/her) is a Lambda Literary Award-nominated writer of young adult science fiction and fantasy. Her works include the Sidekick Squad series (Duet Books) and *Ben 10 (Boom!)*. CB loves to write about queer teens, magic, superheroes, and the power of friendship. When not nationally touring as an educator, writer, and activist, CB lives in Los Angeles, where she can neither confirm nor deny being a superhero. You can learn more about her and her adventures as a bisexual disaster at http://cb-lee.com and follow her on Twitter @author_cblee.

Katherine Locke (she/they) lives and writes in Philadelphia, Pennsylvania where they are ruled by their feline overlords and their addiction to chai lattes. In addition to contributing to *Out Now*, they are the author of *The Girl with the Red Balloon* (2018 Sydney Taylor Honor Book), *The Spy with the Red Balloon*, a contributor to *Unbroken: 13 Stories Starring Disabled Teens*, and co-editor and contributor to *It's A Whole Spiel: Love, Latkes and Other Jewish Stories*. They secretly believe most stories are fairytales-in-disguise. They can be found online at KatherineLockeBooks.com and on Twitter and Instagram at @bibliogato.

Hillary Monahan (she/her) lives in Massachusetts with her husband, hounds, and four cats. She loves horror, humor, feminism, and makeup. The inspiration for *The Hollow Girl* came from her Roma-born grandmother. Her YA book *Mary: The Summoning* hit the *New York Times* ebook bestseller list, and she is currently working on more dark things.

Candice Montgomery (they/them) is a YA author, teacher, and classical dancer based in Seattle. When they're not writing, teaching or dancing, you can often find them messing around on Instagram and Twitter. Their debut novel, *Home and Away*, is a part of the YA launch list of Page Street Publishing.

Mark Oshiro (he/him) is the Hugo finalist (in the Fan Writer category) creator of the online *Mark Does Stuff* universe (Mark Reads and Mark Watches), where he analyzes book and television series unspoiled. He was the nonfiction editor of *Queers Destroy Science Fiction!* and the co-editor of *Speculative Fiction 2015* with Foz Meadows. He is the President of the Con or Bust Board of Directors. His first novel, *Anger is a Gift*, is a YA contemporary about queer friendship, love and fighting police brutality, out now with Tor Teen. When he is not writing, crying on camera about fictional characters, or ruining lives at conventions, he is busy trying to fulfill his lifelong goal: to pet every dog in the world.

Caleb Roehrig (he/him) grew up in Ann Arbor, Michigan, but has also lived in Chicago, Los Angeles, and Helsinki, Finland. His hobbies include eating and sleeping, but he also loves to travel, and has been lucky enough to visit thirty-five different countries. A former actor and television producer, Roehrig has experience on both sides of the camera, with a résumé that includes appearances on film and TV—not to mention seven years in the stranger-than-fiction salt mines of reality television. In the name of earning a paycheck, he has: hung around a frozen cornfield in his underwear, partied with an actual rock star, chatted with a scandal-plagued politician, and been menaced by a disgruntled ostrich.

Meredith Russo (she/her) was born, raised, and lives in Tennessee. She started living as her true self in late 2013 and never looked back. *If I Was Your Girl* was partially inspired by her experiences as a trans woman. Like her character Amanda, Meredith is a gigantic nerd who spends a lot of her time obsessing over video games and *Star Wars*.

Eliot Schrefer (he/him) is a *New York Times*–bestselling author, and has twice been a finalist for the National Book Award. In naming him an Editor's Choice, the *New York Times* has called his work "dazzling…big-hearted." He is also the author of two novels for adults and four other novels for children and young adults. His books have been named to the NPR "best of the year" list, the ALA best fiction list for young adults, and the Chicago Public Library's "Best of the Best." His work has also been selected to the Amelia Bloomer List, recognizing best feminist books for young readers, and he has been a finalist for the Walden Award and won the Green Earth Book Award and Sigurd Olson Nature Writing Award. He lives in New York City, where he reviews books for *USA TODAY*. You can find him at www.eliotschrefer.com, or on Twitter @eliotschrefer.

Tara Sim (she/her) is the author of the Timekeeper trilogy and the upcoming *Scavenge the Stars* (Disney-Hyperion, 2020) and can typically be found wandering the wilds of the Bay Area, California. When she's not chasing cats or lurking in bookstores, she writes books about magic, clocks, and explosions. Follow her on Twitter at @EachStarAWorld, and check out her website for fun extras at tarasim.com.

Jessica Verdi (she/her) lives in Brooklyn, NY, with her partner and young daughter. A graduate of The New School's MFA in Writing for Children program, Jess is the author of several contemporary novels for young adults—including *And She Was*, *What You Left Behind*, *The Summer I Wasn't Me*, and *My Life After Now*—and a picture book, *I'm Not a Girl* (co-written with Maddox Lyons). She loves traveling, seltzer, hot sauce, TV, vegetarian soup, flip-flops, and her dogs. Visit her at www.jessicaverdi.com and follow her on Twitter and Instagram @jessverdi.

Amazon bestselling author **Julian Winters** (he/him) is a former management trainer who lives in the outskirts of Atlanta, Georgia and has been crafting fiction since he was a child, creating communities around his hand-drawn "paper people." He began writing LGBTQ character-driven stories as a teen. When he isn't writing or using his sense of humor to entertain his young nephews, Julian enjoys reading, experimental cooking in the kitchen, and watching the only sports he can keep up with: volleyball and soccer. He debuted with a soccer-based novel, *Running with Lions*, in 2018, followed in 2019 by *How to Be Remy Cameron*.